THE PRICE OF REBELLION

MICHAEL C. BLAND

This is a work of fiction. Names, characters, places, and incidents are products of the author's imagination or are used fictitiously and are not to be construed as real. Any resemblance to actual events, locations, organizations, or persons, living or dead, is entirely coincidental.

World Castle Publishing, LLC
Pensacola, Florida

Hardback ISBN: 9781958336892
Hardback Case ISBN: 9781960076847
Paperback ISBN: 9781958336908
Paperback ISBN: 9781960076748
eBook ISBN: 9781958336915
First Edition World Castle Publishing, LLC, May 16, 2023
http://www.worldcastlepublishing.com

Cover: Dorothy Mason
Editor: Karen Fuller

Dedication

To Dad. You inspire in more ways than I can count.

My name is Dray Quintero. You may have heard of me.

You may have heard I'm an enemy of the state, that I killed law enforcement personnel to evade custody. That I caused my younger daughter's death.

If you follow science news, you may have heard of my former company, Gen Omega, and the innovations I engineered—including a surveillance network linking every camera across the country. The software was meant to keep you safe.

And maybe you heard my broadcast. Our government has been hijacked, those pretending to be our elected Congresspeople hiding behind the technology implanted in our heads. We have to take our country back.

Which is why I've joined the Founding Fathers, one of many rebel clans determined to free the government. The rebels seem the best option, but I don't know if I can trust them.

If we fail, generations will pay the price.

Timeline to Rebellion

Year

2030 The OCB1 virus escapes the thawing permafrost. Highly contagious, the virus attacks humans by crystalizing the lenses in their eyes before consuming their brain tissue over a nine-week period. The infection rate is 97.7%. Within months, over 1 billion are blind worldwide, and 40 million are dead. Although human travel, commerce, and interaction virtually cease globally, infections continue to rise.

2030 Unable to create a vaccine in time to save humanity, scientists discover that OCB1 is affected by medical-grade steel. They propose a radical plan to world leaders: replace every citizen's lenses using the same procedure as cataract surgery and install a permanent steel rod into citizens' brains to neutralize the virus.

2031 In the greatest mobilization of resources and healthcare providers in history, countries across the planet follow their scientists' advice. Billions are saved. The United States, however, becomes mired in political posturing and lawsuits. Though a percentage of Americans opt for the procedure, most refuse. Millions needlessly die. Sensing America's expanding weakness, foreign terrorists begin to attack U.S. cities, killing thousands. During this time, American innovators begin to modify their implants.

2033 As U.S. deaths reach 32 million, more Americans decide to adopt the OCB1 procedure. The country starts to emerge from its darkest days but finds itself left behind by the rest of the world as China, Russia, India and others expand their influence and eliminate their reliance on the West.

2034 Following the success of those early American innovators, Congress passes the Personal Integration of Vital Organized Technology (PIVOT) Act, which mandates that instead of simple silicone lenses, each citizen be implanted with lenses that have clear computer screens—and the implanted rods expanded to contain neural nets, offering a way to save lives, as well as make the U.S. competitive and innovative again. After some resistance, the law is embraced by tens of millions.

2035 Adoption reaches 85% of the population, but PIVOT mandates every citizen receive the modified lenses and neural nets. The law includes severe penalties for noncompliance, including forced implantation. Even so, the U.S. government struggles to achieve 100% adoption and enlists the National Security Agency (NSA) to help.

2037 The U.S. once again becomes the dominant country on the planet. The NSA grows in size, as many still refuse to get the new implant, though terrorist attacks in Chicago, Miami, and Los Angeles strain resources. The attacks culminate in the Daisy Chain Massacre when multiple bombs explode in cities from L.A. to Atlanta. 4,300 people are killed, and 21,000 are injured. Dozens of separate security cameras capture video of the terrorists responsible, but by the time the footage is compiled, they've fled the country.

2037 Dray Quintero's company is commissioned to link the country's security camera systems into a unified whole. Dray oversees the project, completing it in under 10 months. Crime plummets, and terrorist attacks stop.

2038 The NSA morphs into The Agency, the government's domestic enforcement body. Under new leadership, The Agency unleashes drones and other surveillance equipment, begins physically enhancing its Agents—and starts using everyone's implants to spy on people, further tightening its grip. Within six months, virtually every citizen is implanted.

2038 When Congress reconvenes, a group of Congresspeople implements a coup d'état. No one outside the Capitol witnesses it, as the Agency uses people's lenses to hide their takeover.

2040 Kai Spencer, a former NSA/Agency employee, claims the government was overthrown. He posts a shaky video to support his accusation and agrees to do a live interview but is murdered fourteen seconds before his feed links with CNN's network. His killer is never found, even though five separate surveillance cameras guard his apartment building.

2042 Two women claiming to be Agency employees post statements supporting Spencer's claim and upload documents—schematics, computer code, and other information—to prove their assertions. News agencies pick up the story, but the women disappear. Though The Agency quickly erases the documents, the story strikes a chord in those who have felt something's off. Individuals from Schenectady to Eugene locate copies of the documents—nothing is ever completely deleted online—and as they decode the data, they realize they have to fight back against a ruthless enemy. The rebellion is born.

CHAPTER ONE

Invading The Agency's office was reckless. Suicidal. But I was desperate.

We stood at the bottom of a metal stairwell in a high-rise in Los Angeles' New Downtown: myself, my nineteen-year-old daughter Raven, her boyfriend Jex, and Senn, one of my self-appointed bodyguards.

"You sure 'bout this?" Jex muttered as he pulled on his poorly-grown "playoff beard", his Creole accent thick with doubt.

I didn't have a choice. I'd called for a damn uprising against the United States.

The Agency protected the government's secrets with highly-trained, augmented Agents as their enforcers. They'd hunted Raven, killed my other daughter Talia, and nearly killed me, yet their office could reveal the locations of their broadcast nodes—which we needed to take back the country.

If the intel Jex had gathered was right, no Agents should be there, and the rest of the office were analysts and worker bees. Or so we were told.

I nodded to him. "Go."

Using a palm-sized controller, he activated his spider-like robots, which began to scurry up one of the whitewashed walls of the open stairwell. When they reached the bottom of the landing overhead, they turned and followed the stairs up. We stood just outside of view of the first camera that guarded the stairs; from my angle, I spotted the lead robot descend the wall behind the fixed camera and crawl along its body, stopping just behind the lens. I couldn't see the others, but I knew they would move into the same position on every floor.

It would take precious seconds to blind all fifty-three floors.

As they rose, Senn bent over, his legs straight, and touched his toes.

Raven elbowed him. "You already stretched in the van."

"Gotta stay loose. Don't want to pull a hammy."

I shifted my heavy backpack, full of the same nervous energy. "The Agents should be at their Van Nuys facility, running their invasion simulation—"

"But we don't know for how long," said Jex. We spoke quietly. We knew the risks. Actually, we didn't. No one had dared something like this.

The sensation of having a target on my back, which I'd had since learning the government's lies, felt far heavier than my pack. Our enemies—the men and women who'd taken the identities of the Senators and Representatives from both sides of the aisle in D.C.—used our neural nets and the clear computer screens in our eyes not only to hide the damage done to our environment but the coup they'd orchestrated without anyone's knowledge. Because I'd tried to reveal their actions, I was one of the most wanted men in America.

"In and out in eighteen minutes," I reminded them.

"Almost ready," Jex said, the sounds of the robots' scraping fading as they crawled higher. He eyed my right temple. Worried about my implant.

"It's covered." We all wore knit caps interwoven with wire that blocked our implant signals.

The silver-dollar-sized neural nets implanted into our skulls granted access to the depth and breadth of the digital world, but as I and others learned, the nets, linked to the cameras that rested on our retinas' blind spots, not only hid the coup in D.C. but tracked and monitored everyone.

The implant I was saddled with, however, could betray the rebels.

In addition to the caps, we wore gloves, sealed clothing, and tinted masks laced with energized fibers. I'd crafted the masks so no person or camera could see our faces, but we could see each other's as the tinting was phased to offset when gazed through one into the other.

I glanced at Raven, her golden-brown hair pulled into a ponytail. "For Talia."

Her jade eyes softened. "For Talia."

Jex's handheld controller flashed.

"Do it," I said.

Jex touched the controller.

Moving in synch, the fifty-three robots swiveled forward and covered the stairwell's cameras with tiny screens. If anyone was watching the cameras' feeds, at most they'd catch a flicker before their monitor returned to depicting empty stairs.

Stepping to the center of the stairwell, we removed our grapplers from our belts, raised them, and fired. The titanium bolts disappeared as they rose, trailing red nylon ropes. Seconds later, four thuds echoed softly as they pierced the ceiling over five hundred feet overhead. I exchanged a glance with Raven—who had a large pack strapped to her back, at her insistence—and thumbed the device. The motor pulled the rope tight, then lifted me into the air.

I rose up the stairwell, the others just beneath me, passing floor after floor in a quickening blur. Before I could get used to it, the motor quit, preprogrammed to stop at our destination: the forty-seventh floor.

The others stopped around me, gently swaying.

This had to work.

We climbed over the railing onto the landing and unhooked our grapplers, abandoning them to swing in the open space.

Jex approached the door to the level. "Uh, problem," he whispered.

There was no lock for him to pick. The metal door handle

was smooth, certainly reinforced.

Beside the door was an old-style card reader.

All eyes turned to me.

I knelt in front of the reader, which was similar to what I'd installed at Gen Omega's building. I'd packed a hard-wired, two-way transmitter, though I hadn't expected to need it. Removing it from my pocket, I slipped the curved end under my knit cap—which made my team tense—and touched it to my implant. I then touched the transmitter end to the reader.

Kieran, the Agent who'd nearly killed me, had soldered this implant into my head so I couldn't remove it. Unblocking it threatened a swift visit from a swarm of federal thugs, as the implant pinpointed my location in seconds via my identification codes—and, I suspected, recorded everything I saw, which The Agency could use to find our operations, learn our secrets, destroy our rebellion.

That didn't mean it was useless, however.

The computer in my implant hooked into the building's system via the transmitter wire, the readout streaming across the clear lenses in my eyes. With a dataring, I pulled up the program guarding this floor and entered a code I'd had for years, which used to work on this model.

The door didn't open.

I cursed under my breath and searched for the subroutine that dictated user protocols.

"Dad," Raven whispered, her voice tight, as I scanned the program layers.

I knew. I was taking too long.

Senn made a slurping sound as he sucked on a Life Saver. "You got this, boss. Feel it."

"Need me to step in?" Jex asked.

I ignored them as I searched for an override.

Before I could, I heard a click, and the door opened.

Senn patted my shoulder—though it was more of a punch. A former personal trainer, he was the most muscular rebel I knew. "Booyah."

I jerked to my feet. "I didn't unlock it." It could've been a fluke in the building's software, but I didn't buy it. Agents could know we were here.

My group pulled their weapons.

I pushed Senn aside and opened the door, fearing Agents had learned of our plan.

But an empty hallway greeted us.

Still uneasy, I led my team forward, scattered office sounds drifting toward us.

We extracted bio-stunners, and I made sure my cuffs were handy.

Moving silently, we exited the hallway, Jex and Senn to the right, while Raven and I went to the left. Light-gray cubicles grouped in small clusters greeted us, along with offices lining the outer wall. From the sounds they made, I estimated six or eight workers.

A hallway branched off to one side, leading to the reception area and elevator bank.

I motioned Raven toward the nearest cluster of cubicles before stepping past toward a second set.

A man sighed as he typed.

Behind me, Raven activated one of the bio-stunners and rolled the metal ball toward the cubicles I'd indicated. I did the same, rolling mine toward the other cubicles, the metal ball's glowing yellow lights spinning as it rolled into the cube and disappeared. The next moment, there was a puffed charge, followed by slumping as the electrical discharges knocked out the workers, each ball boasting a fifteen-foot stun radius.

The workers would be out for twenty minutes, maybe less, depending on metabolism.

I hurried forward to check the offices. The first two were empty, but the third contained a man in a suit. He wasn't an Agent—his hair wasn't silver—but he was still a threat, unaffected as his office was outside the stunner's range. I tasered him before he could look at me, and he crumpled.

The corner office was Kieran's. I paused, the memory of

standing in front of his onyx-slabbed desk asking for help like a punch to the throat. I couldn't tell if the empty office was still his. After what I'd done to him, I doubted he was still with The Agency.

Jex and Senn approached. "No Agents," Jex said.

Our plan had a chance.

When we passed the all-glass receptionist desk, we found pictures of Agents projected along the back wall. Employee of the Month pictures. Kieran dominated the award frames.

I wanted to smash his pictures, but I told myself he was gone. I'd defeated him.

I took in the other portraits as I fought my anger. A woman occupied most of the other frames, including the most recent, her silver hair cut in a stylish bob, her blue eyes intense, the name under her portrait identifying her as Sari Britt. A man with almost no neck occupied two other frames, his silver hair short, his nose bent. I wondered what kind of force could've broken it. His name was listed as Thys Gunnar. That fit.

"Are they really that lame to have an Employee of the Month?" Jex asked.

"More like Psychopath of the Month," Senn said around his Life Saver.

Raven didn't laugh. Neither did I.

"Bet you I'll find the nodes first," Jex told me with a lopsided grin.

"You're on." I glanced at Raven and Senn. "You know what to do."

As the team split up, I searched for a computer. We needed to leave before the workers woke. My lenses showed we had thirteen minutes left.

The far side of the floor contained more cubicles, along with communication bays, datatanks, and servers.

The broadcasting nodes were used by the government to maintain control by sending their lies to everyone's implants.

Our hackers had tried to find the nodes virtually, but whatever firewalls had been erected to separate the implant network from the internet were impenetrable. I'd found the location of the node here in L.A., which The Agency since relocated. It's where I'd revealed our enemies watched everyone from their own eyes—and had hijacked the country. But my broadcast had gone out via The Agency's network, which meant it had been limited to Los Angeles and northern San Diego, as that was the area covered by the node I'd commandeered. And it hadn't been recorded. As a result, Washington quashed the riots and outrage that had followed my broadcast, and even though protests continued in both cities, the rest of the country seemed to believe the government's fabrications.

And I became part savior, part pariah.

I needed to go bigger this time, find a map of every node—which was why we'd invaded the office—but I didn't want to find them to send more messages. We needed to destroy them. If we did, every citizen would see the truth. They would rise up.

I entered one of the offices, which seemed to be part storage room, a desk to the left, boxes stacked to the right, a copier machine on the inside wall, windows comprising the far wall that presented the cityscape.

I noticed the body next. A young woman lying on her stomach, brown hair, nose ring, edge of a tattoo peeking out from a business-appropriate blouse. She lay near the windows as if she had been gazing outside when she was zapped, the charge enough to disrupt biorhythms but too weak to damage any of the computers.

I sat down at her computer, a cutting-edge box of security-protocol-laden connectivity, and the screens came to life. Her login hadn't timed out.

I was in.

I hadn't known if I would be able to get into their system. We'd brought password-cracking devices, though we didn't know how layered The Agency's systems were—and thankfully didn't have to try. Our plan to come during the day had worked. We'd risked The Agency staff triggering an alarm before we could knock them out, but their computers were logged into.

Ready to access.

If Jex did as instructed, he would've located another logged-into computer. I didn't care which of us found the info we needed. We had to find it. Fast.

Raven and Senn passed my doorway carrying the large canvas bag she'd brought up. They set it in front of the windows at the end of the main hallway and began to unpack our getaway.

As they worked, I searched The Agency's mainframe. Vast amounts of data ran through this office, surveillance and monitoring information, files on potential suspects, video archives, and so on. I tapped into a system that was similar to the LAPD's, which made me think of Talia when she'd hacked the cops' system. Pushing aside my sadness, I searched the system for the node network. My efforts grew desperate as I came up empty over and over, and nearly gave up before I found a potential access point hidden in a concealed sublevel. I tried to access the sublevel—and a login screen appeared.

I plugged in my password-cracking device, but it failed to override the software.

Shit.

I pulled off my mask to think. The system at the node building I'd invaded weeks earlier hadn't required a password. Maybe The Agency had figured armed robot sentinels made passwords superfluous. But I understood why they'd have them here.

This operating system was similar to the one I'd created to link the country's network of public and private security, traffic, and other cameras, so I tried the backdoor login I'd installed for that OS. It didn't work. Neither did the password from my old job at Gen Omega.

I opened the desk drawer, hoping to find a user ID and password written somewhere, when I heard a noise behind me. I jerked around—and the young woman on the floor ducked her head. She was awake.

I swiped my mask to cover my face. "Guys," I yelled. "We have a problem."

Jex and Senn ran in, tasers drawn.

"Don't shoot," the woman said in a Russian-accented voice, keeping her head down.

"I thought you checked everyone," I said to my teammates as I secured my mask.

"He checked her," Senn said.

"I thought you did," Jex said.

The woman said, "I saw balls bouncing past and heard people getting electrocuted. I didn't want to get shocked, so I faked it."

"Should I stun her?" Jex asked.

"Too late now. Check everyone, make sure they're really out," I said.

They left, and the woman cautiously peeked up at me. She looked to be in her late twenties, attractive in a punk way. "You're the one who took over my eyes."

She'd seen my face, which, because of her implant, meant I'd show up on facial software. Agents—who we called Silvers because of their hair—would be alerted. Probably had *already* been alerted.

I turned my back to her. "She scanned me," I called out. "We have two minutes, tops."

"What do you mean, 'two minutes'?" she asked, her curiosity overcoming her fear.

"Long story." Focusing on the computer, I tried variations of old passwords. None worked. I glanced out at Raven, who was now by herself, Senn having returned to the reception area to keep a lookout. She'd nearly completed our getaway. A black metal frame was braced inside one of the windows, and the defuser that would reduce the glass to sand was already in place. As I watched, she lifted the launcher that would send a zipline to the roof of the parking garage across the street.

"You claimed the government watches everyone," the woman said. She'd gotten up. "I started snooping around. You're onto something. Data doesn't add up."

I tried passwords that worked on other software but still

couldn't get in.

"Your hacking skills are not great. What are you trying to access?" she asked.

"None of your business."

"Kind of is."

I pulled up the root operating system, hoping for an administrator-level access. When I linked my admin-right request to the node software, I heard her inhale sharply.

"Ballsy," she whispered. "Type Alt+G+Control+F9."

"That's not a thing."

"I made it one."

I did as she suggested—and got into the sublevel. The screen filled with everyone's streaming data, one line for each citizen.

"What is that?" she asked, stepping closer.

"What's your job here?"

"Forensic research."

I pulled a random feed. A box appeared, showing the view from someone's eyes: a pair of young hands reached into a purse and pulled out a wallet, the view lifting to a woman sleeping in a bed then back to the wallet. The hands pulled out four twenties, then returned the wallet. "I'm more than 'onto something.' The cameras in our eyes betray us like I showed in my broadcast. That's why we're wearing masks."

"It's really true." Her shock was evident in her voice.

Of course The Agency wouldn't share their violation with every employee. "Complain to your boss. Actually, don't. They'd kill you."

"We have company," Senn yelled. "Coming up the elevators."

I scanned the screens before me, on the verge of getting up—and instead requested diagnostic systems analysis to try to find the nodes' physical locations.

Jex appeared in the doorway. "I disabled the elevators, catchin' two Silvers in a car, but they won't stay trapped—and SWAT teams are headin' up both stairwells. We gotta go."

"Not yet." A datastream appeared on the screen to my left, but before I could follow it, more data appeared, what seemed like a second 'stream but wasn't. There was overlapping information; some was the same, but others were different. As I watched, more repeating data appeared.

Senn raced past my office to join Jex with Raven. "About time," I heard her say. "Ready?"

"Oh shit," Jex drawled.

His tone—and Raven's gasp—made me turn. A dozen feet past her, hovering outside the window, was the female Agent Sari Britt, sitting on one of my old company's hoverbikes with a strange-looking rifle jutting from a holster strapped to the bike.

Before we could react, Britt raised a pistol and fired. The first bullet cracked the window, the next two shots widening the cracks.

I ran to Raven, who backed up as Britt continued to fire, and the window exploded as I reached her, throwing us both back and pelting us with shards of glass.

Jex and Senn stood over us as they opened fire, forcing the Agent to veer off. She flew past the building out of sight.

"What now?" Senn asked.

"We run," said Jex.

I straightened, the outside air swirling around me. "I need more time."

Raven grabbed my arm. "You want them capturing us?"

I shook my head.

As we ran for the hallway, the woman who'd given me the passcode called my name. I stopped in the doorway. "You need to knock me out," she said, averting her gaze. "I'll look less suspicious."

She'd seen the feed, the datastreams. Still, she was right.

Jex tossed me an unused discharger, which I used on the woman. After she collapsed, we ran for the stairwell. When we reached it, Raven quickly climbed over the railing. I heard footsteps below us. One of the SWAT teams.

"Come on, goofballs," she whispered. She leapt—and

grabbed a dangling grappler as my heart stopped. Jex went next, and the two swung our grapples toward Senn and me.

As we hung forty-seven floors above the ground, Jex dug into his pack and withdrew three flash-bangs. He keyed them one-handed, then let go. I closed my eyes before they went off in quick succession as they fell, the sounds deafening in the enclosed stairwell.

We dropped before the SWAT team could recover. Floors passed in a blur, our grapplers not engaging until right at the end, when they slowed us just enough that we didn't break anything when we hit the ground floor. As soon as we did, I grabbed Raven and lurched for the door while gunfire rained down.

I steered the group to a side door that led outside. We'd planned to zipline to the garage across the street, but this would have to do. "Ready?" When they nodded, I left the building, the rest following.

The street was clear—although more SWAT teams would appear any second.

We ran toward the eight-story parking garage, but as we neared, I slowed.

"What's wrong?" Raven asked.

I considered running in the other direction to lure Britt away from the others, but Raven would come after me. If we were going to fight, our only chance was to do it together. "We have to set a trap."

Jex and Senn exchanged nervous glances. "Okay," Raven told me, looking the way she had the day Talia was killed.

"Get inside the garage and be ready." I scanned the skies as they did, my heart pounding. I knew one day I'd face another Agent. That didn't mean I was ready.

The hoverbike appeared—and after Britt saw me, I ran after my team.

The garage's first floor was level with the street, encircled with a waist-high wall. I plunged inside and dashed down the center toward the far end—though I knew I wouldn't reach it.

The roar of jets grew behind me, then faded as Britt landed.

I stopped and faced her.

She'd parked just inside the garage. Now she climbed off the hoverbike, slid the shotgun-like rifle into a holster over her shoulder, and started toward me. There were four of us—five if Bhungen, who drove us here, had jumped out of our getaway van to help—but I feared it wouldn't be enough.

We had seconds before more Agents arrived.

She extracted a pistol as she walked. "I know who you are. The Agency's Director wants you. I'm going to hand you to him myself."

There was a click to her right as Jex cocked his pistol. Another click followed, to her left, from Raven, who stood ten feet from me.

I raised my pistol as well.

Britt stopped a dozen yards away. "Your speed won't take out all of us," I said. As an Agent, she would be augmented, able to move faster than nature allowed.

She glanced at Raven, then Jex. "I like your new faces." Shit. She must've somehow shifted her vision's harmonics to see through their masks.

She swiveled to Raven and raised her gun.

Without thinking, I leapt at Raven to shield her, tackling her. Gunshots rang out, though not at us. Britt had swiveled back and fired at Jex instead, who'd barely managed to duck in time.

The Agent faced me with a smug grin—then flinched as Bhungen appeared from behind a pillar and shouted. She spun and fired at the Taiwanese rebel as he ducked back, but when Senn stepped out from behind an SUV, she was exposed. He shot her twice, the first clipping her side, the second nailing her left arm she raised almost too fast to see.

She stumbled back, hurt but still dangerous. I could tell she reassessed Senn, recognizing his shooting ability as a threat.

I got to my feet, my gun pointed at her. "Drop your weapon."

Jex had recovered, and Raven stood as well.

Britt scanned us—we had her nearly surrounded—seemed

to gauge her odds, then tossed her pistol to the side and held up her hands.

We approached cautiously, all except Jex, who went for his bag.

I extracted the handcuffs from a leg pocket and turned them on. If my calculations were right, they'd hold her.

Nearing, I got a good look at her. Same slender neck as her picture, same intense eyes. She had a runner's body and was almost my height.

I reached out to grab her wrist—and in a single motion, she stepped back, pulled the shotgun-like device from its holster and swung at Senn and Jex, knocking them down, Jex's pistol flying. She then kicked me so hard I was thrown backward, landing awkwardly.

Bhungen was too far away. The only one left nearby was Raven.

Britt didn't sound even slightly winded as she approached me. "Kieran will be ecstatic that I caught you. Traitor."

I felt a flash of anger at hearing his name.

With a battle cry, Raven attacked her, firing repeatedly as Britt tried to dodge the attack—and caught the Agent in the left shoulder, disabling her wounded arm.

The next moment, Britt grabbed Raven's throat with her good hand.

I jumped to my feet, my gun trained at Britt's head.

"Drop it, or I squeeze," she said. She'd read my file. Knew my weakness.

Behind her, a hoverbike landed in the street outside the garage. A burly Silver, his short hair glinting in the bright sunlight, got off the bike. It was the other Employee of the Month. Gunnar.

He dismounted and leisurely started for us, assured in our demise. I understood why. The guy was even bigger than Senn.

Before I could do as Britt ordered, Raven angled her Glock and shot the female Agent in the thigh. Britt gasped in pain and let go of Raven—who then kicked her, driving her to her knees.

Gunnar paused just inside the entrance, confused by the

turn of events, then started faster toward us.

As Senn ran to us, I went to cuff Britt's wrists, but she lashed out, knocking me back, then swung at Senn and caught him in the side of the face.

"Stop," Raven said, her Glock aimed at the woman's head. Britt was still on her knees. Her speed wouldn't save her.

I saw the fury in Raven's eyes change to conflict and fear. She began to shake.

Before Britt could react, I raised my Glock, but Jex was faster. He fired his taser, which he'd cranked to the max setting, the charge like a mini lightning bolt—and knocked her out.

Raven kept her gun aimed at the woman, her arms shaking.

Gunnar was closer, a lumbering mass of impending death. Behind him, SWAT teams poured out of the office building.

I wanted the dark matter sphere in Britt's hoverbike, but there was no way to get it in time.

I ran to Jex's bag instead, snatched a zapper grenade—brought in case this all went to hell—flipped it on, and tossed it at the hoverbike. Then I took off for the far side of the garage, my team beside me. When we reached the wall on the back side of the garage, I turned back—and spotted Britt on one knee, aiming the shotgun-like weapon at us. Jex must've seen her as well, for he leapt as if to shield me and crashed into me.

The next moment, the grenade exploded, the shockwave laced with a digital scrambler.

Multiple car alarms went off as the ground shook, and black smoke filled the air.

I stood as the smoke cleared. Neither Agent was visible, the SWAT team driven to the ground.

"Are you all right?" I asked Raven, helping her up.

"Didn't lose any body parts."

Bhungen was back at the van, which he'd parked down the street. We quickly joined him, piling in the unfinished back as Bhungen started the engine.

"Are you hurt?" Raven asked Jex, running her hands over his chest.

"Must've missed me." He gave her a quick kiss, then used a handheld remote driver to trigger two preprogrammed vehicles we'd planted. The vehicles raced out of the garage in different directions as decoys. Bhungen drove off as well, only going a little over the speed limit.

"That hoverbike's a bad sign," he said as he drove. "If there had been more, it would've been a slaughter. Speaking of, why didn't you shoot that chick?" He glanced back at Raven, brown eyes questioning.

Jex spoke up to cover for her. "We have to be better than 'em."

Senn frowned at Jex's leg. "What is that?"

Jex looked down, and his smile faded. "Don't know."

I knelt beside his leg. A rounded piece of metal stuck out of his calf. It had a bulbous end and five prongs, like spokes of a wheel. The ends of the prongs jabbed into Jex's skin as if supporting the device, which seemed to be a projectile, though unlike any I'd ever seen. It must have come from the Agent's weapon.

"Was he shot?" Raven asked.

"I think so." To Jex, I asked, "Did you feel anything?"

"No."

I extracted a metal blade and slipped it down the length of the protrusion to pry it out—but the bulbous end moved, lifting up as if to puncture something deep into Jex's leg.

Shit. I dropped the blade and grabbed my Glock.

"Wait," Jex said. "What are you—?"

"Don't move," I said. Before he could react, I shot him.

CHAPTER TWO

Jex yelled as he clutched his leg.

Raven shoved my gun away from Jex's body. "Dad! What is *wrong* with you?"

I regretted shooting him but held onto his ankle to see if the bullet had taken out the bulb cleanly. If I'd stopped it from injecting whatever it was going to inject.

I was vaguely aware of the van accelerating as I scanned Jex's leg.

Whatever the device was, I couldn't find any remnants, though the blood seeping out didn't help.

I holstered my pistol and moved his leg out of the way to search the van's floor, which caused him to yelp.

Raven punched my arm. "Stop hurting my boyfriend."

"Sorry, kid," I said to Jex as I searched the floor. The bullet had made a hole, and both it and whatever device Britt had imbedded in Jex's leg were gone. Still, I ran my fingers along the painted metal, running them through the thin coating of blood to see if I could locate anything.

"Stop moving me," he said through gritted teeth.

The van shifted as Bhungen took a corner too fast.

Shit. Our escape.

I let go of Jex's leg and slapped the electrostatic discharger we'd brought.

The discharger triggered with a throaty buzz—and

knocked out every person's feed in a three-block radius, along with my own network. The two fake getaway vehicles would've triggered their own dischargers at the same time as ours, adding to the chaos.

It gave us a chance, but the dischargers would only blind The Agency for thirty seconds.

"How much further?" Senn asked Bhungen.

"It'll be close."

"Go faster."

Jex whacked his damaged leg into the metal wheel well as Bhungen took another corner and yelped again. Raven shot me another glare.

"You saw he was hit," I told her as I reached for the first-aid kit.

"I saw something, then you shot him."

I opened the large kit and pulled out three thick pads.

"You sure you didn't feel the thing hit you?" I asked Jex.

He shook his head, wincing. "Felt your gunshot, though. Got any pain meds?"

Raven snatched the kit from me, but I managed to grab the syringe pre-filled with nanobots, its large needle gleaming.

"Ah, hell no," he said.

"Did you two find anything in The Agency's computers?" Raven asked to distract him.

"I found a bullet. In my leg."

We took another corner, the three of us shifting.

"Don't move," I told him.

Before he could protest, I grabbed his leg and jabbed the needle into the hole I'd made.

He muffled his cry.

I emptied the syringe—though it wasn't enough to heal the wound, just slow the bleeding—as Raven comforted him, then she and I started to bandage his leg. Droplets of blood covered the three of us.

A cell phone rang.

"Don't answer that," I said.

"I was told to call in," Jex said, grimacing.

"Don't, and don't answer. Just leave it."

Senn spoke up. "We got problems."

I raised my head. The world visible through the windshield and front windows looked harmless enough, a typical part of downtown Los Angeles, the buildings only a couple of stories in this area. Yet nothing was harmless nowadays. The software I'd created years ago linked every public and private camera to track potential crimes, but The Agency had commandeered it to help retain control, which meant the dozens of cameras covering nearly every block could be used against us. And with the implants we all had, anyone who saw our faces unintentionally revealed our presence via the cameras in their eyes.

It wasn't just the cameras and people. This area had been scarred by the riots that stemmed from my broadcast. Two lamp posts had been pulled down, the traffic signals and cams ripped from their perch, and many of the windows remained boarded up. A temporary stop sign stood on the corner up ahead—next to a DNA scanner.

Shit.

I glanced at Jex. "Have they linked your DNA to you?"

"I got arrested once."

Which meant yes. "Bhungen, can you pull off somewhere?"

Bhungen shook his head. "There's a cop behind us."

"We need to seal the wound," I told Raven. She nodded and wrapped tighter.

I snatched a pad from the kit and jammed it into the bullet hole in the floor, unsure how much had dripped out, if any clung to the undercarriage. A thin layer of blood was smeared in a streak across the painted-metal floor. I used more pads to soak it up, but tiny droplets containing his DNA would still be hanging in the air from the gunshot.

"Slow down," I said to buy time and grabbed our packs.

"I can't go any slower," Bhungen shot back.

He was cocky and always brought too much shit—which was why I opened his pack first. I pawed through energy bars and a change of clothes, pushed aside a pair of bolt cutters, ignored a wad of cash, and found an old-style canister blowtorch next to a lighter.

I snatched up the blowtorch and quickly twisted the knob to unleash the gas.

"Uh, aren't you forgettin' somethin'?" Jex asked, eyeing me nervously.

I waved the canister in the air to spread the rapidly-releasing gas.

"Everyone, cover your face." I set down the now-empty canister, grabbed the lighter, covered my face with my arms, and flicked the lighter.

There was a loud *poof* and a flash as the gas ignited—someone yiped—and immediately flamed out, hopefully destroying any airborne particles of blood in the process.

I dropped my arms and scanned the others. Thankfully, Raven didn't use hairspray on her long hair. Other than some singed tips, it was fine, and she was unharmed. Same with the others, though Jex's shirt smoldered a little.

We neared the DNA scanner. Even from inside the van, I heard the device's clicking sound as it drew in pockets of air to test. None of us moved as we rolled past, forced to slow further to drive over a speed bump which had been installed next to the scanner. Raven and I shared a look as the clicking grew loud, then faded as we passed.

Senn leaned forward to watch the side mirror. "The cop's slowing down."

Probably getting a readout from the scanner.

Since the van only had windows in the front, the cop shouldn't have seen the flash unless he happened to look at one of the side mirrors at the right time. He hadn't reacted so far, yet we remained tense. Bhungen took the next left, then both he and Senn relaxed, which told me the cop had continued on. Seconds later, we pulled into a large, multi-exit parking garage. Senn jerked away from the window right as we pulled in.

"What is it?" I asked.

"I spotted a hoverbike."

Agents would be combing this area. I'd heard they had increased their hold over L.A. since the night of my broadcast six weeks ago, which meant we had to get out of the city as quickly and quietly as possible. "Did they see us?"

"Not sure," he said as Bhungen drove down one level.

We pulled into a spot. "Ready?" he asked.

"One second," I said.

"We don't have time."

"Get in the other vehicle. We'll be right there."

While they climbed out, I helped Raven finish bandaging Jex's leg, aware of the blood on us. I handed her strips of medical tape, which she wrapped around the top and bottom of the stretched gauze. As she finished, I pulled off my jacket to leave it behind, revealing my gray undershirt and told them to do the same.

"Come on," Senn hissed from outside.

I pulled out my ion blade and grabbed Jex's leg. Ignoring his protests, I cut away a strip of his pant leg that had been stained.

Our efforts weren't perfect, but they'd have to do.

Senn opened the van's sliding door and helped Raven with Jex. I wanted to torch the van to hide evidence, even though The Agency already knew who we were, but a fire would draw attention.

We'd parked next to what appeared to be a small, ivory-colored refrigeration truck, the name of a fake ice cream company displayed on the side. Bhungen was already behind the wheel. After making sure no one was around, we got in, Raven first, then Jex awkwardly, struggling to get past the front passenger seat into the back, then me. Because of my modifications, the only way into the rear was by climbing into the front seat and then ducking through a row of clear, thick plastic strips we'd kept in place that separated the front from the rest of the interior.

The rear was dark and narrow. More of my modifications. Jex and Raven squeezed to one side to leave me space.

"We need to get him to the med unit," she told me as I

sat, pointing at Jex's bandage, which was already soaked through with blood.

Senn settled into the front passenger seat as Bhungen pulled out of the space.

"Kinda dizzy," Jex said.

"Here, lay down," I said. We moved around to give him room.

As Bhungen approached the exit, his phone rang again. "Don't answer it," I said.

Senn glanced at me hesitantly, his worry etched on his chiseled face. When I nodded, he triggered the electrostatic discharger we'd hidden in the truck, which masked our exit and also scrambled the incoming call. The phone fell silent.

A minute later, Bhungen muttered under his breath. "Crap."

I pulled the plastic curtain aside in time to see two police cars shoot past, lights flashing but sirens silent. Searching for us.

The next intersection contained the entrance ramp to the 110. Due to the bulk of our vehicle, Bhungen had to slow before taking the ramp, though he accelerated quickly. The modifications I'd made should fool the sensors imbedded in the road of the multi-lane highway, but we were far from free.

We picked up speed as we joined the flow of traffic. The ride was rough but manageable.

I started to settle back when Bhungen swore again and began to brake.

Through the windshield, brake lights flared across all lanes of traffic.

I pushed aside the plastic. "Is there an accident?"

"Not sure."

Senn leaned forward, scanning the road—and was the first to see them. "Drones!"

Scout drones swooped down a quarter mile ahead. Dozens of them. Then hundreds. The drones slowed as they neared the vehicles ahead of us, gliding between each one, scanning. They'd check not only vehicle VINs but each passenger's neural net feeds.

And they'd have infrared scanners.

I let go of the plastic strips, which settled back into place.

Jex tried to sit up, but I put a hand on his chest. "No one move." He settled back, frowning, while Raven appeared afraid yet focused. "Let us know when," I called out.

"Fifteen seconds," Senn said.

To Raven and Jex, I said, "Don't forget to cover your mouths."

"Five seconds."

I covered my mouth with my collar, then reached for the button I'd installed.

"Now."

When I pressed the button, the motors I'd installed initiated the mixture of chemicals I'd layered into the truck. The chemicals reacted, rapidly leaching the heat out of the ceiling, walls, and floor that made up the rear compartment. Within seconds, our portion of the vehicle mimicked an actual refrigerated truck.

While I had included a layer of insulation in the floor, the temperature still dropped, and Jex arched his body to try to avoid the sudden cold against his back.

Both Raven and I pushed on his chest to keep him still, though all three of us trembled from the cold.

Through the blurred view of the plastic curtain, the drones approached; they looked like a massive octopus-like creature spreading its arms down each row toward us.

Beside me, Jex breathed rapidly, struggling with the temperature.

The front edge reached us, the drones slowing to inspect us before continuing on. But these drones would scan repeatedly, one after another, at multiple angles and different wavelengths.

We had to keep still.

More drones passed, a few gliding up over vehicles, including ours. I thought I heard others circle behind us for further inspection. Maybe they were. They could be underneath as well.

I didn't dare breathe.

Jex clenched his fists as he forced himself to exhale slower, his shirt, which he'd pulled over his mouth, dissipating the heat from his breath.

The chemically-induced cold, which hid our body heat from the drones' sensors, wouldn't last long. The vehicle was too big, the California sun too strong.

More drones congregated around us. Two rose in front of the window to scan Bhungen and Senn. Their sensors could see through the curtain. If we moved one inch, the heat differentials would tip them off.

Bhungen and Senn claimed The Agency didn't know they were rebels—they'd never been arrested or questioned—but we weren't 100% sure.

A moment went by. Two.

Then the drones rose up out of sight, the pack dissipated, and vehicles started to move.

Bhungen started forward when he was able; he and the other drivers proceeding cautiously. After a few seconds, I saw why: parked to the side of the road were three vehicles. I couldn't tell the types or whether they were damaged but didn't need to. Through the plastic curtain, I saw the silver hair of three Agents. They'd initiated the roadblock.

Even as we drove past, I knew The Agency wouldn't give up. Agents would hunt us until they destroyed us—or we somehow defeated them.

As Bhungen picked up speed, I heard the buzz of a cell phone. Different from earlier. Senn removed a burner phone and checked it, his slurp of his Life Saver ending abruptly. He pushed aside the curtain and held out the phone to me, which displayed a text. "It's from Valor," he said.

The message read: *Get back to HQ right away!*

CHAPTER THREE

Fluorescent lights whipped overhead as we drove through the tunnel that punctured one of the Sierra mountains in eastern California, the lights catching the edge of where Anya had burned a hole in my left lens when The Agency temporarily blinded me a month ago. This time of night, we were the only car on the two-lane highway.

Senn pressed a button on the dash, and with a clunk, the projector trolley disengaged from the undercarriage of our truck, drove out from under us, and activated its hologram as Bhungen slowed. I watched for a moment as the 3D rendering of our vehicle continued on, a dummy that projected our image and metal signature that wouldn't stop until it reached a pre-planned location miles north of here and hid in a culvert. We could retrieve it later when it was safe.

Bhungen cut across the highway and aimed for what appeared to be the side wall of the concrete tunnel. The next moment, he drove through the hologram and stopped in the small receiving area, which was large enough for six cars. A guard lowered his machine gun when he recognized us and waved us to an empty space.

Though we arrived in one piece, we spent the entire four-hour trip scanning the skies and road behind us. We were wary, tired, and didn't know what awaited us.

After we got out, Jex limped away from the truck, then

stumbled. Raven caught one arm, and I grabbed his other. He'd lost more blood than I'd realized. We carried him toward an arched pathway that led deeper into the mountain, avoiding the round, blue mass-projectors that hung from the center of the walkway, which added the illusion of density if the government ever scanned the area.

We exited the tunnel into the central hub of the rebels' headquarters, a circular room that was eighty feet across. The entire complex had been fashioned out of a former salt mine; a wide tunnel pierced the hub, creating a large hallway that stretched off to the north and south with living quarters, meeting rooms, offices, storage rooms, and training areas fashioned out of what had been carved before. Cables ran along the walls and edges of the ground everywhere. Even with our tech, we still depended on cables for power and connection.

Vents ringing the central hub and burrowed into other strategic spots throughout the complex prevented the place from smelling like six hundred people lived here. The vents were only a few inches wide and auto-masked at night to block even ambient light from leaking out, another protection. There wasn't a single indication that we were here. We leached electricity from multiple sources, and the water pipes and sewer had been constructed decades ago when the mine was established, the records long since destroyed.

Though it was late at night, nearly two dozen people were grouped in the central hub, viewing one of the screens screwed to the rough-hewn walls. It was how we received warnings, news feeds, and other information.

An uplink-blocker hung by a thick column from the ceiling that arched thirty feet overhead, supported by four metal cables bolted into the ceiling. The blocker had been stolen from a shuttered middle school—all schools needed powerful blockers to prevent students from cheating on tests—so we wouldn't have to worry about our implants revealing our presence. Even so, I kept my feed-blocking cap on.

Behind me, Bhungen and Senn sighed in relief as they

removed their caps. Raven followed suit, unhooking a more subtle implant blocker we'd created, a curved, silver disc that covered an implant but made it look unshielded. She tossed her blocker into a box by the entrance that contained hundreds and grinned as she looked around. She was in her element.

A Black woman larger than me with muscle, attitude, and hatch-mark tattoos burst from the crowd. Her frown lines were deep, corn rows swinging, eyepatch covering her left eye. Her right eye was pretty, though I didn't think it was appropriate to tell her that. A former artist and amateur bodybuilder, she called herself Valor, and she was my other self-appointed bodyguard. I didn't think she and Senn knew each other before they joined, but both took their role seriously. She wore street clothes like most everyone else, though she carried a pair of chrome-plated plasma handguns she'd etched with intricate carvings. "I can't believe you left without me."

"Senn told me you were busy," I said.

She growled at him. "I'm going to twist your exercising ass into a pretzel."

Before Senn could reply, Jex sagged in our grasp.

"Med unit," Raven said to me, the concern on her face echoing my own.

We carried Jex to the five-bed med unit, which branched off the central hub, ignoring his weak protests.

After we carefully situated him in one of the beds, our resident surgeon appeared, her translucent face and short blond hair making her look like a Scandinavian goddess. I'd met Anya—Dr. Nystrom—when she operated on Raven two months ago. Anya had been the one who'd inadvertently revealed how the government watched everyone. She'd pretty much saved my life, patching me up after Kieran stabbed me and restoring my sight. She even helped me broadcast my message to everyone in L.A., and in the process, became something more. What that was, I wasn't sure yet, though I had hope.

She quickly took in Jex's condition, then began to unwrap his bloody bandages. "What happened?"

"Boss man shot me," Jex slurred.

Senn and Bhungen chuckled, but I didn't. I wish I hadn't hurt him, that I hadn't had a reason.

"Where did this happen?" Anya asked.

"In a parking garage in L.A.," Raven told her. "We invaded one of The Agency's offices."

Anya looked at me incredulously, then scanned all of us. "Anyone else shot?"

"Just him," Raven said.

Anya finished removing the bandages. The gunshot wound was clean; the bullet had missed bone, though it had taken more tissue than I'd realized, possibly due to the spokes.

Senn leaned over as Anya cut away the rest of the gauze. "Battle scar. Nice."

"You can take off your cap," Raven whispered to me.

"Later." I explained to Anya what happened, then added, "There may be fragments from whatever began to burrow into him. I want to analyze them."

Jex struggled to sit up. "Is *that* why you're hangin' 'round?"

I rested my hand on his shoulder. "I am sorry. I'll make it up to you."

"You've got to work on that bedside manner," Anya told me, her sky-blue eyes smiling. "You're lucky you all weren't shot."

"I was banged up a little," Bhungen said.

"Oh please," Raven said.

I stepped closer to Anya. "Need any help?"

"Trying to get on my good side?" she joked, then turned serious. "You aren't hurt but not telling me, are you?"

I lowered my voice. "If that's an excuse to get handsy with me, I'll allow it."

She grinned, though it faded. "Unfortunately, you won't have time to be disappointed," she said, nodding at Valor.

I frowned as the bodyguard approached. She was one of the toughest people I'd met, having walked across Death Valley to join the rebellion—while evading two Agents who'd hunted her halfway across the country—yet she looked shaken.

"You need to see this." She held up a vid screen and played a slightly-jerky clip that revealed a gathering inside the central hub, what looked like the entire mountain population packed together. Isiah Lafontaine, one of the rebel leaders, stood on the small platform carved into the rock.

"The second revolutionary war is upon us," he declared, the other leaders clustered behind him. "We're going to launch a full-scale attack on one of the Army's bases here in California. It'll be a great strike that will capture the hearts and minds of our citizens. They will discover our righteous purpose and will know we fight for them."

A cheer went up as the clip ended.

Raven, Bhungen, and Senn, who also caught the vid, were stunned, as was I.

"They said your broadcast failed, and this is how we'll win," Valor added.

"By attacking the Army directly. The U.S. Army," I said angrily. "I knew the leaders wanted to make a big statement. I didn't know they were so goddamn reckless."

"They announced it while you were out, so you couldn't object," Raven said.

"If we pull it off, it will be big," Bhungen said.

"Nothing about this is right or just," Valor said. In addition to protecting me, she acted as our moral compass at times.

I said, "There are over a million and a half active military in this country versus what, a thousand of us? Maybe two, counting the other clans?"

"It's what you wanted, isn't it?" Raven asked me. "To defeat the government?"

"Not like this."

"Then what was your call to rise up about?"

I instructed my team to get some sleep, told Anya to let me know if Jex's condition worsened, and then left, but I didn't head to my room. I took the med unit's other exit instead, a carved archway that led through a supply room to the north hallway that extended from the central hub.

The wide hallway, like the rest of the facility, normally bustled with energy and purpose. Due to the late hour, the hallway stood empty, though tension permeated the cool air, voices and the clink of glasses audible from various rooms I passed.

The hallway widened further as one side curved outward. A pair of double doors stood at the apex of the curve, the doors the entrance to the leaders' chamber. I'd only been inside once, to make my case before them. Other than Amandez de Vera, the leader of my eighty-six-member clan, I'd never spoken to the other six leaders before yesterday, though I knew who the main ones were.

The rebels were divided into "clans" that had formed over the years in different parts of the country. I was part of the Founding Fathers clan, though it wasn't the biggest. That designation went to Earth's Redeemers, which Lafontaine had established seven years ago, making it one of the oldest. He'd been a minister in southern Missouri with a congregation of over twenty-five thousand. After he learned the truth about the federal government, he told his flock. Few believed him, but those who did followed him out west, zealots who took his every word as gospel. He'd attracted a swarm of believers since reaching California and even owned this mountain, bequeathed by one of his people.

Lafontaine wasn't the most powerful rebel leader. Nash Perenko held that position, his cartel-like resources and cunning outshining the others. Yet Lafontaine had grown more influential over the past few weeks. The clan leaders planned to meet sometime soon to select one of their own to spearhead the rebellion, a modern-day George Washington. I suspected Lafontaine was angling to become that leader, regardless of how many people died for his ambition.

I lifted my fist to pound on the door.

A rough voice spoke. "Don't bother."

I turned to face Cole, who leaned against the far wall. "I need to wake them."

"Their quarters are elsewhere—but even if they were inside, you're smarter than that." The broad-shouldered rebel colonel almost smiled, though it would've been crooked. The wound he'd suffered the night of my broadcast was healing, though the gunshot had taken a part of his jawbone, which saddened me; the injury not only reflected his suffering, it clearly identified him and, unlike his other scars, was virtually impossible to hide. "You pushed them to do this—at least, that's how they see it—so you're the last person they'll listen to. They want to make a statement."

"You mean Lafontaine does. The Army will crush us—and we'll risk hurting civilians, which could make us actual terrorists."

"Nothing you say will change their minds. They've made their decision."

I closed my eyes, exhaustion washing over me as the colonel, who'd hated me once, approached.

"Rest up, Dray. You'll need it."

* * *

The upper-level hallway was almost as empty as the main level. Those few still up nodded as they passed, but they left me alone. Maybe they'd heard of my failure. Or they saw my frustration.

I wasn't naïve enough to think our enemies would simply give up their power, even if every U.S. citizen marched in protest. We would have to fight. But I feared it would tear the country apart unless we did it the right way—though I wasn't sure what the right way was.

Strips of scuffed LED lights embedded in the walls were my companion as I walked, along with one or two people who followed me. Groupies, spies, I didn't know. They stayed back, though.

I approached my room, which had been carved out of the salt and rock. The door was unmarked, yet people still found it. Knickknacks had been placed on either side of the entrance: flowers, letters, a pottery bowl that looked like it had been made by a child, and a couple of items I was wary to identify.

A young man slept against the wall next to my door, his blond hair hanging in front of his face.

I gently shook him awake.

He scrambled to his feet and held out an empty dinner plate with a geometric pattern painted on its surface, his nerves evident. "Hello, sir. I brought you this."

"Why a plate?" Though I suspected the reason.

"It's from your kitchen. I thought you'd like it! A comfort from your old life."

There was a chip on one side—which Talia had made after she'd swiped Raven's softball bat when she was ten and raced past the dining room table, the bat clipping the plate and shattering two glasses.

"You inspired me to join," the young man said. "I had no idea I was being manipulated until I saw your broadcast. I also brought the tie you wore the night of the fusion reactor lighting, but the rebels took it."

"The Agency has microphones and trackers that are so small you can't see them. Clothing is the easiest place to hide them. So, teams burn everything to keep us all safe."

"Oh."

I unlocked my door and stepped inside, then gave a small grin. "Is my house just wide open at this point?"

"No. The front door was double-bolted. Don't worry, I locked it back up."

"Too bad about the tie. It was my lucky one."

I closed the door, then placed the plate with the others I'd received. At this point, I almost had the entire set, as others had brought individual plates like a strange gesture of thanks for me opening their eyes to The Agency's lies.

My space contained a small table with two chairs, a bed, a nightstand, and a rickety dresser, with numerous shelves carved out of the rock walls filled with other random objects from my house. Cables strung along the ceiling brought power to the lights.

Thousands had caught my broadcast, but it hadn't led to the huge swell in fighters I'd expected. The government had labeled my claim a hoax, twisted the message, and slandered me.

Not only did our government watch us from the cameras in our eyes, they used our lenses to disguise a dirty secret: the world was running out of oil. The planet's leaders chose to avoid panic by using additives to extend the remaining supply, but the additives poisoned the air. Washington used our lenses to hide the growing smog—then either the same leaders who decided to let the environment choke or some other group, we didn't know which, overthrew Congress and took their victims' personas digitally, projecting the faces of the defeated onto our lenses. No one knew it happened, as the next day seemed like any other, the same faces entering the halls of Congress—at least, that was what was portrayed on citizens' lenses.

Taking off what looked like a simple, black bracelet, my only jewelry other than my datarings, I faced the fact it was too late to fix my failure. I had bet so much on finding the nodes—and instead of finding them, I'd nearly gotten my team captured.

Now we were going to attack the U.S. military.

What had I started?

My team had struggled to defeat a single Agent—and the fact Agents had more hoverbikes concerned me, as that gave them another edge.

Although I was in my room with fifty feet of rock overhead and the uplink blocker providing additional safety, I removed my wire-infused knit cap—which blocked all transmissions to and from my implant—with caution. The computer screens in my lenses flickered, as if my implant was coming online, which made me stiffen. Unlike everyone else here, the implant Kieran saddled me with was permanent, with ID codes that threatened my freedom every time I connected to the digital world.

Because of this, I almost put my cap back on. Instead, I placed it on the table as my implant failed to connect and sat on the bed, then reached over and turned on the device that rested on my nightstand. A hologram appeared of Talia's likeness. The small image was precise in detail, perfectly rendered, though tiny cracks were visible.

I felt a rush of emotions: an easing of tension mixed with a swelling of love and pain, memories dancing at the edges of my thoughts. I understood why Mina had made an avatar of our dead son Adem and pretended he was still alive. I missed Talia so much, her cleverness and independence and goofy heart. I had only been able to grieve her death for a few days; our enemies didn't let me take any longer. It was a part of me now, an ache I wasn't sure I wanted to fade.

The memory of my failing her never would.

What would also never fade was my anger toward Kieran. I wanted to inflict as much pain on him and every other Agent as he'd exacted on me. The memory came hard: the sound of the gunshot, Talia on the ground, blood escaping her twelve-year-old body, the fear in her eyes as she died, and Mina's cries as Kieran held her back. He had manipulated her, using her grief to betray us by convincing her that he could have Adem's files uploaded to a new implant.

She'd chosen her dead son over her live family.

I didn't have a holographic bust of him. I should have. I should've done a lot of things.

For reasons unknown, The Agency had given Mina access to my implant, which I didn't discover until I uncovered it once far away from headquarters. She'd sent messages, layering them with images and videos of Adem. I'd only uncovered my implant twice since then, as each time I risked The Agency capturing me, but when I had, stacked messages had flooded my 'net.

The last time I uncovered my implant, though, no messages had awaited me.

Though I needed to come up with a plan to stop the rebels from fighting the wrong enemy—and, failing that, protect as many of our people as I could—I stared at Talia's image.

If Mina could somehow watch my feed through the bedrock and blocker, she would see our daughter.

CHAPTER FOUR

Two hours later, Anya knocked on my door.

"Were you asleep?" She'd changed out of her doctor clothes into jeans and a teal shirt.

Surprised to see her, I stepped aside so she could enter. "No. Too much to absorb." I closed the door, went to my nightstand, and turned off Talia's bust. "I didn't know you knew where my room was."

"The shrine clued me in." She took in my bed, unfinished furniture, and various possessions.

"Want a drink? Jex left some tequila."

"Must not be good if he left it."

"He said I needed it more than he did."

She gave a soft chuckle. "Do you?"

"Only when he looks at Raven the way he does."

She held up a bag. "I brought food."

I grabbed plates as she pulled two sandwiches from her bag, along with some chips and other basic items the kitchen staff set out every night.

Although I was glad to see her, my surprise didn't just extend to her sudden appearance. I was still adjusting to her return.

After we finished the broadcast that fateful night six weeks ago, Anya and I had searched for Raven. It had been perilous traversing the city, for my announcement had triggered riots.

We drove the van we'd stolen halfway across town before traffic forced us to abandon it. As we continued on foot, we spotted people yelling at each other, others using mirrors to search for the cameras hidden in their eyes. Soon after, a group surrounded us. When they ripped off my mask, I feared they would lynch me. Instead, they helped. Cops came, as did three Agents, which led to a multiple-block fight. Anya and I wouldn't have survived if those strangers hadn't protected us.

We'd made it, though, first to one of the Founding Fathers' camps, then here. Anya and I had grown closer during that time. Then she'd left three weeks ago without a word.

Two days ago, she'd returned.

"You couldn't mention you were going to go invade The Agency's office?" she asked as I poured two fingers' worth of tequila into a couple of glasses.

"It came together pretty fast."

She narrowed her eyes in skepticism, which I ignored as I sipped my tequila. She mimicked me, then focused on her sandwich.

After a few bites, she said, "Jex is stable. I gave him a liter of blood and sewed up the wound. He'll have a limp for a little while, but he should be fine. The night nurse is watching him."

"Did you find any fragments in his leg?"

"No, but there were gouges in the entrance wound I've never seen before, five of them spaced evenly apart. What hit him?"

"Whatever it was, it seemed like it was going to inject something into his bloodstream."

"Did it?" she asked, alarmed.

"I think I got it in time."

She took another bite. "It's horrible about Lafontaine's announcement. I know you have to fight, but the thought of people getting hurt sickens me."

"Is that why you left?"

She flushed. "I had some loose ends. Rebellion-joining had not been on my to-do list."

"'Loose ends'? Anything I need to know about?"

"A woman's gotta have secrets."

"Secrets aren't always healthy." Though I kept my own.

"Says the man with an entire set of dishes. Wanna talk about that?"

I shifted in embarrassment. "It's just a gesture of thanks from some who caught the broadcast."

"I don't even get a salad bowl? You've told these worshipers I was there, haven't you?"

"I'll send them all to you from now on."

"I'll settle for a bowl." Anya took another sip, then sat back with a mischievous grin. "Tell me something about yourself, something few people know."

"I went into space once. Our first Gen Omega rockets worked, but their readings showed anomalies we couldn't figure out. The others convinced me to ride in the next launch to discover the problem. It was a test run, so we didn't announce I was onboard. I was only in space for eighteen minutes before the capsule returned to earth."

"What was it like?"

"During the ascent, I could tell something was wrong. I was so focused on finding the problem I nearly forgot where I was. Then at apogee, I unbuckled myself. I knew to expect weightlessness, but the view outside the window, sunlight glinting off the atmosphere, nearly overwhelmed me. It was one of the best experiences of my life."

"Did you figure out the problem?"

"Yeah, with about twenty seconds to spare. I wasn't completely buckled in before the capsule started its descent. I nearly got thrown out of my chair."

"What did you want to be when you grew up?"

"Never thought about it. Didn't even plan to go to college, though when I did, I was recruited by the football team."

"You're serious."

"I wasn't good enough to play professionally, but they gave me a scholarship."

"And being on the team got you the ladies."

"The quarterback got the ladies. I got ice baths," I said, which made her laugh. She hadn't seemed jealous, just curious. When I'd met Mina, she'd needed reassurance. And validation. Anya, on the other hand, was confident, smart and grounded, qualities I liked. "Your turn."

"Well," she said, drawing out the word as she thought. "I tried for a double major in undergrad: biology and applied robotics. With nanotech playing a bigger role in the health field, I figured if I couldn't get into medical school, I could help people through robotics." She cringed. "I hated it. I admire what you do, but working on tiny little machines was *so* boring."

"Okay, what else?"

"I'm a horrible card player."

"That's all I get? A bad card player?"

"You gave me a space mission."

"Fair." I considered. "After Raven was born, I was so afraid of her getting hurt I drove to a baby store and bought every blanket and plush toy they had, then padded her crib so much that the stuff I'd bought nearly swallowed her the first time I laid her down. I had to remove everything, so I placed the blankets and toys in spots around the house I thought were dangerous, even though she couldn't move on her own for months."

Anya smiled, then took a breath. "Teen romance movies are better than historical romance movies. I don't always like the patients I save. And I'm very cautious, which is great as a surgeon but makes life outside the OR challenging."

She seemed vulnerable. Or conflicted. Gently, I said, "You came with me to save Raven. If you hadn't, I wouldn't have survived."

She stared into my eyes, and I felt something shift between us. "You're smooth. But nothing's going to happen between us tonight."

"Did I seem like I want something to happen?"

"You are a man."

"I'm glad you noticed."

"Have a good night, Dray." She went to the door, then gestured to the device that projected Talia's image. "If you turned that off for me, you didn't have to."

* * *

The next morning, the nurse was in the med unit bent over Jex's body, running a violet-colored, subsurface laser over his wound to accelerate his recovery.

His bed had an additional, adult-sized depression. By its contour, I suspected Raven had slept beside him. Since Anya hadn't mentioned it, I wondered if Raven had waited until she'd left.

"How is he?" I asked, keeping my voice low.

"He woke up around three with a fever. I gave him antibiotics, and more pain meds, so he'll sleep for a few more hours, but he's improving. So long as the fever doesn't return, we'll release him later today."

I wished Anya would let him stay longer. He was exhausted. I suspected he would be mad at me for shooting him for a while, which was too bad. I'd grown to like him. I still didn't know if he was right for Raven, but that wasn't my choice.

"He shouldn't have a scar, at least," the nurse added, indicating the laser.

"Let him. He'd like it."

She frowned at me. "What is it with you people?"

I was surprised to be lumped in with a scrappy eighteen-year-old fighter, especially since before all of this, the most physical battling I'd done the last few years was with Amarjit on Gen Omega's racquetball court. But that didn't alleviate my concern, especially since Jex had been shot with a weapon I'd never seen before. Anya hadn't found any fragments, but that didn't mean there weren't any clues. I leaned over his leg and saw a faint discoloration along one edge of the bullet wound. "You have his chart?"

"You his doctor now?"

I raised my eyebrows, hoping my status—however much I had—would work. She sighed and turned away to retrieve Jex's chart. As soon as she did, I flicked on my ion blade and sliced a tiny piece of skin that included the discoloration, then captured the piece in a gauze pad that had been resting on the nearby tray.

"What the hell are you doing?" the nurse demanded.

"Helping with the scar," I lied.

"Get out."

* * *

As I left the med unit, I found Valor leaning against the wall. "What are you doing?" I asked.

"Have to watch over you."

She'd been waiting for me. "Not necessary," I said, starting off.

"Could be worse. Could have both of us. I convinced the angry exerciser to give you some space."

She and Senn were fanatical about guarding me, which was both touching and exasperating. Some days, they alternated. Other days, I got both.

While her tone was light, she was tense. Ready for anything. I needed to be, too.

The leaders' declaration of war hung over us—and was already transforming the place, which buzzed with anxious energy. A team of rebels assembled weapons racks in the central hub, while technicians laid down more cables along the edge of the hallway. Higher-level commanders hurried past and headed up the north hallway to where people gathered near the leaders' chamber, and the message boards filled with assignments for training, logistics coordination, and other preparations for war. Clenching my jaw, I led Valor into the south hallway, where more men and women passed, some in full battle gear.

Three hundred feet down, the hallway split, both pathways busy with activity. We took the righthand fork and passed a couple of Lafontaine's men who stared at us suspiciously, especially Valor and her eyepatch.

Speculation ran high about the patch. She'd confided to me it hid a camera hardwired to her optic nerve. The camera was closed-loop, but she risked the leaders kicking her out if they discovered it—especially since I suspected she'd used it to record Lafontaine's announcement. Yet she was one of only a few in this country who didn't have a neural net, though she'd had one in the past. We'd crafted a broadcaster for her that mimicked a 'net, but it wouldn't pass scrutiny if The Agency ever captured her. How she'd had her implant removed and lost her eye, she wouldn't say, though she did make a game out of me trying to figure out what happened.

As if reading my thoughts, she asked, "New guess?"

"You were in a dart-throwing contest and stepped in front of a player at the wrong time."

She snorted, though the edge of her mouth curled upward. "You're not even trying."

The air thumped with gunfire as we followed the passageway past training rooms and tactical simulations, all of which were noisier than usual, the air thick with what felt like desperation. Or maybe it was just me. I didn't think we stood a chance against the U.S. military.

"Sir," a man with neck armor and shielded arms said as he passed, then two men in their twenties with thick facial hair approached. "Mr. Quintero, it's an honor to see you," one said.

Groupies. Beside me, Valor made what sounded like a growl. I thanked them and propelled her onward.

Our passageway led to the motor pool, the largest space in the mountain, what had once been the loading area for the salt mines. Instead of continuing down, we took a side passage that led to two rooms. The larger one contained the production equipment Garly's assistants utilized to generate the multitude of weapons, implant shields, and other tech we relied on.

I didn't go to that room, stopping in front of a soot-stained door instead. "Coming in?"

Valor shook her head. "I'd break something. I'll hang here."

I ran my thumb along the ridge of the handle to unlock the door before me, twisted the knob, and entered Garly's lab.

The room, three times as long as it was wide, was crammed

with robotics, drones, plasma generators, electrical enhancers, clean boxes, and leftover food. We'd reinforced the wall at one end so we could shoot devices to see how well they worked, leaving it scarred with indentations, gouges, and scorch-marks. Lab stations gripped the walls toward the center of the room, containing bottles, sketches, 3D printers, and a mess of equipment and gadgets.

Garly sat in front of a small mound of electrical components, wearing a black armband over his lab coat. For Talia. He'd worn it since I told him.

He stood when I entered, unfolding his six-and-a-half-foot frame, his head nearly hitting the ceiling as his bushy goatee stretched into a smile. "The only and greatest! Welcome back to the abode, my Yoda."

"Good to be back."

"How'd it go? I bet Bhungen coinage you'd get clinked."

"Nice vote of confidence."

"Didn't hope it, but they were choice-o odds." A line of small, five-legged robots, each about the size of a key ring, linked together behind him. They moved awkwardly, as if they were still learning how to use their appendages, although four of them were managing to drag a liquid-core motherboard behind a printer. I also spotted clusters of various-shaped magnets being manipulated by a trash-can-sized robot. Nothing that could help me.

I needed to fix my failure, find the nodes, convince the leaders to wait. "I couldn't hack in."

"That's unbelieves! Their system must've been lights out."

"Are you aware of The Agency overlapping data?"

"You sure it wasn't some anomaly?"

I shook my head. Before he could reply, an energy coupler suddenly turned on. Six of the linking robots dangled from the lever that activated it.

"Oop," Garly cried as he lunged and flipped the lever off, jerking it so hard he sent three mini-bots flying. I reached out, caught them as they curled into a loose ball, and handed them to him.

"Sorry," the twenty-seven-year-old said. "They don't mean harm."

While he tried to herd the growing spread of linking 'bots, I set up his microscope analyzer and transferred Jex's skin sample. We had bigger issues, but I had to see what The Agency was up to. As I readied the slide, I told Garly about Jex getting hit by The Agency's strange weapon, me shooting him, and that I'd obtained a sample of skin.

Garly dumped a handful of linking 'bots into a container I realized held hundreds. "Did Nurse Snarly give you that?"

"Why do you ask questions you don't want the answer to?"

The sample appeared on the attached monitor, with the results of a spectral analysis displayed next to the image. "There are traces of liridecane," I said, surprised. It was a fast-acting agent, numbed skin on contact. I scanned the rest of the results. "There are traces of aluminum and a coating agent. No gunpowder, though."

"The projectile was fragilio in some way."

My team, the rebels, depended on me, yet I didn't understand what the object had been—or what it was for.

Raven entered the lab, jaw tight. We'd barely spoken since the med unit. "Did you have to shoot Jex?"

"He was hit with something."

"So shooting him was the answer? You didn't do it because we're together?"

"If it was, I would've shot him weeks ago," I joked.

Her eyes widened in disbelief. I suspected she was trying not to laugh. Then her gaze shifted to the monitor, and her face slackened. "Is that his *skin*?"

"I'm trying to help," I told her as Garly nervously started fiddling with a miniaturized electrical decharger.

"You can't treat him like this, Dad."

"I like the kid. He's loyal, and he makes you happy. Just… give him a razor, would you?"

She tensed as if to argue but didn't, a ghost of a smile appearing instead. "Don't shoot him anymore."

I smiled back. "Did you come here to yell at me?"

"And let you know Cole had to go on a recon mission. The hackers claimed one of their dark-web servers went offline." The hacker group used a series of servers scattered across the country that had been around for years. One going offline was cause for concern.

She picked up one of a pair of thin, brushed-metal objects that each curved around a set of fingerholes, what reminded me of futuristic-looking brass knuckles. "What's this?"

Garly puffed his chest. "Made it myself. First of its kind. It's a glowing blade, chi'."

He showed her the switch, then stepped back so she could activate it. The tightly-woven laser energy glowed as it spun along the curved edge of the seven-inch-wide device, the glow highlighting the joy in her face. The curved blade was a powerful weapon, able to cut through nearly anything, but would it have helped when we fought Britt? The Agent had overcome our tech, knew who we were, and nearly defeated us.

We needed a better solution. And I needed to protect Raven, both against The Agency and the Army.

Garly handed her the blade's twin, which she also activated. Standing in the lab, feet planted, Garly's glowing weapons in each hand, she looked formidable. I didn't know how I felt about that.

She turned off the blades, though her smile remained. "You know I'm taking these."

Garly chuckled. "They're for you. Gifts for the huntress."

"Let's talk about this," I said.

"Talk's lame," she said. She kissed my cheek before heading to the door, blades in hand. "Don't work too hard."

I threw Garly a harsh look as she left, but he seemed too pleased with himself to care.

With an irritated sigh, I gazed about the lab, taking in sound condensers, a laser Garly hoped could turn water into a weapon, charge emitters, and portable dischargers. He'd become obsessed recently with large-scale harmonics. I'd been obsessed with finding the nodes. I feared my efforts had been a waste, however.

One of the tiny robots bumped into my hand. It seemed unsure, though one of its pointy-tipped legs was hooked with another 'bot, and that one to a third, the three seeming to have wandered off from the main group Garly had corralled.

"They're getting brave," he said. "I'm linking their command protocols to the user's emotions. It's quicker than trying to link them with users' intellect, as emotional signatures are more uniform, though it's grisly to tinker. Got the idea the other day when de Vera was all puffy."

The tiny 'bots had been his idea, a hive-robot-network he wanted to explore, but together we'd built surveillance robots—from high-flying recon drones to ant-sized roaming ones—and a defensive 'bot. They didn't feel enough. None of this did. We had one lab compared with who knew how many the government owned.

"Sorry about your new broadcast," he said.

I had recreated my call to rise up, and we had posted it online three weeks ago. "Why are you sorry?"

"Lafontaine ordered the hackers to turn it off. Did that yesterday, before his big speech. Thought you knew."

"No, I didn't," I said, unable to mask my frustration. I was proud of the video.

Garly looked distraught, though his face lit up after a few seconds. "I forgots. The hand shields you conceived are ready-o."

He extracted a pair of gloves from a high shelf, the backs covered in electronics, with support bands across the center of the palms and wrists.

He smiled. "Take 'em for a spin."

I slipped on one of the gloves and activated it. The phased-array projectors emitted high-compression, multi-layered, eddy-current-derived waves to form a curved shield two feet in front of my wrist, almost like a trapped concussion wave. As I watched, the curve became visible, the waves capturing light and tinting the shield a faint, dark-violet color.

The gloves made me feel marginally better. "Have you tested them?"

"Worked like a charm." By our calculations, bullets lost ninety-nine percent of their momentum when they struck the shield, melting as they tried to punch through. "They deflected plasma blasts as well."

The projection—smaller than screenshields but providing better protection—was bulky and slowed my movement, the intense waves blocking the air more than gliding through it. I opened my mouth to tell him, but from the arch of his eyebrows, I could tell he hoped I liked them. He didn't need accolades from anyone. Yet he wanted them from me. "They're a little heavy, but good job."

"Think they could've flipped the tide yesterday?"

I hesitated. "Probably not. The Agents had hoverbikes, which means The Agency probably has dozens."

Garly's face fell. I could relate. We'd developed a number of weapons, but we didn't have anything that directly countered hoverbikes, which gave The Agency superior mobility and expanded the battlefield to the skies. Except for drones, we had nothing that was airborne.

"What about the cuffs? They worked, right?" he asked.

"She moved too fast. Which reminds me, I want to build an emitter strong enough to disable an Agent. I wrote some notes." I searched for the app in my implant, multiple icons appearing in my vision.

"We've got no time to tinker. We have to gear up for the battle. They're deploying in three days."

I felt a touch of panic. "I thought it was a week."

"Teams gotta get in position. I could use your help. I'm flooded with 'I wants.'"

Since the night of my broadcast, I had been so focused on Agents, I hadn't even considered large-scale battles. It was a completely different approach, one I hadn't thought we would be foolish enough to pursue. "What's on your list?"

"Everything! Leaders want stealthy gear and power-punch weapons. If I had time, I'd make self-functioning robots, save some people's bits. The battle they announced will be massive."

I frowned. "How massive?"

"They're gonna swarm Fort Irwin. It's a training base southwest of here." He hesitated. "The base usually has 7,000 soldiers holding up there."

"Against 600 of us. Tell me you're joking." There were more rebels scattered across the country, but I assumed Lafontaine would limit the fight to those staying in his mountain.

Garly shook his head. "I need your help, chi'."

It was going to be a goddamn slaughter.

CHAPTER FIVE

After a long night with Garly and his team developing tech for the coming battle and a few hours' sleep, I made my way through the rising pandemonium. Each of the seven clans had a portion of the mountain to call their own, with barracks, training areas, and supply depots grouped together. As I passed through each area, teams worked on different projects, the areas of engagement already assigned: air defenses, gunnery, and so on.

A series of foot-long, metal cylinders laid in a row near a six-wheeled vehicle. As I watched, one end rose five feet into the air, drawn by focused, overlapping magnetics, and attached to a thick protrusion on the side of the vehicle. The other cylinders followed, rising one at a time to form the barrel of a powerful-looking cannon. The cylinders then glided apart and slipped under the vehicle for hiding. Further along, a group of warriors wearing sand-colored gear lifted their arms and winked out of existence. I paused in surprise until I realized the wall behind them seemed pixelated. The team reappeared and began complaining to a flustered girl off to the side. Camoshields. They might be effective, but they needed fine-tuning.

Rooms I passed displayed various schematics of Fort Irwin, with routes drawn out and satellite patterns indicated. Others showed recon feeds, the rebels' drones kept at a distance to avoid detection.

Minutes later, I reached the Founding Fathers' area.

Like the rest of the mountain, the hallways buzzed with energy. Commanders barked at aides rushing past. Squads of men and women practiced advancements. And weapons, packs, attack drones, and other items were laid out along the main corridor in preparation.

The war had started, and I couldn't stop it.

Angling toward a metal door that stood open, I tried not to estimate how many around me would perish.

I stepped out of the crowded hallway and into the room where de Vera, the leader of The Founding Fathers, sat at a desk. "We need to talk."

The woman raised her head, revealing her leathery face and thin lips. She came from a family that had been wealthy until they spoke out against the government. While they didn't reveal the coup d'état that had taken down our elected leaders, their rhetoric had been exceedingly critical of the political leadership. Within three years, her family's wealth was drained by investments that soured, her two siblings mysteriously vanished on a ski trip, and her father died from a cancer so rare it had never been documented before. De Vera's mother finally told her of The Agency and their coverup, and de Vera fled their home that night, hours before it burned to the ground with her mother inside.

"You had your chance, Dray," she said in her raspy tone. "We can't wait on principled uprisings any longer."

"We have to focus on The Agency, not taking on another enemy."

"We'll deal with Agents in due course."

"You think they'll wait for us to get around to them?"

"We'll fight them, but we committed to this attack."

Desperation seeped into my words. "At their office, I found some weird overlapping data—"

"I don't care. We can't stay in this cave forever." She snatched a piece of paper and stood. "We need your wizardry to pull this off. We need screens, comm disrupters, rapid-fire plasma emitters—are you writing this down? Garly mentioned something about shields."

"Did he mention that Agents have hoverbikes again?"

"The Agency shouldn't be your focus, Dray. Not right now."

I heard her barely-restrained impatience, yet I couldn't give up. "The Agent we fought used a new weapon, which means they have technology we're not aware of."

"I'm sure they have all kinds of gizmos. That's why you're here, to counter them, but for now, focus on defeating the Army."

"Soldiers aren't the ones hunting us."

For the first time, she looked uncertain. "If we don't engage the military, we'll be perceived as weak."

"If we attack, every branch will come after us. We'll lose those we love, and for what? A moment of false glory before a million soldiers hunt us down?"

Her gaze shifted away.

"We have to defeat our enemies the right way, by exposing their actions and having the country rise up with us."

Her uncertainty changed to derision. "People won't rise up. They're sheep."

"Don't underestimate them."

"After PIVOT became law, parents swore their kids would never be implanted, even though that damn virus supposedly will never go away—until other kids got them, which meant their precious offspring might never get their own high-end kitchens and big-screen TVs. So they shoved their babies under the knife. They're sheep."

"If we attack that base, we'll be portrayed as murderers slaughtering innocent servicemen and women. We need to be seen as liberators."

She leaned forward. "We have to do more than random attacks no one pays attention to. We have to do something big."

"You want a big gesture? Let's invade every Agency office in the West—and we'll broadcast their crimes at the same time. It'll be a dual strike that will—"

A male voice spoke behind me. "It won't work, Quintero."

Lafontaine entered the room with two of his huge bodyguards. The clan leader stood six feet tall with large eyes, thin eyebrows, and a wave of painted gold in his hair. The gold wasn't like the Agents' coloring; their silver hair masked multiple implants scattered around their skulls. His was a status thing, though it looked dumb to me.

"Our invasion will catch our enemies by surprise. My plan, our fighters, and our technology will crush their soldiers before they can respond," he said. "In the process, we will grab the country's attention. It'll generate the uprising you've wanted."

I clenched my fists. "Sir, with due respect, your plan is miscalculated."

"You called for war."

"I called for people to stand up and fight."

"Well, they didn't listen." In that instant, I could see how much he disliked me.

I looked to de Vera, but she had sat back down and was rubbing the sides of her head, her posture resigned.

To both of them, I said, "The Agency won't stop. If you go through with this, we'll have two forces coming after us instead of one."

"You're a tech guy. Do tech stuff. Help us win the day." He turned away dismissively. To de Vera, he said, "Do you let all your people act this way? No wonder your clan is the shakiest."

"Killing innocent soldiers won't defeat the government," I said, my voice rising.

He spun back around. "Get out."

We glared at each other. Though we were roughly the same size, I was a lot thicker—but fighting him wasn't the answer. Besides, his guards shifted behind me. If I flinched, they'd tackle me.

I relaxed my stance.

Lafontaine started to smile, then pointed a finger at me. "You're not allowed to leave this facility without my permission. I shouldn't have allowed it in the first place. If you would've been caught, it would've been catastrophic, what with your" —

he waved at my covered implant— "disability."

* * *

A few hours later, I stepped out of the mountain and quickened my pace across open land to the nearest tree, the sun blasting me like a massive spotlight. My heart gave two sharp thuds as I reached the tree, bark scraping my calloused fingertips as I grabbed the trunk. I scanned the sky, didn't see any drones—or, god forbid, hoverbikes—and stepped toward the next tree.

I was defying Lafontaine's order, but it was a small defiance.

My feet crunched the occasional twig as I moved through the grove of trees that stood near the base of the mountain, each sound making me wince.

Although the area was miles from civilization, I couldn't shake my uneasiness.

Each tree had a decent-sized canopy of branches, hopefully enough to shield me from any satellites or high-altitude drones that might be watching, though I couldn't tell. The leaves should've been augmented, which would help; the entire grove had been designed to look natural.

Past the trees, a long meadow sloped down toward a forest that stretched into the distance; a faint passageway leading into the thick forest was just visible from where I stood.

"Hey," a Creole voice said.

Jex stood near a large sycamore, dressed in shifting camouflage, a small toolbox by his feet and a camouflaged bag over his shoulder. I was glad to see him out of the med unit, though he was favoring his good leg. His face was pale—even more so than the paleness all of us mountain-dwellers sported.

I nodded at his bandage. "How's the...?"

"Gunshot wound?" He gave a rogue's grin. "Hurts. You should feel terrible."

"I have more bullets."

His face fell, then he snorted. "Kick a man when he's down."

"Seriously, you okay?"

He limped a little as he moved to lean against the tree. "Yeah. Leg should be normal by tomorrow, accordin' to the nurse. Whatcha doin' out here?"

"I could ask the same thing."

He shrugged. "Improvin' some things. Where are your 'bodyguards'?"

"Left them by the door." They weren't happy when I told them to stay back, but having them with me would increase the risk of being spotted. "No one's supposed to be out here, you know."

"You shouldn't talk, what with your…" He nodded at my implant, nearly mimicking Lafontaine.

The knit cap that blocked my feed pressed tight against my skull. "It's covered."

"I know." His eyes darted away, though he rubbed his brow to hide it. He was wrestling with something.

"I want to apologize. If I'd known my broadcast would've led to Lafontaine thinking he needed to one-up me with this attack, I would've done something else."

"It's the path we're on now." His voice was shaky.

I'd thought he would've reveled in me apologizing. I considered. "What do you think of de Vera?"

"What do your instincts tell ya?"

"She'll follow the pack."

"My thoughts, too. She won't stand up to Lafontaine. 'Sides, he and Cardoza are united. They'll walk over anyone who resists."

Selina Cardoza was another one of the leaders; originally from Pichilemu, a small surfing village on the Chilean coast, she looked like a surfer with blonde hair and sun-scarred skin. Her clan Los Que Ven—Those Who See—occupied northern California, though clans weren't limited to geography. While this led to friction, some leaders like her and Lafontaine occasionally teamed up.

I liked how perceptive Jex was. He kept that ability to himself; I'd only recently discovered it. He masked a lot of his abilities, as well as his feelings, hiding both under his scruffy beard and Louisiana charm. Having both parents murdered at fourteen and forced to survive on his own must've had an influence.

His comment confirmed what I'd suspected. "You know I didn't shoot you on purpose," I said.

"Well, I am shackin' up with your daughter."

"Calling it 'shackin' up' doesn't help."

He gave a half-smile. "I want us to have kids—in like ten years or so."

Amazed he'd admit that to me, wondering what Raven thought about that—and bothered by the thought of Raven being a mother—I asked, "Are you going to marry her first?"

"Lord yes," he blurted, his face reddening. He avoided my gaze, though he seemed to want to say more. He shifted the bag on his shoulder, and I heard a muted clink.

"What're you really doing out here?" I asked as he picked up the tool box.

"Wanted to feel safer. Not used to hunkerin' in one spot this long." He stared off for a moment. When he looked back, tears ringed his eyes. "Shit's gettin' real. We're actually goin' to war."

"I'm trying to come up with an alternative."

"Train's left. And hey, don't worry about Agents. Our luck, they'll show up on the damn battlefield."

"You going to do this? Aim a weapon at another American and fire?"

He looked miserable. "It's what I signed up for."

"Is the fight worth the cost? Up to and including dying? If so, then that's what you need to hold onto."

"Is that what you believe?"

"It doesn't matter what I believe. It's each person's choice. But if it means anything, I support you either way."

His voice turned contemplative. Almost wistful. "I would've married Raven. Had you as my dad."

"You will—if she'll have you."

He snorted again, though he looked grateful for my lame joke.

"Do you think Raven would leave this place?" I asked.

"What, to hide somewhere? She said you wanted to."

I felt a glimmer of hope. "Would she go if I did?"

He grinned crookedly. "Yeah, to wherever you wanna take her—then after she's sure you're safe, she'll leave ya. You two are so damn similar." He stared at me, then started toward the door. "I liked it better when us three were on the run."

Chapter Six

I gripped the metal skin and pushed upward while Garly held the large drone in place, both of us straining not to damage the propellers. We'd cut the skin to the correct size, but its thickness fought me. With a grunt, I forced the metal to bend further, pushing the edge backward the last inch I needed, then slipped the edge under the lip, snatched my ion blade, and melted the lip to seal the metal into place.

When I finished, we set down the drone with a sigh. The skin would protect the multiple plasma bolt-emitters we'd attached to the underside. We'd built two of these drones, each one designed to work autonomously to protect our troops.

"Did you catch any winks?" Garly asked as the Foo Fighters issued from a media player I'd scrounged, the volume lower than I'd wanted.

"Couldn't." We'd stayed up until midnight working on various devices, hampered by time and supplies. We'd managed to create over a dozen chillers the forward teams could use to conceal their approach to the base, yet we needed more.

After my chat with Jex, I'd worried if Raven and others struggled as he did. I found her running invasion simulations of the Army base with her squad. The first attack, she ran in too quickly, and holographic forces gunned her down, which shook me to my core, her bodysuit simulating the gunshots. The second time, she got two others taken out. The third time, their enemy pinned her down as she'd helped a squad mate.

Her inexperience showed.

Which was why I'd made the drones.

And why I hadn't slept.

"Think two are enough?" Garly asked, eyeing the drone and its twin.

"No. We need more air support."

"I got something new I crinkled. It'll take a bit." He inspected me like I was a half-broken respirator. "You're spectral. Go grab some food. I'll clean up."

Vaguely surprised neither of my "bodyguards" was around, I started up the corridor toward the mess hall. I passed the entrance to the lower level, where sounds of teams running simulated assaults echoed up, and reached the main corridor. I spotted Jex as he stepped out of a side room, what I'd thought was a storage area of some kind, dressed in camouflage like the day before.

"You going back outside?" I called as loudly as I dared, but he didn't acknowledge me as he exited the complex via a side door.

I could tell he needed time alone, whether to focus on his task or grapple with what was coming, I wasn't sure.

I proceeded up the tunnel toward the center of the complex.

I passed other clans making shields, enhanced rocket launchers, and other tech, each group haphazardly crafting objects that might or might not work.

I tried to come up with an alternative to attacking Fort Irwin. The best I came up with was searching Los Angeles' permit archives for evidence of the buried cables used to perpetuate the government's lies, in the hopes of finding the new L.A. node, but that would take too long.

As I approached the mess hall, Senn rushed over, wearing a red tracksuit of all things, hair damp with sweat. In the distance behind him, a crowd had gathered. "Boss, we got a problem. The Agency invaded the Founding Fathers' main base."

The news shook me. That was where Cole had planned to

take us when we'd escaped San Francisco. I could've been there. Raven could've been there.

Lafontaine's voice floated toward us from the hub, his words faint this far away. "We have a team already loading up."

"There aren't any survivors," Senn told me.

I frowned. "He just said he's sending a team."

"It's too late. That's not all. There was another assault, a safe house near Irvine. He's sending a couple of people there, but a couple isn't enough if there's trouble."

Over the years, the clans residing in the mountain—the Founding Fathers, Lafontaine's Earth's Redeemers, Cardoza's Los Que Ven, the Rough Riders, Twin Beacons, New Americans, and Spencer's Warriors—had built bases, training facilities, safe houses, and other locations to recruit and rebel. Each had developed in their own way, the Founding Fathers originating outside of Portland, the Rough Riders in western Utah, Earth's Redeemers rising from Lafontaine's Missouri congregation. Each had created networks to expand their numbers in preparation of launching a revolution against our false leaders. Now it seemed The Agency had developed a way to find these hidden locations.

"Stay focused on our goal," Lafontaine told those who'd gathered, his voice echoing down the hallway. "Squads start heading to Fort Irwin tomorrow night."

His timeframe made me tense. "How many people were lost?"

Senn's sorrow was evident. "Twenty at the base and six more at the safe house. The leaders aren't clearing anybody out, not at the other bases or houses or anywhere."

"Why the hell not?"

"De Vera claims we need to 'maintain a presence along the Coast', which means keeping our spies in place. It's Lafontaine bullshit."

I recalled seeing a monitor in the leaders' chamber that displayed every one of the various clans' locations in California and Oregon. There were over three dozen spots, with probably four to five times that number of rebel fighters. "If The Agency found our base and that safe house, they can find more. Lafontaine won't listen to me, nor Cardoza. Do you think we can convince the other leaders to clear out their people?"

"You've talked to them. I'm just a grunt." He glanced down the hall as the gold-streaked leader droned on. "Man, he's pompous. When will God smite him?"

"That's not how it works."

I considered approaching de Vera and the other leaders. We needed to search for survivors and protect the others, but I was forbidden from leaving this place.

As I weighed my next move, Senn bent down and grabbed a leg to stretch.

"Why the tracksuit?" I asked.

"Never skip cardio."

Cole appeared in the hallway, leading a four-person team clustered around someone. From what they were wearing—dark clothing varied enough to avoid looking like uniforms yet reinforced with woven Kevlar lining, flex plating, and enhancers—I could tell they'd just returned from their excursion.

As they neared, I made out the person they surrounded: a petite woman with a sack covering her head and cuffs encircling her wrists.

I was surprised. She was the first captive we'd taken. I wondered who she was.

Selina Cardoza followed the procession, along with a small but growing crowd drawn by the intrigue of a prisoner being brought to the mountain.

Cole walked across the hallway past me, his team right behind, toward a side passage I hadn't noticed.

As they passed, the masked woman spoke. "I want to join Dray Quintero's rebellion."

Cardoza scowled at me. Some in the crowd murmured.

"*My* rebellion?" I asked skeptically.

The prisoner stopped and swiveled toward me. "Dray, let me join you."

She'd recognized my voice—and there was a familiarity

with her response as if we'd met before.

Cole shot me a pointed look, then pulled his captive forward, leading his group into the passage.

Senn popped a Life Saver and leaned toward me. "Think they found her at the dark-web site?"

"Why do you say that?"

"It's where Cole went." His concern was evident; I was concerned as well. The captive, whoever she was, threatened everyone here.

Which made me question why Cole had brought her.

Senn and I entered the passage, the air thick with the rock-dust/salt smell that permeated this place. We followed the narrow tunnel past a sharp turn and stepped through a doorway into what had been offices for the former mining company. The far wall had been converted to contain a large plate-glass window, what I identified as a two-way mirror into the room beyond. Through it, I watched Cole direct the captive to one of two chairs in the room and handcuff her to the table in the center. She'd been placed in an interrogation room. I'd had no idea Lafontaine's mountain had one.

After Cole secured the prisoner, he removed the sack covering her head. Senn nearly choked on his Life Saver when he saw her.

It was the nose-ringed young woman from The Agency office, the one who'd helped me with the Agency computer. She wore jeans and a dark denim jacket, the low collar revealing a falcon tattoo on her neck.

I had just seen her two days ago. Not only had she found our server location, she'd done so seemingly in an instant—and if she could find our site, The Agency could, too.

Cole would've made sure he wasn't followed back, aware of the surveillance out there, but it improved every day. We barely managed to stay ahead of it.

Cardoza confronted me. "Why did she mention you?"

I had to be careful. I didn't know what the young woman might say. "She probably saw my broadcast, like millions of others."

Cardoza turned to two members of her entourage. "Go find out what she knows."

As she watched the two disappear into the interrogation room, I spotted one of Cole's team, an ex-soldier named Monroe. Cole had introduced us once before and often spoke of him, as they'd fought together in Brazil and Turkey. Monroe was extremely fit, in his late thirties. His hair had grown out of a buzz cut, but his body language betrayed his military background.

I approached him. "Where did you capture her?"

He hesitated as he gave me a flat expression. "At the server location, waiting for us. We couldn't determine whether she touched anything other than one power cord. She told us how to get the servers back online, even offered to do it."

"What does she want?"

"To join you, supposedly."

While she would've been searched before being brought here, she could still be dangerous. The fact she'd found—and taken down—our site worried me.

I considered asking for more details, but Monroe's stance made it clear he wasn't interested in talking further.

As I backed away, I caught a snippet of the conversation from the interrogation room. "If I'd wanted to incapacitate all of your servers, I could've," I heard the prisoner say.

"We start collecting people, we're gonna need a bigger cave," Senn said under his breath.

As four more guards entered the room, joining the two already there, Cardoza huddled over her handheld tablet, communicating with someone. Everyone seemed tense, unsure who the captive was or what she really wanted, me included.

"She's probably talking with Lafontaine," Senn said quietly with a nod toward Cardoza. "They're together, you know. Not officially, but she's in his room most nights."

I hadn't known, though it explained her willingness to support Lafontaine's battle plan.

"...the media is full of lies about Quintero," the prisoner

said to Cardoza's men and Cole, her voice issuing from a speaker in front of the two-way mirror. "They claim he's a terrorist, but he's not. He was part of the Gang of Five!"

Eyes bounced between me and the mirror, the dozen or so who had followed us in judging me. I avoided their gazes. Now wasn't the time to think of my old business partners.

Four of Lafontaine's guards entered the offices, shooting everyone looks as if we were enemies. Cardoza approached them. "We need to dispose of her," she said.

I called out to her. "I met her once."

"Whatcha doing, boss?" Senn murmured.

Under my breath, I said, "Getting all the allies I can get."

"Who is she?" Cardoza demanded.

"A possible asset. Clearly, she knows something about the dark-web, enough to find our servers. She could help us."

Senn nudged me. "Maybe it's a sign she found us. You said she did some hack at The Agency's office?"

I didn't respond, aware of his line of thinking. If the prisoner joined our group, she could help fight for our cause online. In a weird way, it felt like I'd be replacing Talia, who could hack into seemingly everything, including the LAPD's network, the FBI's, even my former company's, to my amazement. If she had lived, she would've become one of the top hackers in the world—and probably many other incredible things.

Cardoza faced the room. "Everyone leave."

Those gathered began to depart, but I didn't move.

She smirked. "You think you're gonna have a little pow-wow with the prisoner?"

Her tone slowed the exodus. Lafontaine's guards turned their attention to me. I recognized one of them by his cleft chin: he was one of the guards Lafontaine had brought to de Vera's office. The guy, who was only a year or so older than Raven, looked ready to fight me.

"I'm the best person to get her to talk."

The guard sauntered over. "Let the adults handle this."

Senn shoved him hard. He stumbled back but smiled as

his clan members formed behind him, hands on their weapons.

I hoped Monroe would stand with us, but he remained where he was, his teammates looking to him for guidance.

"Back off, all of you," Cardoza said sharply. She stepped between us. "We don't need your help, Quintero."

"She could have information—"

"If she does, we'll get it. You're not one of us, Quintero. You're not a believer."

Chapter Seven

I swung hard and fast, the augmented sleeves I wore magnifying my blows. Sweat coated my face, my breath quickening. Blows as powerful as mine came hard and fast in return. My chest plate absorbed the majority of the energy I failed to block, but the hits still hurt.

I activated my left-hand shield to protect my stomach, the vibrations shaking my arm and thickening the air in a cone before me—though not as badly as before—and punched over top of it with my right. The move caught Cole off-guard, but he blocked my next punch and continued to drive at me, forcing me back.

Yesterday's confrontation with Cardoza was still fresh in my mind.

I'd tried to beg off training, exhausted from working on tech for the coming battle while trying to figure a way to stop it. Cole insisted we stick to our schedule, though I almost didn't show, as the first troops were scheduled to deploy tonight. But Garly had modified the hand shields. They were more flexible now. They wouldn't stop bullets completely, but they slowed them enough to render them harmless. To offset the reduction in rigidity, he'd modified the projectors to surge when something struck their section, which meant the shield flared at the point of attack. He'd even waterproofed the gloves.

I deactivated my shield, spun past Cole's swing, which made him stumble, and came at him again. My sleeves, which had self-bracing, multi-jointed carbon "tendons" that extended up my arms and wrapped around my shoulders to add power to my swings, responded perfectly; my next blow lifted him off his feet a little. They took a toll, though. Tomorrow my shoulders would throb.

After fending off my next attack, Cole swung one arm high, another low, a move that would've taken me by surprise weeks ago. Instead, I caught both arms, swiveled and pinned an arm, exposing his midsection, and struck.

The blow drove him to one knee.

I stopped. Cole wasn't the person I wanted to punish. The rebellion I'd joined had spun out of my control—and threatened those I loved.

My concern nearly made me miss his expression as he glanced up at me. It was one I hadn't seen before. Like I was no longer a trainee.

I helped him to his feet.

"Got your aggressions out?" he asked, not unkindly.

I chuckled, which released more tension, though I still felt insulted by Cardoza's treatment—and troubled I had enemies I hadn't been aware of. "For the moment."

I deactivated the hand shields and removed them, both gloves soaked.

Cole's training room was an old, upper-level storage area he'd repurposed. He'd selected a few students for one-on-one practice, though he trained me the most. Maybe it was to make up for when I'd been captured before my broadcast.

"The leaders agreed to let you invade The Agency's office because the odds were you'd fail," he said. "Best case, you'd find information that could help. Worst case, you'd be killed—but you would've made a damn good martyr."

"So now I'm just a problem?"

"You threaten their power. Many like you, Dray. Some will follow you if they think you can actually free the government."

"Would you follow me?"

He smirked—or maybe smiled, his disfigured jaw making

it hard to tell. "I still don't like you."

Monroe approached from the far side of the room.

I tensed, remembering his unwillingness to help Senn and me in the interrogation area. "How long have you been there?"

"A few minutes." He looked past me to Cole. "What did you want me to see?"

Cole said, "The three of us need to talk about the upcoming battle."

"You sure about this?" Monroe asked the scarred commander.

Cole nodded as he removed his augmented sleeves, the shiny-black "tendons" retracting into the sleeve cuffs. "Dray, we need to stop them from launching this battle. Lafontaine thinks the Army's soldiers will have rubber bullets in their guns since the base is a training facility, but they only switch their clips before starting a simulated battle and always switch back to regular ammo afterwards. When we attack, their weapons will be lethal."

"Have you warned de Vera?" I asked.

"She wouldn't listen."

"The other issue is the battle itself," Monroe said, his aggression thickening his voice. "Fighting a trained army is unlike anything most of our people have experienced."

"Worse will be the scar of killing innocent Americans," Cole added. "We make an unprovoked attack, we will be forever stained."

"Are other people questioning Lafontaine's plan?" I asked.

"Not sure. One word to the wrong person could lead to accusations of treason."

I ignored the irony of him using that word. "Why does he want to take on the Army when we can't even defeat The Agency?"

"His ego," Monroe said.

"And to create confusion," Cole said. "His team will plant evidence that The Agency is behind the attack. They want the Army and Agency to tear each other apart."

That surprised me. "Will that work?"

Cole looked at Monroe, who seemed reluctant to respond. "Doubtful. The Army could become an ally if approached the right way."

Two spots on his brow caught my attention: infrared sensors. I activated my shields. "Who are you really?"

"What're you talking about?" he asked, though he shifted into a fighting stance.

Cole stepped between us. "Dray, he's on our side."

"Kieran had the same sensors in his brow," I said. "So did Britt, and Thys Gunnar. Maybe Monroe is a Silver in disguise."

Monroe relaxed his stance, though just slightly. "The military installed them."

"Other veterans here don't have them."

"Only career infantry soldiers get them."

Cole told me, "Agents are former soldiers. Each one is a highly skilled and disciplined fighter who tried to qualify for Special Forces but failed. Their failure crushes them—and the Director of The Agency plays on that. He recruits them, then subjects them to multiple surgeries, reconditioning, and genetic modifications. In the process, he strips them of their humanity."

I turned my gaze back to Monroe. "And you?"

He ran his hand through his hair to show he didn't have hidden implants. "I didn't fail."

I deactivated my shields, though I was still tense.

"No one knows who the Director is, but he's created an army of fanatics," Cole said. "He's the reason Agents are modified. Anyone who refuses the process is killed."

Monroe added, "He's created his own little kingdom. The military would be a threat to him."

Which we could use if we didn't attack them. "What about going over Lafontaine to stop him? Can you contact the head leader, that Perenko guy?"

"He doesn't know me, and he probably only knows you through your broadcast, so he'll look at you as a threat," Cole said.

"Every leader looks at you that way," Monroe added bluntly.

Which meant they wouldn't listen. "They're going to get us all killed."

"That's why I'm hoping you have a plan," Cole said.

"I'm trying."

Monroe scratched the skin near one of his sensors. "I'm not impressed, Colonel. He knocked you down with his fancy tech, but I expected a lot more."

"He can make a difference. You saw his broadcast," Cole said.

"You know I'm still here," I said.

Monroe looked at me, then him. "He doesn't have the training for what you want, and this isn't enough. Sir."

"What's he talking about?" I asked Cole as Monroe left.

The colonel faced me with reluctance. "You need to know something. Raven was promoted last night. She's going to head the lead unit. She'll be one of the first ones to enter the base and open fire."

* * *

I quickly left Cole's and headed down a back passageway. I needed to talk to de Vera. Plead with her. Anything to keep Raven out of danger.

Jex had said that she would run off with me to make sure I was safe. I could try to keep her away. She'd be furious, but she'd be alive.

As I debated where I could take her to hide, a clattering of machines drew my attention, issuing from a room farther up the narrow, rough-carved passage. I approached the open doorway and found a handful of rebels overseeing twenty automated sewing machines laid out in a five-by-four grid. They were fashioning identical outfits. Military camouflage outfits. The same uniforms the soldiers at Fort Irwin wore.

Lafontaine's plan became clear. The forward units—including Raven—would slip in and act like Army soldiers until they attacked, their clothes providing camouflage until our other forces came behind them.

I returned to the main level and was passing the entrance to the mess hall when I spotted Raven. She and Jex sat at one of the tables, talking as they ate breakfast, she in her training outfit and Jex in camouflage, his toolbox at his feet. I'd never seen her so taken with someone before. Though they'd only known each other a short time, they were clearly in love.

As I watched, she rested her head on his shoulder.

Maybe he could convince her to run.

I approached, my face grim.

Jex tensed with an old wariness, but Raven lit up. "Dad, guess what? I got promoted! I'm now a second lieutenant." She twisted her body to show me the holographic mark on her sleeve.

Her promotion meant a lot to her, but seeing confirmation of Cole's news was like a blow to the gut. "Do you know your assignment?"

"Not yet, but my squad and I head out late tonight. It takes a few hours to get to the base. Once we get there, we'll hide until the rest join us."

I motioned her outside.

As Jex took their trays to empty, she followed me to the hallway. "You don't know what they've going to make you do," I told her.

"Whatever it is, I'll do it. I'm a soldier." She touched my arm. "I want to change things. This is how."

I recognized her expression: a youthful belief in her actions. I struggled to find the words that would get her to listen and remembered something that had bothered me. "When we were in that parking garage, you hesitated to shoot that Agent."

Raven's confidence faltered. "The angle was bad."

"No it wasn't. You started to shake. You can't hesitate—"

"I'm fine."

A group of fighters passed by, chatting excitedly. Their uniforms looked like vaguely matching casual wear, but they had infrared insignia that troop commanders could see and track.

She took Jex's hand as he joined us, his limp nearly gone.

"Gotta go." She hurried after the fighters, dragging him with her.

I should've asked her the same thing I'd asked him: if she could fire at Americans. Unless I did something, tomorrow would pit her belief in the rebellion against her desire to make the world safer for others. I didn't want her to have to make that kind of decision. For all she'd been through the last two months, she was still a kid.

I changed course and headed for Garly's lab.

As I neared, Valor appeared at my side. "I can't leave you alone for a minute." I was going to ask where she'd been, but she wasn't smiling, hands on the grips of her chrome-plated pistols.

When we reached the lab, she guarded the door as I went inside.

The room was a mess, supplies strewn about and half-dismantled devices lying around like discarded toys. Augmenters, quantum boards, and compression motors covered the rear work area, while a partially-constructed emitter of some kind lay in sections on the work area in front of Garly.

He didn't look much better. His hair spiked out in every direction, and bags hung under his eyes, his armband hanging low on his bicep.

"What is that?" I asked, indicating the emitter.

"Cover for the battle. Fashioned the idea last night."

"Did you hear about Raven?"

"She came by to show off her stripes. She was rad giddy."

"Garly, they're going to send her in the first wave."

His eyes widened. "We need to protect her."

I described the uniforms I'd discovered. "They're just regular cloth. What can you make that she can wear under it?"

"You wanna bubble of protection?"

"Yes, a body-sized shield. I can bring back the hand shields—"

He waved away my offer. "I should have enough projectors. I can zip a bodysuit and slather it with projectors. She may not be able to move fastlike, though, depending on how many I stick on."

"Use every one you have. Will the suit be thin enough to go under her uniform?"

He nodded. "The battery will be bulky, though."

"She can strap it to her back."

He drew sketches of the shield-suit with an air pen, the design first appearing on the top of the work area next to the emitter as if he actually sketched it onto the surface, then rising into the air when he flicked the pen.

"When do you think you can have it ready?"

"It could take all day."

"I'll help."

"The first part is better solo. Help me this afternoon when the sheep come after me." He pantomimed resting his head on a pillow.

I understood a fully-covered bodysuit would take time, but cutting it that close made me anxious. The first units would head out later today, which meant Raven would deploy tonight or tomorrow morning.

"I have good bulletins," he said. "I noodled an equation to counter the hoverbikes: a depth shield. Totally rad if it works. And I reworked the cuffs. I added a zapper inside them so you can subdue whoever you clink."

"You did all that?" I was impressed.

"Would've tried a couple of other tweaks, but a supply run didn't show."

Anything could have happened to it. Still, my paranoia level rose.

Garly retrieved a plastic box the size of my palm. "One more thing. For you."

I opened it to find a black electronic device, three inches across and almost an inch thick. The device was covered with a multihertz antenna, battery pack, liquicore processor, and a hole, probably for a microphone, while the underside had a smooth section in the middle, which I realized would attach to the curved, exposed part of an implant.

"I stayed up all night to finish it. It's a broadcaster! Now you can 'cast from anywhere to recruit people."

"I can broadcast my message?" I felt a glimmer of excitement. I'd been more disappointed about the takedown of my broadcast than I'd admitted to myself.

"Yeah, and in real-time, if you want. You'd have to leave this place, though, as it broadcasts directly to other implants. It taps into your specific 'plant, since your codes don't shake, and zips it out to everyone linked to that node's area. Not sures if it can pop to other nodes. It should, though if The Agency glimpses any of your blasts, they could throw down blockers, so it doesn't spread-like to other areas."

Talia would've liked it, but as I returned my gaze to the broadcaster, I remembered what Cole said. "Hide it. If a leader finds it, it could be misconstrued."

Garly looked hurt. "In what way?"

"They'll think I want to stir everyone up to steal control. I could use it to communicate with their people behind their back, try to recruit them or get them to mutiny."

"Would that be so bad? There have been more sneak attacks, but the leaders have stayed mute: a recon team got wiped out, and another safe house. We need a fresh take. Build your own squads and use 'em to fight Agents while the others play war."

"The leaders are already wary of me. If they find that, they could banish me or worse."

CHAPTER EIGHT

I entered the motor pool with Valor at my side, the banging of wrenches and whining of drills filling the grease-scented air. Nearly two dozen vehicles occupied much of the large, brightly-lit area, parked in a haphazard manner: surveillance and fake delivery vans, tank-like vehicles, two full-size buses, a half-dozen SUVs, a slew of motorcycles, and a couple of modified sportscars.

The long wall opposite the vehicles was actually a multi-sectional door reinforced with metal supports. Lafontaine's team had built it years ago to enclose the space, the door camouflaged on the outside to blend in with the mountainside, the same mountainside I'd walked past when I'd talked to Jex.

"Senn tell you about Lafontaine and Cardoza getting freaky?" Valor asked as we walked past a red '38 LeMans Electro-Sport. "It's summer camp romance."

"They're adults."

"They wanna play lovers, do that, not start a war." When I didn't respond, she said, "You haven't guessed about my badass eyepatch in days. Wanna try again?"

I shook my head.

"Don't act gloomy. It makes me jittery."

I relented. "Your parents gave you a BB gun when you were little, and you shot your eye out."

"What's a BB gun?"

When we reached the hackers' room just past the motor

pool, she took a spot beside the door as I walked inside.

Gear and rebels filled the space, with black cables hanging from the ceiling and hackers clustered around tightly-packed workstations. The stations contained monitors, though the razor-thin screens were more for the benefit of Xenon Saito, the manager of the group. Most of the hacking occurred via the rebels' implants. Anonymous web connectors adhered to their nets, their lenses flashing as they typed with their datarings.

The clicking of random connector switches, one of the many layers of discovery protection they'd installed, filled the warm, humid air.

A young woman glanced up at me. "Saito!"

Within seconds, the manager weaved his way over. He had wispy hair, thick hands, and the skin of someone who'd given up seeing daylight.

"Garly said you wanted to see me," I said.

Saito leaned close. "You have a phone call."

I lowered my voice to match his. "We have phones?"

He steered me toward the far side of the room. "There's a broadcast being sent out across the web, calling for you. We followed the signal to a website that requires you to answer a question before you can access it."

I suspected I knew who was reaching out. I didn't have any interest in talking to her, but Saito steered me to his computer, which was separate from the others, the dual screens private. When I sat down, I saw the question: *What was Adem's favorite toy?*

An old sadness welled up.

Saito plugged in a retro-style headset and handed it to me. "I've set multiple layers so you shouldn't be tracked, but don't stay on longer than thirty seconds. Just in case."

After he stepped away, I donned the headset and entered the answer, which connected the call.

"Dray?"

Mina. My wife, whom I'd once loved more than anyone. "What do you want?"

"You still need me. Always and forever, remember?"

I cupped the microphone. "Our marriage is dead."

"I can help you, but you'll have to do the unthinkable. It'll bring you peace." Her voice turned shaky. "Bring us all peace."

I told myself she struggled with the loss of Adem and Talia, as I did.

"I'm in trouble, Dray. Please come find me."

I heard a commotion in the background, then the call abruptly ended.

* * *

My footsteps were heavy as I left the hacking area.

Unbidden, a memory came: our wedding night, the last dance of the evening before the remaining guests left and we went to our suite, the anticipation of being alone together making my body thrum. Yet I wanted the moment to last. The part of Mina's back not covered by her gown was warm to my touch, her eyes glowing as our bodies swayed, the classic "When a Man Loves a Woman" caressing the air.

It was one of my favorite memories, the start of the family I'd longed for but had surrendered until I met her. My surrogate brothers—Nikolai and Brocco and Zion and Tevin, who with me would later become known as the Gang of Five—watched us from a nearby table, drunk from all the toasts they'd given.

Mina's call bothered me. It was the first time we'd talked since she'd betrayed me and the girls. She'd sounded lucid but scared just now, a contrast to the messages she'd sent to my implant, which had seemed to be her justifying her actions.

I couldn't pretend she hadn't called. She'd once been my world and would always be the mother of my children. I didn't know if I should help her, not only because of the upcoming battle but because of what she'd done. But if Raven found out her mother had asked for help, and I didn't try to find her, I suspected she would never forgive me.

Driven by the memory of Mina's past lies and deceit—though whatever game she was playing would have to wait—I aimed for the north passageway, Valor a coiled presence beside me, her hidden camera a faint sound as it scanned our path.

"You don't have to follow where I'm going next," I told her.

"I suspect I do."

We wove our way through the rising mayhem of soldiers hurrying in either direction and headed to the main hallway.

"Another location went dark," she told me. "One of the training camps this time, in Lancaster. All thirty-eight inhabitants dead or captured."

Though I didn't know any of the rebels there, I mourned their loss, a feeling that had become all too familiar.

We continued up the main hallway. The first troops would be leaving for Fort Irwin any minute. My efforts to stop the attack had failed.

Motioning Valor to stay back, which earned me a scowl, I slipped into the side corridor that led to the interrogation room.

The passageway was empty, but when I stepped into the office, I discovered the first room was not. A young kid, one of Lafontaine's zealots, sat at a nearby desk, the barrel of an assault rifle sticking up past the desktop. "Can I help you?"

Past him, I spotted the prisoner through the two-way mirror, resting her head on the table.

"I came to see her. You're relieved."

"No one's allowed to talk to her."

"A war is starting. You didn't expect to stay here forever, did you?" I asked. "You need to suit up."

"Now?" He stood—then narrowed his eyes. "Lafontaine said you were banished from here," he told me as his hand slid toward a taser clipped to his belt.

"He had a divine vision or something about me getting intel out of her."

The kid wavered, then shook his head. "I gotta call this in." He reached for a landline phone, one of only a few I'd seen in the facility.

As the kid dialed, I walked past him as if heading toward the interrogation room—then spun, hooked the back of his shirt, and before he could rip free, snatched his taser and zapped him.

The jolt knocked him out.

I lowered him to the floor, put the handset back on the phone's cradle, and hurried to the outer door. "Valor," I called as loudly as I dared. When she appeared, I led her inside.

"What the hell did you do?" she asked.

I lifted the kid and held him out to her. "Hide him somewhere."

"This is wrong on so many levels."

"Judgment later. Redeemers will show up any minute."

She hooked an arm around the kid's waist and left, holding him as if he'd passed out drunk—though his feet dragged along the stone floor.

I locked the door behind them and approached the two-way mirror. A voice-activated recorder hung beneath it. I unplugged it, which severed all comms. Satisfied, I entered the room.

She pointed at the ceiling.

"I deactivated it. Why are you here?" I asked, sitting across from her.

"To join you. My name's Nataly Tskovski," she said, her Russian-accented voice a little hoarse. I wondered how well they'd treated her. A cot stood against one wall, the mattress covered with only a thin, green blanket. She still wore the denim jacket she'd arrived in, though it didn't look very warm.

I wasn't sure if I could trust her. "How did you find our dark-web site?"

"It's what I do. Yours are nearly undetectable, but not for me. I found three of your sites and picked the one that was far enough away I would've known if Agents tailed me. I figured they'd track everyone who was at the office when you broke in, so I swiped one of their jamming devices to block my implant's signal, grabbed my bike, hid my face, and followed power lines from east L.A. to Bakersville, then Visalia. I know they track targets via cameras, feeds, drones, and satellites—and our eyes—so I biked at night and used the power lines' pathways to avoid detection."

"Over the course of two days?"

"I was motivated."

"All so you could join us."

She nodded. "Though it won't be very fun if you screw up. The Agency is fixated on you. They've launched spiders to search for your implant signature. The moment they find you, Agents will strike. You're the face of the rebellion."

"Why should I believe you? You joined The Agency."

"I wanted to see the world."

I stood up. "You're wasting my time."

"Wait." Her sarcastic smile disappeared. "I love the thrill of the unsolvable, of the impossible, but I don't agree with what The Agency's doing. They hired me to trace dark-web sites. After you invaded our office, I erased my research and ran. I can help you hide your sites so even I wouldn't be able to find them."

"What about this place? Did you find it as well?"

"No, or I would've come here instead. Whatever you guys use to link to the sites is untraceable. Do you use quantum-folded comms?"

I didn't admit she had guessed correctly. Just observing our chatter made the data disappear.

Her demeanor, cockiness backed by talent and cut with impatience, reminded me of Talia.

Nataly took a breath, hope and uncertainty flickering in her eyes. "Did you really mean what you said in your broadcast? '*Make your future. Fight for it.*'"

"Every word."

She nodded as if to herself. "You sure no one is listening?"

"As sure as I can be in this place."

She smiled again, a hint of her earlier cockiness returning. "I didn't wipe what you did at the office, or they would've known I helped you. Besides, it's not like you found what you were looking for."

"Did you?"

"No." She frowned. "The Agency is hunting every rebel

they can find using a new kind of tech. It's a network of super tiny drones that create a three-dimensional grid, their sensors able to penetrate wood, stone, steel, just about anything."

I went cold. "I know that system. Kieran developed it."

"He got demoted for the way he handled you—and for failing to stop your broadcast. But there are others determined to succeed where he failed."

I didn't believe he was no longer active. Kieran wasn't the type to accept being pushed aside, even if I'd hobbled him. Did that mean Nataly was lying? "If we're in danger, why are you here?"

"I can give you access to that network, see where it's spreading. But I want to join. It's cool you zapped me at the office. Could've warned me, though."

"Where's the jamming device you use?"

"The guy took it, the one with—" She scrunched one side of her face, indicating Cole.

She glanced at the door. I heard it, too. Voices. Lafontaine's people were coming.

She quickly told me the name of a website and rattled off a username and complicated password. I pulled up the notes feature in my implant and used my dataring to save the info. "I'm loyal just to you," she said. "Your broadcast shattered my life."

The voices grew louder.

She leaned forward. "Why haven't these people let me talk to you? Because they don't trust you—so I don't trust them." She straightened as the door to the three-room suite burst open and adopted a slightly bored look. "The Agency has deployed streaking drone-ships with scanners. They may have ground penetration radar, DNA collectors, and other tech I wasn't able to discover."

The door to the interrogation room flew open, and two of Lafontaine's guards entered, both armed, the lead one the cleft-chin guy from the day before. "You're forbidden to be anywhere near here," he told me. Before I could react, he grabbed me and pulled me from the room.

As he dragged me toward the exit, I glanced through the mirror. She was looking at it as if trying to see me, her worry evident.

Cleft-chin tossed me into the passageway, then frowned. "Where's the other guard?"

"The place was empty when I got here."

"You come in here again, I'll lock you up."

I raced to Garly's lab, Valor joining me along the way.

He opened the door when I pounded on it, hair even wilder. For once, Valor followed me inside. "You're hooked to the internet, aren't you?" I asked Garly as he closed the door. I'd spotted a display monitor earlier.

"Help yourself." He shuffled back to the work area where thin, carbon-fiber-laced cloth stretched to the floor. Suddenly he lunged forward, snatched a picture frame I hadn't noticed before, and clutched it to his chest, covering the photograph of an older couple.

My implant. If I was ever caught, their images could be downloaded. They could be used against him. "I barely looked at it," I assured him.

As he put the picture away, I went to his monitor and pulled up the website Nataly had told me about. The welcome screen was spartan: no identification or emblem, just a login and password prompt. The typeface and layout screamed government. I referred to my notes and logged in.

The website revealed a real-time map of the United States. It was zoomed in on southern California, with the southern tip of Nevada and a sliver of Arizona visible as well. Overlapping dispersal graphs, what looked like shaded circles, hovered over a large area that extended from Los Angeles to San Diego. Per the legend along the side of the screen, each circle reflected the placement of The Agency's 3D tech: tens of thousands of tiny drones that could stay in place for months, maybe years, loaded with facial recognition software, pattern behavior sensing, and audial recording data, while wielding the radar Nataly had described.

The circles hovered over most of the main areas that had received my broadcast. They covered not only the first rebel safe house that had gone dark, but the camp that had been attacked, two dark-web centers the rebels had used, and notable meeting locations. Tens of millions of people were now under The Agency's inescapable gaze.

And now that the system Kieran had shown me two months ago was up and running, it would be easy for The Agency to add to the network. Their drones would catch us all.

"You have the map of every safe house and training camp still operating?" I asked.

Garly bounded over and pulled up one of the mountain's internal systems.

I compared the two side by side.

A safe house in Bakersfield was sitting in the growth path. It would be discovered, its people killed.

Unless I got there first.

CHAPTER NINE

I considered running from Garly's room to try to convince Lafontaine to send our troops to the Bakersfield house and the other locations in jeopardy, but he wouldn't listen. None of the leaders would. They were too focused on starting their damn war.

I turned to Garly. "What weapons do you have?"

He extracted two pistols from his various piles, energized pellets, the hand shields, and a modified missile launcher of all things. "I wanna ride with."

"You're too valuable." To Valor, I said, "Find Cardoza, have her try to contact the safe house. Let me know if she gets through."

"I'll wake up the guard, too, have him tell Lafontaine what we found."

I almost told her not to bother, but between Cardoza and Lafontaine, I figured they would have to send some kind of reinforcements to help.

A knock on the door made Valor pull her chrome pistols. If Lafontaine sent his fanatics after me for knocking out his guard, we were screwed.

Garly cracked open the door to see who it was, then opened it to let in Jex.

"What's goin' on? Bhungen spotted you runnin' here," the Creole asked, not wearing his camos for once.

I conveyed what I'd learned, speaking quickly as I jammed Garly's weapons into a sack.

"You stay here. I'll handle the safe house," Jex told me. I shot him a look, and he threw up his hands. "Had to try. I'm goin' with, though. I don't deploy until tomorrow."

I glanced at Garly. "Make sure Raven stays here, no matter what."

His eyes widened. "How am I supposed to finagle that?"

* * *

Being out in the open again—even if in a car—was nerve-wracking. I wore my plastic mask over my knit cap, shielding both face and implant, and Jex was shielded as well, yet we were risking our safety. The Agency could spot us from cameras in doorbells, in vehicles, hanging from street corners, from drones, satellites, anyone's eyes—and soon we would have the 3D grid to worry about as well.

Valor sent a message to my burner phone along the way. The phone at the safe house was disconnected, and Cardoza was unable to get a hold of anyone stationed there.

Jex drove faster.

Lit by the midday light, the safe house, located next to an empty, grass-covered lot, was a nondescript, two-story structure in an old section of town, the greenish-blue siding and tan trim similar to others on the street.

As we passed the darkened house, I discovered the structure had been built on a slight rise, allowing good lines of sight, and had multiple ways to vacate in case of trouble.

"Where's the lookout?" Jex asked. "There's always a lookout, either on the porch, walkin' the street, somethin'."

The street seemed quiet—not the type of quiet when everyone was at work, but the quiet I was familiar with, of hiding in the hopes a pursuer wouldn't find me. That's when I spotted something, my muscles so tense they felt like rocks. "There's a body."

"Where?"

"In the lot near the back." I'd nearly missed it, as the grass was overgrown.

I directed him to turn down the next street to circle back around. As he did, I heard something overhead. Drone streakerships. Three of them in a cluster. I thought we just missed them scanning us, but they'd be back, for they ran sweeping patterns over prescribed areas.

Jex turned onto the street behind the safe house, and I unbuckled my seatbelt. "After I get out, drive over a couple of blocks and park. You know what the Agency is capable of. You see anything, you leave. I don't come back in five minutes, leave." He started to argue, but I cut him off. "The leaders need to know—and Raven needs you."

"I'm goin' with you."

"Stay in the car."

He pulled over. "Or what, you'll shoot me again?"

I grinned. "Exactly." I got out, and he reluctantly drove off.

Stepping into the open was dangerous; just being here was dangerous. The 3D tech had almost reached this area. I had to hurry.

I stood in front of a brick ranch house with a carport that leaned to the side, the safe house visible beyond it. I thought I heard a vid somewhere, maybe inside the ranch, though I could've imagined it.

"For Talia," I whispered.

Hiding a pistol against my stomach, I approached the ranch and slipped between it and a neighboring garage. When I reached the backyard, I extracted my discharger. I also had a pocketful of pellets but only one discharger. I needed to make it count.

The alley past the backyard appeared clear, the back door to the safe house forty feet away, the screen closed but the solid door left open. This could be a trap, the body and open door left to attract others. But I had to risk it.

I dashed into the alley and across to the body, aware of how exposed I was to the windows of houses in multiple directions.

When I reached the man, I dropped beside him, but he was dead, his neck twisted. *The lookout*. He hadn't been fleeing. He'd been neutralized.

Everyone inside was in danger.

I scrambled to my feet, took the six steps as quickly but quietly as possible to the back door, opened the screen, and stepped into the kitchen. It was basic—small portable island, bamboo cabinets, recycle-fridge—and empty.

The house seemed normal, but I knew better. It didn't have the monitor trim that tracked vitals, movements, health factors and voice tones, no alarm system, nothing that could be used to track or record those who hid here. The pictures on the wall were sparse and generic. All cover.

A doorway on the far side of the kitchen opened to the rest of the house: a dining area, then a short but wide hallway with a stairwell to the left, followed by a living room with a broken table and two broken lamps, the front door visible past that. Lying in the hallway a dozen feet from the kitchen, back pressed against the faux-plaster wall, was a bloodied man with curly copper hair and a scrawny beard, aiming a gun at the stairwell. As soon as he saw me, he swiveled the weapon, a Beretta 92, and aimed at me.

Sounds echoed above our heads: grunts, blows landed, and an occasional crash. The second floor.

I took off my mask, hoping his implant was covered. "I'm on your side," I whispered.

He didn't recognize me, more focused on my feed-blocking cap. I lifted it away on the opposite side of my implant to show him my hair color. When he saw it was black instead of silver, he reoriented his gun on the stairwell.

A heavy thud shook the house.

I joined him in the hallway; we could only see half a flight as the stairs turned at a landing before continuing up. "An Agent?" I mouthed.

The man nodded, trembling slightly. "He must've taken out our scout. Didn't see him coming. The others ran upstairs. He left me here, made sure I couldn't go anywhere fast." He nodded at his right leg, which appeared to have multiple fractures. He'd crawled to this spot to lie in wait for his attacker.

Someone raced along the upper hallway toward the stairs, heavier footsteps following—though the footsteps suddenly stopped, followed by a muffled cry and then a pop. A thump came next as something dropped to the floor.

The rebel flinched in response. From the sound above us, I suspected he'd become the house's remaining survivor.

Seconds later, a person bounded down the stairs and appeared on the landing: the heavily-muscled Agent from the office invasion. Gunnar. He looked bigger than I'd remembered, his frame nearly filling the stairwell.

The rebel and I aimed our pistols at him.

Gunnar eyed me. "Is this what finally drew you?" he asked as he took the first step toward the main floor. "A body in the yard? I'm doing the planet a favor."

The rebel fired—but before I could join in, the Agent was on us and snatched the rebel's gun. I lowered mine before Gunnar could snatch it, aimed at his pivot leg, and squeezed the trigger. Gunnar howled in pain, slammed my gun away, and then raised both of his massive fists over his head. I activated my hand shields and thrust my arms up as he came down. The force of his blow drove my arms back, wrenching my shoulders, but I deflected his fists to either side of my shields, his face inches above mine.

Before he could react, I drove the edges of both shields up into his exposed neck.

The Agent stumbled back—then grabbed my right shield in both hands and threw me into the living room.

I landed with a grunt, the shields cushioning some of my fall, but my lenses suddenly lit up as my implant connected with the world and information flooded in, the air turning clearer except for the spot that had been burned in my lens. My landing had caused my cap to slide off of my implant. I yanked my cap back down, cutting off the information—and saw him running toward me like a silver-topped wrecking ball.

Gunshots rang out behind him, and he arched, slowing his charge.

I'd dropped the discharger during my flight into the living room, but I had the pellets. They'd been developed to take out the 3D surveillance drones. Didn't matter. I reached into my pocket, activated a pellet by squeezing it, then scooped out a handful. As minuscule lights flickered on, I threw the pellets at the Agent. They hit him and unleashed their energy, discharging over five hundred combined volts of electricity.

He collapsed.

I scrambled to the discharger and activated it. An electronic pulse shot out, knocking out the feed going to my implant and any others in a three-block radius. Then I stumbled toward the rebel, who appeared stunned that I'd been able to drop the Agent. "Come on, he'll only be out for a minute."

The man opened his mouth to say something but froze, eyes swiveling past me. Before I could turn, an ear-splintering boom erupted behind me. A second quickly followed, the front door shredding from the blows to reveal a man-sized robot, wide as a linebacker, forcing its way through the doorframe. After it stepped through, the mechanical weapon shifted to the side to reveal the female Agent, Britt. Another Agent was behind her, dark eyes cold and ruthless.

"You really are here," Britt said to me. My implant. It had alerted them before I'd zapped the signal—or she'd seen me through Gunnar's eyes.

I turned to the rebel. "Run."

He leapt to his good foot and hopped as quickly as he could toward the kitchen, but we were too slow. Agents were enhanced. Gunnar was already waking up; if he'd been a normal man, he would've been out for hours.

The rebel paused. I glanced past him—and saw Jex in the kitchen doorway, missile launcher resting on his shoulder.

"Get down!" he yelled.

I tackled the rebel.

As we dropped out of the way, Jex triggered the missile,

which screamed as it shot over us and exploded with such power the house shook, the brilliant-white detonation deafening me and scorching my back.

The missile destroyed the front of the house: the couch was half incinerated, the other half on fire, the rug held flames, and bits of ceiling fell down in front of the gaping maw where the entrance had been. The Agents' robot was gone—but through the smoke, I saw flashes of silver. The Agents had been blown out of the house into the street.

As I watched, Britt sat up.

Jex grabbed my arm. "Move!"

I helped the rebel to his feet, hooked his arm over my shoulder, and we hurried to the alley where our car waited, doors open, engine running. I started for the car, but the rebel, who I suspected managed the safe house, pulled from my grasp and hopped toward the body instead.

I went after him. "He's already dead."

My words made him stop.

As he turned back, gunfire erupted from two different spots, and we both dove to the ground. Two cops had parked in front of the safe house and fired at us over their patrol cars. In the distance, my ringing ears caught more sirens.

Police drones descended and took positions to either side. More would come: drones, men, Agents.

I reached for my gun but paused, remembering Cole's training. I needed a distraction.

"Dray," Jex called.

He was just visible on the other side of the car, gun in hand. He flicked his eyes upwards. The drones.

He'd remembered my pellets. Luckily, I hadn't used all of them inside. I extracted my remaining supply, activated them, and glanced at the rebel, who lay next to his fallen guard. "Get ready."

We moved as one. Jex stepped out from behind the car and started firing as I hurled some pellets at the two sets of drones, then stood as the drones shorted out and threw the rest at the cops' cars. The charges stunned the men in blue, who had ducked to avoid Jex's gunfire, the electricity throwing them back.

I reached for the rebel, who grabbed the body. "No time," I said, pulling him away. His arm over my shoulder, we lurched toward the car as Jex climbed behind the wheel. I heard a tiny exhalation, we scrambled into the car, then I heard a second exhalation followed by something hitting our car. Jex took off, and I glanced out the back window. Just past the house, Britt lay crouched, aiming the same strange weapon she'd used on Jex days earlier.

Seconds later, she disappeared from view. Streets whipped past, the combustion engine straining.

A dozen blocks later, he slammed on the brakes and wrenched the wheel, nearly sliding into a delivery van. "Get out."

"What the hell?" I asked.

The delivery van's rear doors opened to reveal two people in masks I recognized immediately: Raven and Senn. She wore a trooper outfit, the dark fabric in contrast to her golden-brown hair, while Senn wore his tracksuit, though the mini-cannon he held was new.

So much for keeping Raven at HQ.

Jex and I helped the rebel to the van. We closed the doors as soon as we got inside and Valor, also masked, drove us out of town, detonating another discharger along the way to hide our escape.

Raven fitted the man I'd rescued with a cap to block his implant before removing her mask. Jex must've messaged her in some way. I gave him a withering look, but he didn't flinch. "Have you met your daughter?"

She punched my bicep. "Stop trying to protect me."

I rubbed my arm and turned to the rebel. "I'm Dray."

"Thought I recognized you. Nipsen," the mop-haired guy said, his curls now contained by the cap.

"I need to inspect you."

He gave an amused grin. "Seriously?"

When I didn't return his grin, he agreed. We maneuvered

around each other as best we could. As we did, Jex asked, "This isn't the same thing that made you shoot me, is it?"

"What?" Nipsen asked in alarm.

The rebel seemed clean, but then I spotted it. His lower back, just under his shirt line. "You've been hit."

Raven, Jex, and Senn huddled close, taking in the five metal prongs spread out from the aluminum base.

I looked more closely at the reinforced-glass capsule in the middle. As I'd feared, it contained an object of some kind.

"I don't feel anything," Nipsen said.

"It's moving," Raven said.

She was right. The capsule shifted, rising a fraction. Nipsen reached back, but I grabbed his wrist before he could touch it. "Don't. I'm going to try to remove it."

"Is it transmitting?" Senn asked. "It's doing something. Throw a cap over it."

We needed to get to HQ, but we were two hours away.

I had Nipsen lie on his stomach and pulled out my ion blade. When I activated it, I paused. The end had sunk deeper into his body, nearly flat with the surface of his skin—and was empty. "Shit."

"What?" Nipsen asked worriedly.

"The capsule injected something into your body. Don't move." I couldn't slice into the guy, especially not here, not with Valor driving like a madwoman. I searched the cab, saw a dangling wire, and ripped it loose.

"Does the van need that?" Senn asked worriedly.

"Give me your plasma gun."

He handed it over as Valor took another corner. I quickly disassembled it, the glowing energy core casting weird shadows. With the core free, I stripped both ends of the wire, jabbed one end into the hole in Nipsen's back and touched the other end of the wire to the conductor, sending a stream of plasma down the wire and into his body.

He shook violently, inadvertently kicking me and Raven—then collapsed, no longer breathing.

CHAPTER TEN

We arrived at headquarters among a whine of brakes, my team shouting for a gurney the moment we stopped. I barely paid attention as I was focused on maintaining CPR on Nipsen, hoping I had the rhythm right.

Doors opened, throwing light from our base's hidden entrance. I kept pushing on his chest. "Dad, stop," Raven said. I did, moving aside so Jex and Senn could pull him out of the van and onto the gurney as the nurse barked orders. My arms throbbed, and my wrists were stiff from the near-continuous CPR, but I managed to get out of the van as the cluster—nurse, Jex, Senn—steered Nipsen into the entrance tunnel.

Raven and I caught up with them as they reached the central hub. I was surprised at how packed the hub was with soldiers and weapons and onlookers, though I didn't slow as I followed my group into the med unit.

As my team moved Nipsen to one of the beds, Anya entered from the supply room. "What have we got?"

"Male, approximately thirty, in cardiac arrest," the nurse said as she administered CPR.

"Was he shot?"

"I did it," I said.

Anya turned at the sound of my voice. "You have to stop shooting people."

Jex joined us. "He did one better. He zapped the guy with

plasma."

She raised her eyebrows at me. I quickly explained.

"So shooting wasn't enough," she muttered. With the nurse's help—and some injectable capsules—she got Nipsen's heart beating after a couple of tense minutes.

Anya said, "Help me flip him over."

We did, exposing the wound, and she grabbed a handheld MRI to scan it. The dual-sensor MRI projected a three-dimensional feed like the image I saw when she'd operated on Raven's skull back when this all started. "You scarred his vein, but if I follow it—ah, I found the electronics." To the nurse, she said, "Grab my surgical kit."

She remained focused on the readout until the nurse returned with a portable kit, then spread a blue sheet with a hole in the center across Nipsen's upper back. As she did, Valor and Senn left, though I suspected they wouldn't go far.

With a practiced motion, Anya cut into Nipsen. "Whatever this thing is concerns me. With the right device, an Agent could turn someone catatonic—or worse."

"Don't expect me to thank you," Jex said to me.

"Luckily, this one didn't reach its destination," she continued as she cleared away blood. She flickered her eyes at me. "Is there a reason you keep doing stuff like this?"

"I wanted an excuse to see you work."

She lowered her head, but I caught her grin.

Over the course of a few minutes, she removed the pieces of the device that had adhered to the side of his vein, injected nanobots, sewed the incision and covered it with foam.

As she turned her attention to his fractured leg, I inspected the remains she'd extracted, which she'd dropped into a tray. "It's a mini-bot," I said. It was fried, though. The plasma had melted its components.

"What was it supposed to do?" Raven asked.

Anya rubbed a fingernail, thinking. "You said the capsule moved, which means it's designed to inject its contents into the bloodstream. As far as that thing's final destination, it could have been anywhere: spine, heart, brain. It could stop a heart, or if it nestled into the cortex, it could paralyze the person. It wouldn't need much energy."

"I bet it was designed to burrow into the brain," Raven said. "That would make it harder to remove, and it could be another way to see through our eyes."

The others offered their opinions as Anya and the nurse set Nipsen's leg, but without an undamaged capsule to study, it was all conjecture.

"You said an Agent shot him?" Anya asked. When I nodded, she said, "I encountered a couple Agents while I was gone, but none carried the weapon you described. This seems to be a new tactic."

The rest of my team headed for the exit, where I heard growing murmurs on top of the normal chatter.

Anya stepped beside me, her head down as she made notes on a med pad. Though the circumstances weren't ideal, it felt good to be near her.

"Speaking of while you were gone, did you finish whatever you needed to do?" I asked quietly.

She nodded, then fidgeted. "I missed you," she whispered without looking up.

Her words shot through me.

I wanted to respond with something more than an echo of what she'd said. I also wanted to ask about the Agents she'd encountered. Before I could either, she nodded toward Raven, who hovered near the exit. "Someone's waiting for you."

"Let's continue this conversation later."

She smiled. "Play your cards right."

I went to Raven. "You okay?"

She hugged me, then punched my arm again. "I swear, this is the last time you do something like that without me."

"You have enough to think about with deploying tonight." An event I couldn't stop worrying about.

She looked away—and I caught a blinking in the corner of my vision. When my cap had been pushed off my implant, at least one message downloaded. I suspected Mina had sent it sometime in the recent past. I wasn't sure I wanted to hear it.

I knew I should tell Raven about her mother's call. The two had been close, arguably closer than she and I, but Raven didn't need the distraction right now.

The reason why made me edgy.

Garly had assured me her protective suit would be ready in time, but he could run out of materials, the projectors could malfunction, or some other issue could come up. I needed to make sure he was on track—and tell him about the linebacker-sized robot we'd encountered at the safe house. We needed a defense against them, which wouldn't be easy, as each probably weighed three hundred pounds.

The 3D drones were the bigger risk. Garly and Lafontaine's guard should have told the leaders about the danger—yet they hadn't sent anyone to help us save Nipsen.

"You're going to do something risky," Raven said, watching my face.

Instead of replying, I led her into the central hub.

The cavernous room was barely-organized chaos. Troops clothed in black assault attire selected weapons from various racks while team leaders barked at them to hurry up. Other troops received pep talks or divided up to take the various vehicles being used to reach Fort Irwin.

Applause suddenly broke out.

A group of our clan members, along with some people I didn't recognize, cheered me, nearly a dozen in total.

"What's all this?" Raven asked.

The young man who normally guarded the entrance stepped forward. "People heard what you did saving that guy."

I thanked those who applauded us, then started for the north passageway. "Don't like the accolades?" Raven asked, staying by my side.

"No time."

Whether it was my words or my tone, some of those who'd cheered us followed as I headed to the leaders' chamber. Without knocking, I opened the double doors and went inside.

The chamber, ten times the size of my room, contained a ring of chairs on one side and display screens on the other, with maps displaying troop movements, safe houses, camps, assumed enemy positions, and targets.

A couple of guards stood near the doors, their hands reaching for their weapons when we appeared, though they didn't draw them when they saw the size of our crowd.

The seven leaders—Lafontaine, Cardoza, de Vera, and the other four who had moved their teams to the mountain—clustered around one of their coded maps, though they looked up when we entered.

"What the hell is this?" Lafontaine asked.

"The forces heading to Fort Irwin need to be redirected. Every safe house and base is in trouble," I told them.

"Our locations have gone undetected for years," de Vera said. "The ones that were found were just flukes."

"No, they weren't." I quickly described the 3D drones and their capabilities. "They'll find all of us, even in here. None of us will be safe anymore."

Beside me, Raven gasped. "My god."

Two of the monitors lit up, the icon for a safe house flashing red, followed by a second, a third, then nearly a dozen.

"Multiple attacks," Cardoza breathed.

"San Diego, L.A., the whole southern part of California is lost," Raven said.

The leaders exchanged uncertain glances as a third display began to list the locations, men and women who'd sacrificed for nothing.

I faced the leadership. "Redistribute your troops. Send them to every location that's in danger to save whoever's left—"

"No," Lafontaine said. "We'll warn the remaining locations, but we're not deviating from our plan. Otherwise, we'll lose the advantage."

"What advantage?" I asked, exasperated.

Cardoza said, "We're already started deploying teams,

all of whom are operating under radio silence. The only way to recall them is by using the emergency beacon, but that could expose them. They could be traced back here."

I could feel the anger emanating from Raven, Jex, Senn, Valor, and the others who'd entered the chamber with me, which matched my own. "Use the beacon," I said. "We need to rescue everyone we can, then head east, get somewhere safe."

Lafontaine said, "You're out of line."

"The Agency will find this place. When their drones expand here, they'll expose us."

"Just because you did some broadcast doesn't make you a military expert."

"I've fought an Agent face-to-face. Have you?"

"I've fought them for years, sacrificing everything I have."

"Except your identity."

My crowd inhaled sharply as everyone hid their identity from the government—except for me.

"You attack my guard, knock him out, and now you dare barge in here?" he asked.

"You wouldn't let me talk to your 'prisoner'. If I hadn't gone in there, we wouldn't have known about the drones. We would've lost another fighter."

Cardoza spoke up. "You saved one of my captains. Thank you."

The other leaders began to waver.

Lafontaine pointed a finger at me. "Your damn broadcast sped up our timeframe. Now The Agency is coming for us."

"They were already coming for us." I turned to the other leaders. "Save your people. When I was at the safe house—"

Lafontaine cut me off. "You left this facility? Is that what you meant by almost losing another fighter?"

Shit. "I had to. There was no time."

"I hope it was worth it." He motioned to his guards. "Arrest him."

Raven and Jex began to object, stepping in front of me—but Lafontaine's men raised their weapons at us.

"Isiah," Cardoza objected. "He saved one of my people."

"Not only did he *attack* one of my men, he broke my rules," Lafontaine said, then started to grin. "His punishment will be righteous."

Valor strode forward with her chrome pistols aimed at Lafontaine's men. "Back off!" Senn joined her, his Glock raised.

More guns rose, this time from Lafontaine's side.

"They have the numbers," I told my team. "Stand down."

As Lafontaine's men disarmed them and the rest of my group, de Vera yelled at Lafontaine. "You don't have the authority to do this."

"Say another word, and you join him."

Chapter Eleven

Iron cuffs—god knew where Lafontaine got them—dug into my wrists, secured by a steel chain his men had threaded through a ring they'd pounded into the rough-hewn wall.

Four of Lafontaine's men had pointed machine guns at me the entire time it took to chain me up. The soldiers preparing to leave watched in confusion, many looking like they wanted to rescue me, though I shook them off. I didn't want more to suffer because of me.

Raven, Jex, and the others had avoided being locked up, although Lafontaine had told de Vera, "Make sure they're all deployed on the front lines."

I had to protect them—but couldn't.

Lafontaine had planted me in the central hub on purpose, between the tiny stage and the entrance tunnel, to broadcast my new status as his prisoner. At least the chain was long enough that I could sit on the floor, which I did.

Anya had tried to stop his men from chaining me to the wall, to no avail. After they left, it took some time to convince her to return to the med unit, though she eventually did, her fear and uncertainty evident.

No one else approached. That didn't bother me. What did was what Lafontaine might do next—as did whatever Raven, Jex, and the others might face for standing with me, assuming they survived the base attack.

Dire scenarios ran through my mind as soldiers cycled through the process of getting ready, loading up, and deploying, each taking an implant blocker from the box as they exited. The leaders would kick me out. Hopefully, that's all they would do—but they had to deal with my implant. If they were smart, they would either try to drill out the insides or rip it from my head. Both options would likely kill me, but Lafontaine wouldn't care. Destroying my implant would protect his base.

More rebels entered the central hub to start the deployment process, though they were subdued, either due to my presence or their growing fear. I was about to look away when Raven, Jex, and both of my bodyguards emerged from the south tunnel in full battle garb.

The four moved without speaking to anyone, slipping between soldiers to grab assault rifles and ammunition. Valor also shouldered one of the packs loaded with food and medical supplies.

Seeing Raven threw me into a panic. She hadn't been scheduled to deploy for hours—which meant Garly's suit wasn't ready. I couldn't let her battle the goddamn Army without it. I pulled on the chains, though I'd already tried them.

She spared a glance at me before looking away.

She didn't look upset. Nervous and focused, but not upset. Resolved.

That's when it hit me. She was leading a team to break me out. That's why she wasn't wearing one of the fake Fort Irwin uniforms.

Lafontaine's men had retreated to either side of the hub but hadn't left. They would arrest or shoot anyone who tried to free me.

I climbed to my feet. I needed to create a distraction, stop Raven and the others from acting.

Before I could, a commotion arose, what sounded like a garrison march-stepping.

As the sound grew, Lafontaine and the other leaders appeared from the north tunnel. I wondered if this was going to be my court martial or whatever the rebels called it. But the vibe wasn't right. Excitement, trepidation, and arrogance filled the air. The next moment, a group of people I'd never seen before emerged from the entrance tunnel. Then I recognized one of them: Nash Perenko, the most powerful rebel leader on the West Coast, maybe the entire country. Average height and bald, Perenko wore a gray suit, a sharp contrast to most everyone's military or casual attire. Five men and women followed, not as formally dressed though they carried themselves with poise. Other leaders. Guards emerged behind them, their weapons prominently displayed.

The rebels in the hub fell silent.

Lafontaine stepped forward, his voice echoing off the uneven dome. "Welcome to my sanctuary. We are blessed by your presence, though we didn't expect you for another week."

He must have been referring to them choosing a leader to spearhead the rebellion, who all of the individual clans would report to.

"We're not here for the vote," Perenko said. "We came because of your plan to attack Fort Irwin. Did you think I wouldn't find out?"

Lafontaine's smile turned condescending. "I didn't try to hide anything. It was time to strike. Any decisive leader would've known that."

Cardoza flicked her gaze toward me though she kept her face expressionless.

"Watch that attitude," Perenko warned. "You're no longer on the pulpit, and God won't protect you from me."

"I got tired of waiting while you line your pockets with your underground trade routes. How much money is enough, Nash?"

"Your ego could destroy our chance to overthrow Washington. I'm shutting this down."

Raven, Jex, Valor, and Senn stepped forward, submachine guns in hand, though they didn't point them at anyone.

Perenko's guards raised their weapons in response and

moved in front of him.

Raven nodded toward me. "We're not here for you. Just him."

Perenko followed her gaze and raised his eyebrows. "Dray Quintero."

Raven pulled an object from her belt and tossed it to me. My ion blade. I caught the handle and thumbed it on. As the particle-blade glowed faintly, I hesitated, aware I would sever any chance here, though that was already gone. I pulled the chains tight and sliced through the iron cuffs, the cut metal clinking to the ground.

"How dare you," Lafontaine shouted.

More rebels had gathered, no doubt drawn by the news of Perenko's arrival.

The powerful, suit-wearing leader took in the growing crowd, walked toward me—making me wonder if he was going to shake my hand or something—and angled toward the stage. He put his foot on the small step, causing his pant leg to lift—

And that's when I saw it. The star-shaped dots, made by the spoke-like prongs, with the now-healed hole in the center. The same pattern created by The Agency's strange device.

Perenko had been tagged—and whatever device they'd injected into him was now inside our headquarters.

I must've gasped because everyone turned to me, conversations stopping.

And in the silence, a new sound grew: metallic legs scraping. Clawing.

Echoing.

Oh god, the vents.

CHAPTER TWELVE

"What the hell is that noise?" Perenko asked as the metallic scraping grew louder.

I strained to interpret the foreign sounds. Whatever was causing it seemed to just come from above us, though there were vents scattered throughout the complex that were too far away to hear.

The scraping grew louder—then tiny robots, each four inches across, crawled out of the vents, the lead 'bots dropping the broken pieces of auto-shields that had masked the shafts. Each robot controlled a tiny laser, but even though people cried out, the robots didn't go after them.

Instead, they scrambled up the walls. Heading toward the ceiling.

Where the uplink blocker hung.

"Stop them," Lafontaine shouted.

The thunder of gunfire filled my ears.

The invaders fell as the two dozen guards and soldiers shot them, their tiny, shattered bodies twitching as they landed, but more poured out of the vents. There were too many, crawling toward the thick column that suspended the blocker like destiny arriving to drag us to our demise.

The blocker prevented our implant feeds from escaping the mountain. Even under all this rock, if the blocker went down, our feeds could connect with the network and reveal our presence.

Thirty additional rebels rushed into the hub to join the fight.

As the crawlers began to descend the column, I turned to three of the rebels, two women and a man who stood nearby. "Guard the entrance," I yelled over the gunfire and rising shouts. They took positions, faces pale. I got others' attention, nearly a dozen more, as the ex-soldier, Monroe, entered the hub.

Before I could wave him over, the robots' ascent took on a different sound as they crawled down the column. They stopped when they reached the blocker and activated their lasers, bathing the machine in destructive light—

And as the blocker exploded, my vision turned blinding white.

Rebels cried out in fear and confusion.

With the blocker destroyed, The Agency had accessed our implants and turned every rebel's computer-enhanced lenses opaque, blinding all of us with white light.

I'd been through this before, though the memory still scarred me. Anya had burned a hole in my lens to combat the same blindness after Kieran captured me and left me for dead.

They were coming. Kieran. The Agency.

As the realization gripped me, black letters appeared across my vision. *Dray Quintero. Join us. What we have will change everything.*

Like hell.

I quickly adjusted my vision, using the burnt hole in my left lens to take in the view around me. The gunfire had stopped. Rebels staggered about, clutching their heads, unable to block the command that blinded them.

The Agency would be here any second. Raven. Anya. They and others would be captured—or slaughtered.

We were the torch-bearers of the truth. If we were wiped out, I doubted anyone else would discover the lies we'd learned.

I spotted the box of implant blockers.

I ran toward the entrance, swiped the box, slapped a blocker against the side of my head—the blocker ill-fitting but still erasing The Agency's cryptic message and restoring my vision—and ran back to the soldiers who'd taken position to shoot at the entrance tunnel. In seconds, I gave them their sight back.

Movement caught my attention. Monroe was tracking me, face creased in concentration, probably using the sensors in his brow. I flung a blocker at him, which he caught and placed on his implant. He nodded in appreciation as he sighted himself, so I scooped a stack of blockers and lobbed them to him. He caught them and started to distribute them. I did as well.

A new sound grew: heavy robotic steps, along with human footsteps.

"Hurry," I said as I placed blockers in people's hands. "Get ready to fight."

I was foolish. We were blinded, caught off guard, hundreds of our forces already sent out to the goddamn desert. I should've told everybody to run.

"Dad," Raven yelled. She and my other rescuers huddled by the south entrance, frozen in their blindness.

"Blockers, here, take these," I said, distributing to those nearby. More swarmed me, drawn by my voice, reaching into the box. Sighting themselves. Then grabbing blockers for others—or turning toward the entrance, weapons raised. The kid who'd brought the plate from home appeared beside me. I slapped a blocker onto his implant, gave him the box, and scooped three handfuls of blockers, shoving one in my pocket. "Hand out as many as you can."

I covered another soldier's implant and gave him one of my handfuls. "Get others. Bring as many as possible."

We were running out of time. The sounds were louder, the footsteps doubling. About half of all of the rebels in the hub wore blockers, but that only totaled forty. It wouldn't be enough. I ran to Raven, who stood her ground, submachine gun gripped tight, though she was shaking, her eyes wide as she tried to see. Jex stood beside her, faring no better. I placed a blocker over Raven's implant, and she nearly slumped in relief. Before she could say anything, I said, "Grab Valor and Senn and get us a ride out of here."

"We have one, in the motor pool," she said as I sighted Jex.

"Then get there. I'll meet you. Be careful!"

I could tell she wanted to fight, to save me, but she handed me a pistol, grabbed some of my blockers, and hurried to Valor and Senn.

As she and Jex helped them, I pushed my way past blinded soldiers, telling them to get down. I didn't use my remaining blockers on them. Had to choose. Against the back wall, the leaders huddled, Lafontaine, Cardoza, de Vera—and Nash Perenko, half-laying before them, all wiping at their white eyes. I capped de Vera's implant first, then Cardoza, even Lafontaine.

The footsteps grew louder. Rebels shouted to each other, getting in position.

Lafontaine grabbed my arm, his vision sharpening on me. "You betrayed us!"

I pulled free of his grasp, grabbed Perenko's leg and yanked up his pant leg to reveal the telltale scar. "He brought them here!"

A ripple of metallic sounds—machine guns being readied—alerted me, and I turned to the entrance.

What I'd started with my broadcast and what I'd been unable to stop since then arrived at our hideaway.

War.

Gunfire roared as rebels opened fire on the entrance.

A man-shaped robot, similar to the one that had attacked the safe house, emerged from the tunnel, its metallic skin sparking as bullets struck it. Two more robots appeared behind it, the three stopping a few feet past the entrance to create a quasi-barrier. Thys Gunnar appeared next, gripping a semi-opaque, four-foot, black-and-gray riot shield in each hand, his face covered in recent burn scars. The Agent stepped out from behind the robots on one side, Agency soldiers from the other, men and women in black with stylized "A"s on their shoulders and returned fire, blue-white plasma lighting up the cavern.

While the soldiers weren't enhanced like Agents, they

were still highly trained, well organized, and they poured out of the entrance.

I turned back to the leaders. I'd planned to give them my last blockers—I had about ten—but didn't. "What're you going to do?" I yelled at them.

Without waiting for a reply, I stood and opened fire, taking out three of The Agency's soldiers. Return fire made me drop to the ground, hiding behind a fallen rebel.

To my right, two dozen rebels huddled against the back wall, blind, confused, vulnerable. I hurried to them, crouched down, and handed out half of my blockers to those with weapons. "Get the others out of here," I yelled, not sure if they could hear me. Plasma strikes laced the wall above us, the sounds of battle deafening. To my left, Cardoza fired at the Agency forces as de Vera grabbed fighters and directed them. Lafontaine glanced at me, then stood and began to fire at the invaders. Perenko remained blinded, eyes white as he pressed against the back wall.

I couldn't see much from where I was, rebels crouching in front of me, some blind, others fighting. I stood—and saw more forces emerging from the entrance. Gunnar was a tornado, using his shields to slam through clusters of rebels, bludgeon them, and drive them back. He was bleeding in spots, but he didn't seem bothered. More soldiers poured in behind him, twenty, thirty. Just as I was about to duck back down, one ran toward the med unit. My breath caught as he disappeared inside. *Anya.*

I ran across the hub, plasma and bullets zipping past me, a thin cloud of pulverized salt rock and gun-smoke filling the air while cries of pain lanced through the thunder of mechanized death. I felt a flicker as something grazed me but didn't slow, the north tunnel nearing. Amidst the chaos, I glimpsed Monroe firing at our enemies in a detached, precise fashion before I plunged into the north tunnel and skidded to a stop.

The entrance to the med unit's supply room was a few feet away.

I stepped inside and spotted Anya immediately, pressed against the corner between two shelving units filled with supplies, clutching her field medical bag. Her blinded eyes darted to me when I entered, her expression fearful. She'd known to hide—and that someone was coming.

I couldn't hear the soldier in the next room; the gunfire from the central hub was too loud. But he was coming. I raised my pistol, and the next moment the soldier appeared: black-clad, helmeted, MP5 submachine gun raised and ready. I fired a split second before he did, my shot throwing him back and causing him to miss.

But he didn't go down.

Before he could recover from the shot, I tackled him, adrenaline flooding my veins, and drove him to the ground. I snatched the barrel of his machine gun, held it down, then raised up as he struggled and fired my pistol.

After swiping his submachine gun from his still fingers, I went to Anya. Her fear was still there, but when I used a blocker to restore her vision, astonishment colored her fright.

"You came for me."

"Of course." I grinned. "Didn't you come back for me?"

She flashed a smile. "If I told you, where would be the fun?"

I wanted to banter more. No time. I jammed my pistol into my pocket, took her hand, and led her to the hallway.

The central hub was a warzone. Bodies lay everywhere, blood stained the ground, and the cloud of smoke and pulverized rock had thickened. The air reeked of gunpowder, salt, and burnt plasma, along with the tang of blood. Plasma bolts came sporadically; bullets from both sides were more prevalent. The three robots no longer guarded the entrance. They'd moved deeper. As I watched, one ripped the machine gun from a fighter's hands, unfazed by the gunfire, and shot her. Gunnar was in the middle of the room, bleeding from his face, stomach, and legs, still holding one shield while he punched and grabbed and threw our soldiers with his free hand. Two more Agents emerged from the entrance. Unharmed. Dangerous.

I needed to get Anya away, but to reach the motor pool,

we had to cross the chaos. Then I realized: with the area blocker knocked out, The Agency would detect signals coming from the motor pool. They'd discover there was another entrance.

"Stay low," I told her.

I pulled her into the hub.

The gunfire was loud, bullets zinging nearby, reminding me of the battle that took Talia's life. Anya and I ran, dashing past a cluster of fighters shooting at the black-clad forces, two rebels falling in succession as we darted past. I glanced at the entrance—and spotted two Agency soldiers aiming at us, drawn either by our movements or their recognition of me. Letting go of Anya's hand, I brought up my weapon, though there was no way I'd get a shot off in time.

Gunfire a dozen feet behind me punctured the noise in the room, and the two men fell. It was Monroe, dusty but otherwise untouched. He hurried to us. "Come on," he yelled, leading the way across the room. We reached the far side—and Lafontaine appeared before me.

"Get everyone to retreat," I told him.

"They'll kill us all."

"They already are!" I glanced back. De Vera tended to someone while Perenko huddled against the wall. I realized Cardoza was the one de Vera was tending to; she'd been shot in the shoulder. Anya went to them, knelt, and removed a small medical nanobot syringe.

I turned back to Lafontaine. "Get to the motor pool. *Now.*"

Without waiting for his reply, I turned and faced the room. "Retreat," I bellowed. "This way." I turned back to Anya as she administered the nanobots, took her arm, and pulled her toward the south entrance. She reshouldered her pack, pale face set, as she followed.

Before we'd gotten a few feet, Senn came racing toward us—though he wasn't looking at us. He ran past, leapt, and tackled Gunnar, who'd appeared from out of the carnage and had nearly reached us.

My bodyguard was bigger than most people here, yet he

was half Gunnar's size. The muscular Agent managed to stay on his feet from Senn's attack, though he stumbled back. As Senn punched at him, he raised his shield as if to strike—but Senn grabbed the shield, lifted himself up like a crazed gymnast, and kicked Gunnar in the throat. The Agent collapsed, taking Senn with him.

Senn moved with surprising speed, knocking the shield out of the way and straddling the Agent. He glanced back at me. "Go!"

I wanted to help. To protect him. But others looked at me: Anya and Monroe and one of the leaders holding Cardoza and dozens of soldiers, those who, by some miracle or training or karma, had survived the initial attack. I glanced back at Senn to give me a look, let him know how difficult this was for me, but he'd already turned away, fighting the silver-haired monster who'd invaded our headquarters. Sacrificing himself, for he had no chance of winning.

My throat tight with grief, I pulled Anya toward the south hallway.

We hurried into the tunnel, the gunfire behind us dropping as first a few rebels, then more, followed my lead.

We raced down the wide, empty hallway, exposed. Our only chance was to reach our vehicles and get away—although I didn't know what awaited us outside. If The Agency had brought an army, we were dead.

I suddenly pulled Anya to a halt. She swung toward me, her eyes wild. "What's wrong?"

"We need to free someone." It wouldn't make up for Senn, but Nataly would be killed if caught. I led Anya into the side passageway and hurried toward the interrogation rooms.

When I reached the door, I opened it—and jerked back as a young rebel soldier, blinded by his lenses, swung a gun in my direction. "Don't shoot, it's Dray," I said.

The soldier hesitated, then lowered his gun. "I can't see."

I moved past him and entered the interrogation room. Nataly, pressed against the far wall, flinched when I entered, white eyes searching. "It's okay, it's me," I said. I placed a blocker onto her implant, returning her sight.

She exhaled in relief, then narrowed her eyes. "The Agency's here."

"Come on." I led her and Anya into the side passageway, handing a blocker to the young rebel along the way.

Before we reached the main hallway, we heard an explosion. I stiffened and glanced at them. "The motor pool." The Agency had found it.

Raven.

Anya, Nataly, and I dashed to the main hallway. When we reached it, rebels were running past, a few firing over their shoulders as they ran. They were in full retreat. The three of us joined the flow and raced for the motor pool.

A part of me realized I was probably tearing Anya's arm out of her socket. She kept up, though, Nataly right behind. We wove through the crowd, a few injured, everyone armed, Agency forces following in the distance. Our enemies didn't seem in a rush—which frightened me.

Up ahead, I spotted Garly with an implant-shielding cap jammed on his head and hurried to him. He wore a large backpack and carried a duffel bag, the thick canvas stretched tight. The way he hunched over, I could tell it was heavy. "You were supposed to be in the motor pool."

"I'm bookin'." He gave Anya a shaky greeting, then stumbled when he saw Nataly. I introduced them and kept them moving.

Among the growing surge of people, Cole emerged from a secondary hallway with two of his men, all three with caps on. I called him over as we continued to retreat. "The hub's lost."

"Whole damn place is lost," he said.

"What was that explosion?"

"Has to be the motor pool. I was training these two when it went off." He grew visibly upset as he took in the soldiers around us, his eyes lingering on the wounded ones.

We kept up with the flow, which slowed when we neared

the motor pool, our forces taking positions to either side of the opening, pressed against the walls.

I let go of Anya's hand and moved closer.

Past the scattering of vehicles, The Agency had blown a hole in the door on the end farthest from us, charred pieces from the explosion scattered across the formerly pristine stone floor. Sunlight streamed in, making the rest of the massive space seem dim. Agency forces had climbed through the hole and spread out, nearly twenty men from what I could see, although they weren't advancing.

A few bodies lay scattered about, all rebels. One Agency soldier holding his side sat against the blasted door.

I stared at the downed bodies and spotted Bhungen. His unblinking gaze tore at me.

A scanner moved among the dead and wounded, taking DNA samples.

To the far right, Raven stood pressed against the back of a van Garly had modified. From the outside, it looked like a suburban family's conversion van. The inside had been gutted, however, with benches installed along one side, a mini-lab drilled into the other, and containers and cubbyholes filled with materials, portable fabrication equipment, and weapons, the windows bulletproof.

Raven looked unharmed, weapon held high, though she was breathing heavily; when she glanced at me, she looked like the scared nineteen-year-old she was, barely holding it together as gunfire chipped at the van's edges.

Cole pulled me back. "We split in groups, head for the vehicles that are armored—Chevy, Audi, the two Jeeps—and use those positions to take out the bastards."

"We need to reach the van," I said.

He took a quick look. "OK, the van too. We gotta move fast."

I nodded, clenching my fist. We'd be lucky to survive.

Lafontaine appeared behind us, his gun gripped tight. "Here's the plan—"

"Don't bother," Cole growled. He began directing the thirty or so men and women huddled with us. A few more rebels arrived, which Cole steered into a group before turning back to me. "Ready?"

The frequency of the gunfire in the passageway behind us slowed, though the gunshots grew louder. Agency forces were approaching. I wondered where the rest of their assets were but didn't wait. I told Anya and Nataly, "Stay close."

"Uh, me too," Garly said. "I can help shield you."

Movement past him. Agency forces from the central hub were nearing, the silver hair of two Agents just visible.

Cole saw it, too. "Go," he barked.

We rushed into the motor pool.

Gun raised, heart pounding, I stepped into the large room in concert with fellow rebels. We split off as planned: some went to my left, others to my right, Anya's fingers touching my back as we hurried across the concrete floor toward a mountain-green Jeep, the SUV a third of the way across the room. The lead rebel to my right suddenly opened fire, taking down four soldiers in one sweep. The remaining soldiers shot back, the gunfire loud in the space, plasma blasts lighting the entire area.

I grabbed Anya's hand and ran toward the Jeep, using it to block us as gunfire swung toward us. When she, Nataly, Garly and I reached the vehicle, we nearly slammed into it, not slowing until we were close.

Others weren't as lucky. Gunfire took out six rebels, a seventh crying out and diving behind a stack of tires, clutching her leg.

Four rebels joined us, taking positions to my left. Valor suddenly appeared behind me, almost crashing into the back of the Jeep.

As sweat coated my body, my heart beating so fast it hurt, I attempted to peer around the side of the vehicle, but a burst of bullets pulled me back. Glancing through the windshield, Raven and I locked eyes. She gave a quick nod.

I took a breath. Tried to ignore my trembling hands.

"Okay, be ready," I told my group.

Raven swiveled out from her hiding spot and opened fire.

I charged out from behind the Jeep, gun raised, leading my group out in the open.

The vast room seemed to grow, the distance expanding even as we ran toward the van, toward my daughter, who continued to fire, the machine gun jerking her body. And toward our enemies, some of whom ducked back, a few diving through the hole they'd blown in the door, others returning fire.

Anya ran behind me, Valor pulling slightly ahead, Garly bending forward as he ran, Nataly behind us.

Gunfire crackled the air.

The distance to the van slowly narrowed.

I could barely catch my breath but didn't slow. A bullet tugged at my sleeve, death inches from me.

We reached the van, winded.

Raven stopped firing and gasped.

Angling to look over her shoulder, I managed to see the far end of the motor pool. The doors to the hackers' room had opened—and Kieran stood in the doorway.

The man responsible for Talia's death. For manipulating Mina. An anger deeper than any I'd ever felt flooded through me. He'd nearly killed me before I beat him and ripped out his primary implant. I'd neutered him. Ended him. Yet here he was, leading two Agency soldiers out of the room. He didn't have the swagger he used to have, but he was still dangerous.

He wore a strange contraption, a metal framework I'd never seen before that contained two bands of bright metal encircling his head and pieces of tech spaced in three different spots.

"Oh god," Raven whispered.

I forced my eyes from Kieran to take in the room he'd exited. I spotted bodies. Blood. Computers smashed, cables ripped out, stations overturned. He'd destroyed everything and everyone. Saito. His team of hackers. Gone.

Bellowing in anger and grief, I lifted my gun, desperate

to destroy the bastard—and he lunged forward as I unleashed a string of bullets. He wasn't as fast as before, but he was still fast. Before I'd gotten off three shots, he dove through the hole The Agency had created and disappeared outside. Beside me, Raven opened fire at the two soldiers, taking one down, but the other made it through the hole as well.

I shouted again, this time in frustration.

Gunfire exploded around us, aimed at the soldiers positioned near the hole.

The van rocked slightly; someone was in the vehicle.

When I pulled back from firing on The Agency's men, I saw Valor inside, a half-dozen packs scattered about. "Where the hell are the guns?" she shouted.

Before anyone could reply, a loud mechanical groan filled the air. The garage doors suddenly rose, and sunlight poured into the massive garage. Rebels ducked under the rising doors and yelled as they ran off into whatever awaited them, others rushing the opening as well, a growing mass of escapees.

Valor threw open the rear doors. "Come on, let's go," she barked before climbing over the gear toward the driver's seat.

"Where's Jex?" I asked Raven as I scanned the chamber, fearing he was hurt.

"Outside. He ran out after the attack started." She removed a commlink from her ear, her face pale and streaked with dirt, turned up the volume so I could hear, and pressed the transmit button. "Babe?"

Jex immediately answered, his voice strained. "I'm by the defense panel. Didn't get a chance to hook in all the new stuff to the remotes. There's an army out here."

My heart sank at his words.

Garly leaned over the commlink. "You remember how to trigger everything manually?"

"Yeah. Should I do it now?"

A strange thud alerted me. It came from outside, followed by three more. Then four others. The mass of rebels outside slowed, then started to retreat back toward the motor pool. Not understanding, I stepped forward. The next moment, a thick metallic plate, four feet wide and eight feet tall, dropped vertically out of the sky and slammed into the ground in front of one of the lead runners, who'd made it nearly fifty yards from the motor pool. Five additional plates fell rapidly around him, entrapping him. Other plates imprisoned who knew how many others.

The runners scattered, some racing back toward the mountain, others heading to either side of the road.

More plates rained down. It wasn't haphazard, though it looked like it. The plates were targeted.

"Tell Jex to wait," I said.

Raven hooked the comm to her belt. "I'll get him." Before I could argue, she said, "When we leave, we won't have time to stop for him." She kissed my cheek, then dashed toward the back of the garage where a motorbike remained.

I hated the idea but knew she was right.

My MP5 in hand, I ran to the entrance, bullets and plasma bolts piercing the air as I moved, dropped down when I reached the open doorway, and stared in wonder.

As I'd noticed when I'd talked to Jex the other day, the land sloped downward away from the motor pool, the road leading into the forest visible below—but fifteen or more Agency vehicles stood in a curved line to stop us from entering the forest. They remained back, nearly one hundred yards from the motor pool exit as if giving us room to surrender. Or acting as containment. More ominously, a large structure hovered in the sky overhead, suspended by dark matter or propellers, I couldn't see from my angle. As I watched, four more plates dropped, capturing another fighter.

Then I saw her, silver bob glinting in the sun: Britt on her hoverbike. She remained stationary, hovering eighty feet off the ground and a hundred yards or so from where I knelt, intently focused on the runners. She made a hand gesture, and more plates dropped.

Behind me, the tone of gunfire shifted. The Agency forces from the central hub were nearing the motor pool.

We were pinned.

Chapter Thirteen

More metal plates slammed into the ground, sometimes capturing two or three rebels. A couple of plates crushed their target instead of capturing them. More madness.

As the sounds of Agency forces advancing behind me grew, I searched the skies again for Britt. Spotted her to the south, confident in her advantage.

Bringing up my MP5, I aimed, exhaled like Senn had taught me—triggering a pang of sadness—and squeezed the trigger, the bullet striking the front of her bike. I'd been aiming for her, but the result was the same: the strike shorted power to the bike, and she dropped out of sight.

Cole appeared beside me. "Good shot. I'll take out the floating barge overhead."

I'd seen his look before. Determined. Ready to sacrifice himself.

Outside, the mass of rebels angled to the side to avoid The Agency as they rushed once more toward the forest. This was followed by a discordance of engines as our drivers prepared to head out.

I patted Cole's shoulder and stood to return to the van—but it pulled up beside me. "Get in," Valor shouted as vehicles drove past, engines thundering, one nearly hitting Cole in the driver's desperate scramble to get away.

The back doors swung open, and I climbed in. Garly and

Anya made room for me, most of the open space occupied by our bags. As soon as I shut the doors, Valor took off, Nataly riding shotgun.

We exited the mountain, and for one brief moment, the world expanded, a sliver of time before war crashed in. The next instant, Jex triggered the mountain's defenses. Hidden doors on trees opened to reveal vertical lines of gun barrels that unleashed hails of bullets at The Agency's forces, the high-caliber bullets shredding the front row of reinforced SUVs, the barrels swiveling to spread their destruction.

Rebel vehicles raced to the side, curving around the men and women still running, though many had already gained the forest, using the trees—real and fake—as cover. We were near the back of the line, the Chevy and a couple of motorcycles the only ones behind us.

Our defenses stopped firing as the front edge of our caravan reached The Agency's line. The first vehicle, a reinforced Ford Explorer, slammed into two Agency SUVs blocking the path to the forest hard enough to shove them out of the way.

We had an escape.

Rebel vehicles ahead of us drove through the break in The Agency's line. "Hang on," Valor yelled. She drove us through the gap, gunfire pelting the van's sides as we passed between the wrecked SUVs.

I stared out the van's rear windows as we surged away, searching for Raven and Jex. Seconds later, they emerged from the forest, descending the tree-covered hill with Jex driving and Raven holding on. He angled their motorbike toward the gap—but before they reached it, Agency forces appeared on ATVs, over two dozen of them, with an Agent in the lead, racing to fill the gap we'd driven through.

"Slow down," I yelled at Valor.

She did, and I raised my machine gun to bust out one of the rear windows.

"Wait," Garly cried. He lowered the window instead.

I glared at him, then stuck my machine gun out the

window, aimed, and fired at the lead ATVs. I took out one driver and shot another in the leg, which caused others to slow, and Jex and Raven made the gap.

"Okay, go!" I yelled.

Raven and Jex stayed close behind us as we raced farther away from the mountain, but The Agency's forces followed, the ATVs keeping up—and a flicker of shadow drew my gaze upwards. Drones swarmed overhead, not the same type that had struck Free Isle, but long-distance tracker drones.

My heart sank. Even if we got away from The Agency's forces, the drones would follow us.

Gunfire pinged the back of our van.

I returned fire on the ATV drivers, as did Raven, swiveling on the bike, one arm around Jex's waist, the other gripping her submachine gun. She fired a short burst and took out the front vehicle. The ATVs behind it swerved to avoid the carnage, though two crashed into each other. Coming up through the ranks, passing one ATV after another, were two black sedans, both driven by Agents.

Garly peered out the window. "No bueno."

Nataly shouted from the front. "Look."

She pointed at another Agent, a thin male flying a hoverbike. He flew in tandem with the tracker drones, either controlling them, or they were augmenting his efforts.

Valor shouted back at us as more gunfire pinged our vehicle. "Do science stuff."

Garly began rifling through the containers he'd brought. "When I say, stop the van."

He glanced through the front windshield, then pulled out the device I'd previously seen him working on: it was the emitter he'd previously had in pieces back at his lab. Shaped like an oversized, pop-up sprinkler head, the brass-covered device was two feet long, with a generator occupying the bottom half. Based on the way he held it, the device appeared heavy. "Okay, stop," he barked.

The van lurched as Valor slammed on the brakes. Before

we'd stopped sliding, Garly leapt out and scrambled toward a spot in the middle of the road. I got out as well.

The Agency's forces were approaching, the Agent-driven sedans now in the lead, gaining on Jex and Raven as they neared us. Jex slowed as Garly set down the emitter with a thud.

"Keep going," I yelled at Jex. I lifted my MP5 and fired at the lead sedan, making the driver slow, the ATV engines like a swarm of hornets.

"Here it comes, chi'," Garly said as Raven and Jex drove past. He triggered the device, and with a *whoomph*, sound waves burst forward in a thin line, fifty feet across, creating a force field in an arc that sliced through tree branches and kicked up dirt. The field wobbled with a low thrumming sound, the bottom edge etching at the ground, digging into it.

He saw me staring. "They're high-pressure harmonics." He shrugged. "Supposed to be elevated-like. Should be okay. Made it to protect our peeps at the Army base from airborne blasts."

The dirt got captured in the sound waves, obstructing our view, but not before the first vehicle slammed into the force field, the debris further covering the view. We heard two ATVs slam into the force field as well.

The road we were on extended through a gap in the ridge. The Agency wouldn't be able to go around the field to get to us. He'd blocked them.

"I'm impressed," I told him over the noise. "How long will it last?"

"A half-hour or so," said Garly.

"Wow," Nataly said. She'd gotten out of the van, though she stayed near the door, Anya visible behind her.

A shot suddenly rang out, and Garly's shirt flicked from what seemed to be a near-miss. I yanked him behind the van. "Get inside," I yelled at Nataly. Two more shots rang out, though the van protected us.

Nataly opened the front passenger door but used it as a shield as she searched for the shooter. "It's Britt!"

I peered around the side of the van. The female Agent had taken a position partway up one side of the ridge. She must've crashed nearby.

Raven and Jex circled around behind us, slowing when they saw our distress.

"Watch out," I yelled. I grabbed the MP5 to provide cover as Garly and Nataly both climbed back into the van.

Jex took off, heading in the only direction he could: toward the gap. They'd be vulnerable. I aimed at Britt and fired repeatedly, forcing her to duck behind a boulder. But it's all I could do.

Jex and Raven continued forward, Raven firing one-handed, her left arm wrapped around his waist—and the next moment, I heard a gunshot. Raven cried out as her machine gun went flying and slumped to the side, then started to slide off. Jex snatched her forearm as their bike veered, straightened their ride, and gunned the engine. Raven crumpled over, my last living child hurt. The next moment, they disappeared around a bend.

I fired at Britt, though I couldn't hit her where she crouched. I drained the MP5's clip, then climbed into the van. Valor floored it as soon as I got in, and we drove into the gap, chasing after Jex and Raven. Britt raked our van with gunfire as we passed, though we didn't slow. Seconds later, we were away.

"What about the drones?" Nataly asked.

I nearly yelled that I didn't give a damn about the drones. I just wanted to reach my daughter. But she was right. Wherever we went, they'd track us.

Garly snapped his fingers, then reached for the heavy canvas bag he'd hauled to the van. He directed me to stand by the rear door. "Here," he said, pulling out a replica of a hoverbike's handlebars. He then pulled out a black, insect-like robot, no more than an inch and a half long. It looked familiar. "Ditch your shield and cover your implant with this."

I put aside the empty MP5. "Why?"

"It'll glean from you, like communicating but without formal commands. They figure out what you want."

I removed my shield—The Agency knew where I was at the moment anyway—stuck it in my pocket, and placed the robot over my implant. Though I was temporarily blinded again, I could feel the tiny 'bot shifting into a circle as I brought it near. Settling the robot over my implant, it covered it completely, cutting off my stream so I could see again.

A few streams of data flickered in my lenses, too fast to catch.

Garly zipped the bag completely open to reveal a shifting black mass.

"What—?" I started.

"Hold the bar straight-like."

I did as he instructed, not sure if I'd regret it—and the black mass rose from the bag in a narrowing column to connect to the fake handlebars. I realized the tiny robot covering my implant was one of the thousands that made up the black mass that was now forming before me. They were the interconnected robots I'd seen in his lab. As the mass rose and thickened before me, I saw flashes of bright metal, what looked like tiny jets. I started to ask what they were doing when the mass slipped between my legs, pushing them outwards as more of the connecting robots filled the space behind me. Then a foot-long metallic structure emerged from the bag, lifted by the black mass. "Is that a jet nozzle?" I asked, perplexed.

The next happened in rapid succession: Garly opened the rear doors, the four tiny jets lit, the robotic mass rose beneath me—and I found myself suspended inside the van. Then the large jet nozzle swiveled into place behind me.

Jesus, the robots had formed into a hoverbike.

"You only have three minutes of fuel," Garly shouted, shoving a plasma pistol into my pocket. "Make it count."

"For what?" I yelled.

"Taking out the drones."

The large jet ignited—and I shot out of the van back toward the ridge. I pulled on the handlebars, not sure if they'd work, and the robots responded, either due to my actions or the connection with my implant. I quickly rose, the mountain range appearing before me, forests nearby, the arid valley behind me. I hadn't planned on flying, on going after the drones—but he was right. If we were going to have a chance, I needed to take them out.

My height made me concerned about the thing I was on. I couldn't call it a hoverbike, or anything, really. I was being suspended by interlocking robots, what I thought of as swarmbots. I wasn't sure how they even connected together, whether it was designed like puzzle pieces or if they were just holding onto each other like two men shaking hands.

The shell of the bike rippled under me, which didn't reassure me.

I searched the skies for my target. It took a few seconds, more than I had, but then I found them. The tracker drones moved in synch, trailing what I surmised was our caravan of getaway vehicles. I cut across the sky, forty feet above the forest floor, heading for the lead drones. I didn't have a weapon other than the plasma pistol, I realized as I neared, although I had an idea. If it didn't work, I wasn't sure what to do.

I approached the long cluster of drones, treetops undulating beneath me, the Agent spotting me but too far away to intercept in time. I noticed he had the same strange rifle Britt had used on Jex. The thin Agent brought it to his shoulder and aimed, so I pushed the wide handlebars to angle away before he could fire—but felt the slightest sting in my left index finger. Shooting to the side, I noticed the encapsulated end of the burrowing device jutting out of my finger as I gripped the handlebar. Only one of the five prongs had actually pierced the skin, the second digging into my nail, the other three extending past my finger. It must've been why I felt a sting, as what I thought of as the numbing needles had mostly missed me.

I jerked on the handlebar to free my hand, as the central needle, much longer than the others, had embedded itself into the handlebar. When I freed my hand, the central needle jutted out from the end of my finger. The tiny electronic device that the projectile injected into people's veins was still in the encapsulated end; the needle didn't have anything to inject into. I'd been lucky. As that thought went through my head, the needle began to retract—no doubt searching for flesh to inject into. I let go of the handlebars completely and yanked the device out of my finger. The electronic capsule was still in place.

If I survived, I could study it to find its purpose.

I jabbed the device into the side of my heel for safekeeping, then reoriented myself. The caravan was farther away, the Agent near the drones.

I grabbed the handlebars again and pushed forward, triggering the jet.

Within seconds, I closed in, aiming for a head-on collision with the drones.

I sent what I hoped was a command to the robot affixed to my implant—and my 'hoverbike' expanded outward, the front edge widening into a curved net. I shot through the cluster, the drones slamming into the robot-fashioned net, jarring me as they splintered apart, the bits of Agency tech falling to the forest floor.

Within seconds, I'd wiped them out.

I searched for the Agent—and ducked as he shot past, nearly hitting me.

The swarmbots reformed into a hoverbike, and I triggered the main jet as the Agent arched through the air toward me. I shot forward, out across the descending forest, away from the rebel group, the Agent on my tail and gaining. I fired at him, using the pistol Garly had given me, though I was going too fast and at too poor of an angle to get anywhere close. Growing desperate, I flew in a random pattern, leading him further away, but was nearly out of fuel. I was down to seconds' worth; there wasn't a gauge anywhere, but the robot attached to my implant must've sent me a signal of some sort. Whether accurate or not, I had one choice.

As the Agent got closer, I felt something shift under me. The robots moved the main jet assemblage under their collective body and placed it at the front of the constructed hoverbike. With it in place, I yanked back on the handlebars—triggering a blast from the jet that arrested my forward momentum, nearly giving me whiplash—and let go. Thrown backwards, I twisted in the air, the swarm bursting apart from under me, and I reached for the Agent, who flew straight at me, too stunned to duck away in time. I slammed into him, throwing him from his bike, the swarmbots a cloud it flew through.

We fell.

Swarmbots fell with us.

As I dropped toward the forest, the 'bots that could reach each other formed around me—and protected my body as I crashed through the branches of a tall pine. The limbs grew thick enough to slow my fall, though the multiple impacts tossed me about. I landed hard, the swarmbots barely able to cushion the blow. But other than some bruises and an ominous twinge in my back, I was uninjured.

The swarmbots dropped away from my body, and I stood, though I was a little unsteady. Maybe I was more injured than I'd realized. The rest of the 'bots, which had been too far away to help shield me, pelted the ground, though they seemed unfazed by the fall.

The Agent wouldn't be far.

I found him crawling across a pile of dead needles toward a Smith & Wesson pistol, one leg twisted, a broken tree branch three inches in diameter jutting from his stomach. I pointed my plasma weapon at him. "Don't move," I said.

The Agent looked at me, his features slack, then continued for his gun.

I dropped to a knee beside him as he grabbed the gun and swung it toward me. I caught his arm easily, which told me how much his injuries had weakened him, and pressed my pistol against his chest. Fury rose inside of me. "You people killed my baby girl."

"Then she deserved it."

I fired, the plasma bolt too close for his enhanced skin to slow.

His eyes remained open, though he was dead.

I closed his eyes to block the cameras resting against his retinas and stumbled back. The events of the past hour gripped me: the invasion, Kieran's return, Raven being shot. I wasn't sure where or when The Agency would come again. They'd seen the rebels' faces. We were exposed, flushed out; even with the drones destroyed, there were more ways to track us, more ways to defeat us.

I bent over, my hands on my knees. Senn, Bhungen, Saito, and dozens more, maybe hundreds. Dead. Others captured. And Raven injured, possibly dying.

Kieran would hunt her, hurt her, to get to me.

I had to get away from the dead Agent. His multiple implants were uncovered, so The Agency would find him, even out here.

I searched for the hidden button on my bracelet and turned it on. Because I couldn't use my implant's tech, I'd designed the bracelet to emit a crude, three-dimensional image: a topographical map that looked like something out of the late 2020s. When it formed, I spotted the red dot immediately. It took me a moment to orient myself, but with it, I determined Raven's location. They were farther south than I would've guessed, down in the foothills.

I stumbled to the Agent's hoverbike, my legs stiff and my body beginning to ache. The shell was cracked, but it should still work. I climbed on, the familiar tinge of weightlessness caressing me when the seat depressed, but the engine didn't start. The fuel gauge showed empty—and that's when I smelled it. Jet fuel. A quick check confirmed that the tank had ruptured in the crash; the fuel had seeped into the ground.

Shit.

I approached the swarmbots, which sparkled in the sunlight. I didn't want to leave them. As if they read my thought, the robots clustered together, stretched for my hand, grabbed it, and crawled up my arm to my shoulders. In seconds, they settled into place. They were heavy, though I managed the weight.

Remembering, I checked the heel of my boot. The capsule

had broken, probably during my fall, and the electronic device was gone.

Grimacing, I checked the map again and hurried away.

* * *

Twenty minutes later, sweaty and tired, I stumbled to a stop.

The trees parted to reveal a two-lane, deserted road. Walking the paved surface would be quicker, though it would expose me.

I hesitated, then peered at the robots on my shoulders and pulled up a program icon I'd noticed in the corner of my vision. Options appeared on my lenses, what I realized were shapes they could make: a pyramid, a man, and so on. One expanded, an apparent suggestion of theirs: a black bear.

A confused chuckle escaped my lips. "What the hell do I do with that?"

CHAPTER FOURTEEN

The growl of a combustion-engine disrupted the forest's quiet.

Seconds later, a wide-grilled, seventy-year-old pickup truck appeared. I marveled it still ran.

The growl grew loud, a trail of smoke issuing from the tailpipe. From my hiding spot near the road's edge, I caught a glimmer of gray hair from the driver and passenger. The vehicle was fifty yards away and closing fast. Thirty. Ten.

I glanced across the road. In the shadows, a body formed.

A high-pitched squeal cut through the growl as the driver suddenly braked. The truck slid past me, stopping a few feet away. The bots' calculation had been damn-near perfect.

I shifted forward as the driver opened the door. "Don't get out," a woman called from inside the cab.

"Shush it," a man replied. They both sounded old. In the side mirror, I glimpsed the passenger's head, her curly-white hair bobbing as if she was scanning the shadows on the opposite side of the road for a small black bear—which I hoped she was doing.

"Close the door at least," she said.

"Quiet. You'll scare it off."

The driver stood by his open door. I could just see the top of his head. If either turned, I'd be busted. Even at their age, they'd have implants. Cameras.

I crawled out of my hiding spot onto the warm asphalt road. I stayed low, my gaze switching from the side mirror to the back of the driver's head, risking a glance at the sky as well, then slipped behind the truck, the exhaust puffing in my face as I passed it. The swarmbots would've already collapsed out of their bear-shape and crawled through the brush. I had seconds.

"Where'd it go?" the driver asked.

"Get in the truck, Sal."

I stood, exposing my presence as I grabbed the back of the pickup's tailgate. The driver and passenger were still staring at the spot where the swarmbots had been, but they wouldn't for long. The woman fidgeted; she'd lost interest. If she looked back, The Agency would find me.

As I climbed into the pickup bed as quietly as I could, the driver began to turn. I dropped down and hid inside the bed, ears straining for a shout. Instead, the driver's door slammed shut.

"You saw it too," I heard the man say.

"Did not."

Knowing I only had seconds, I rose up enough to stick my arm over the back of the tailgate. The swarmbots scurried across the asphalt, darker than the road, and rose up in a stretched-pyramid shape for my hand. I reached down farther, and the highest section of 'bots wrapped around my wrist. As soon as they did, the rest began to climb up my arm, and I pulled them in.

Settling back as the truck started forward, I checked the bracelet's map showing Raven's location. I was about thirty minutes away.

The bed was scratched and dirty but empty, which would make my departure easier, though still risky. I lay back, the swarmbots nestling next to me with their dagger-tipped feet inward, and I brought up my display screen on my lenses, which I'd kept minimized since the day we'd invaded The Agency's office. I wasn't broadcasting, which meant the robot was securely covering my implant. Then I saw them: messages in my inbox.

I wasn't sure I wanted to read them.

I gazed at the sky, though the "2" hovering over my Messages pulled at me.

As the truck rattled, I pulled up the messages. Both were

from Mina. The first pierced my heart. It was Talia's eighth-grade picture with words across the bottom: *You don't understand.*

I closed the message, then opened the other. It was a voicemail, the words turned to text. "Dray, it's Mina. Find me." She left a phone number, which stunned me. She had to be with The Agency—they wouldn't have let her out of their sights—yet she wouldn't have left a phone number if Agency staff could hear her.

Or so I assumed. She was better at this than I was: the intrigue, the political maneuverings.

I'd considered searching for her, but not now. The message flashed on my lenses told me who was really behind her communications.

I deleted the voicemail, though the phone number remained etched in my memory.

* * *

The projected map indicated that I had nearly reached Raven. Her tracker hadn't moved in the last ten minutes, which stoked my worst fears.

Aware the driver could see me if he looked through his rearview mirror, I dared not rise up to look over the edge of the bed. Instead, I focused on the truck's movements to determine the best time to escape. A minute later, the truck angled upward as it ascended a hill.

This was my chance.

Concentrating, I envisioned what I wanted the swarmbots to do—but they didn't move.

I'd have to handle this myself.

I lifted my body over the bots, pressed against the tailgate—aware I was even more exposed to the driver—reached over the top and felt for the truck handle. When I found it, I pulled it—and struggled to lower the gate quietly, though even an errant squeak from the gate was less risky than climbing over it. As soon as I finished lowering it, I scooted to the edge. Before I could focus on the swarmbots again, they moved over me and covered my body, including my face, adopting a lattice structure to cushion me. They'd read my intent, after all.

With a shift of my weight, I fell off the tailgate.

I landed in the road but didn't bounce or roll. The 'bots absorbed the blow, then continued to cover me as I lay still, blocking the sunlight from my view. The truck's engine, muffled now by the 'bots, faded as the vehicle crested the hill. Seconds later, it was gone.

I sighed, hoping I hadn't endangered the old couple.

The swarmbots slid off and pooled before me. I frowned, not sure if they'd ignored my command or had known I was going to jump, so wanted to protect my fall. Both answers disturbed me.

I stood, then reached down so they could crawl up onto my shoulders. Once they settled into place, I checked my map, turned to the right, and plunged through the tree line.

I snaked my way through the shadowed forest as clouds began to fill the afternoon sky, not slowing until I found a dirt road with a dozen or so vehicles—including Garly's van, to my relief—hidden under canopies of vegetation and heat-shielding material. I could smell the bleach used to destroy the DNA left in the vehicles. More assets we were forced to abandon.

The meetup spot was a former tree farm, the fields reclaimed by nature, the formerly-whitewashed house struggling to remain in one piece as the elements eroded its foundation. My relief was short-lived, though. While the place appeared big enough to hold five or six bedrooms, it appeared deserted.

As I reached the front steps, the front door opened. I pointed my pistol, then lowered it as Valor rushed out with a plasma rifle slung over her shoulder. "You made it." She hugged me, squeezing tight. "Thank god you're alive."

"Raven. Where is she?"

"Inside with the others—those who are left."

She led me toward the front door. "What's on your shoulders?"

I explained about the swarmbots. "I'm sorry about Senn."

"Is there any chance…?"

I shook my head. They'd bickered like a married couple but had been dear friends.

The interior of the house was in the same condition as the exterior, with peeling paint, little furniture, and no electricity. I heard a couple of harsh whispers but didn't see anyone, tension heavy in the air.

Her eyes downcast, Valor led me to a small room that contained a stained mattress, a pile of what seemed to be discarded clothes in the corner—and Raven, Jex, and Anya. Raven sat on the mattress, Jex by her side, with Anya kneeling before her. All three appeared exhausted.

I hurried to Raven, stepping around the medical supplies Anya had laid out and hugged her gently, relief and fear washing through me.

Raven trembled in my embrace, holding her right arm out to the side. "I wanted to find you, but Jex wouldn't let me—"

"You would've bled all over the forest," he drawled.

I pulled back. "Where were you shot? How bad is it?"

She stood, thrust her hand in my face, and my relief at finding her alive evaporated. The index and middle fingers of her dominant hand were gone. Anya had sprayed Raven's hand with antiseptic and had been in the process of wrapping it, but even with the covering, the significance of her injury was evident. There was also a deep gouge along her forearm, but that could be fixed. Her fingers couldn't be.

Raven struggled to maintain her composure. "Hurts worse than it looks," she tried to joke.

"Do you have tiny robots on your shoulders?" Jex asked, who'd also stood.

I explained about the swarmbots, then pulled Raven aside. "How are you really?"

When she replied, she spoke so softly I almost couldn't hear her. "You were right. I failed to shoot Britt in that garage. She reminded me of that Agent on Free Isle, the one I killed."

During our escape from the fake island, an Agent had burst into the armory and would've killed me. She'd shot him before he could—though she'd dropped her gun in horror after he'd collapsed. "You saved my life that day," I reminded her.

"He wasn't able to react in time to save himself. She couldn't, either. What if that happens to me?"

"Raven, this is war. You have to be prepared at all times."

She held up her wounded hand. "I deserve this."

"You don't have to be a soldier. You can help in other ways."

Anya took Raven's shoulders and steered her back toward the mattress.

"No, Dad," Raven said as she resisted Anya's efforts. "I need to fight."

"Sit," Anya told her, her voice tired. For the first time, I noticed the stains on her shirt. The plastic bags piled in the far corner were filled with bloody rags. Raven wasn't the only one who'd been injured.

As I tried to process what we'd suffered—and the damage to Raven, both physically and emotionally—Anya knelt once more before Raven, though she looked up at me. "I'm glad you made it."

Jex hugged me. He was vibrating, whether from anger or anxiety or something else, I couldn't tell. "We have a bad habit of being chased," I told him as he let go.

"How'd you find us?"

Before I could respond, Raven stiffened. "Wait, did you put a tracker on me?"

I tried to give a disarming smile. "Remember the injection the nurse gave you for that additional round of virals?"

"You *injected* me?"

Jex shook his head as Anya's eyes widened.

"I told the nurse that de Vera required it," I admitted.

"Take it out."

She looked angry, which she had every right to be. "I will. I promise." To Jex, I asked, "How long before The Agency finds this place?"

"I didn't think they'd find the mountain, so who knows.

Couple hours?"

"We can't leave yet," Anya objected. "Raven's in shock. She needs to rest. We all do."

"We have to go," I said. "The Agency knows we're on the run."

She set her jaw and opened a gauze pad. "Give me five minutes."

As I stepped out of the room, I felt Senn's and Bhungen's absence. If they'd lived, they would've bantered with Raven, their jokes masking their concern—and they would've anointed themselves as her bodyguards, though it would've annoyed the hell out of her.

I was heartbroken that she'd been permanently disfigured. Not only would it be a forever reminder of this war, not only did it put her at a disadvantage, but it would become another way to identify her. To hunt her down.

"Surprised you didn't make a comment about my rifle," Valor said as she stood in the empty hallway.

"Looks nice."

"What would be nice is having my pistols. I'm so pissed Lafontaine took them."

"Where is he?"

"Left. Claimed he's got some 'friend' who can help us, so that's where everyone's heading. Not sure it's a good idea."

"So, he survived. What about the other leaders?"

"De Vera made it, though she's hurt. And Cardoza. The others were killed or captured—including Perenko. No one's heard from Cole."

I hoped the cantankerous colonel survived, though it was unlikely. And with over half the leadership gone, we were even more vulnerable. "What about the teams that went to Fort Irwin?"

"De Vera and Lafontaine sent messages to them, but I don't know if they've heard back. Kind of scared to ask." She dug into her pack and handed me a machine gun. "For when we leave."

Two rebels I didn't recognize stepped into the hallway

and disappeared outside via a side door. Even though I only saw them for a moment, they looked shaken from The Agency's attack and our desperate escape.

Another person appeared in the hallway: Garly, carrying two large bags. His cheek was covered by a bandage that stretched to his ear. He hurried over. "You rise again. So relieved, my padre."

"What happened?" I asked, indicating his cheek. He stood slightly hunched as well, favoring one side, and he had bags under his eyes.

"After you flew off, Britt almost clocked me out. We skedaddled before she could try again. I brought you a present."

He pulled my hand shields from one of his bags.

"Did you use them during the escape?"

He gave a chagrined look. "I forgot I had them."

Nataly approached, pale and frightened, though she looked relieved to see me. After making sure she was okay, I turned to Garly. "Do you happen to have my cap?"

He produced it from his bag, and I slipped the shield-blocking knit cap over my head, then removed the swarmbot attached to my implant, careful to keep my implant covered.

With his and Nataly's help, we transferred the robots from my shoulders to the canvas bag he'd carried them in. After they were zipped up, I rolled my shoulders, which ached from having carried them. The robots rippled inside the bag as if in response.

Garly smiled again. "They bonded to you. They shouldn't need your implant anymore, at least not when they're close, cause they borged to your frequency. You're linked now."

"That's disturbing."

Cardoza appeared with three bodyguards. "What's she doing here?" she asked, indicating Nataly.

"She's invaluable. She may be the only hacker we have left," I said as Garly moved close to Nataly.

"Come with me," Cardoza told her.

"I'm with Dray."

Frustration and annoyance crossed Cardoza's face.

A thought occurred to me. "Have you told everyone to check each other to make sure they haven't been tagged?"

"Of course. We are not fools. Make sure your own people are checked."

"Our group's clean," Valor said.

Cardoza looked as if she wanted to argue but left, taking her bodyguards with her. The next moment, Raven, Anya, and Jex appeared, Raven's hand bandaged and sealed.

We were the last ones in the house.

I didn't trust Lafontaine, but I didn't know where to go from here. We could take one of the vehicles, but we didn't have supplies, resources, or a destination. At least, not yet. So I followed as they exited via the side door Cardoza had used, five steps leading to a grassy field that stretched toward the seemingly endless forest surrounding the place, the trees dark in the late-afternoon haze. Cardoza was in the field, leading her bodyguards toward the forest, with a cluster of rebel soldiers, the last ones other than my group, visible past them.

The field looked odd, though.

"It's OK, chi'," Garly told me. He stepped in front of us and into the grass—where his feet disappeared, the grass unchanged. "I laid down a hologram. The whole field's covered."

"To mask our escape," Jex said. "Nice."

"The Agency will find the 'gram, but it'll give us time."

Jex kept a hand on Raven's good arm as she descended the steps. Garly and Nataly huddled close to help until Valor glared at them and stepped to Raven's wounded side. I moved behind Raven, wanting to help as well.

We started across the field grouped around Raven, the hologram warping the ground at our feet, a faint glow to the fake grass adding to the distortion. When I lifted my gaze to scan the forest, I spotted Monroe watching us. We locked eyes. He lifted his chin, then turned away.

Anya lagged a little, her medical pack almost dragging on the ground. "Need help?" I asked.

When she saw I carried only a small pack, she handed hers

over. "If you think this gets you bonus points, you're right." She rubbed a shoulder muscle. "For the record, being a badass fighter isn't the best way to woo me. I prefer flowers."

"Hard to find a good florist these days."

She smiled, then nodded at Raven and dropped her voice. "There was nothing to save. The rest of her hand is bruised but should be fine, and her forearm will heal quickly with the nanobots I injected."

I understood her message. The 'bots would heal the wounds on Raven's hand and arm but couldn't regrow her fingers. She might've shot left-handed once or twice, but right now, she was a soldier who couldn't fire a weapon with any skill.

If she found the courage to fire at all.

CHAPTER FIFTEEN

Conversation faded as we moved deeper into the forest, each of us instinctively quieting in the hopes of avoiding detection from The Agency.

We couldn't run forever, and we couldn't hide. Not anymore. All of the rebels besides myself had been ghosts before, having hid their identities, but now The Agency knew what everyone looked like. They'd code their software to alert them whenever we appeared on camera. And they'd search their records. Make connections to family, friends, contacts. Tighten their noose until they captured or killed everyone.

We caught up with the other rebels after twenty minutes. Some of them looked confused and shellshocked, mourning their fellow soldiers—and their lost sense of security. Others were wounded but determined. The rest seemed angry, searching for someone to fight, furious that The Agency had blindsided them.

I hesitated to speak to any of them, not sure what I'd say or if my words would be welcomed, so I focused on my group. We stayed close, making sure no one fell behind, providing brief touches and words of encouragement, each of us keeping an extra eye on Raven. She kept up, though she trembled more as her shock wore off and the pain set in. Anya offered her meds, but Raven only took one of the pills offered.

Those with weapons held them at the ready, aiming ahead and at the sky as they walked, though they didn't slow.

I understood their fears as I aimed the machine gun Valor had given me. The trees hid us—but hid dangers as well.

"Garly," I said quietly, pulling him and Nataly from their whispered discussion. "You have any recon drones?"

The three of us stopped. He squatted, pulled a six-inch drone from the backpack he carried, handed it to me, then stood and picked up the duffel bag containing the swarmbots. I saw him grimace. "Want me to carry that?" I asked.

Garly shook his head and handed me the drone controller. I almost insisted but dropped the topic as the rest of our team joined us. Instead, I sent the drone skyward. It crested the ocean of trees, and at my direction, scanned the entire area.

"Well?" Jex asked.

As the camera panned, a large, trapezoidal-shaped object slid into view on the controller's screen, hovering a mile or so away, one side pockmarked with dark circles. I zoomed in and could just make out a mist of some sort emanating from the circles.

My team clustered around the screen. "What is that thing?" Raven asked.

"It's dispersing something," I started, when it hit me. "Kieran's 3D drones. The Agency has to be deploying thousands."

"Dray," Jex said. The camera had panned away from the disbursement vehicle, and two tiny objects appeared in the sky.

Garly eyed the screen. "Hoverbikes, I think."

I commanded our drone to return to us, then we hurried to the others. "The Agency is coming," I told the rear unit. "Stay together and move quickly. The smaller footprint we make, the better." At least until The Agency unleashed reconnaissance drones that flew close enough to spot us—but one problem at a time.

The fighters spread the word, and the groups picked up the pace, their unease palpable.

My team and I continued to check on each other as we followed. Jex noticed Anya was uneasy moving through the forest, so he talked quietly with her for a few minutes, giving advice and encouragement. He helped others as well, sharing the knowledge he'd built up over his four years running and hiding from The Agency, including making sure everyone had good socks; he carried extra pairs in his pack.

The whole time, he kept a close eye on Raven. I noticed because I did the same, alternating my focus between the forest around us and her. She kept her head up, though her shoulders betrayed her despair.

Rebels clustered up ahead; they'd stopped to look at something. When we reached them, I signaled to my group to stay back and made my way through the crowd.

I found Lafontaine squatting near a ridge that revealed a portion of the forest dropping away directly ahead and then rising toward the next hill in a frozen ocean of green, other hills visible in the distance. Cardoza squatted beside him.

"You survived," he said to me. Without waiting for a reply, he handed me a pair of binoculars, the enhancers about an inch thick, and indicated a hill farther away.

I focused the binoculars, not sure what he wanted me to see, until I caught motion. A six-legged robot appeared on an outcrop of sand-colored stones that jutted from the hill and crouched on the edge.

"It's a crawler," I said, returning the binoculars. The robots were one of many types The Agency had, according to rumors I'd heard.

"Do they know where we are?" Cardoza asked.

"Not yet. They're searching."

"Maybe the damn thing will slip and fall."

"I doubt that would damage it," Lafontaine said. He retreated from the edge. "Everyone keep moving. We don't want those things spotting us."

As his group followed his orders, he told me, "We'll need masks now that we've been exposed. Not rubber ones. Agents spot them a mile away. When we reach our destination, have Garly work on it."

"Have you heard from the teams sent to Fort Irwin?" I

asked quietly.

He frowned. "Gauging from reports we received, over ninety percent were killed or taken. I triggered the beacons during the attack, but The Agency must've already known their location."

I could've accused him, but it wouldn't bring back those we'd lost. "I'm sorry, Isiah," I said, using his name for the first time.

He paused, his face turning inscrutable. "Make sure your group keeps up."

When I rejoined my team, they looked tired, but Raven looked exhausted. "You okay?" I asked her.

"Don't have a choice."

Jex was squatting beside her, attaching a gun holster to her left hip, though she looked uncertain. He finished, slid a gun into the holster, and stood.

Without looking at anyone, she started after the other forces, and we followed.

The ground sloped upward toward where the trees began to thin. I held my team back so others could go ahead; the more we clustered, the greater the chance The Agency would spot us.

Garly had brought a dozen of the chillers he'd made for the assault on Fort Irwin, eight-inch disks that hung from nylon handles and absorbed heat when activated. They'd mask us from The Agency's infrared sensors, but they only worked within a ten-foot radius, which meant each group assigned to a chiller would have to stay close together. We'd need them if we continued walking after sunset.

When the path cleared before us, I led my group up the hillside. Anya shifted to help Raven, who struggled but kept up. Garly stumbled, but when I went to him, he motioned me forward, his expression strange. He was sweating. I took his duffel bag to ease his burden though he objected, then continued forward.

The ground dropped off to our left. As we ascended, more of the rippled landscape appeared due to the expanding erosion.

Nearing the apex, I heard a drone, then spotted it: a JN-4 military drone. Whether it had spotted us or was flying a predetermined flight pattern, I didn't know, but the armed tracker was heading toward us, visible due to the erosion around us, which revealed the undulating landscape.

Unlike the 3D drones, this one actively hunted targets, designed to fly for hours with a reinforced body and various weapons, although its communication relay was my biggest concern. I wanted to shoot it out of the sky before it spotted us but knew that would make things worse.

Movement against my leg startled me; the swarmbots, shifting inside the duffel bag.

As I lifted my gaze, Jex raised his machine gun. Valor was aiming at the drone as well. I hissed at them, and they lowered their weapons, though they both remained tense.

The JN-4 appeared to be flying a predetermined path, as it maintained its elevation and would fly just behind us unless we alerted it. We stayed still, watching it near—and then Britt appeared on her hoverbike from behind one of the taller hills and headed toward us.

My heart sped up. A drone, even weaponized, was one thing; if Britt spotted us, she could signal The Agency's entire army—then drop out of the sky to attack us.

She flew hunched over the handlebars, intent and angry. She had to have discovered the Agent I'd killed.

She didn't slow, arcing over us, my eyes catching a glimmer of red as she did. Blood. She had bandages as well, but even if she was wounded, she remained lethal.

Her path would take her directly over the rest of our army. I couldn't tell if she'd picked up anything—she had enough tech in her head to synch in real-time with satellites, high-level scouting drones, and God knew what other surveillance they were running—but the closer she got, the more I worried.

The JN-4 flew over the terrain behind us; it would find any clues we'd left.

Britt flew over the army's position, then banked to the left;

if she looked over her shoulder, she would see us.

Garly, who'd hidden behind one of the trees, continued to breathe heavily. He looked pale. I frowned, but he pointed past me. Britt had straightened out; as I watched, she banked the other way. Her back was to us.

"Come on," Raven whispered. She led the way, leaning on Jex as we dashed across the apex and down the back side, nearly tripping and falling in our rush to get into deeper cover.

We didn't slow until we spotted the tail end of the main group, mostly clustered together but some smaller teams spread out from the rest.

"Did she see us?" Jex asked quietly, craning his neck to look behind us as he supported Raven.

Britt didn't appear, so we seemed safe—for the moment.

"We need to knock her out of the sky," he murmured. He glanced at me. "Have any gizmos that can do that?"

I shook my head.

Movement in the sky drew our attention. As Britt flew back over the way we'd come, a second hoverbike flew past on our other side. We froze until the Agents flew out of sight.

Cautiously, we continued on.

"Lafontaine better come through with that 'friend' of his," Jex said. "Otherwise, we're toast."

* * *

Our eyes adjusted as the sun set and night descended.

We traveled in silence, making decent time—until the forest suddenly ended. Past it was an open field rolling gently toward the horizon.

"Rest for a few minutes," Lafontaine declared, his voice carrying through the crowd. "Turn on your chillers. We'll continue soon."

Stopping for even a short time was risky, a feeling echoed in the expressions of my team. "I'll find out what's going on," I said as they and other groups activated their chillers to mask our body heat, the devices pulling the warmth from our clothes and skin.

I started for Lafontaine, pleasantly surprised when Raven came alongside. She'd leaned on both Jex and me the last two miles. "How's your hand?"

"I took a second pain pill." She glanced at me. "I still feel the fingers I lost."

I searched for words to comfort her but couldn't find any good enough.

We made our way through the crowd of men and women, each team grouped around their chiller. A perimeter watch was established, though unless they had night specs, they'd be mainly staring at shadows.

The temperature dropped quickly, though that was due as much to the chillers as the dry air.

Raven and I found Lafontaine talking to de Vera. "What's the plan for getting across?" I asked.

"When I say go, we go." He held up a finger as I started to ask how much further. "Our ride is on the other side. We make it, we'll be set."

"That's a big if," Raven said.

He pointed at her hand. "That thing sealed? If you're trailing blood, don't come with us."

"Our surgeon wrapped it. It's not leaking," I said, though I couldn't tell in the darkness.

He looked as if he wanted to argue but dropped it. "Fifteen minutes. Be ready. We won't wait for anyone."

We repeated his words when we returned to Jex, Garly, Nataly, Valor, and Anya. "He's a charmer," Nataly said.

Garly chuckled, then wheezed. He acted wobbly, his ivory skin nearly glowing in the faint light. "Something's going on with you," I said.

"Just winded," he said, though he stumbled as he tried to lean against a tree. Nataly grabbed his arm to steady him, which earned her a smile.

Anya approached. "Let's take a walk." She led him a few steps away, then sat him down.

"He did that earlier," Nataly told me. "He won't say

what's wrong."

She looked worried in the faint light, weighed down by fears we all shared and concern for Garly, probably wondering whether staying with us was a good idea, though she had as few choices as the rest of us.

"What else will The Agency use to find us?"

"Drones and Agents aren't enough?" She frowned. "Their physical weapons aren't their greatest strength. They track everyone's digital activity and cross-match it with pattern information captured from their camera networks. Teams of psychiatrists interpret the data, and if someone is tagged as a threat, The Agency eliminates them.

"No one in Washington can help us," she went on. "Their checks and balances have been neutralized."

Which meant The Agency controlled them. I didn't know if Congress and the White House controlled The Agency or if it was the other way around. Either way, we had to take them down.

She rubbed her arms. "I read blogs and amateur-reporter posts from people who lived in D.C. nine years ago to try to find when our enemies took over. They all abruptly stopped writing around the same time, so I searched backup systems and found an old Amazon server someone forgot to shut off. As I'd hoped, there were additional posts, though not many. One talked of armed crews working in underground spots late at night, which I think was The Agency. Another mentioned an entrance to a tunnel the blogger thought linked to an area being worked on, but I couldn't find anything else. The Agency covered their actions. They knew what they were doing."

I didn't know whether to try to create a mass uprising, fight The Agency directly, or just hide somewhere far away from our enemy's reach, if that even existed.

I felt responsible for us running, for all of this—including whatever was wrong with Garly.

Anya was still huddled with him. Not good.

"You angered the worst Agent," Nataly told me. "The

other Agents in my office worship Kieran. He made the team number one in the country, and he was marked for great things until you came along."

"Does that include Gunnar?"

She gave a sharp nod. "He worships Kieran because Kieran never forced him to do paperwork or anything else he hated. They all blame you for Kieran's demotion, especially Britt. She and Kieran are lovers."

Angry lover. Jesus.

I pulled out the search drone. "Can you see if she or any other Agent are still up there?"

After she took the drone, I went to Garly and Anya. "What's going on?"

"He's been lying to us," Anya said, opening his jacket and slowly lifting his shirts.

"She's great, isn't she?" Garly asked, nodding to Nataly. He wore an undershirt as well as an outer shirt under his loose jacket. He moaned as Anya pulled his shirts higher. Both were stained with blood. Large, self-adhering bandages crisscrossed the side of his chest.

I squatted beside him, partly to see better, partly to hide his injury from view. "What the hell happened?"

"Took a whizzo during our dash from the mountain."

"A 'whizzo'? You mean a bullet?"

"When I triggered the harmonics."

"He told me it just grazed him," Anya said, her voice tight. "I didn't even check him, just gave him some bandages."

"Didn't want to seem whiny," Garly said.

I'd thought Britt's bullet had missed him.

Anya pulled away the bandages. "It did more than clip your side. Damnit." She began to search her pack.

The bullet had entered his upper back almost two inches in. He was lucky it hadn't punctured his lung—or traveled all the way through.

Anya used a pocket scanner to check his side. "The bullet broke one of your ribs. At least it was a clean break."

"You can leave me. I'll keep mouse-like."

"Don't be foolish."

I agreed. "How quickly can you patch him up?"

"Five minutes. I'll staunch the bleeding and set some nanobots to work on his ribs," she said.

He squirmed, so I said, "Just pretend you're at the nurse's office back in high school."

"Went there oodles," he said, watching Anya as she extracted supplies she'd need. "I grew too fastlike as a runt, kept having the wobblies when I skated. Had to sayonara the parks. Then scholarships made me sayonara the rest of Santa Monica to join Ivy peeps."

He never looked away from Anya as he rambled.

To distract him, I relayed Lafontaine's demand that Garly make masks for everyone. "He said rubber ones don't work."

"They're not organic, which triggers Agents' bells. Lost good warriors until we stopped using them. We'd need to craft faces with tissue bits. Fake skin doesn't work. It's not alive."

"Maybe a thin bio-construct, enough to change our features yet maintain elasticity, wrapped in a membrane of some kind."

"Know of anything like that?" When I shook my head, he said, "Me neiths. Hey, if Cole shows up, don't alert him about my hole. He's rescued me enough."

Anya glanced at me but didn't comment as she wrapped his injury with bandages.

I saw Nataly eyeing Garly worriedly, Valor beside her, near the chiller, with a faraway look. Raven stood a few feet away to the other side, watching our surroundings with a fearful expression, cupping her injured hand, the pistol neglected at her left hip. Past them, de Vera reassured what appeared to be one of the leaderless clans. I couldn't see Lafontaine, though his gold streak should've made him easy to spot.

I checked on Raven. She assured me she was okay, though she didn't seem interested in talking, so I didn't push. I joined Jex instead, who'd stopped doting on her a few minutes earlier and stood away from the others.

"Even if we get to whoever we're meetin', it could be too late," he told me in a low voice, his drawl thick.

"You think The Agency is setting up roadblocks?"

He nodded. "We need to hustle outta here."

I glanced at Valor, who was the closest to us, but she wasn't listening. Even in the darkness, I could tell she was mourning those we'd lost.

Everyone was drained, reeling from the attack and struggling from the lack of food and water.

"We have a dirty secret, us rebels," Jex said quietly. "We've never won a face-to-face battle with Agents. I think our fight in the parkin' garage is the closest we got."

"How the hell did Lafontaine think we could take on the Army?"

"Probably hoped you had somethin' up your sleeve." He smirked. "You're a better leader than him. You should make a clan. I mean, you kinda already have one. Then you could fight for control of this whole sad bunch."

"I don't want to fight for control. It's what doomed my company. The five of us each thought we were right. We ruined what we had—and that was a business. Everyone here is risking their lives."

"What if the wrong person is actin' as leader?"

Lafontaine saved me from answering. "Time to go," he called out.

Within minutes my team was ready, even Garly. Raven stood beside Jex, protecting her arm, and Valor and Anya moved to my side, each carrying a pack. I shouldered Garly's pack—damn thing weighed a ton—and picked up the duffel bag.

The forward scouts activated camoshields as they headed off. The shields, originally planned for Fort Irwin, masked them in three-dimensional shadows that blended with the surroundings, the faint images disappearing within moments.

"Did you see anything when you launched the drone?" I quietly asked Nataly.

"It's too dark," she whispered. "But they have night

drones. I hope these chillers work, or they'll locate us quickly."

At some unseen signal, our forces stepped out of the forest and into the dark clearing of night.

I scanned the dark, rolling hills behind us. Far in the distance, I caught two tiny dots gliding among the tree-covered hills. I hoped I was wrong, but they looked silver.

* * *

We started across the vast meadow in bands of ten, each one grouped around a chiller. The teams moved in unison, emerging from the trees with weapons out and eyes scanning the skies. My team joined the exodus, the seven of us clustered around our device, while far ahead, Lafontaine and Cardoza shared a chiller with a group of four elite fighters. Just under one hundred rebels.

No one spoke, though we made noise: the rustle of fabric, the rattling of supplies, the snapping of brittle reeds as we walked. The sounds couldn't be helped, but they would alert our enemy if their sensors got close enough. The slightly uneven ground, treacherous at night, added to the noise—and our efforts. We had used a half-hour of the chillers' capacity waiting for nightfall. Each contained a capacity of six hours, depending on the circumstances. As we exerted ourselves, the devices' effectiveness would continue to shorten.

The terrain ahead consisted of a series of hills cast in gradients of grey that sloped downward toward what I hoped was another forest, though it was so far away it looked like a black smudge. A tiny grid of lights clung to the horizon, one of the towns that occupied the valley far below: possibly Visalia or Porterville.

I alternated my focus on the darkness around us and the ever-shifting ground under my feet as we walked. Jex carried our chiller, Raven walking doggedly beside him. She'd pulled her pistol and held it in her left hand. Garly kept up, eyes on the ground to watch his footing, Nataly by his side though she surveyed the skies. Valor seemed to scrutinize everything; her tension was an almost physical presence. To my other side, Anya kept an eye on both Garly and Raven.

I thought to say words of encouragement but didn't. Better to stay quiet.

Amidst the sounds of our traveling and heavy breathing, I heard something. So did others. Many of us scanned the skies as we hustled, and I slowed my group to hear better. That's when I identified them: Drones. Most of the buzzing came from the north, though it seemed one or two more came from the west as well.

"Shit," Raven said, her voice barely audible.

"Anyone see them?" I quietly asked my group. Everyone shook their head.

We hurried forward as one, though Raven's breath hitched. Dark circles had formed under her eyes, and her stride echoed the pain she was suffering. I reached out to help her, but she waved me off as she kept pace.

Other groups heard the drones. They accelerated, weapons raised. Then Valor hissed my name. To the east, what looked like three red lights moved in unison across the cloud-covered sky. By their formation, I knew what it was: a DNA scanner. I didn't know how effective it was from that altitude, but teams began to break up as individual fighters ran faster to get away.

"Stick together," I said, my words echoed by others. Most of the teams reformed, but we were all jogging now, though our destination didn't seem to move any closer.

Garly's pack and duffel bag, along with my own pack, weighed me down. Grimacing from the burden, I continued to switch hands carrying the duffel bag, the swarmbots heavier than I remembered. I considered using them but wasn't sure how they could help.

Climbing and descending the next three hills took a toll, and the teams started to slow. Lafontaine's voice floated back to us. "Keep moving. Our ride won't wait."

"Stop," Jex whispered, halting in the grass. We did as well, the other teams hurrying on ahead as he angled his head to listen. I held my breath, tried to ignore my pounding heart, and focused on my hearing. There was a faint sound in the distance, then the crack of a tree branch. A hydraulic whine.

He and I looked at each other. "Crawlers," he said.

They must've caught our trail and reached the edge of the forest, one stepping on a fallen branch. Though there was a lot of distance between us, others would be with it—and there was nowhere to hide.

Raven faced him. "Run."

The grasses were shorter here, but our breathing, pounding feet, rustling clothes, our heartbeats, all worked against us. "Stay tight," Garly wheezed. Anya slowed down slightly to stay close to me; I glanced back to make sure we remained near the chiller, my team within arm's reach of each other.

We crested another hill, went down the back side, then up the next, this one shorter but steeper. I'd been aware of Raven's location the entire time—behind my left shoulder, footsteps mostly in synch with mine—so when she stumbled, I reached for her before she could fall. She nodded at me as our group slowed, staying together.

"You go on," she said, her voice weak.

Jex handed the chiller's nylon handle to Anya. "Don't let it touch you," he said as she took it. Then before Raven could object, he lifted her off the ground, his hands under her thighs which caused her to wrap her legs around his body and glanced at us. "Let's go."

I didn't like how he was carrying her, but he had a pack slung across his back—and this wasn't the time to argue. I switched the duffel bag to my other hand and followed, the rest of our group behind me.

We were the farthest group back, the closest team one hill away.

When we crested the next hill, the forest appeared closer, the ground sloping down toward it. No more hills. But then I realized I could see it better, not only because it was clearer but because the sky was beginning to lighten.

Dawn was coming.

"Hurry," I said.

We sprinted toward the forest. The last team was halfway there, the ones ahead of it disappearing into the trees.

As we ran, I heard a soft beeping. "Dray," Anya huffed, holding up the chiller. A yellow light was blinking.

"It's almost out," Garly said.

Something in his voice made me look back. He was slowing, his arms hanging loose, face sweaty.

Two hundred yards remained, but it seemed like two miles.

"The rest of you, keep going." I handed the duffel bag to Valor. "Take this."

They took off for the forest, Raven's head slumping as Jex carried her.

I reached for Garly—and noticed Nataly remained at his side. "Go with them."

"I'll help."

We each hooked one of Garly's arms over our shoulders, though he was too damn tall to carry, and the three of us hurried toward the trees.

The sky grew brighter, the meadow becoming clearer; with the coming dawn, a handful of birds chirped in the distance.

Sweat soaked my shirt, the weight from Garly's pack and mine resisting my need to get us to safety. Garly grunted as we ran; I could tell he was pushing himself.

The sound of an engine reached us across the field, followed by a second. "ATVs," he gasped without looking back. I didn't, either. No time.

Three figures emerged from the forest and ran toward us.

Garly started to slow, but I forced him to keep up, a hand behind his back. The figures grew closer: Jex. Valor. With Monroe in the lead.

They nearly collided with us when they reached us. Valor grabbed my arm to pull me away from Garly, and Monroe took my place. "Come on." The three had cross-shaped objects in their hand. As one, they triggered them—and the camoshields formed.

The others winked out of view from where I stood, then faintly became visible as they started forward.

Valor pulled me with her, and we hurried toward the forest's edge.

"Thanks for coming back for us," I panted.

"Had to yell at Raven to stay in the trees."

Monroe grumbled behind me. "Tallest guy in our group, and you're out in the open."

"I like grand entrances," Garly said, the weakness in his voice robbing his joke. He sounded like he was going to pass out.

We reached the tree line. Raven stood just outside of the forest, her gun trained on the land behind us, though she held it awkwardly in her off hand. Anya waited behind her. They met us, and we entered the forest.

Forced to slow to a walk, I scanned the area. "Where are the others?"

"Leaving," Monroe said. "Follow me."

He handed Garly over before angling through the trees, picking up speed as a diesel engine whined to life.

Garly slumped and passed out.

I lifted him, Monroe rushing back to help, and we carried the scientist through the brightening forest.

The trees parted to reveal a semi-tractor trailer with the name RITE TIME MOVING COMPANY painted across its length, parked on a two-lane road with the side doors open. The last of the rebel army was climbing inside; when we appeared, those who spotted us waved at my group to hurry.

We rushed toward the semi, which jerked as if shifting into drive, though the driver didn't pull away before we reached it. Anya and Raven scrambled into the trailer first, with Jex helping Raven, and Monroe and I nearly threw Garly inside before climbing in using the metal rung under the doorway. After helping Nataly and Valor in, I grabbed one of the doors, Monroe grabbed the other, and we shut them, casting us into darkness.

The trailer lurched forward and picked up speed, though no one was relieved. We had no explanation of who'd picked us up or where we were going.

Worst was the conviction that if I and my team had been a few seconds later, the others would've left us.

That's when I realized something I'd been ignoring: these rebels weren't the answer I'd hoped for.

CHAPTER SIXTEEN

The trailer doors swung open, letting in the first sunlight we'd seen in hours.

We found ourselves inside a large airplane hangar, an open section before us, a cordoned-off section behind it, with a handful of rooms in the building's rear. The hangar entrance closed behind us.

Lafontaine stood a dozen feet away. "Everyone, stay away from all doors and windows and keep your voices down. The Agency's still hunting us. Get some rest, but stay sharp."

I quickly exited the trailer. "We can't stay long," I said as others climbed out behind me.

"I know, Quintero. This time tomorrow, we'll be in a different time zone."

"Where are we going?" I asked, but he walked off, his cleft-chin guard and another guard eyeing me as they trailed him.

Anya touched my arm as the rebels continued to offload. "What did he mean by a different time zone?"

"I think he's flying us out on a private jet," Jex said.

A familiar voice chuckled nearby. "In your dreams," Cole said. He stood near the cab, arms crossed, a wry grin on his disfigured face, clothes only slightly more scuffed up than the last time I saw him

"You're here," I said in surprise. Nipsen stood by him, favoring his good leg. I was relieved the curly-haired captain had made it as well. I felt bad for zapping him after we'd rescued him.

Jex saluted Cole, then gave him a hug.

"How did you two get away?" I asked.

"Managed to cause enough chaos after we took down their floating platform. Garly, that huge screen of yours helped," Cole said. "The Agents couldn't get near it. The sound waves bothered their heads for some reason."

"Maybe it's all the holes in 'em," Jex said.

"Could be." Cole patted him on the back. "Great job back there. If you hadn't beefed up our defenses outside the motor pool, we all would've been toast."

Our teams settled in, forced to wait for whatever Lafontaine had in store for us. His "friend" who had arranged the hangar was nowhere to be seen, so we were dependent on the rebel leader. The packs of food and water set out for us—which we quickly snatched up—weren't enough to settle my concerns.

Munching on a protein bar, I inspected the hangar, which stood two blocks from the midsized airport, an occasional plane taking off or landing as I walked around. While the structure had an automated package sorting area, offices, and storage, it didn't contain any areas where we could truly rest and recharge.

I grew worried that we'd be found, but others relaxed; some even slept, like Raven had during the however-many-hours we'd been in that trailer. Our group had watched over her and Garly during the ride, Anya checking their vitals and injecting both with more nanobots and meds as they slept, yet they needed more time to heal. We all did.

I encountered Anya setting up one of the offices as a triage area. "Can I help?"

At her direction, I gathered the medical nanobots we had, gauze, and other supplies. I glanced at her as we organized our collection. Even on the run, she looked good.

The thought caught me off guard.

"I am aware you're a married man," Anya said as she sorted the supplies. She'd noticed me staring at her.

"Just in name."

She glanced to the side, then grinned. "What kind of example would I set for your daughter?"

Before I could respond, Raven spoke from the doorway. "She's got you there." She suppressed a smile, giving a glimmer of her old self before she slipped away. I turned back to Anya. The fact she'd evoked that reaction from Raven made me like her even more.

She gazed at me expectantly before refocusing on her supplies.

I was horrible with this stuff.

"Hey, jefe," Garly said, appearing in the doorway. "I'm not, like, interrupting anything…" He wagged his finger between us.

"Not unless he admits it," Anya said playfully.

I almost said, "Admit what?" but I wasn't that dumb.

Garly asked, "Where'd you plant my pack? I can snag it so long as we don't marathon again."

"You should get more sleep," she said.

"Actually, we want your assist. Nataly has an idea for Raven, but we need your input."

They left, Nataly looking uncharacteristically hesitant when I spotted her.

Now that we had a moment, I wondered again about what had looked like a parallel network at The Agency office. Maybe they'd constructed it to hide their activities from the rest of the government. Although I was exhausted, I commandeered one of the other hangar offices. Valor parked herself near the door but left me alone, focused on etching patterns into the barrel of her Glock. As she worked, I brainstormed scenarios of why and how The Agency's other system might operate.

I was still at it when Jex found me. "Interrupting?"

"No," I said, wiping the synth paper I'd been using. All of my scenarios were just conjecture. I needed more data.

"I, well, don't know how to tell you. Here." He handed me his datapad, which was paused on a broadcast. Mina's face filled the screen, the caption "Exclusive Interview" occupying the upper corner. I was startled to see her face. The last time I had, she'd betrayed us.

When I hit PLAY, a woman off-camera spoke. "Mrs. Quintero, your husband has been reported as being delusional. What do you say to that?"

Words appeared across the bottom of the screen. *Prominent inventor/businessman made false claims, may be dangerous.*

"Dray betrayed his family," Mina said. "His decisions led to everything we suffered. I'm glad we didn't have more children. I can only take so much heartache."

I listened to the rest of the thirty-second snippet but couldn't focus, too thrown by her lie. After it ended, I dug through my pack until I found my burner phone.

After it turned on, I dialed the number I'd memorized, even though I knew I was doing exactly what she wanted. Being manipulated increased my aggravation—and the words of caution from Jex and Valor didn't help. "What was the meaning of that bullshit interview?" I nearly yelled when the call connected.

"We need to talk," Mina said. "Find me—"

"We're done. What you did, pretending Adem still lived, destroyed our marriage."

"You couldn't handle his death, either. You hid in your work, though none of it mattered, did it? Not when our son was gone, unable to admire your creations."

I squeezed the phone so hard I risked breaking it. "How dare you."

"See what I see, Dray. I beg you."

I hung up and quickly powered the phone down.

I didn't want the memories, but they came anyway. Adem's funeral, the tiny coffin, stifling air, my black suit like a weight of penance. Mina had held Talia's hand, and I'd wrapped my arm around Raven, all of us shellshocked. I didn't realize until years later that Mina and I hadn't grieved together, not like we should've, for we each felt we'd failed the other.

A second flashback: Mina at our dining room table, begging me to give her another child two years after Adem's funeral. My grief had been so deep, I couldn't muster an answer. Before I could decide, she closed off again, burying herself in her career.

A third: Mina straining to break Kieran's hold so she could run to our fallen daughter, her cries piercing my ears as the light left Talia's eyes.

Valor closed the door to the office. "You all right?"

I didn't answer.

Jex faced me. "I consider you family, you know? I see where Raven gets it. Doesn't confide in me, either. She hasn't said a word 'bout Talia's death, what her momma did, you, any of it."

I raised my head, a cutting response ready, though when I saw his earnestness, I sighed. "She may never say anything. You have to accept that."

He nodded. Grimaced. "We need to fight back, or we won't survive. And we need to lean on each other."

* * *

It was late the next morning when I saw Raven again.

I'd slept fitfully, haunted by my children, so I rose early and developed an electricity absorber, though it took longer to determine how to make it rapidly draw electricity from an object than I'd hoped. Once I worked that out, I screwed an adherer to the collection side. Hoverbikes had plexiglass bodies, so I had to use an adherer instead of a magnet. If my aim was true, the device would stick to a passing hoverbike and drain its energy, turning the 'bike into a huge paperweight.

I was tired when I finished, though when I saw Raven, I perked up. She looked elated. Anya flanked her, as did Garly and Nataly, all three grinning.

"Dad, are you ready?" Raven asked. She held up her right hand. Where her index and middle fingers had been, two metallic, multi-segmented replacements stood in their place. Metal bands wrapped around her wrist to secure the smooth-metal contraption.

She wiggled her fingers—including the metal ones.

"I commished a portable printer for the bands and the

outer layers," Garly said. "Normal digits aren't enough for the royalty, though. Nataly and I fashioned parts out of a mini-plasma gun for the core."

I blinked. "A gun?"

"Yeah," Raven giggled. "It actually works."

"Nataly did most of the creation. The firing mechanism is a little tricky, though Raven will get the hang," Garly said. "Each finger holds a mini-cartridge. Crafted her some backups, too."

"You fashioned this? In one night?" I asked Nataly, who blushed.

"I took classes on prosthetics at university."

"We made a good team," Garly said, which made her blush deepen. He looked slightly better; he must've gotten some rest as Nataly worked, and I suspected Anya had pumped him—and Raven—with more meds.

"We wanted to show you before we wrap it so she can travel," Anya said. "What do you think?"

I wasn't sure what I thought. "She could risk tripping sensors."

"None of us are just skin and bone anymore."

"We can swap digits, too," Garly said. "She can Swiss-knife it, even swap for non-metallic versions if she needs."

Jex came over. "That's awesome, babe. I can call you Finger Guns now." When Raven frowned at him, he said, "It's better than Stumpy."

"You do that, you're sleeping alone."

She yearned to make a difference in the world, for her life to have meaning, and the finger-shaped weapon fitted her need. "What if your body rejects it? Or you develop an infection?" I asked her.

"The redness is normal," Anya said. "The main concern is whether her body reacts to the metal, and so far, it hasn't. I need to beef up the neural connections, but she's taking to it well."

Garly added, "Once I re-conk a lab, I'll farm some fake skin and noodle better bands. Maybe you could help."

They looked at me expectantly. The engineer in me

appreciated their efforts, but seeing the prosthetic fingers hammered home the fact that my only surviving child had been permanently injured. And I'd failed to prevent it.

I thanked them, though I felt heat rise in my chest.

Raven followed as I started back toward my office. "Dad. What is it?"

I took in her fingers. "Is it worth this?"

"Our cause is worth dying for."

"What if your fight involves shooting those you're trying to save?"

A sudden boom reverberated through the hangar.

She stared at me as people rushed toward the rear of the immense space, her eyes wide with shock.

"Come on," I said gently, taking her good arm and leading her toward whatever had caused the sudden noise.

Past the offices, a forty-foot-long, red shipping container rested on a flatbed that had been backed into an open space. Behind it, the hangar doors closed with a deep thrum.

Jex and de Vera stood to one side, both looking stunned. "What the hell?" Jex asked as we joined him. Around us, others had the same reaction.

Lafontaine appeared from behind the container. "We're leaving—in this! Our enemies are watching every passenger flight, so we need to make ourselves cargo."

"I liked your idea better," Raven murmured to Jex.

"Airport facilities are guarded," I called out to Lafontaine. "Their robots will catch us when we land."

"That's why we're parachuting out over Kentucky."

"Jump out of the plane? You kiddin' me?" Jex asked.

"That's risky, Isiah," de Vera said.

"You mean bold," Lafontaine replied. "Don't worry, I'm going with you. The container is insulated, so we'll stay warm, and we added a side access panel. While we have a higher power with us, one of my soldiers will use the panel mid-flight to open the container's doors, as we'll be locked inside."

I didn't like his plan or condescending attitude. "We need

to consider every variable before we do this," I said.

"A Lockheed C-130 just landed and will take off in two hours, with this in its belly. Get in or get left behind."

CHAPTER SEVENTEEN

I clung to the inside of the container with my pack over my shoulder and parachute at my feet as the cargo plane took off with a shudder and roar.

We'd been herded into the rectangular-shaped Trojan horse, the metal container barely able to fit all ninety-seven of us, Lafontaine the last inside before the driver of the flatbed locked us in.

Holding onto a side wall with one hand, I put the other against Anya's lower back to keep her beside me as the container trembled from our climb, though there was little room for her, or any of us, to move. Soldiers pressed against me from behind, and Jex and Raven stood inches away.

After grabbing our things, along with the goggles and parachutes Lafontaine's clan offered—a leap of trust in itself—we had snagged a spot by the access panel he'd mentioned, a three-foot-square section of wall that slid open.

My worries grew as we climbed. Though we left California airspace, I wasn't confident in Lafontaine's plan, which was supposed to sneak us past the Agents and cameras and software that hunted us. This flight—and the planned jump—came with so many risks, the main one being that we were nearly helpless, barely able to move, let alone run or hide if we were found.

As I kept my hand against Anya's back, Cole's words floated through my mind.

"I saw your wife's interview," he'd said before we boarded.

"She's not my wife anymore."

"Everyone thinks they're the hero of their own story, but sometimes they're the victim."

"She's not a hero."

"You're right. She's a victim. If you're not careful, you will be, too." He shifted his gaze to Lafontaine, who huddled with de Vera and Cardoza.

"They're setting me up to be a scapegoat, aren't they?"

"You saving them when The Agency invaded HQ carries a lot of weight with their troops, which means you've become a threat to those who think they're the next George Washington."

His words, spoken as the rebel fighters lined up to climb into the container, cast Lafontaine's actions, the fighters' smiles, their attitude toward me, in an uncomfortable light.

My future no longer rested with them, but striking out on my own, or with those who might follow, was treacherous. We couldn't overcome the network my fellow citizens and I had allowed to be built, nor did we have even a fraction of the firepower our enemies possessed.

The plane leveled off, and the sounds of flight decreased to a loud hum.

"We will join with a local clan when we land," Lafontaine announced from the end of the crate, nearly shouting over the engine noise. "From there, we will plan our attack. Our target is Washington D.C.!"

He continued with basic instructions, though he avoided any details about where exactly we were supposed to land or what clan would meet us.

When he finished, Jex cracked open the access panel, letting in a sliver of light.

I took in my team as cold air seeped in. They looked anxious, avoiding each other's gazes. Garly stood tall though his head was bowed. Whether from pain or concern, I couldn't tell. Nataly pressed against his unwounded side, biting her lip and eyeing those outside our group. Cole stood within arm's reach,

Valor wedged between him and Jex with her plasma rifle hooked over her shoulder.

Taking in the rest of the crate, I only saw a few rebels wearing their parachutes, as space was a premium, the rest clamping them between their feet.

Lafontaine spoke again. "Make sure your implant shields are firmly in place. We don't want them coming off during our drop."

Jex shuddered. "Our 'drop'."

Raven was strangely silent. She held her modified hand to her chest as if trying to protect it. Or accept it.

Anya leaned against me for warmth.

I liked her against me, but I was uneasy. Our entire rebel force was in this one plane.

The next two hours passed in a bored haze. There was nowhere to go, nothing to do but wait.

"I can't take this," Raven suddenly told Jex.

He whispered something I didn't catch. Instead of replying, she opened the access panel completely, letting in more light, cold air, and engine noise.

"Tell me when to open the crate," she shouted at Lafontaine. She grabbed the edge of the access panel and climbed out.

At least with the noise, I couldn't hear Lafontaine's objections.

Jex held up her coat, which she took. Then he held up her chute. Her gaze flickered to me, then back to him. "I'll get it later." She slid the access panel most of the way closed, reducing the outside light and sound.

I warred with myself. She seemed to need space, though the sadness in her eyes ate at me. I wanted to help her somehow.

"Did you fight Gunnar during the headquarters attack? That big Agent dude?" Jex asked Cole. From Jex's expression, I could tell he was warring with himself, too.

"Senn did," Valor responded.

"He saved my life," I said.

Anya turned to face me, causing my hand to slip down to

her waist.

I only partly listened as my group talked. I was worried about Raven, about our futures, but Anya's smile distracted me. I wasn't sure if it was okay that I was touching her waist. Then I realized her arm was around mine.

Her hand shifted against my lower back. She frowned.

"What?" I asked.

Fingers played across my skin near my kidney. I realized the area felt numb.

Her face tightened. "You were hit. Some time ago. I can feel the pattern."

I'd been hit by the same thing that had hit Jex, Nispen, and Perenko, what I thought of as a burrower.

My hand went to my back, my fingers brushing over the patterned scar. Nausea, anger, and panic flashed through me.

The Agent I'd killed must've done it. After he shot my thumb, he must've fired a second projectile. They could've followed me since then. Knew we were on this plane. I was risking every person here.

I struggled to keep my voice low. "I have to get away from everyone."

"I'll go with you."

"No. We'll meet up soon. Keep an eye—"

"I will."

We hugged.

"What's going on?" Cole asked.

I slipped off my backpack and let it fall from my grasp. Felt the seconds slipping. Looked at the others. Jex stood near the access panel like he wanted to dive through it, Garly fiddled with a camoshield projector while Nataly watched, and Valor locked eyes with me as if she could read my goddamn mind.

"Watch out," I told Jex, ignoring his protests as I gently moved him aside. I slid the panel open, pulled myself out of the container, the cold air and growl of the engines assaulting me, sat on the bottom edge of the opening, then swung my legs out and stood. When I faced the opening, concerned faces peered at me, Valor's chief among them. I didn't ask for my parachute as I didn't want her or others joining me, instead sliding the panel closed.

Our container was the only cargo in the hold, the side of the airplane a few feet from where I stood.

My goggles around my neck, I made my way toward the front and stepped past the edge of the container. I spotted Raven immediately on a seat built into the wall that separated the hold from the cockpit, rubbing the skin beneath her metallic fingers with a worried expression.

She sensed my presence and hid her hands. "What're you doing out here?"

I lifted my shirt to show her the burrower markings. "I need to leave. The Agency will know where we are."

Before she could say anything, we heard a shriek—and a thunderous explosion temporarily blotted out all other sound. The plane lurched, and I could see daylight through several gouges in the fuselage down toward the tail.

I made sure Raven was okay, then approached the largest hole as close as I dared and peered out. I smelled it before I saw it: fire. One of the plane's four engines had been destroyed; a smoldering husk was all that remained.

I looked behind our plane—and found a fighter jet tailing us, what I thought was an F-35 Lightning VI.

Our plane was pilotless; the onboard computer wouldn't know to fly evasively. Besides, there was no way the Lockheed had the maneuverability to shake a fighter jet.

Sunlight glinted on what I thought was the pilot's helmet. Then I realized. It was silver hair. Bob cut.

Britt.

She kept pace behind us, probably watching to see if we'd try to escape.

"What's going on?" Anya yelled. She'd slid the panel open, Jex, Cole, and Valor huddled near her.

I ran to them. "Give me your rifle," I said to Valor. Her eyes wide, she quickly handed it over.

"Everyone, put on your chutes," I yelled, aware Britt was probably tracking my movements. Before anyone could react, I shoved my arm into the opening, stretched my hand toward the floor, and snagged Raven's parachute.

I hurried over and thrust it into her arms. Giving it a quick inspection, I realized the pull cord was on the left side of her chest. "Can you manage the cord?"

She gave a frustrated nod.

I approached one of the larger holes. I found Britt had dropped back a little. She was lining up for another shot. I quickly raised the plasma rifle, aimed for the cockpit, and fired.

The angle and windspeed carried the discharge away. I wasn't even close.

Another missile dropped from under the plane, then launched toward us.

Desperate, I angled the rifle down and held the trigger, sending a constant stream of super-heated plasma down past the plane. The missile curved toward the stream but managed to avoid it and angled under us.

Where it exploded.

The force of the explosion shoved the plane upwards. I was launched into the air, as was Raven—and the container. Debris shredded the plane's belly. I landed on the deck, pain flared, the container slammed to the floor of the cabin—

Then crashed through.

A cry lodged in my throat as the container fell through the bottom of the plane, the ground visible miles below. Raven did cry out as the container plummeted, our friends—Jex, Anya, Garly, and others—locked inside.

Raven was crouched on the deck close to the front of the plane, unharmed, clutching her chute. "Jump!" I yelled at her. "Get to safety."

Then I stood, pulled my goggles over my eyes, and jumped out of the plane without a parachute.

CHAPTER EIGHTEEN

The plane seemed to whip up past me, the shredded rear edge nearly slashing me as it shot up. The next moment, my perspective righted as I plummeted toward the ground roughly six miles below, the Rocky Mountains like jagged teeth growing by the second.

The container grew smaller as it fell through the air, swaying in the wind though it remained mostly level.

Gravity accelerated me at 9.8 meters per second per second, less whatever drag for wind resistance. With my weight, I had forty-five seconds, max.

Jex, Anya, Garly, and the others were trapped, the hatch too small for anyone wearing a parachute, and the double doors on the end unable to be opened from the inside.

My only hope was to use wind resistance to my advantage.

I angled my body downward, face-first, arms at my side. An arrow. The altimeter in the corner of my vision spun like crazy as I shot downward. I ignored the numbers, willing myself to go faster.

The container grew larger. The ground inched closer. I focused on the container. My friends.

I had one shot at this. If I missed, I'd lose precious seconds—and I needed my momentum. It was their only chance.

The container grew larger, still swaying. I was sixty feet away. Forty. The container seemed to rush toward me. Twenty.

Aimed for the end opposite the doors.

I ducked my head and slammed into the container a quarter of the way from the end. Pain flared. The forty-foot-long vessel swung down, though its momentum slowed. Still, I slid toward the edge, wind buffeting me, trying to stop it from tilting upward. I reached the edge—and shoved, throwing myself outward, the force of my shove just able to tip the scales.

The container angled straight down. And picked up speed.

I grabbed at the container as the air buffeted me, managed to grab onto the edge, and crawled my way up.

Time was running out.

I shoved myself upward the last few feet, snatched the upper edge—pain lacing my fingers as the wind tried to shove me away—and crawled onto the doors, what was now the top of the falling container.

Two metal bars, both the height of the doors, kept them closed.

I grabbed the handle—and a figure slammed down onto the doors beside me, startling me. Raven. Her hair streamed behind her, eyes protected by goggles. She wore her parachute but hadn't opened it.

I yanked on the handle—but I didn't have the angle. The bolts were designed to be lifted upward while the container was on the ground. Besides, there had to be a hundred bodies pressing against the doors from the inside.

Movement caught my eye. The Lightning VI flew at us, angling downward to try to match our descent. Flickers of light emitted from either side of the cockpit. The next moment, bullets slammed into the upper half of the container, the last two shots passing just over our heads.

The jet flew past, but the damage had been done. People in the container had been killed.

Fury gripped me, adding to the fear I had battled since leaping from the plane. I tried the handle again, unable to budge it.

Raven shifted around. Gripped the edge at the "top" of

the container. Held out her free hand—the bandaged one.

I grabbed the bottom part of her palm, shifted, and together we pulled.

The handle didn't budge.

I strained as hard as I could, knowing I was hurting her, pulling with all of my strength, my altimeter turning yellow—

And the handle slid upward.

I twisted it, unlocking the doors—

The double doors burst open, flinging both of us from the container, and people burst out in a chaotic stream, the air from the access hatch forcing them out.

As they rose, the rebels opened their chutes. Ten, twenty, more.

But some didn't. Four of them rose motionless, trailing red mist, moving too fast for me to identify.

I was sickened. They'd been helplessly slaughtered.

Garly emerged, his size and the duffel bag strapped to his front giving him away. Nataly was with him, his backpack strapped to her front. As I watched, he reached over to pull her cord, but she did it first, nearly taking his hand with her. He then pulled his own cord—and I saw him shout though I couldn't hear it as the chute jerked him upward. Somehow, he managed to hold onto the duffel bag, the two rising up away from me.

I spotted Anya, her platinum hair a beacon. She was holding something in her hands. My parachute.

I angled toward her as the flood of rebel escapees ended, sliding over across the top of the container. As I did, I glanced down. A cluster of people huddled in the bottom of the container, hurt or fearful or unable to get out, I didn't know.

Before I could consider my actions, I dropped down into the container, the wind gusting in from the hatch slowing me. I angled toward the nearest wall and pushed off to descend further into the container. There were six people, eyes wide with fear, gripping the metal walls. They all wore parachutes but were frozen in inaction.

I mimed to them to hold hands, which they did. As soon

as they were all linked, I pulled the chute of the one closest to the top. The wind caught his chute—and yanked them all out of the container.

Satisfied, I prepared to leave when I spotted a parachute pack in the darkness beneath me, the straps entangled in the legs of a dead rebel. I didn't have time to mourn the person or discover his identity. I reached for the pack instead, quickly untangling it, and launched myself upward, the wind catching me and pushing me the rest of the way up and out of the metal deathtrap—and nearly snatching the pack from my hands.

My altimeter began to flash. Almost out of time.

My adrenaline in overdrive, I fought to put on the pack. Anya angled toward me to try to help, but I waved her off, then twisted in the air as I struggled with the straps before snapping them into place.

Resettling, I gave her an okay gesture. She let go of my parachute, put an arm around her medical bag that was strapped across her front, and pulled her cord.

I watched her shoot upward with relief; above and past her, shrapnel descended in an arc from the wounded cargo plane, which somehow continued to fly as it spewed black smoke. Other chutes littered the sky above, while debris and bodies seemed to hover in the air around me as we fell, the container moving farther away as it descended.

The debris and plane would attract attention. We'd need to distance ourselves from it.

I spotted my backpack a dozen yards away.

I angled over and snatched it. That's when I noticed Raven. She and Jex continued to fall, keeping level with me, watching me. I gave her a thumbs up, which prompted her to pull her cord. Jex followed, both jerking up and away.

I rolled over to face the ground. It was too close, racing toward me, Denver's mega-complex disappearing behind the easternmost mountains.

I grabbed my cord and pulled.

My chute opened above me, jerking me so hard I nearly

lost my grip on my pack.

As I slowed considerably, the bodies and various debris from the container followed it the rest of the way down.

I etched the spot where the bodies landed in my memory, then angled hard to the east.

The group followed my lead, though I only had time to glance back once. The ground was coming too fast, the top of a rocky peak leaping at me as I flew past, the mountainside dropping away toward a series of green hills. I glimpsed a smattering of houses directly ahead as I descended, so I aimed for what I hoped was a deserted area away from any structures.

Trees and rocks and brush swooped past me as I fell, the ground straightening and quickly rising. I pulled on the cords to slow my descent but landed hard in a deserted meadow, rolled, and finally, mercifully, stopped.

My body thrummed in pain, my brain ached from the adrenaline and fear that had pummeled it, and I swore never to fly in a plane again.

We had to get moving.

As I picked myself up, my team landed around me, the rest of the survivors descending behind them. I pushed the button to retract my parachute, then straightened and smiled as Anya headed for me, a strange, determined look on her face.

She neared, barely slowing, threw her arms around me and kissed me. Passion flooded through me, taking me by surprise. I returned the kiss, the world around us skipping into obscurity for a few precious seconds.

Her kiss softened, and I felt a flicker of disappointment as she pulled back.

"Is that all I had to do for a kiss?"

Her grin was the sexiest I'd ever seen. "Next move is yours."

My team landed around us.

I steered them into the woods, then helped Anya make an assessment as more joined us. Many were hurt, some from the missile explosion, others from the descent and landing. Blood coated Garly's side, his wound reopened; he was clearly in pain and had a limp. Raven, praised for her effort in helping me save everyone, shielded her modified hand, only letting Anya see it to inspect it for injuries. Jex was banged up as well.

The worst were those we'd lost: de Vera had been killed by Britt's gunfire, along with a half dozen others. I wanted to find their bodies and bury them, acknowledge their sacrifice, but couldn't risk it.

As Anya focused on Garly's injuries, I went to Raven. "You shouldn't have risked yourself."

"I wasn't going to just pull my chute and have a leisurely ride to the ground."

We hugged, holding each other tight. More rebels filtered into the woods around us.

As we let go, Monroe came up. "What you did up there."

"No choice."

"Have you noticed yet?" He leaned in. "Commander."

I frowned at him and his damn smile.

Lafontaine headed toward us. We all looked windblown and discombobulated, though he seemed more so. He appeared disoriented—and weakened. His arm was clearly broken.

Cole stepped in his path. "Why didn't you have any defensive measures on that plane?"

"They shouldn't have been needed."

"We need to go," I said.

"You know where we can hide?" Cole asked Lafontaine.

"No, I don't. We were supposed to be in *Kentucky*." He took a calming breath. "We should head east. Let's move."

The soldiers weren't looking at him. They were looking at me.

Lafontaine noticed it, too. He seemed to consider his words. "Dray, we owe you a debt of gratitude."

"Saved your ass," Nataly said.

Lafontaine glared at her as Cardoza and a few of her people joined us. "You don't want to leave? Fine. Stay here."

I spoke up. "He's right. We left a debris field that points

toward where we're standing."

"Let's go, people," Cole said. "Make sure your implants are covered."

I needed to get away from all of them.

Anya slipped her hand into mine—the first time she'd ever done that—looked at me with caring and concern, then flicked her eyes to the crowd. Many had started to move, but over half watched me. Waiting.

For me to lead them.

I was wary of the responsibility. Yet I feared I had little say in the matter.

Cardoza inspected me, though for what I didn't know, then led her group away.

Anya and I started off with Raven and Jex beside us.

Those who had watched me began to follow.

CHAPTER NINETEEN

We hurried east toward Denver, moving as fast as the scruffy wilderness allowed.

The terrain was unfamiliar—and had more open areas than we'd faced in California. Which meant higher odds of getting caught. We followed a trail that angled north, but the tree cover quickly fell away, which forced us to dash from one patch of trees to another, our weapons at the ready.

Though a couple dozen people now followed me, I had to protect them.

"I can't stay," I murmured to Anya.

"I'm coming with you."

Raven and Jex moved up beside me. "I told him," she said quietly.

Before I could respond, Cole approached, arm around Garly, who continued to limp. "Whatever you're all whispering about, it's distracting the others."

"Yeah, what's the dealio?" Garly asked as Nataly also joined us.

"Don't react," I said, then lifted up my shirt to show them the burrower scar. It was only fair. When I dropped my shirt, they looked at me with distress.

"Could nanobots extract it?" Anya asked Garly.

"Not if his parasite is anchored."

"Can you remove it?" Cole asked her.

"At a hospital, maybe, if I knew where it was lodged."

I looked at both men. "Don't even think about it. I'll take off north, lure The Agency away from everyone." They argued to go with me, but I refused.

Anya touched Garly's arm. "I need a wire, the thinnest one you have."

As he rifled through his pack, Raven said, "Won't your cap shield their device?"

"I wore my cap during the flight, but they found us anyway."

"Do you have my jamming device?" Nataly asked Cole. "That could block it."

He unhooked his pack and dug through it. After a moment, he held up a disc-shaped device. The black-and-gray object had a readout on the bottom, the transmitter making up the majority of its bulk. "I never took it out after we captured you."

The battery level was thirty percent. I turned it on.

Jex said, "Now you can stay, right?"

"I don't know for sure it's jamming the burrower's signal," I said.

Raven asked, "How will you find us?"

I held up the bracelet linked to her tracker, which I'd used to find her at the farmhouse.

"I hate you right now," she said.

Anya and I started north, while the rest reluctantly headed after the others. I tried to convince her to go with them, but she refused. "I need to disable the burrower."

We followed the terrain, using any cover we could find. When we reached a ridge, I scanned the skies and spotted tiny movements to the west. Drones. Probably The Agency's.

We found ourselves in a park, the trail following a fence that separated the park from private residences. A small structure was visible on one of the properties, just past a wooded area. Before I could stop her, she climbed the fence. "Come on."

Within minutes, we approached what I'd thought was a shed, but it was more than that. The ten-by-twelve-foot structure had solar panels, a window on either side, and double doors that were locked. In the distance, a house stuck up over the edge of a hillside.

"You sure about this?" I asked.

"I can work on you in there."

I picked the lock and ushered her inside. Fluorescent lights turned on to reveal assorted lawn equipment plugged into outlets that connected to the roof. A desk stood at the far end of the room, next to a small bathroom.

Anya strode past the equipment, unshouldered her medical pack, and set it on the desk. "Have a seat."

As I settled in the desk chair, she removed the handheld MRI from her pack.

"The burrower will probably be in the heart or head. That's the direction Nipsen's was heading," I said.

She turned on the MRI and pressed it against my back. "Something's wrong with the readout."

"Must be the jammer." I retrieved the device, went outside, and propped it against the concrete foundation to block the interference. After I sat back down, she tried the MRI again. "Better?"

"Much." She quickly scanned my body, pausing when she angled the scanner up under my cap to inspect my brain. "Found it."

She began to unwrap Garly's wire, which was so thin I could barely see it.

"You gave me the idea." She nodded toward her backpack. "There's a surgical kit in the top pocket. Grab that and the portable defibrillator."

"I have a bad feeling about this," I said but did as she ordered, then unzipped the kit to reveal a selection of scalpels, which made me uneasy. I retrieved my own first-aid kit and held up the pain meds.

"No, I need you alert." She doused the wire in rubbing alcohol, washed it off in the sink, then approached me. "Lose the shirt and lay your head on the table." When I hesitated, she ran her fingers through my hair and gave me a quick kiss, which turned my uneasiness to worry.

"You aren't going to be able to remove it with just a wire."

"This is the next best thing."

Shit, she wasn't going to remove it. She was going to try to disable it by frying its circuits.

Reluctantly, I removed my shirt.

"Nice," she said, eyes roaming my exposed skin.

"If this was a ploy to get my shirt off, it worked."

"Can you blame me?"

My smile faded as she donned surgical gloves.

She touched my upper back. "I can't make an incision in your carotid artery as you could bleed out. This means I have to go farther."

I fought my urge to pull away as she made a small incision between my spine and shoulder blade and then began to thread the wire into my vein. I could feel it sliding into my body, my heartrate increasing as I forced myself to stay still.

I now had an idea how Nipsen had felt when I did this to him. At least Anya was a professional—and we weren't in a fishtailing delivery truck. I caught her reflection in the window, along with the three-dimensional image of my veins. I could just make out the wire as it moved upwards, which magnified the tugging I felt.

She paused to wipe away the blood that trickled from the incision.

I stayed quiet so she could concentrate. But not for long. "What was it you needed to do back in L.A.?" I asked, referring to when she'd left HQ for two weeks.

She continued to feed the wire, the sensation growing into a searing pain. "As I said before, I hadn't planned to join a rebellion. I had responsibilities, patients, things I couldn't just abandon.

"I reached out to a couple colleagues about the neural nets. I didn't tell them why, or that you opened my eyes, so to speak. They have no idea the lenses are being used against everyone. I don't think anyone knows, except the rebels."

"I thought you might've had second thoughts about, well, us."

"I needed to clear my head. For a while, you were all I could think about."

I started to turn around—and the pain sharpened.

She grabbed my shoulder. "Don't move." She repositioned me, then continued to work.

"What kind of thoughts were you having?" I asked.

"I'm definitely not answering that."

I fought the urge to turn again, to get her to say more.

She finally did. "You come with a lot of baggage, including being on the Most Wanted list. I had to make sure I wanted all of this." She paused and pressed the MRI against the base of my skull. "The burrower settled in your frontal lobe."

"Can you reach it with the wire?"

"Yes, luckily—if there's anything lucky about this. The burrower didn't go too deeply into your brain."

She grew quiet as she worked the wire, using the MRI as a guide, her movements concise, her breathing steady. She finally spoke. "I have the wire in place. Stay perfectly still."

I heard rustling, then the whine of the defibrillator.

She gave me a reassuring touch. "I'll do a quick jolt."

She'd have the defibrillator at the max setting, although since it was a portable version, it probably maxed out at 360 joules. Typical electronics could withstand upwards of 500 joules.

"Hold the trigger for as long as you can, at least five seconds," I said.

She inhaled sharply as she considered. I assumed she was balancing my suggestion with what my body could take.

She stepped back to create distance, pressed one paddle against my skull, the other to the wire sticking out of my back, took a breath—

And triggered the device.

Electricity erupted inside of me, locking my muscles as it seared my cells.

* * *

I opened my eyes to discover night had fallen. Other than faint moonlight filtering in from one of the windows, the shed was dark.

We were on the floor, lying on my sleeping bag, Anya against me.

I felt her shift as she woke. "How's your head?"

After she'd zapped me, my skull felt like it had been split in half. She injected nanobots to remove the burrower's remains, then I had to rest.

I'd only meant to take a short nap.

"Better," I said, though my head still ached. We couldn't tell if the burrower continued to operate, but no device that small could've survived an extended charge like that.

"We should rejoin the others."

I remembered the jamming device. When Agents begin looking for us, their active scans would discover an area being jammed, so they'd concentrate their search to that location—which I could use to our advantage. I had the search drone Nataly had used during our escape. It was smaller, but it should bear the jammer's weight.

While Anya rolled up the sleeping bag, I extracted the drone, keyed in instructions for it to fly northwest—staying fifty feet off the ground at all times—then attached the jammer and sent it off.

As the drone's buzz faded, I turned to her. "Ready?"

We struggled to move quickly in the dark, although we picked up speed as our eyes adjusted, aided by the moonlight. I used Raven's tracker frequently, impressed she and the others had apparently traveled nearly five miles from the crash site.

Because of the terrain, it took us until daybreak to reach them.

We found them holed up at the visitor's center for the Lookout Mountain Nature Center, a brick building perched on a hillside. The rebels nearly filled the building, from the nature info-displays on one end to the admin offices on the other.

Jex appeared out of the crowd. "You're late."

He steered us into the building's gift shop. When we stepped inside, we found the remaining members of the Founding Fathers standing in a rough semi-circle, fourteen in all.

"There you are," Cole said with a grin, the sun cresting the mountains behind him. "Dray Quintero, by unanimous consent, we have chosen you as our leader."

Gary and Nataly clapped as if I'd performed a magic trick while the others smiled and nodded.

"You didn't even know I'd be able to rejoin you," I said.

Jex chuckled. "You jumped out of a plane to save us. We knew you'd get here."

I wasn't sure I wanted this. I'd led teams before, responsible for multiple divisions at Gen Omega, but I knew what it was like when leaders clashed. It derailed futures.

Lafontaine walked in. "What's the clapping about?" Instincts honed from years of opposition sharpened his gaze as he turned on me. "They made you leader?"

The role tied me tighter to a cause I wasn't sure I believed in anymore, but I cared for those who'd chosen me. "Yes, they did. I don't report to you, though. You don't control all of the clans."

"Yet."

Jex spoke up. "You almost killed all of us on that plane."

"The *government* tried to kill us," Lafontaine said. "We'll make them pay."

"How?" I asked. "We need a full-scale uprising, but even if we do succeed, who can you trust? There are people in Washington, good people, who know how the systems operate. Unless you want to dismantle every aspect of this country, you'll need them, and that's where the ones in power could stay in power."

"We'll weed out all who pose a threat. We're not naïve—and I don't have to answer to you."

"You sound naïve."

He spotted Cardoza, who'd entered the shop at some

point. "You agree with me."

When she didn't answer, Cole asked, "Who would you follow? If you had to choose between these two?"

She considered Lafontaine, then me. "Neither. But what you did saving us was the bravest thing I've ever witnessed." Her gaze lingered on me. "We're heading to Denver to meet with a regional leader. Colorado rebels are tough. Most have lived their entire lives in the mountains. They have their own code of acceptance, so we need the leader to vouch for us. I'll ask him to vouch for your clan, too."

As she left, Lafontaine shook his head at me. "Just because you saved everyone doesn't qualify you as a leader. It took no planning. No sacrifice." He faced those who'd gathered. "Don't forget, fellow believers, his parachute was in the shipping container. How do you know he wasn't just trying to save himself?"

"I could've stayed on the plane," I said.

He gave me a sad smile. "Well, the truth will come out in the end."

After he left, my clan assured me his claims didn't change their decision. "This might," I said. I told them how I might have been tracked by The Agency. If they wanted me as their leader, they needed to know about the burrower.

The group fell quiet as they absorbed my words.

"Did you know you were tagged before you got on the plane?" Valor asked.

I shook my head.

"Then you didn't do anything wrong."

Jex swore under his breath. He'd brought up his tablet. "Guys. I left a mini-cam where we landed." He flipped the tablet around to show us. The camera had been positioned to capture a wide swath of meadow. Figures moved in the background, dressed in black, a stylized "A" on their shoulders. The next moment, Britt walked past the frame.

The Agency had found our landing site, which meant they would pick up our trail.

We couldn't rely on them chasing the jamming device. The stakes were too high.

* * *

We slipped through the trees, keeping quiet as if our pursuers were already close. With The Agency's resources, we didn't take mere distance for granted.

The brightening sky as the sun rose higher added to my stress. But I wasn't one to ignore reality, which meant I needed to step up as a leader. I should have earlier, at the rebels' headquarters. I should've gotten everyone out of that damn mountain as soon as I'd learned of the 3D drones.

Nataly walked nearby, smiling. I angled toward her, hoping for some positive news. "You're in a good mood," I said quietly.

"Garly offered to replace my implant so Agents can't track me."

I wanted to ask if they'd become more than friends, but it wasn't my business. Instead, I said, "Keep an eye on him." He seemed to be moving better—he'd probably slept the entire night at the visitor's center—but he needed more rest. We all did.

"Did he tell you? I boosted your broadcaster."

She pulled out the black object and placed it in my hand, her face expectant. I'd forgotten about the communicator device Garly had made me.

"Now you can recruit many others," she added.

"I'm not sure I'm comfortable trying to convince people to risk their lives."

"To *rescue* their lives. That's a job of a leader, no?"

I didn't have an answer. Not a good one, at least.

I slipped the device into my pocket. When I did, my hand brushed something. The burner phone. The device couldn't be tracked when it was off, but I'd forgotten I still had it. I dropped back, hesitated, then turned it on. One voicemail. I played the message.

"Go to Texas," Mina whispered. She sounded desperate. "We landed outside of Dallas, so we're in the northern part of the state, though I don't know where. We drove for hours. The facility we're in has barbed wire and doctors, with farms in every direction. Please, find me before it's too late."

Her message didn't make sense, accusing me on television while now begging for help in private. I turned off the phone, broke it in half, and jammed the pieces into my pack.

Nipsen hurried down the trail to me. I'd sent him forward earlier to keep an eye on the leaders. "The Redeemers found buses, but something doesn't smell right."

My clan and I followed him up the hillside. I checked the machine gun Valor had given me, which I'd stuck in my bag, and made sure the safety was off.

Cole appeared ahead, more tense than usual. Past him, the rebels clustered together, nearly all of our ninety-odd forces. As I watched, someone near the front disappeared as if they'd fallen. Then another.

Lafontaine came over, a smile on his lips. "This is how it's done," he told me before moving into the crowd, which parted just enough for him to slip through.

"What's going on?" I asked Cole.

"He got us a way out. He's an insufferable narcissist, but he has his uses."

The cluster of rebels thinned out enough for me to see that the land sharply dropped down a dozen feet or so to a parking lot that served as the starting point for a public trailhead. Two old school buses stood in the otherwise empty lot, the words Church of the Northern Plain stenciled on their sides, the white letters contrasting with the buses' dark green paint. Rebels amassed before both doors, though Lafontaine directed them to form a line in front of each one

The buses' engines started.

"Thank god," Anya said.

Those in front of us slid down the embankment.

When it was our turn, I slipped my machine gun into my pack as Raven slid to the bottom, her damaged hand elevated. Jex followed, so I slid down awkwardly after him, weighed down by my pack, Garly's, and the duffel bag. Anya and Valor were next, with Nipsen right behind, nodding nervously at the buses.

Garly bounded ahead with Nataly, the two giggling excitedly.

We followed, slowing as we neared the line to the second bus. Lafontaine approached, barely acknowledging us though he motioned Garly to get in line. He did, Nataly following his lead, the two standing so close together they nearly touched.

Both unaware of Lafontaine frowning at her.

As more rebels moved into line in front of us, two of Lafontaine's men suddenly appeared behind me, one grabbing Garly's duffel bag. As I turned in surprise, the second removed Garly's pack from my back. "Just helping out," the man said, though as he walked past me toward the bus, I realized it was the guard with the cleft chin.

"Dray," Anya said cautiously.

I felt it, too. As I opened my mouth to object to Lafontaine—though I didn't know what, exactly, I was objecting to—he boasted to the crowd, "These buses are courtesy of a long-time worshiper of mine. He moved to Wyoming a few years back, but when I called him, he immediately came to our aid, as the good book says."

"Why didn't he tell us help was coming?" Anya asked me.

As the clans continued to board, I directed my team to get in line, though I wondered if I should tell them to stay back.

Garly and Nataly were near the front, ready to board. Catching Valor's eye, I waved to her, and she pushed her way into a spot behind them. Anya remained by my side as the three boarded—which heightened my concern.

Raven followed our lead, waving the last of our clan into line, then she and Jex stepped up behind us after we moved into a spot at the end.

The first bus finished loading, and the doors closed.

I scanned the lot and hillside behind us, but we were the last of the rebels. At least we'd get out of the godforsaken forest.

We shuffled forward as more boarded the second bus.

Monroe was visible through one of the bus's windows; past him, Valor stood in the aisle, following the others to the back of the bus. From her expression, she wanted me on board, glaring at me through the windows. Before her, Garly sat in one of the seats, Nataly presumably next to him.

When we reached the door, Lafontaine appeared before us and blocked our entry. "You're not getting on."

I went for my plasma pistol, the one I'd used on the Agent—but paused as Lafontaine's guard aimed his machine gun out the window at us.

Lafontaine had planned this. Not only the buses but who got on.

My anger ignited as he took the pistol from my pocket. "I saved you—and you," I snapped at the guard.

"Then you'll be fine on your own," Lafontaine said.

He faced the two buses. "Dray Quintero was sloppy when he went to Cardoza's safe house. He led The Agency to our headquarters, which caused the deaths of so many of our brothers and sisters. Our brethren in Denver will help us, but not if he's with us."

Voices rose inside the second bus as my people tried to get off, Valor and Garly included. Lafontaine's men held them back while two aimed pistols at Monroe to keep him in place.

"That's a lie," Jex shouted.

Lafontaine turned back to us and dropped his voice. "Does it matter?"

I searched the windows for Cardoza. She knew the truth. But she looked away. He must've gotten to her somehow. Others, though, began to fight, Cole and Valor chief among them, the bus rocking slightly.

I started forward, cocking my fist—but before I could swing, Lafontaine jabbed a Subdue-R into my stomach. The device weakened victims; if used too long, it could kill them. "You're trying to take my place, everything I've sacrificed for," he muttered to me.

"You can't do this. We'll be captured," Raven told him

as Jex and Anya stiffened beside her, having seen Lafontaine's weapon.

Behind him, hands pulled Valor out of sight, and an arm hooked around Cole's neck.

"We're fighting the same cause," I told Lafontaine.

He leaned close. "No one carves statues for second place."

Chapter Twenty

We backed away as the two buses drove off, our kidnapped clan subdued—though Valor appeared again in a window. She fought but couldn't shake off her captors, her voice breaking as she shouted my name.

Seconds later, the buses disappeared around a bend.

"Come on," Jex said. Only he, Raven, Anya, and I were left.

He shepherded us back into the woods. Once inside the relative safety of the forest, he crouched down and sighed.

Raven plopped down beside him. "We're fucked, aren't we?"

We didn't have Garly's gadgets, didn't have any protection other than the branches over our heads. I worried about the rest of our clan, especially Nataly with the way Lafontaine had looked at her, but so long as they kept their cool and he didn't turn on them, they should be fine. Raven, Jex, Anya, and I were not.

"I can't get Lafontaine's smug expression out of my mind," Anya said. "Just leaning against that tree like we were his playthings."

"Leaning against a tree?" Raven asked.

"Yeah, when everyone was sliding down the embankment. He almost had his arm around it."

Jex and I shared a look. "Does he strike you as the leaning-against-a-tree type?" I asked.

We scrambled up the short, steep hillside and hurried to the tree Anya pointed out. A small device clung to the bark, a tiny light blinking among the covered electronics.

"It's a simple-band broadcaster," I said.

"You know what it's gotta be broadcastin'," Jex said.

Raven paled. "Dad's implant codes."

I pulled out my ion knife and destroyed the broadcaster.

"Why would Lafontaine set you up to get caught?" Anya asked. "Your implant can reveal their faces."

"The Agency already learned what everyone looks like when they invaded the mountain," I said.

"We're gonna have company real soon," Jex said. "What weapons do we have?"

We did a quick inventory. He and Raven had pistols, and I carried the machine gun along with the energy absorber and a few other items, though we only had two full clips between us. "My pack only has medical supplies," Anya said apologetically.

Three weapons with limited firepower.

"We need to move, use the terrain in our favor," Jex said.

A noise drew my attention: an electric vehicle approaching.

We hurried away from the tree Lafontaine had used, moving through the forest to circle around the edge of the parking lot before stopping. Jex pulled Anya back behind a tree while Raven dropped to her stomach, aiming her pistol with her left hand at the clearing, her bandaged right hand keeping the weapon steady. I dropped beside her and extracted my machine gun right before a black SUV with tinted windows appeared. The vehicle stopped in the middle of the lot, and four Agency soldiers jumped out, poised for attack. They each carried machine guns, their uniforms Kevlar-reinforced and biometrically synched with a central command, an additional level of monitoring the Founding Fathers had discovered during an encounter outside of Oakland.

The soldiers scanned the area, their movements coordinated and efficient, then headed toward the hillside, bounding up it effortlessly.

We had seconds.

"Which way you wanna run?" Jex murmured as the men disappeared.

Raven and I exchanged a look. We had the same idea.

"We're taking their car," I said.

"We better be fast," she said.

Anya's eyes widened as Jex chuckled. "Baller."

We raced out of the woods to the car, trying to be quiet, feeling exposed in the blacktopped space, and opened the doors, which they'd left unlocked. I climbed in and reached under the steering column as Raven and Jex aimed their weapons at the spot where the men had gone. No one closed their doors, not wanting to tip off the men; a light breeze caressed my forehead as I ignited my ion blade and severed the signal blocker from the column.

"Come on," Raven whispered, standing next to the rear driver-side door.

"You want the yellow wire," Jex whispered.

I reached up where the blocker had been, pulled the ends of the yellow and white wires, and touched them together. "Ready."

Jex triggered the scrambler he'd built for this car line—and the dash lit up. The engine was on.

He, Anya, and Raven climbed in as I twisted the wires together, and we softly closed our doors.

I put the car into gear and started forward, making a quick U-turn and accelerating away from the area.

"The GPS," Raven said.

I reached under the dash as I drove along the blacktopped road toward the state highway. "Dammit," I said when I felt the box. "It's reinforced."

Jex stretched forward. "Watch your leg."

Before I could ask, he jammed the barrel of his pistol flush against the GPS transmitter and fired, the sound deafening.

* * *

My ears finally stopped ringing five minutes later.

As my hearing returned, I turned onto a two-lane highway that followed a valley between rock-capped mountains, heading east. There was little traffic as the road twisted and slowly descended, though we remained on alert.

With the early-afternoon sun beating down on us, I spotted a sign listing a series of upcoming exits for Golden. I took the second one, cresting the exit ramp and turning onto the main road.

"Dad, what are you doing?" Raven asked.

"We have to switch cars."

Anya touched my shoulder. "People will see you."

She was right, even with the SUV's tinted windows. I used one hand to hide my face as I drove. In the back seat, Jex and Raven crouched out of sight.

The longer we remained in this vehicle, the greater the chance The Agency would find us. Drones would already be in the air looking for the SUV.

Anya handed me a pair of sunglasses she'd found, though they only concealed my eyes.

The town wasn't ideal. Small houses, lots of space. In another life, I would've enjoyed its Western charm. I considered turning around but had committed; I followed the street as it dipped and rose toward a central business area where an arched sign welcomed us to Golden.

"Dray," Anya whispered, hiding her face as well.

"I see them." Tourists. Dozens of them. Sitting in outdoor restaurants, window-shopping, a handful casually walking across the street ahead of us. Each a moving camera.

I also had my network to contend with now that we were in a populous area.

I slowed, not sure the best way to try to get away if Agents suddenly showed up. Then I spotted what I'd hoped to find: a parking garage.

"I know I'm being paranoid, but check yourselves for burrowers. I don't want to get caught by surprise again," I told them as I turned down the side street. I approached the brick-covered garage—but a sign indicated the lot was full, a parking arm blocking the entrance. Swearing under my breath, I drove past.

Raven and Jex twisted in the back seat as they checked themselves and each other while Anya ran her hands over her body. I pulled into a small alley just past the garage, drove down to the far end, and pulled into a small loading area a dozen yards from the street. After I shut off the engine, I did a quick sweep of my skin and checked Anya's back for her. She did the same for me as the kids climbed out and closed the doors.

Anya leaned forward. "Was this a ruse so you could touch me?"

I felt myself blush. "Hey, I only touched your back."

"Yeah, disappointing."

As she reached for the door handle, I asked, "What about me being married?"

"You going back to her?"

"No."

"Well then." She gave me a quick kiss, and we got out.

The four of us might be free of burrowers, but we were far from safe. Cameras, drones, people—all could be watching me. Watching us.

We approached the end of the alley. The street opened before us, with shops, microbreweries, and restaurants in both directions.

"What're we going to do?" Raven asked. "We can't hide our faces."

"What 'bout masks?" Jex asked. He was serious, body tense, eyes scanning everywhere.

"It's not Halloween."

"We need to decide where we're going first," Anya said.

"Let's go to the garage and get another car."

Anya and Jex agreed—but Raven interrupted. "Check that out."

I risked a glance down the street. She'd indicated a local sports bar that flew a Denver Broncos flag, the front painted blue and orange. Then I saw it: a party bus. It was an older model, one of the first self-driving commercial buses, with the bar's name—West Willy's Sports Bar—plastered over the windows. Patrons decked out in Broncos' jerseys milled near the bus, waiting to board. From the time of day, their outfits, and their overall lack of sobriety, I suspected they were going to a Broncos game.

"You're not serious," Jex said.

She turned to us. "Lafontaine mentioned that leader in Denver, right? That's where we need to go. We'll take the bus to the stadium, then go find the leader."

I pulled them back into the alley. "It's not a bad idea. It'll get us into the city, and the windows are covered. So long as we hide our faces, we'll have a chance."

"How the hell do we get to the bus without you three being spotted?" Anya asked. "You see the cameras."

Even in a smaller town like this, a dozen or more cameras occupied spots along the block we'd have to walk to get to the bus. I'd spotted six, but there'd be more.

"Wrap our faces in gauze?" Jex suggested.

"Once again, not Halloween," Raven said.

I held up a hand. "We can't avoid the cameras, but maybe we can give them an aneurism."

They frowned at me. "You havin' one yourself?" Jex asked.

"When I connected the cameras' software systems together, I thought of them like a brain. Neural pathways grow over time from experiences and learning skills, but they don't form fully connected to other areas. Our brains have to link these different areas by associations. That's one reason why smells and songs link to memories. I designed my system similarly, linking data that's consistent across all software—the video streams themselves—then worked backwards to create links."

"Let's give Big Brother an aneurism," Anya said.

I gave a quick nod. "I need some supplies."

"There's no time," Raven said. "They'll start boarding any minute."

"We can't just walk over there."

"I'm tellin' you, we need disguises," Jex said.

Anya removed her medical pack. "I have an idea." She handed it to me, eyed my backpack, then hurried out of the alley.

We watched anxiously as she jogged down the street away from the pub, then ducked into a Walgreens.

With a start, I remembered Kieran knew what Anya looked like, though he might've dismissed her as a captive instead of a rebel.

Turning from the street, I searched my pack for an energy source to fry the cameras on the street but came up empty.

More patrons had gathered by the bus; when I glanced back the way Anya had gone, I spotted a traffic camera hanging at the next intersection. Though its sentinel eye angled away from us, I pulled Jex and Raven deeper into the alley. They looked at me questioningly, but before I could explain, footsteps rose. The next moment, Anya returned with a tote bag she'd stuffed with supplies. "At least it's the right time of year."

"What're you talking about?" I asked.

She pulled out a Broncos shirt. "Disguises. They only had two of these, though."

"The bus is startin' to board," Jex said, peering around the corner.

Raven took the Broncos shirt and began to remove her quasi-military jacket. Anya handed a red-and-black checkered shirt to Jex, shrugging that it was the best she could do, then gave me a XXL "Golden - Gateway to the Rockies" T-shirt.

I looked at her in confusion. I wasn't small, but I didn't need a shirt that big.

"For your backpack," she said, as she pulled out a Broncos shirt for herself.

I adjusted my pack so it hung over my stomach instead of my back, then put on the shirt.

"Nice beer belly." She then plopped a blue-and-orange wig on my head.

"Seriously?" I asked.

"Let's go, Broncos," she said with a grin.

We barely looked normal, Anya's purchases unable to mask our commando-type pants. Raven unhooked the gun holster from her belt and ditched it along with her jacket, then slipped her gun into her waistband and hid it under her new shirt. Jex hid his gun as well.

We started up the street. I leaned on Anya as if I was drunk, the gaudy-ass wig hanging over my eyes. Anya's tote bag, into which she'd stuffed her backpack, draped her other shoulder. Raven and Jex followed, our Broncos gear our only disguises. I didn't risk looking around.

As Anya steered me to the bus, voices grew louder, though one man talked over the crowd, directing the patrons. We joined the end of the line, yet my heart hammered as more riders closed in behind us. More eyes to see us.

The line moved slowly. Damn drunk people.

Finally, we stepped onto the bus.

The voices were louder in the enclosed space, the air thick with the aroma of beer. I kept my head down, though I was forced to let go of Anya when we topped the steps, for the aisle was only wide enough for one person. As I followed her, I risked a quick scan. The bus had two seats to either side of the aisle, each seat facing forward. Old-style flatscreens hung in spots to appease the partying patrons, the screens tuned to the pregame show. The rubber floor was sticky.

Anya found an empty pair of seats near the back and took the one by the logo-covered window, I sat beside her, and Jex and Raven took the seats behind us.

My back to the aisle, I started to pull off my wig, but Anya stopped me. "Leave it," she whispered.

Acquiescing, I looked through the gap between the seats. Raven and Jex both looked apprehensive. "You guys okay?"

Raven leaned forward. "What if someone tries to talk to us?"

"Ignore them. Focus on each other—and keep your face hidden." I was glad her bandages masked her metal fingers.

She pulled back, and I shifted in my seat to look at Anya,

who smiled and put a hand to my cheek, effectively hiding my face. Then she leaned in and kissed me.

What started as gentle turned passionate for both of us, the ruckus inside the bus fading away. Emotions rose up inside of me, feelings I hadn't experienced in a long time. Everything about her was amazing, including the way she kissed me.

It was only after she broke the kiss and nestled into me that I realized the bus had started. We were already on the highway, heading east.

I glanced between the seats. Raven gave a tiny smile. She seemed happy for me.

Someone shouted, "Hey, turn that up."

The TV screens no longer showed the pregame broadcast; instead, each screen displayed Richmond Holland, the President of the United States, sitting in the Oval Office. The bottom of the screen declared this as an important announcement.

The President's voice suddenly erupted from speakers throughout the bus, causing Anya to sit up. "The government is not out to get you," Holland said. "We serve you. Every Congressperson and I were elected to better this great country. The broadcast that aired in Los Angeles eight weeks ago is a lie. Dray Quintero is an expert videographer and skilled engineer, and a terrorist. He wants to overthrow the government and rule you all.

"We will find him and his followers and punish them. By law, your implants cannot be tampered with. My administration takes this very seriously. That is why we will not rest until they've all been captured."

The goddamn President had just thrown down the gauntlet.

I kept my back to the rest of the bus, afraid to show even a sliver of my face. Anya stared at me, the bright Colorado sun breaking through gaps in the letters that coated the window to highlight her.

Raven whispered between the gap in the seats, asking if I was okay. Just hearing her voice cut me. I was vaguely aware of the pregame show returning, of conversations restarting. I reached into my pocket, my fingers grazing the communicator device Garly had given me, pulled out the fragment of Talia's cap I kept at all times, and rubbed it like a talisman. I worried that my actions since the night of the fusion reactor had been all wrong.

Our fellow passengers grew rowdier as we pulled off a multi-laned highway onto a four-lane road packed with people. Cameras hung everywhere. Cops. Eyes. An overlapping grid I couldn't escape. We had a few weapons, but they weren't enough to escape this. My muscles were so tense I could barely move.

More and more people became visible walking on either side of the street, lanes of traffic filled with vehicles.

Within a minute, the bus turned again, and the stadium came into view. People packed sidewalks that led toward the stadium, and vehicles filled the parking lots, the sounds of music, cheers, and car horns muted inside the bus. Cops stood near patrol cars parked in strategic locations, while other cops directed buses like ours down a cone-lined street toward a drop-off point in front of the stadium. I'd hoped we would've stopped on the outskirts of the complex, but instead, we were going to have to exit the bus into the sea of people flooding the area.

As our bus slowed, Raven leaned forward. "They have DNA monitors." She pointed toward the wide concrete-and-brick walkway that led from our road to the stadium itself, the walkway lined with trees, commemorative half-arches—and a half-dozen, innocuous white poles topped with triple collectors.

"What do we do?" Anya asked.

"We can't risk goin' out there," Jex said.

The bus swung onto the road parallel to the stadium, stopped, and the doors opened. "Everyone, please disembark," a recorded voice stated. The patrons around us stood, a few wobbly, a herd of blue-and-orange heading out.

I looked at the fear in Anya's eyes, then took in the view outside the windows. People swarmed toward and around us, a massive army that could take us down.

"That's it," I breathed.

"What is?" Raven asked.

"A way to fight back." I reached into my pocket and pulled out Garly's communicator. "Every one of these people are oblivious. What would they do if we showed them the truth?" I looked at Anya. After I had shown her the truth, she began to follow me. Others might, too.

I stood. "Follow me." My eyes flickered to Raven, who looked skeptical and anxious. "For Talia."

I led them out of the bus, following the drunken crowd, only marginally hiding my face. Music drifted toward us from the stadium, an undercurrent of sound augmenting people hawking items, patrons talking and laughing together, and cops shouting at the few human bus drivers to move their vehicles.

Instead of following the others toward the stadium, I moved to the side and faced the bus, using it as a temporary shield. As Raven, Jex and Anya huddled around me, I pulled out the communicator Garly gave me and slipped it under my cap to attach to my implant. Using my datarings, I accessed the program he'd installed, which searched for feeds to connect to. The program design echoed the one I'd written that linked the camera systems together. I searched the settings; he'd defaulted the "number of feeds to link to" at just one. Yet it could go up to fifty thousand. I set the feeds at the maximum level, then removed my cap, exposing my implant.

I felt both Raven and Jex stiffen beside me. I smiled, though I made sure not to look at either of them. "Move over to the side. I don't want either of you in the shot." I touched Anya's arm, also not looking at her. "You too."

"I want to help."

My smile widened, and I shifted my gaze to her. "Okay, then I'll use you first. Stand over there."

She gave a nervous grin as she walked five or six yards, stopped, and faced me. I attached the removable microphone Garly included with the communicator, set the software to run closed captioning so everyone could see my words on their lenses—and hesitated. The people around me, men and women, families and friends, were living their lives safe and oblivious. But we couldn't fight alone. We needed to go bigger in a way that couldn't be ignored.

I'd thought people would've responded to my revelation that the government used their own eyes to watch them when I revealed it in my first broadcast, but I hadn't. I'd focused on my daughters. Yet this fight was for everyone.

I removed the wig and Golden T-shirt, slipped off my pack, then stood tall and faced Anya, the stadium, the cameras and anyone who looked in my direction, the feeds from my implant coming online as I hooked back into the digital web of our lives. I accessed the communicator; in seconds, thousands of selections scrolled down a section of my vision, each anchoring to my code. I focused on Anya, the software instantaneously connecting to her.

It was time to stop hiding from the technology and use it instead.

I activated the communicator's software.

In less than a second, my face appeared on the screen in the right eye of everyone here, and my voice took over the speakers in their ears—as well as the stadium's sound system.

"Hello. My name is Dray Quintero," I said.

Anya smiled as she looked at me, the camera in her left eye filming me, the bus behind me creating a space in which we could stand among the crowd.

"President Holland claimed my broadcast, where I exposed his government, was a lie. Here I am, minutes after his announcement, live outside of a Broncos football game. Let me show you the real lie."

A man in a faded Kansas City Chiefs shirt and spotty facial hair glanced back at me as he and his friends angled past. With a flick of my dataringed finger, the feed changed from Anya to me and then to him, the apparent "camera" pivoting each time. My face was just visible before the man turned back around. He stumbled to a stop, his left eye broadcasting what he saw to everyone else, including me, though I retained voice control.

"Your government watches you from your own eyes," I said. "Your implant, the cameras in your eyes, are to control you. They see what you're now seeing through this man's eyes." The feed switched to an older woman with black hair. "Now hers." It switched again, moving closer to the stadium, now to a young boy. "The government uses the tech in your head to record everything you see. Twenty-four hours a day. Seven days a week."

The camera lifted again, only this time, it pulled in a second feed, from a heavily-bearded vendor, so for a moment, the two feeds merged, the view became three-dimensional, the "camera" hovering between the man and boy. Then the view lifted away from both of them, pulling in two, three, four feeds at once. The composite view began to glide like a bird over the crowd, down through the turnstiles and into the stadium, curving as it soared down among the fans, the software taking composites of the various feeds and turning the individual people translucent, ghosts in their own world.

From the burnt hole in my left eye, I saw that everyone had stilled around me, mesmerized by what I showed them.

"Because we believed our leaders in Washington, we've let them invade every second of our lives."

Another turn brought the camera up between lines of people waiting to buy food and beer, then past them and down a passageway that led to the interior of the stadium itself. When it exited the passageway, the multi-layered view lifted up as it shot out over the edge of the rows of seating, then up, the feeds from those already in their seats, the thousands of cameras in thousands of eyes combining as the feed lifted outward, upward, the stadium revealed in all its three-dimensional glory. The view swept down and across section after section, hundreds of faces passing every second, the floating composite camera-view angling up to the upper section. The image then arced down to the football field, taking in the feeds from players and coaches and referees to give a ground-level view.

"This is the access they have," I sail. "It's how they control you. Nothing you do is secret. Nothing is private."

The collective view took off again, only instead of taking in the stadium, it went through it, the software using every feed to make the physical structure fall away, revealing just the people. Along with the view of fans in their seats and staff at work, other activities were glimpsed: a football player injecting himself with a syringe in an unused shower; patrons using the public bathrooms the next level up, their urinations and wiping revealed to everyone; a mother smacking her crying son; a couple having sex in a private suite while a man in a wheelchair slept unaware in the next room.

"You can't hide—and they're launching even more penetrating technology. Why? To shackle you in surveillance. You'll never break free, nor will future generations. We have to stop them now."

The view plunged downward to the level below the stadium, the security guards and support personnel, the camera moving past a room that was oddly without any feeds—so it stood out as black to the rest of the faded structure, though two men guarded its door—then back outside, the sports structure laid bare, before heading towards me.

The view returned to Anya, settling, so the software used just her feed to focus on my face. "Make no mistake: we are at war. Choose your side. I choose freedom."

CHAPTER TWENTY-ONE

Anya hugged me with tears in her eyes. "That was amazing."

I reveled in her embrace, adrenaline feeding my veins—then hands grabbed me, ripped me from her, and threw me against the side of the bus. "Dray Quintero, you're under arrest." A stunstick pressed against the back of my neck as hands patted my body. Cops. Two of them. If the cop behind me activated his stick, the charge would knock me out.

"Let him go," I heard Raven shout. The pressure against my neck eased as the cop who'd pinned me backed away. I turned. Jex had an arm around the man's throat, a gun pressed against his head. Raven gripped the second cop's collar and had her gun pressed into his back.

"We won't harm you," I said, "unless you give us a reason." When neither responded, I handcuffed them, removed their pistols—and tensed as people approached from all sides, a growing crowd of blue and orange. Past them, shouts rose from the stadium that drowned out the pregame music. There was movement as well: fans exited the structure and headed our way, while others clustered along the promenades encircling the stadium, staring down at us.

I pulled Anya behind me, facing the threat with Raven and Jex, but the crowd didn't attack. Instead, they swarmed us with questions, fears, how to help, what to do.

They not only heard my message, they embraced it. I could

see the effects, the football game forgotten, the crowd turning to me instead.

"Spread the word," I told them as Jex ushered the cops I'd handcuffed away from the crowd. "Question what your vision tells you, demand to see your elected officials in person. Confirm their identity—not only with your eyes but touch their faces, make sure they're who they project to be."

"And be ready to fight," Raven said proudly, her voice ringing out. She glowed with excitement.

Jex rejoined us. "You'll need one of these implant shields," he proclaimed, holding one up. "We can get more, if you join us."

"We have to take our country back by force," I said. "If we don't do it now, we'll never get another chance."

More than a dozen individuals stepped forward, ranging in age from twenty to fifty. "We want to fight," one said.

"Tell us what to do," said another.

A third man, with dark skin and a lean face, frowned, staring up at the four-lane road we'd used to reach the complex. "We're going to get visitors, and not the good kind."

"He's right," Anya said.

"We'll protect you," the first man said, a burly bouncer-type.

"Good, because the fight is coming. We need to organize." To the man with the lean face, I said, "Collect names and phone numbers of those here. Get others to do so as well. The more you gather, the more resources we'll have."

The next twenty minutes were consumed with organization, planning, molding the spark into the beginnings of a movement. I knew every second gave our enemies time to attack, although we had hundreds surrounding us.

There was something else I needed to do.

"My brother-in-arms will give you more detail," I said as I tried to extract myself, indicating Jex.

"I will?"

I leaned toward him. "Teach them how to mask themselves, communicate with us, and what they'll need to do."

"So, Rebelling 101."

"Right."

As he faced the crowd, Raven said to me, "We need to go. The cops directing traffic have stayed back so far, but they will try to arrest us, probably when reinforcements arrive."

"You mean Agents," Jex muttered.

I said, "I'm sure The Agency is on their way. I haven't seen any hoverbikes, which means they'll be forced to drive. Even if Lafontaine's broadcaster shifted their search east, it'll still take them another fifteen minutes or so to get here from the mountains."

"We are not staying that long," Raven said.

"You're right—but I need to check out something."

She scowled, then turned to the crowd, absently rubbing her metal fingers through the bandages. "Who has military training?"

Over three dozen answered in the affirmative.

"How many have connections to military-grade weaponry?" About ten answered. "Use them. You'll need as much firepower as you can."

Twenty or more men ran for their vehicles. I realized they were retrieving their guns.

I took Anya's hand and called out to Raven. "Come on."

She, Jex, and what seemed to be the rest of the crowd followed as I headed toward the stadium. As we walked, Jex handed me his burner phone. "Got a call."

Garly's voice burst from the tiny speaker. "I caught the broadcast. My god!"

"Get over here. Bring Nataly."

"We're close. The traffic's nutso, but your guppies are coming."

"Good. Hurry."

* * *

Minutes later, we approached the door to the basement-level room that hadn't registered any feeds during my broadcast. It either meant it was an empty storage room—though it was guarded—or was constructed with a special material that blocked all transmissions.

The two security guards drew their weapons as we approached. "How many bullets do you have?" I asked.

The guards' eyes swept the crowd behind me—and lowered their guns.

Seconds later, I opened the door to the mystery room.

Hot air greeted me as I entered, Anya, Raven, and Jex right behind me. Datatanks lined the walls, the grated floor with the massive Agency servers below like an old friend. I smiled at Anya. "We found it."

"Another node?" Raven asked. "Seriously?"

"The locale makes sense," Jex said. "Central to the city, yet blocked from easy access."

New recruits entered behind us.

As Jex warned them not to touch anything, I hurried to the command center, which stood on a raised platform like the node Anya and I had found in Los Angeles.

"Having serious déjà vu," Anya said, her eyes dancing.

I smiled. "Remember how the controls work?"

She sat in one of the chairs and began to type. Citizen implant IDs scrolled on one of the screens; as I watched, a few stuttered, their numbers duplicating before combining again. Before I could ask her about it, she said, "I found it." A map appeared on a nearby wall display—one addition the L.A. location hadn't had. The map of the United States contained white dots both spaced out and clustered together that layered the country, connected to each other by one of if not multiple lines.

"The motherload," Raven whispered.

She was right. The map showed the location of every node the government used to maintain their coup.

I approached the display. The nodes, over a hundred, had been placed in every major city—a building near Twin Peaks in San Francisco, underneath a swimming pool complex in St. Louis, three in New York City, including under Central Park, and a node in the top of the Nashville state capitol building.

Others had been placed in the Union Power Station next to the Chicago River, another at the former Six Flags site in Dallas/Fort Worth, and many more locations. Headquarters appeared to be located just outside of D.C., a large glowing dot with dozens of lines branching from it.

Jex looked over my shoulder and chortled. "We just might win after all."

***

Garly, Nataly, Valor, and Cole arrived minutes later, our reunion brief but heartfelt.

Their eyes went wide when they saw the map. As they studied it, I had Jex escort the football-fans-turned-recruits outside to set up perimeters, establish hierarchies, and plan courses of action in case The Agency arrived before we left. The process was good for him. He could go far with the right people under him.

Although I was aware we needed to leave, I wasn't done.

With the room to ourselves, I told the rest of the team, "We have to take out every node. At the same time."

Cole nodded in agreement, though Garly whistled. "That'll be tricky."

"When Anya and I disabled the node in L.A., The Agency activated a new one the next day, which made many people doubt my claims, even dismiss my broadcast as a fluke. If we take out all of the nodes at once, across the country, The Agency will be overwhelmed. People will see the truth."

"One of our new recruits owns a demolition company specializin' in blastin' roadways into mountains," Jex said. "He's got lots of explosives."

"Good. Get everything you can."

Nataly stood so close to the map her nose almost touched it. "Some places appear to be just a node location, like this one, while others have combined a broadcast tower and node together."

She was right. The combined structures were spaced a hundred or more miles apart, covering mostly rural areas. In more densely populated areas, some nodes' coverage areas overlapped, with D.C. the most layered, followed by New York.

"There's a blank spot in West Virginia," Cole said.

"I noticed that," I said. An area that encompassed eastern West Virginia and western Virginia had no nodes, no lines, and no coverage, the only uncovered spot in the country. I vaguely remembered an old radio dead-zone area. That had been decades ago, but the similarity to this one seemingly uncovered part of the country couldn't be a coincidence.

Monroe entered the room. "I had to confirm with my own eyes that you're safe."

"For now," I said. "Good to see you."

"The rest of your clan are on their way. Lafontaine arrived the same time I did, with some of his fighters. They're outside."

"Recruiting, probably," Garly said. "I do *not* trust him. He's bad peeps."

"I'm kickin' his ass for what he did," Jex growled.

"Stand in line," Cole said.

"We'll get our retribution, but he probably has the local leader's ear right now," I said. "We use him, but we limit it. Speaking of which, Cole, help Jex process as many recruits as you can."

"Sure. You know, with even a fraction of those people, you could have the biggest clan of them all."

"Politics later," I said, but I could feel it. He, Garly, Raven, Valor, Nataly, even Monroe—they were looking to me for leadership.

"Speaking of politics, you should get the other leaders involved in taking down the nodes."

"Even Lafontaine?" Jex asked.

Cole nodded. "In a limited way, yes. It'll be a good gesture, and the other teams can share the burden."

Along with the victory. Still, it was a smart play. We couldn't pull this off on our own. "OK, I'll talk to him," I said. "Gather all the information we need so we can get out of here. We're pushing it already. And start reaching out to the other rebel clans. We'll need all thirty-eight to pull this off. Limit what you tell them. Just assign the node location and time of attack."

Cole, Monroe, and Jex left.

"I'll figure out how to power down the station," Nataly said. "It'll stop everyone from broadcasting each other's faces. Then we should smash the consoles."

She and Anya focused on the control panels, while beside them, Garly determined how to access the software's root system to copy it.

Raven, who'd ducked out as Cole and I talked, returned with a tablet to photograph the map and worked with Valor, who zoomed into various sections for her to capture.

Once we took down the nodes, we'd have to contend with the network I'd created, which was nearly as pervasive as the node network. And we had the 3D drone network to deal with, though I suspected it tied into my system in some way.

"Dray," Anya called, her voice troubled.

I walked toward her, my footsteps slowing when an image appeared on one of the panels: Kieran, sitting at some broadcaster's table, as if he was a news anchor. Almost reluctantly, Anya swiped along the bottom of the image to bring up the sound.

"...Quintero is a fraud and a liar," Kieran said, sounding as confident and assured as a professional broadcaster, though the contraption on his head was distracting, the bands reflecting the overhead lights as he moved. "And he's dangerous. Isn't that right, Mina?"

The camera pulled back to show my wife sitting beside him. She looked shaky and troubled. A heading appeared under her identifying her as my spouse.

The broadcast looked hastily put together, the two sitting at a nondescript desk.

She nodded, almost reluctantly. "My husband and his people are trying to rip this country apart. He's misguided and angry."

"Why is she doing this?" Raven whispered. She and the others pressed around me, watching the screen.

I frowned as I watched Mina. "She's scared."

She furtively scratched the edge of her chin. My frown deepened. Back in college, the gesture had been our secret code that she wanted to leave a party.

"President Holland made a statement today denouncing your husband, explaining to the American people that he was trying to manipulate them," Kieran said. "Your husband then sent another fake broadcast. But you're here to tell everyone he's not the white knight he pretends to be, aren't you?"

Mina dropped her gaze. Nodded again.

"He even abandoned his own daughter, didn't he?" Kieran pressed.

Raven and I looked at each other in confusion.

"Yes," Mina said, drawing us back to the screen. She looked up at the camera. "Dray has warped our older daughter and abandoned our younger one, who he thought was dead. But she's not. Talia is alive."

CHAPTER TWENTY-TWO

Unreality washed over me. My mind didn't seem to work. My body felt numb.

"She lives," Mina continued. "Yet Dray abandoned her."

"It can't be," I croaked. It had to be another illusion, like she'd fooled herself with Adem.

"You're sure it's her?" Kieran asked onscreen.

"I know my daughter." She looked at the camera. "I saw Talia's beating heart."

Kieran also faced the camera. "What kind of father abandons his own daughter?"

Anya cut the feed, but I was no longer watching. I was back on that monstrosity of an island, Talia shot, her life bleeding out of her. My world changed that day, my precious, precocious, adventurous little girl murdered before my eyes. I hadn't fully processed her death—out of denial or my need to avenge her, I wasn't sure—but Mina's claim tore me all over again.

I hugged Raven, her tears dampening my shirt.

"I want to strangle her," Raven said. "How dare she say Talia's alive."

"The Agency may have warped her mind," Anya said cautiously. "I've heard whispers of government scientists experimenting with brain scans, psychological warfare—"

"They've been doing that for years," Cole said. He must've seen my face and come over.

"Using little girls?" Raven asked, pulling away.

I glanced at Anya, wondering if this could be true, if they had saved Talia. Could they?

Could she be alive?

If so, I really had abandoned her.

"We need to leave," Cole said. "We have the information we need, and we can plan our attack when we're somewhere safe."

"How many teams will we need to take out the network?" I asked in an attempt to care. To be engaged.

"One for each node, so 112. The size of each team will depend on the location. Most, if not all, will be heavily guarded, so we should plan on two teams for each attack. We've already started contacting other clans. Everyone is willing to help."

Nataly pressed three buttons in rapid succession, and everything turned off: the map, the other two control screens, and the lights on the servers. As she backed away, I ignited my ion blade and slashed each panel, destroying the screens, motherboards, and other tech used to play with people's lives. Bits of glass, silicone and metal pelted me, the smell of scorched electronics filling my nose, but my anger wasn't sated.

Though the node was destroyed, cameras dotted the stadium complex, which meant my network could still track us. As the thought struck me, Cole left the room and began barking orders to disable every camera people could find.

"Let's go," I said.

Valor led the way toward the door.

"Hey," Anya said softly as I started to leave. "If you want to talk, I'm here."

"Can someone survive with a hole in their chest, where you can see their heart?" I'd thought Talia had been shot through the heart, but maybe I was wrong.

Anya pressed her lips together. "If they were in a specialized unit, with the right care, they might. It would depend on so many factors."

We left the node.

For the first time that I could remember, no camera watched me. I should've been elated. Should've felt liberated.

Cole returned from directing new recruits and huddled with Garly, Nataly, Jex, and Raven in the middle of the wide passageway that curved away in either direction, one way following the curve of the stadium underground, the other leading outside. When he saw Anya and me, he stepped back to include us in the circle, none of them meeting my gaze. "This is our chance," he said. "If we destroy the nodes, we'll take their power. And we'll reveal their lies to everyone."

Jex smiled. "It'll change everythin'."

"When will you attack?" I asked. We kept our voices low, though no one was near. Recruits stood guard yards away, and a cluster of men waited farther back. Past them, I heard someone ordering others to beef up the perimeter. Jex had been busy.

"Two days, if we push," Cole said.

"Don't push. I don't want a team caught at some airport. We can't afford to miss a single node." As I talked, a weight inside me shifted. I saw my path. "Use every clan you can reach, along with everyone here. Run small groups, everyone by car, taking every precaution to avoid detection. The Agency will beef up their security after today, so run at least two teams, a point team and a backup. Coordinate them so they strike every node exactly ninety-six hours from now. Four days—and don't hurt any civilians. We have to retain that high ground. After the nodes are taken out, the true uprising will begin."

Jex whispered in my ear, "This is your callin'."

I saw their excitement, their resurgence.

In their expressions, I saw the rebellious life I'd adopted—and those who occupied it with me. Before I opened my mouth, I felt the sharp ache of loss. The feeling didn't arise from my decision. I'd already made it.

The hurt came from what I was abandoning.

I forced as much of a smile as I could. "We killed everyone's feed. Jex, make sure your people understand they're seeing the truth now—and teach them how to hide their faces." He dashed over to a cluster of men I realized were his new lieutenants. I felt proud.

Cole asked me, "You want every team to coordinate through you?"

"No, through you. Everyone needs to get going. With this node shut down, it gives you all a chance to get away. Me as well."

Raven frowned in suspicion. "What do you mean 'Me as well'?"

Confused eyes turned to me. They shouldn't have been. I had to do this.

To Cole, I said, "I relinquish my leadership of the Founding Fathers." I then faced Raven. "I'm going to find Talia."

CHAPTER TWENTY-THREE

Raven grabbed my arm. "Mom's a liar."

I shook my head. "I've received messages from her. I think she's telling the truth."

"What messages? Why haven't you told me?"

"I didn't want to upset you."

"You're doing a shitty job." Her face was flushed, her fists clenched at her sides.

Voices echoed in the stadium's curved passageway from our new recruits waiting for us outside, faint conversations ignored by her and the others in our circle—Jex, Anya, Cole, Garly, and Nataly—as she glared at me and the others stared in confusion and disbelief.

"They must've installed an avatar of her," Raven said. "That has to be it. They tricked Mom." When I didn't respond, she said, "Dad, Talia is *dead*."

"She might be." Or might not, the mere thought powerful enough to clench my stomach. "After I leave, trust your instincts. If something seems wrong, get out of there. And be careful."

I headed toward the exit. Jex followed. "I'm comin' with."

"Stay with the others. I know I'm probably making the wrong decision. But I have to do this."

I said the same thing to Cole when he tried to stop me, adding, "You're the leader now."

"No, I'm not—"

"For this one mission. Take out the nodes. Neuter The Agency. After that, you can hold a vote for your replacement."

Anya was next. I held her. "Just when you and I were getting interesting," she said.

I kissed her goodbye, aware I was jeopardizing the spark we'd kindled, then walked out of the stadium tunnel, the side of my face damp from her tears. I was being foolish. I felt tempted to return to her, to the rebels, to the fight we needed to finish.

But I continued forward. If Talia was alive, I had to rescue her. Or at least try.

When I emerged into the sunshine, there were even more people than before. Many applauded when they saw me; others approached, wanting to talk. I waved them off, though I thanked them for joining the fight.

Monroe came up, a bag hooked over his shoulder. "You leaving to find your daughter? Let me help."

"I'd planned to go alone, though I could use the additional firepower." Besides, if anything happened to him, I wouldn't lose someone else I cared about.

"The war won't end before we rescue your girl. I have a lead on a car. I'll go get it."

Brisk footsteps approached. It was Raven, carrying a small bag and a submachine gun, her damaged hand hidden beneath a black leather glove.

Before I could open my mouth, she snapped, "I'm going with you."

"I forbid it." I never forbade her anything.

"It's not your choice."

"Goddammit, Raven, I said no."

"She's my sister. If she *is* alive, I'll save her. Besides, Mom and I have unfinished business."

"What about you helping others, revealing the truth?"

She looked at the stadium. "I know what I'm giving up. And what we'll probably find. I'm still going. For Talia."

Our personal battle cry cut me. "I can't have you come. I…I can't fail you, too."

Instead of responding, she headed after Monroe.

Before I could come up with a way to stop her, Garly bounded up with a large duffel bag. He set it down, then flung his long arms around me in a bear hug.

When he finally let go, he looked both eager and sad. "I brought stuff in case the local honcho didn't let you in his abode, but, well, there are a lotta goodies that'll help you. I'm glad I brought 'em. I liked that squirt. Oh, and I modified Raven's fingers. She wanted 'em 'full fighting strength'. Nataly helped. She has her curved blades, too."

Valor approached, scooped up the bag Garly had dropped and walked after Raven.

"I didn't say you could go with me," I called to Valor.

"Didn't ask."

I turned back to Garly. "Take care of yourself. And keep Nataly safe."

He blushed. "Is it that obv?"

"Everyone is rooting for you. Just be careful. We don't know if she's been straight with us."

Lafontaine stood off to the side, talking with a band of large men in Broncos jerseys. I didn't approach him. Cole could deal with him.

I started after Monroe—but Jex stepped in my path, pack slung over his shoulder. "I have to go with you."

After what we'd been through, what he meant to Raven, and what he meant to me, I shouldn't have been surprised he would try again. He looked determined, though this wasn't his call. "You have responsibilities, Jex. End this fight. That's your path. Mine is different."

"You need me."

I hugged him. "You have to stay," I told him. "One of my sons has to live."

* * *

We rode in silence: Valor driving, Monroe next to her, Raven to my left in the back seat. Our ride was a ten-year-old, rust-colored SUV, dated but clean. The thrum of its tires on the concrete highway was the only sound.

Raven seethed with anger, and I warred with my emotions, which were so strong I could barely concentrate. If I really had failed Talia, if I'd abandoned her, I deserved Raven's anger and more—but I was upset she'd come with me.

A memory surfaced from just after Talia turned seven. She and Raven had been normal siblings, though they changed after Adem's death. Raven spent more time alone in her room, not only avoiding Mina and me but also Talia.

We'd had a robo-butler, a flat-topped robot bigger than Talia that responded to voice commands and carried tools, snacks, and other objects in various drawers. One day, six months after the funeral, Talia sent it to Raven's room. "Delivery for Mistress Raven," it announced.

When Raven didn't open the door, Talia hurried from around the corner. "No, you're supposed to say it like a real butler," I heard her say from my home office down the hall.

"Delivery for Mistress Raven," it said again in its flat, human-like voice.

"Like this." She repeated the phrase in a bad British accent.

Raven spoke from behind her door. "I can hear you."

"You have a delivery."

With a resigned sigh, Raven opened the door.

The robo-butler reached inside its top drawer. Leaning back in my chair, I watched as the robot lifted a trivia board game from its drawer and held it out to her, Talia smiling hopefully as she stood behind the robot.

"Trivia's lame," Raven said.

"That's 'cause I bean you every time."

"You know that's mine."

"Nuh-uh. I got the game for my birthday."

"I meant the butler. Dad gave it to me."

I had, but the whole family had grown accustomed to using it.

"Then your buddy wants to play with you. Although, I'm not sure how whack of an opponent he'd be. He can't even blat different voices," Talia said.

Raven shut the door without a word.

Talia went to her room and closed the door, abandoning the robot in the hallway.

With an effort—everything felt like an effort those days—I went to Talia. She sat on her bed, hugging her knees, though she snatched up a tablet as I stuck my head in. "You okay?" When she nodded, I asked, "Want to talk?"

She shook her head.

I left, respecting her wishes, though I regretted it. She'd looked so alone.

I wondered how she felt now, abandoned, probably in pain, and a captive of Kieran's. If she really was alive.

I glanced at Raven. She sat rigid beside me, pistol in her left hand, beautiful in her rage and rebel clothes, lethal if she wanted to be.

It hurt me that she'd turned out like this.

It hurt even more thinking that Mina might be telling the truth.

I looked out my window, not really looking at first, though images drew my attention. We'd taken the interstate south; we appeared to be in an upscale part of the city, high-rises and office parks lining the highway, yet smoke rose from three different areas, and as I took in more details, I noted police cars in multiple locations, sometimes two or three together, lights flashing. I also noted at least one cluster of rioters.

Closer to us, cars whipped past recklessly, people shouting at other drivers. We passed a cop on an access road; he'd pulled over and leaned against his car in what seemed to be despair.

"Holy shit," Valor breathed.

We all looked. An open-topped semi passed us heading north, the semi filled with armed men.

"The stadium will be the first battleground," Monroe said.

Raven stared after the semi.

"The fighting will help," I said. "They'll block The Agency from getting access to the node—"

"No," she said. "You don't get to do that."

"Do what?"

"Talk about it. You shouldn't get credit for anything you've done—or anything good that happens from now on."

"Maybe none of us should," Monroe said. "We all abandoned the rebellion."

"Which way?" Valor asked as Raven slumped in her seat. A sign ahead listed the exit for the 470 Loop.

I pulled up the map of the U.S. I'd downloaded weeks ago. "Keep going south."

"You have a plan?" Raven asked almost reluctantly.

"Yes, but we don't have much time. We'll coordinate our efforts to match the attack on the nodes, use it as a distraction." It was our only chance.

Spotting the exit for State Highway 86, I directed Valor to take it.

"East? You sure?" she asked.

Before I could answer, she ducked her face for a few seconds.

"You are okay to drive, aren't you?" I asked.

"Well," she drawled. "I did post some comments about the government. And how great you are." Which meant she had been tagged by Agency software, if not as a known associate, then at least as a sympathizer. Many state and local police departments—which my network tapped into—installed cameras to scan drivers' faces at random access points. If she showed up on a camera, she'd attract unwanted attention.

"I can drive," Monroe said.

"Calm your britches." She took the exit while hiding her face, then headed east, civilization falling away.

The lack of people should've been a relief, but none of us relaxed.

As towns grew farther and farther apart, I tried to remember the grid I'd seen at the node, specifically the lines. I'd need to pick a spot where we wouldn't be seen—and hope I could find the person I needed.

The thought drew me to the duffel bag Garly gave me.

I twisted around and leaned over the back of my seat. The bag lay in the rear, next to Raven's pack and a couple of rolled-up blankets. I found Garly had packed the hand shields, the augmented sleeves, a chest plate, and an emitter that triggered a bolt of energy we hoped would be strong enough to take down an Agent. There was also a repair pack containing a diagnostic reader, mini-tools, wires and a motherboard; a machine gun with ten clips; a handful of implant blockers; a grenade launcher; the energy absorber; two flasher balls; and binoculars.

I checked the implant blockers. They were the standard size, which jammed my feed but didn't fit my implant completely due to the solder. I couldn't risk my implant connecting, so I kept my cap on and returned the blockers to the bag.

An hour later, we reached Interstate 70—which was packed with cars as people fled Denver.

Valor merged onto the interstate and continued east, where columns of smoke rose two miles ahead. They grew larger as we approached Limon, a town of 2,000 or so.

"Uh, guys?" she asked hesitantly.

Directly ahead, state trooper vehicles blocked the road, lights flashing, troopers directing everyone to exit the highway at Limon. Past the roadblock, tanker trucks burned, having crashed and exploded across the roadway, whether as an accident or vandalism, I couldn't tell.

We hid our faces as we rolled past the troopers and down the ramp into town, Monroe pulling his Glock and holding it just out of sight. Raven did the same.

The traffic slowed as we entered town, though police officers directed the glut of vehicles through the stoplights at every intersection.

As Valor drove past the cops at the first intersection, I risked a glance out my window, a hand covering most of my face. The two policemen looked frayed and skittish; behind them, drivers trying to join those of us heading east packed a side road.

At the next intersection, the main portion of town came into view. Debris littered the roadway, police cars blocked the road leading through town as well as intersecting streets, and a dozen people lay face-down in a nearby parking lot, all handcuffed. In the distance, blue light the distinct shade of plasma fire flashed in random patterns.

With his free hand, Monroe turned on the radio and began searching stations.

Raven straightened in her seat as Valor followed the flow of vehicles that headed toward the next I-70 entrance ramp. "We should help them."

"We can't," I said.

"Mom isn't well, Dad. She pretended Adem wasn't dead for years. She chose his ghost over us. Talia is probably a ghost, too. The people here are alive."

Monroe found a local radio station as it reported shots being fired at the Castle Rock Town Hall and a courthouse being invaded in Parker.

Each report made me feel reprehensible, but I'd made my choice.

Valor took the entrance ramp back onto the interstate.

"Duck," Monroe suddenly barked.

We did, although I lifted my head a few seconds later. A wave of military transport trucks drove past on the other side of the interstate, heading for Denver. The last one had a passenger in the front. I didn't catch any details, but the person had silver hair.

Raven saw it, too. "Are you at least going to warn our people The Agency is coming with entire squadrons?" she asked.

"Cole will have moved our teams out of the area—though I'm concerned Agents mobilized so quickly," Monroe said. "They're becoming even more formidable."

Raven looked at me beseechingly as Valor accelerated. "We have to warn everyone."

"We can't," I said. "The Agency will be monitoring every form of communication."

"Dammit, Dad, we need to go back and fight."

"If we expose The Agency's lies, we might be able to defeat them—but it's the *only* chance we have. We aren't strong enough to fight them on our own."

In the side mirror, I saw Monroe frown, but he remained quiet. Valor, though, shot me a look. "Not strong enough? What have we all been doing, then?"

"Surviving."

Raven started to argue, but Monroe cut her off. "We'll have to convince the generals. Even after the broadcasts, they might not accept the truth."

"One step at a time," I said, though I was conflicted. Just as our rebellion finally had a chance to make some real progress, I'd abandoned everyone for what I feared was a fool's run.

CHAPTER TWENTY-FOUR

The multi-hued land rolled past us, the brown and tan swells in the landscape widening as we descended in elevation into western Kansas, the region desolate and harsh.

The more the landscape flattened, and the more vehicles exited the highway, the warier I became, for the more we stuck out. Distance would only help us for so long until The Agency expanded their search.

The haze and dust did nothing to hide us, just clung to our car and scratched our throats.

Monroe pulled a pair of glasses from his pocket, but they weren't ordinary glasses. As he donned them, I realized they flexed in synch with his lenses to magnify his vision. He faced the south and searched the horizon.

It was another thing that surprised me about him. He rarely stopped scanning our surroundings, his head constantly sweeping left to right. Valor, on the other hand, tapped the steering wheel and sang old pop songs under her breath as she drove. I caught snippets of Janet Jackson's Rhythm Nation and Kelly Clarkson's What Doesn't Kill You.

"Drones are being dispersed," he said quietly, as if speaking could reveal us.

To the south, a dark mass seemed to hover in the far distance.

As Raven and Valor hid their faces, I grabbed my binoculars

and focused on what I discovered was a slow-moving armada of drones. As I watched, one broke off from the rest, decelerated, and rose to a spot forty feet in the air. Sunlight glinted off what I suspected was a solar array, which meant the machine could stay in place for months or longer depending on its design and the weather. A boxy protrusion hung from its belly, a transmitter of some kind.

"They might be implant extenders," Monroe said. "My unit used extenders every time we were deployed, with plenty of overlap in case some got shot down."

"You sure the military isn't workin' with the silver-haired freaks?" Valor asked as more drones scattered in every direction, some heading our way.

"They would've fought back. They swore an oath." He leaned back as Valor accelerated. "Dray, we need a plan for when the enemy finds us, because they will. This interstate is one of the only major roadways from Denver."

I nodded as Valor accelerated, causing the drones to fade into the distance behind us. The main cluster also fell back, although they continued to head east, like us.

A massive windmill farm stretched to the north, while to the south, a lone pickup drove down an unmarked road, and a robotic piece of farm equipment churned the earth in a field. Other than that, the land under the brown sky sat still, the fields interspersed with rusted out and wood-dried areas, along with a smattering of silos in the distance.

Nowhere to hide.

The interstate occasionally offered an exit, but besides a few tiny clusters of stores, the exits led to nothing but small roads intercutting the never-ending fields.

"We need gas," Valor announced.

Raven straightened. I did as well. "How far can we go?"

"Dash says twenty-three miles. Why didn't we grab electric wheels?"

The tension grew as we searched for an exit.

Minutes later, a dusty sign indicated a gas/e-charge

station up ahead, at the exit for a town called Goodland.

Raven pressed against her window. "Dad, what's that?"

Something glided in the hazy air, heading toward the interstate from the north. I swung my binoculars around and spotted a long, flat object with an array of sensors hanging from its belly. "It's a reconnaissance drone."

The long-distance search vehicle flew parallel to us, staying north of the highway as we drove. "It doesn't seem to have identified us," Monroe said. Still, he and Raven uncovered their implants—and Valor activated her broadcaster—in case it suddenly headed toward us, as it would expect implant signals to come from each person it spotted. I pressed against the back of his seat, so if the drone scanned our vehicle, his and my heat signatures would hopefully read as one person.

Valor slowed.

"What're you doing?" Raven asked anxiously.

"Gas, remember?"

"If we change our pattern, that thing could decide to inspect us."

"If I don't pull off, we'll get stuck on the side of the road."

The drones disturbed me, but we didn't have a choice. "Do it," I said.

Valor took the exit, pulled to a stop at the end of the ramp—briefly dropping out of the drone's view as the interstate rose beside us—then took a right onto a four-lane road and another right into the gas station. The facility offered four pumps and four charging spaces under a faded Conoco canopy, along with a convenience store. A concrete drive disappeared behind the store, with signs indicating an automated carwash. Past the property sat an RV park, a collection of various-sized trailers parked under large trees. Next to the Conoco station was a decent-sized truck stop. A three-story hotel stood across the four-lane road.

Valor pulled up to an available pump, the second one from the edge facing the highway, and shut off the car. The interior turned stuffy in seconds, the afternoon heat bleeding away the cooled air that had issued from the car's air conditioner.

"I have to pee," Raven announced as she and the others reattached blockers to their implants, each of us scanning the skies for the reconnaissance drone.

I handed her two twenties. "We're pump five."

She got out and headed for the convenience store, using her hair to shield her face—which I hoped would be enough to avoid tripping any Agency scanners.

Valor and Monroe also got out; I did a moment later, though I kept my head down and the door open, my sunglasses in place. The highway rose up past the station to arch over the four-lane road; from our spot, I couldn't see any drones, but that didn't give much comfort, especially since I knew the armada of unidentified drones was heading this way.

There were three other cars at the pumps; the row between me and the interstate was empty, however, except for an old man filling a pair of gas cans. He knelt away from me, so I kept my face pointed toward I-70, careful to stand in a spot where the door shielded my appearance from the cameras hanging from the aging canopy. There was a chance they were closed-circuit, but I couldn't risk them being 'net connected; multiple agencies were looking for me by now, their scanner software among the best in the world.

Beside me, Monroe stood coiled as if ready to attack someone.

Remembering Cole's training, I raised my arm to my face and turned to check my surroundings; between my arm, sunglasses, and cap, my face was obscured.

The other drivers were a mix of the old, the tired, and the lost, some with purpose and others meandering, each helpless to the lies that surrounded them.

The rebels would save them, so long as they pulled off the plan.

I should've stayed to help them.

As I struggled with that thought, a couple eyed us with suspicion, taking in Valor's eyepatch and Monroe's military bearing. The woman also watched the store as if she'd seen Raven walk inside.

The counter on our pump reset.

Valor took the nozzle, stuck it in the tank, and began to pump gas.

"We need to go," Monroe said quietly, his mouth barely moving.

"Can you tell if either is broadcasting?"

He nodded. "The guy is definitely sending a signal. Not sure what, or to who."

Monroe inched his hand toward the Glock under his shirt.

"Let's hope you won't have to use that."

His eyes flickered to me. "I don't see how."

I had to get Raven.

I ducked into the car, pulled a shirt from my pack, and wrapped it around my lower face. Before I could grab a weapon, however, three Goodland police cars pulled to a stop just before the gas station's entrance.

As I climbed back out of the car, Valor quickly returned the gas nozzle to its cradle while Monroe slipped his Glock from under his shirt, hiding it from view as he tracked the cops.

I gauged the distance to the store and prepared to run for my daughter.

Before I could, the cops' patrol lights illuminated, and the cars rolled across the street to block the roadway just past the gas station. The officers got out, opened their trunks, and started to remove patrol drones. The three-foot-wide drones were older and less sophisticated but still posed a threat.

"That reconnaissance drone must've spotted us after all," Valor said. "Let's bust their blockade and get outta here."

"No," Monroe said. "The terrain would benefit them, not us."

From where I stood, I caught the edge of a patrol car parked on the other side of the interstate, the rest of the road hidden by the berms that rose on either side of the road to the bridge over the intersection. "They're blocking both sets of ramps," I said. "I suspect roadblocks are going up at every exit to keep everyone on the interstate. Anyone tries to leave, they won't have any choice but to get back on." Including us.

"Probably to some Agency-erected checkpoint," Monroe agreed. "If we're going to do something, we need to do it now."

The couple had gotten back in their car, the man eyeing me as he climbed in. That's when I noticed their side mirrors were missing.

Monroe was right. "I'll get Raven," I said.

"We can leave a comm for her, have her meet us somewhere," he said, holding up a commlink. "We gotta move."

The police drones rose into the air. In seconds, they would establish our locations and those of everyone else here and begin to track us.

I snatched the commlink. "Get in the car. I'll radio you." I headed for the store, keeping my head down. I looked suspicious as hell with the shirt covering my face but couldn't help it. I didn't have time to confirm where every camera was, whether I could get away with a more subtle move, aware we didn't have backup or anyone who could help us.

A crash sounded behind me.

I spun—and discovered the couple had slammed into the nearest cop car. They backed up and drove into it again, pushing the patrol vehicle back, then took off through the gap they'd made. The cops fired at them as they drove off, one of the officers getting into his car and driving after them. As soon as he left, two cars from the truck stop sped onto the road, turned sharply, and drove up onto the highway.

"Dad," Raven said softly.

She'd come out of the store and nearly reached me—but from her expression, had caught what had transpired. She avoided looking at me and nodded nearly imperceptibly back toward the store; I followed, and she started back toward the store but angled away from the entrance. I realized where she was going.

I lifted the commlink. "Pretend you're getting a carwash," I radioed to Valor and Monroe, who'd stayed with our car.

Before we reached the edge of the building, I caught a sound over the hum of the interstate and my own heartbeat: the buzz of a drone. Heading in our direction. We must've drawn its attention when Raven had reversed course back toward but away from the store, which meant its pattern-recognition software was already running.

My heartbeat accelerated.

We stepped past the building and onto the narrow drive that curved behind the building to the automated carwash. Past the drive was a level patch of grass that ended at the RV park. A road encircled the park, stretching to the left and disappearing, while to the right, it curved where it brushed against the gas station's property and continued into the distance, the road running parallel to the highway. Smaller streets branched off from the road to the right, each lying perpendicular to the interstate.

I'd hoped to duck into our SUV inside the carwash, but we couldn't stay. I paused, not sure where to go or how to meet up with Valor and Monroe, then took Raven's unscarred arm and pulled her onto the tiny lawn. I keyed the comm again. "Drive to the RV park."

We hurried across the grass.

Raven followed my lead, her body tense, as we stepped onto the street that paralleled the highway. I wanted to look back but knew the drone was trailing us. Besides, one glimpse of my face would bring The Agency.

We passed the first street, which was dotted with trees and evenly-spaced RVs. I started to turn toward the second, but Raven grabbed my arm and quickened her step. "Next one." I followed as she led me to the third street and started down it.

I spotted a fairly large tree and realized what she wanted to do. "It won't come close enough."

"We'll bait it."

We broke into a run and reached the tree seconds later, skidding to a stop behind it, the nearest RV ten yards away. As we caught our breath, I heard the pitch of the drone's flight change as it pivoted down the street.

I avoided her gaze as she uncovered her implant. The fact mine was covered was a problem. I was an anomaly—on top of being someone who'd hurried from the scene. "It'll try to ID us," Raven said quietly. "Be ready."

I gripped the bark, unaware if people were watching from the nearby RVs or if cops were on their way.

The buzzing grew louder.

The large drone slowed, then hovered; though we used the tree trunk to shield us, I could tell the machine had paused outside of the tree's reach. Raven could as well. Before I could stop her, she revealed herself by leaning to the side, falling to the ground, and curling into a ball, her face hidden.

The drone tilted and started to approach—but instead of heading for Raven, the drone curved around the tree in the other direction. It would see me, would back away or warn the police of erratic behavior. I carefully stepped over Raven's legs and slid around the tree, keeping the trunk between me and the drone as it moved.

The machine stopped as close to her as it could without flying under the branches, paused, then from the change in tone, I could tell it began to descend.

I backed up a dozen feet, then rushed forward and leapt, planting a foot on the bark five feet off the ground, pushed upwards, and grabbed a branch thicker than my arm that jutted ninety degrees from where I'd started as the drone glided under the tree's branches toward Raven. Because of its descent and planned flight path, the drone's front edge was angled downward, which blocked its under-body cameras from spotting me. Still, I lifted my legs to make sure I stayed out of view—and had to lift myself higher as my weight made the branch sag.

The drone continued toward Raven. Twelve feet.

Risking being caught, I moved farther out on the branch, which caused it to drop further.

The drone began to level out as it neared Raven.

Gauging the distance and timing, I lunged for a branch close to the drone, driving the ends of the branch down into the machine—and a high-pitched whine erupted as the ends caught in the drone's propellers.

I let go of the branch, falling to the ground where Raven had already rolled away, and looked up. The drone had been caught; it hung upside down in the sagging branch, its cameras only able to see the foliage around it.

As I straightened, our SUV appeared at the end of the street. Raven waved it down, and we quickly got in. "Don't drive fast," I told Valor as she accelerated.

Monroe asked, "Did you disable the drone?"

I nodded as I unwrapped the shirt from my face. "We bought ourselves a minute. Maybe two."

"Did it film you?"

"No, we got it." I smiled at Raven, who'd already covered her implant, though she didn't smile back, brushing the dirt from her pants with her left hand instead.

We reached the end of the RV park. Up the four-lane road to the left, the cop cars were visible, along with a line of cars and trucks that had formed in front of the blockade. To the right, I couldn't see the police officer who had chased after the couple who broke through, though I thought I saw two police drones far in the distance aiding the chase. Another car was in a ditch. Sirens drew my eyes to the interstate, where a car flew past, followed by a state trooper.

"That old couple wasn't the only car that didn't like the blockade," Monroe said.

"They're gonna draw more cops," Valor said.

She turned right, away from the interstate, and accelerated, each of us glancing behind us to see if we were being followed. She took the first right a quarter-mile down the road, though in the endless expanse, the cops and their drones remained visible for miles.

We finally drove far enough away that we could sit up. We couldn't use ducking away from the windows as our only defense. Our enemies would see past that.

Raven scanned the rolling fields as Monroe kept an eye on

the road behind us.

"Where to?" Valor asked.

I eyed the sun's position. It was low, but not low enough. "I'll need someone to access the network in order to pull up a map."

Raven gave me a pinched look before extracting a tablet from her pack, a different one than she'd used at the stadium.

"This is Jex's," I said, surprised. "Why do you have it?"

"He built it for you since you can't use your 'net. He kept expecting you to borrow it. He looks up to you, you know."

I did know, but from her expression, acknowledging it would only set her off.

Not sure how to repair our relationship, I turned on the tablet. Using the map feature, I quickly gauged where we were, then shut it off. "Head east."

As Valor turned from one straight, flat, two-lane road onto another, I spotted another drone with the boxy protrusion. The armada had reached and moved past us, its purpose—and ability and who controlled it—unknown.

Chapter Twenty-Five

I made Valor drive twenty miles east, the featureless country road and flat Kansas landscape offering nothing in the way of cover, before heading south again. As the sun reached the western horizon, a line of transmission towers rose like giant sentinels, stretching into the distance, while farm equipment trudged across various fields, silos jutted from abandoned-looking farms, and windmills spun lazily in the distance. "We need to park."

She stopped singing Rachel Platten's Fight Song under her breath. "Out here?"

Monroe pointed toward a small self-storage facility. "How about there?"

I agreed, and within minutes, we backed into a space next to the property, which consisted of two rows of garage-sized units.

As I waited for the sky to turn black, I scanned the area for signs of The Agency's presence.

Beside me, Raven extracted a roll of Life Savers from her pocket, stared at them, and sighed before putting one in her mouth.

I held out my hand.

She glanced at me—but instead of giving me one, she slid the roll back into her pocket.

Valor began a soft tap on the steering wheel. Waiting for the Night by Depeche Mode. "I wonder what life will be like after they strike."

"Much better than this shit," Monroe said.

"Why did you come with us? You seem better suited to taking down the nodes."

Raven spoke up. "He came along to destroy Dad's implant if he gets caught."

The thought startled me.

Monroe turned in his seat to take her in, then looked at me. "I was training off the coast the night of your broadcast. When you started talking, my squad froze. No one moved until after you stopped, and no one spoke about it, though after we returned to base, our lead reported what we saw to our lieutenant. We were told to forget your claims, but we couldn't. You revealed that our Commander in Chief was either a fraud or a pawn. Three guys left that night, and two others the next day. Last I heard, only one had been caught. I left the following day."

"Where are the others in your unit?" I asked.

"In hiding, most likely."

Valor lifted her eyepatch and studied him, her camera squeaking as it ran up and down his body.

He frowned. "What?"

"Don't trust you."

"Dray opened my eyes." He turned and looked at Raven. "Maybe he's opening yours, too."

"Stop hero-worshiping him, both of you," she said.

"It's not hero worship. In fact, when I first met him, I was disappointed. The military makes you think anyone who hasn't served is inferior. But after watching him these past few days, it's an honor to stand with him."

"He's being played."

"Raven," I said.

She turned on me. "Why would you ever believe Mina?"

"Not 'Mom'?"

"Not anymore."

"Her fear is why. She wasn't happy in that broadcast, wasn't excited or worried or even anxious. She was afraid."

Raven scoffed. "I never thought you were gullible. She tricked you—and I'll never forgive you for making me hope that Talia might actually be alive."

She got out of the SUV, slammed the door, went behind the vehicle, and leaned against the liftgate.

"Want me to talk to her?" Valor asked. When I shook my head, she said, "Good. You wouldn't like what I have to say."

Raven could be right. Mina's announcement could be a trap.

If it was, if Mina had lied, torturing me into thinking Talia was somehow miraculously alive, I would make her pay. If I had the strength.

I planned to distract Kieran and The Agency with my hunt for Talia, so our teams would have a better chance of pulling off their attack. But if she was truly gone, I didn't know if I'd have it in me to do a damn thing.

I wished Jex was with us. And Anya. I didn't know if she and I had a future, if this world would let us, but I wanted to try.

Valor broke the silence. "What's the plan here? And don't say it's to find your daughter." Her voice betrayed her anxiety. She always spoke faster when she was nervous.

"We're going to find a man named Brocco Andoletti. He's a wave-spectrum scientist, the foremost expert on communications systems. He used to be my best friend—and he's Raven's godfather."

Valor nodded. "One of the Gang of Five."

"The gang of what?" Monroe asked.

"It was the moniker the media gave us," I said. "Along with Brocco, there was Zion Calloway, a biometrics guru and computer whiz, Tevin Shaye, a cutting-edge astrophysicist, and Nikolai, our energy genius. I handled robotics and translated the others' theories into products we sold. We were unstoppable for a time, until Zion, Nikolai, and Tevin each decided they should lead the company, which led to a wave of infighting. Brocco helped me keep the peace, though it grew too much for him, and he left. That triggered more fighting until Zion quit. Nikolai drove Tevin out a few months later, then eventually managed to get rid of me as well."

"So, we're going to find this Brocco guy?"

"I don't know where he is, though."

"You said he used to be your best friend."

Flickers of the past, of arguments that no longer held meaning, went through my mind. Zion had been twisted by his faith, his father, and his hubris, having been raised in a wealthy but restrictive household, so he rarely listened to reason. Tevin hadn't been the most astute when it came to human relationships, but after Zion left, he and Nikolai fought for control, using board members like weapons until he abruptly sold the software he'd made, cashed in his share, and left. We hadn't wanted him to sell, though at that point, we were barely functioning as a team. Nikolai thought he'd "won" the company, which led to arguments between him and me that lasted until he convinced the other board members to fire me.

"When someone with his abilities doesn't want to be found, he isn't," I said. "But the last I heard, he'd moved to Kansas somewhere."

"Would the others in your Gang of Five know where?" Monroe asked.

"As far as I'm aware, none of us have talked to each other in years."

The night had settled around us.

I opened the car door and leaned out. "We're leaving."

Raven got in without looking at me.

At my direction, Valor pulled onto the road and drove south. "When I tell you, pull over so Raven and I can get out, then find somewhere safe to wait. As soon as we return to the road, come get us."

"You want me to go with you?" Raven asked.

"I could use your help." I grabbed a wire interface from my bag, then glanced through the windshield. "Pull over here."

"In the middle of nowhere?" Valor asked, though she did as I instructed.

Raven and I got out, and Valor drove off.

Perpendicular to the road, one-hundred-foot-tall transmission towers, spaced 1,500 feet apart, marched into the distance to the east and west. Wheat fields pushed against the road to either side of us, seemingly covering every bit of available land, with the exception of the road itself—and the ground under the towers, which was blanketed with grass.

In the silence that descended, I almost felt peaceful. The lack of humanity allowed the Milky Way to shine in its frozen glory above us, countless stars blinking from the distant past.

I led Raven away from the road.

We walked under the nearest transmission tower, the hum from the electricity arching over our heads the only sound other than our footsteps in the grass. We walked until we were halfway to the next tower when I stopped. "This is as good of a place as any."

"For what?"

"Remember the map at the stadium? It not only showed the nodes but the trunk lines that ran between them. To find Brocco—"

"We're going to see him?" she asked with an excitement I hadn't heard in some time.

"I need his address, but I can't risk a normal connection, or The Agency's spiders would find us. This is the next best thing."

"Out *here*?"

I grinned. "Like I've told you girls, don't assume anything."

My words made her turn guarded. It took a moment to understand why. She was worried about what we would find at the end of this journey.

"I don't know what kind of condition Talia will be in when we find her—"

"Don't," she said.

"I'm just trying to prepare you."

"Are you going to kill Mina? You know we'll face her."

"I'll decide when the time comes."

"We need a plan," Raven said. When I didn't respond,

she added, "She'll be with Talia, if she's alive, and she'll want to come with us. We can't let her. She'll betray us again."

I didn't have a response.

I knelt in the center of the field, removed my ion blade, and triggered it, the faint blade bright in the near-total darkness. Moving quickly, I made a U-shaped cut in the earth, then grabbed the grass and pulled it back to reveal a patch of moist dirt underneath. "Help me."

Together we scooped out handfuls of dirt.

Raven felt it first: a buried pipe, fourteen inches in diameter. We removed more dirt to expose the pipe, which was made of a composite material similar to cast iron but more durable.

"This line connects to the nodes?" she asked.

I nodded. "This runs from Kansas City to Denver. The Agency buried their dedicated trunks here because utilities lease the land and require the ground to be free of interference. As a result, there's virtually no risk someone might sever a conduit or even touch this land." I activated my ion blade again and cut a six-by-six-inch hole in the pipe, making sure I didn't cut too deep. Satisfied, I removed the section of pipe to reveal multiple cables: fiber optic, wire, and several large water lines, the water lines being the best conduits for data flow. "Terabytes of information needed to maintain The Agency's deceits run through this every minute. But we can use this to find what we need without them knowing."

I reached into the pipe and focused on the water line that rested on top. I cut a small hole in the black-plastic line, angling my ion blade so I could refit the cover when I was done with my search. When I finished with the cut, I removed the piece I'd created—and brilliant light burst forth, temporarily blinding us. We both looked away until our eyes adjusted; when they did, we both inspected the line. Streaking filaments of light nearly filled the water I'd revealed, the hair-width streaks shooting past in furious, random patterns so fast they were nearly solid, appearing to be rapidly shifting lines of light.

Lies being told in mesmerizing illumination.

The light made us both nervous; I wanted to flee, and from Raven's expression, so did she. But we had a job to do.

Nestled against the right side was a secondary cable, a solid line of light.

I removed my wire interface from my pocket, unraveled it, and slipped the curved end under my cap to my implant. Then I took the other end, which was just a raw metal wire, and slipped it into the water-filled line. I tried to avoid touching the water but couldn't, my fingers distorting the signals that had been shooting past, tiny bits of dirt floating down, causing more distortion. I wasn't sure if it would be bad enough that The Agency's IT group would send a team to inspect the trunk. I slid the end of the wire into the side cable—and my lenses came to life, receiving random bits of data, partial messages, and coded sequences.

"We should hurry," Raven said.

I nodded. The light I'd exposed could probably be seen for miles.

I brought up a software program I'd used countless times for diagnostic work; with it, I created a temporary IP address, accessed the software's search-engine feature, and sent out a request for data on Brocco. The side cable had so much data streaming back and forth, I was able to add my search request to other data. Then waited.

Raven nervously picked the dirt from her leather glove.

Data flashed on my lenses, but it wasn't enough, just an echo of his name. I then sent out a blast search request to every county in the state. Seconds later, responses scrolled down my vision. An address appeared. It had to be it.

I disconnected and replaced both covers. We carefully filled the hole with the dirt we'd displaced, then settled the grass over top of it. Unless someone came looking—which they might—there was a chance the grass would regrow, and the remaining bits of dirt would wash away before anyone noticed what we did.

We hurried to the street. Before we reached it, Valor pulled up. We got in, and she drove off. "What the hell did you find out there?"

I smiled grimly. "Our destination."

CHAPTER TWENTY-SIX

Sunlight greeted me when I opened my eyes. I'd slept longer than I'd realized.

Farms rolled past, their equipment moving purposefully through corn fields. The combines were automated, computers steering them down exacted paths cutting down the wheat and feeding the harvesters, which gathered and bundled the stalks, while other, smaller machines cleaned up behind. On another farm, tall robots herded cows into pastures while wider robots fed pigs in large pens. Though I couldn't make out their details, I suspected both were part of the line of agriculture robots my company used to manufacture.

The sun rose higher in the sky, searing the rest of the grogginess from my mind.

I was hungry and anxious, sensations that were normal these days.

Valor drove with Raven beside her, both alert to the point of being fidgety, Valor's tapping distracted as she constantly scanned the view before us. Monroe, on the other hand, was still as he slept beside me. Though he was unconscious, his battle-hardened muscles gave him an air of danger.

None of them knew I was awake. I hesitated to alert them, welcoming the time alone.

I accessed my implant's memory and brought up Mina's old messages, looking for clues as the sun rose higher. In light of her announcement, it seemed she had been trying to tell me for a while that Talia was alive. Or maybe I was just a foolish father who was letting his enemies manipulate him.

I closed the messages and straightened. "Where are we?"

Valor glanced back, startled I was awake. "State Road 77, heading north. We're almost at the Nebraska border."

"We're pretty close to Marysville," Raven added.

She sounded guarded. As she'd revealed last night under the transmission towers, she didn't know if she could trust me—and this journey had resurfaced emotions she'd suppressed.

"Any excitement the last few hours?" I asked.

"The interstate was the highlight," Valor said. We'd had to cross I-70, so we'd taken a road that drove under the guarded highway. As The Agency was focusing on the interstate, and we couldn't see what might be monitoring the area, we'd taken a risk driving under the interstate, but no one chased us. We'd cheered after a few minutes, the only levity we'd shared.

Monroe straightened beside me. "How much farther?"

"Twenty minutes," Raven said.

We passed through a one-light town, the area seemingly untouched from the modern manipulations gripping this country, though I didn't know for sure. I suspected The Agency's efforts had reached even here.

Monroe distributed power bars to us. They tasted like chocolate-flavored paper, but they were the first food I'd had in two days. He also produced small water bottles, which highlighted how unprepared I'd been.

We had a little over three days before the rebels took out the nodes. Three days to find Talia.

The land began to undulate, though still stretched to the horizons. I searched for drones—and hoverbikes and police and anything else threatening—but didn't see any. I wouldn't be able to see Kieran's 3D tech from inside a moving vehicle, though I didn't think it had been deployed this far. Yet.

Valor let off the gas. Up ahead, the town of Marysville appeared. "What now?"

"Keep going."

We passed small brick buildings as Valor drove us into town. She slowed at the first major intersection, another state road cutting across our path, and glanced at me via the rearview mirror. "Which way?"

Two-story buildings, many bunched together like children clinging to each other for warmth, clustered along the state road, which was probably the equivalent of this town's Main Street. Straight ahead, the street was brick, the blocks worn and chipped. "Take a right."

The town, much larger than the others we'd driven through, had old buildings that held repair shops, banks, government offices, and other organizations. It all looked typical, ordinary, but the more I stared, the less normal it felt.

"Where is everyone?" Raven asked.

There were no cars on the road and few people on the sidewalks. I spotted a wiry woman and a bald, older man who avoided each other's gazes, the man nearly pressing himself against the storefront of a laundromat as the woman walked past. A thin male, possibly a teenager, dashed to his car with a jacket draped over his head. The local sheriff, though, sat in his squad car at the next intersection, closely watching our car as we drove past.

To hide my face, I pretended to sneeze as we passed. I grabbed the shirt I'd used earlier, which was a good thing, as I spotted a camera next to the stoplight.

"What happened here?" Raven asked, shielding her appearance as well.

"Doesn't look like there was violence," Monroe said.

"I think *we* happened," I said. A glimmer of silver hair caught my eye, and I whipped my head to the right. It was an Agent, Britt—but she wasn't in the town. She was on a vid screen playing inside a near-empty bar.

"Raven, can you tune into that broadcast?"

In seconds, she had the program playing on Jex's tablet. "Mr. Quintero wants people to question Washington," Britt stated to an unseen reporter. "That's how he gets power, by fabricating stories to scare people."

I only half-listened as Britt continued her falsehoods about me, my eyes taking in the corner stores and family restaurants that glided past. I'd planned to look for Brocco's influence in the town; instead, I saw only my own.

We passed by a house where people were gathered, their body language stiff. As we did, someone jerked the shade down. Hiding the meeting.

Raven turned off the broadcast.

"Think it's safe to be here?" Monroe asked me.

"We've passed four cameras so far," I said, holding the shirt to my face. "My system can access all of them, linking each to the national network the various law enforcement agencies use, including The Agency."

"Is there a way to turn off your system?"

"It would take a team of programmers. I wove the software into every surveillance system in this country, so any one of them could act as the host for my network."

"How many systems are there?"

"Over two hundred, and my software has multiple ways to defend itself."

"But you can take it down."

"Not easily, and police organizations across the country would unleash teams of forensic programmers to try to rebuild it." I hesitated, then added, "Just severing my network isn't enough. Each camera in town could be tied to a different surveillance system. To truly be safe, we'd have to disable my network, then each individual camera here."

Valor turned off the main street and followed Raven's directions to the address I'd given. The road turned from brick to faded asphalt, the houses a series of small, dated ranches set back from the road. After a few minutes, Valor pulled over before a whitewashed ranch with a one-car garage, the last house on the street.

I frowned. "This isn't what I expected."

"It's not the place," Valor said. "The numbers stop at 939. The address you gave was 3408."

The street ended ahead of us, three metal posts holding a faded, red-and-white striped board that blocked the road. Past it, brush, weeds, and a smattering of trees descended to a tiny creek. "Maybe the numbers go the other way," I said.

Valor made a U-turn and started back the way we came. "It was probably a trap."

Monroe agreed. "Your friend could've hidden a camera here to track anyone who came looking for him."

"I'm getting us the hell out of this creepy town."

I scanned the houses we passed, searching the numbers. They continued to run downward.

"Wait," Raven said almost reluctantly. She'd grabbed her pad and was staring at it. "Two miles north, there's a road with a similar name. I don't see any addresses, but that could be it."

Fifteen minutes later, I clenched my fist as Valor pulled onto what seemed to be an abandoned road, with vegetation crowding in on either side. The more we traversed the road, the more my hopes sank.

Then I saw it: a dirt road disappearing into the forest. It was barely a road, more like a wide trail. There was no number, no mailbox, nothing. But it had to be our destination.

Raven pointed out the road.

"Oh great," Valor said as she turned in.

The forest pressed in on either side of our SUV as we braved the road, branches and brush scratching at our doors.

"Maybe Brocco's become a hermit," Raven said.

A meadow became visible in the distance. When we reached it, Valor stopped at the edge of the forest. "You really want to go here?"

A long house, clad in faded, brown-painted wood trim, stood before us, perched on land that descended from a ridge toward a narrow lake. A walkway extended from the ridgeline to the front door, which I realized was located on the second level of the structure.

No one was visible, but that didn't ease our wariness. Maybe it was the location, or the drawn curtains, or that I'd put my hopes on a man I hadn't seen in years.

"Go ahead and park," I told her. "We need his help."

Monroe leaned against the window. "There's a laser sensor. We continue forward, it'll trigger an alarm. It's not even hidden well."

Which meant there were probably others we'd already tripped, though I didn't tell them. Instead, I nodded to Valor, who did as I instructed.

After she turned off the car, we got out—she and Monroe drew their weapons—and approached the front door. "I don't like this," she hissed. I knocked, then called Brocco's name. When no one answered, I waved to Raven, who squatted down and picked the lock.

"This isn't right," Valor said. "We're breaking into the man's house."

"Which I ordinarily wouldn't do." When Raven stood, I turned the knob and stepped inside.

With the curtains drawn, the interior was cool, almost cold.

As my eyes adjusted to the dim light, I led my group past a formal living room area that contained a dust-covered couch, grand piano, and old-style bar and entered the kitchen. Discarded pizza boxes and empty delivery bags covered the black countertops, while dishes crammed the sink. Past the kitchen was an eat-in area—the table half-covered under stacks of files—an open area with a couch, vid screen, and fireplace, and large windows that looked out onto the lake. A hallway to the side led to a series of bedrooms, while a wide staircase directly ahead angled down to the lower level.

I started for the stairs.

Valor snatched my arm. "You sure this is a good idea?" she whispered.

"Little late for that," Raven said.

"Dray," Monroe said. "How do you know he doesn't work

for the enemy?"

"Put your guns away," I said quietly. After they reluctantly did, I led them down the stairs.

We found ourselves in a small hallway with a wall to our right, double doors ahead, and a couple of doors to the left, one leading to a bathroom.

Sounds came from behind the double doors.

Taking a deep breath, I opened the doors and walked through the doorway.

Windows and a sliding glass walkout directly ahead revealed a patio and steps leading to the lake, along with two generators off to one side. What caught my eye, however, was the room itself. Wood-paneled cabinets had been placed on the floor to the right of the double doors and connected together to create a kind of enclosed work area, the cabinet tops covered with touchscreen displays, electronic components and sensors, cables, papers, and a mishmash of other objects. The wall past the cabinets held a series of floor-to-ceiling shelving, mostly covered with pictures and collectible transistor radios. More electronics occupied the left side of the room, though they appeared to be cast aside.

A figure stood up from behind one of the large touchscreen displays. Brocco. He hadn't aged well, as his face was gaunt. Or maybe it was the lighting. Still, relief washed over me as I took in my old friend.

His eyes flickered in wonder and a hint of old happiness. Then his face hardened.

Before I could speak, he touched something on his display. The most horrific sound I'd ever heard suddenly assaulted us, a high-pitched, throbbing sound that made my bones vibrate and pain flood my body. I covered my ears, which felt like they'd started bleeding, but it didn't help. Behind me, Raven and Valor cried out. I could barely move from the sound; I managed to look back at the others with a mighty effort. Valor looked like she was in mid-collapse, her body locked. Raven grimaced as she plugged her ears, while Monroe gripped his head, his back arched.

I started the long effort of turning my head back to look at Brocco, but before I could, he appeared in my vision, walking toward Monroe. Brocco wore a high-collared shirt, burgundy red, with black slacks and shiny shoes. He carried a dispenser that looked like some sort of nail gun. He approached Monroe and triggered the dispenser; a substance that looked like mercury shot out and coated the pistol in Monroe's holster, then hardened, pinning the weapon in place. As he turned back, I noticed large, foam-like pieces in Brocco's ears. He returned to the console, hit a button—

And the sound stopped.

Valor collapsed. Monroe clawed at his pistol but couldn't retrieve it, then went for Valor's, but I waved him back. Raven went to me. "You okay?"

My ears rang so much I was surprised I could hear her. I nodded. "You?"

"You need to leave," Brocco said.

I straightened. "You just assaulted us."

"You broke in. Armed! And don't act innocent. I've watched you. You're starting a war."

I didn't look at Raven. "Hoping to stop one, actually."

"Right. With someone like him with you." He jabbed a thumb at Monroe, then stepped forward to face him. "I see the infrareds. Where did you serve?"

"Marine Raiders. Did a stint with the SEALs, too."

Brocco turned back to me. "You're not just running around with modified soldiers. I've heard the rumors on the airwaves. You're calling up your fellow terrorists to fight."

I frowned. "What rumors?"

"Militias have been using CB radio bands, calling for citizens to use their 'god given right' to rise up. They and others are arming themselves in *your* name, getting ready to come out of their little holes and swarm government buildings and other places they think they can take over. I've also caught reports of disappearing families and weird call signs."

I'd heard of two military posts being used by groups

in the southwest, but I didn't know what they were doing. Using posts was dangerous. They were layered with active and passive surveillance; the rebels might not know they were being monitored. As far as the other things Brocco claimed, I didn't have a clue. "You think I'm responsible for all of that?"

"You must know about them. Isn't that what all of this is?" he asked with a flutter of his hand. "Should I salute to your new government?"

I didn't answer, and he seemed to tire of his game, his posture sagging. "How did you find me?"

"You were listed in the county database, an old registration for an ordinance change."

He sat, nearly dropping out of sight behind his console. "Now that I know, I'll erase the record. You can leave."

"I need your help."

Though my ears continued to ring, I heard his scoff. "You've done enough, I'd say."

"It's for Talia."

He stood, his expression turning sorrowful. "What did you let happen?"

"The Agency killed her. Or so I thought. They shot her. There's a chance she's alive," I said, while behind me, I felt Raven turn away.

His eyes flickered to her, then me. "I don't want to hear your sob story. The look on Raven's face says it all. Hi, dear. Good to see you after all these years, though I wish it was under different circumstances."

He and the other Gang of Five had spoiled my girls, Raven and then Talia bouncing between the offices when they were young. When we'd all been family. "The world isn't like you think. Everyone is being lied to."

"I watched your broadcast. Both, in fact. I did some digging. Your claims are correct. But what did that get you? Always had to be right."

This wasn't going the way I'd planned. His guard was up. Guard, hell, a massive wall. "Why are you here?" I asked.

"I retired, remember? I'm minding my own business—"

"In the center of the country?"

"The land was cheap, and I could be near people without being bothered by them."

"No, you're here to keep an eye on everyone. It's what you used to do at board meetings, watching everyone."

"I was listening. You should've done more of that."

Raven spoke up. "You know about the implants, don't you? You're blocking them."

Her implant was still shielded, as were the others', but from Brocco's reaction, I knew she'd guessed correctly.

He sighed. "Took longer than I care to admit to find the correct frequency. That Agency of yours watched me do it, didn't they? That's why I built the sound defense I used against you. Still, they'll come after me, maybe quicker now that you're here."

"I need your help," I said again.

"I don't care. You shouldn't have gotten your kids into this." He shook a finger. "This is the first time you've talked to me since I left."

"I called a number of times. You never called me back."

He waved away my words.

"Enough of this," I said. "I want your equipment—and I don't mean these props you've set out. Blocking our feeds takes serious equipment." It's what I was betting on.

"The same goes for the sound you blasted us with," Monroe said, still picking at the hardened metal that encapsulated his pistol.

"I know what you're capable of. I helped you build most of your prototypes." I glanced at Raven, who nodded toward the built-in shelves. "I bet it's in there, too."

Brocco straightened in indignation, then sighed. "You always were a pain in the ass."

He hit a button, and the shelving moved aside to reveal stacks of communication equipment, including liquicore-driven bandwidth manipulators, satellite relays, quantum encryption decoders, and stealth subhertz receptors. I would've been concerned that Brocco's basement was, in fact, an Agency node—the equipment was powerful enough—but there weren't any datatanks, and the map hadn't shown any nodes in this area.

Monroe let out a low whistle, which made Brocco fidget.

"Why do you look worried?" Valor asked him.

It hit me. "You stole all of this from our company." Brocco started to justify himself, but I held up my hand. "It's not my company anymore, either. I got fired."

"Nikolai?" Brocco asked. When I nodded, he actually smiled. "The guy was so pompous."

With Brocco's help, I quickly became familiar with the equipment. He thawed as he spoke, whether because I was dependent on him or that I got fired, I wasn't sure. I recognized his software; it was a system he had developed for us, although upgraded and modified. "You can hook into The Agency's network, can't you?" I asked. "If you're half the scientist I remember, you've already gotten in."

"That isn't a good idea."

"We didn't ask," Valor said, sitting on one of the cabinets where she'd cleared off a space. Monroe stood by the sliding glass door, watching the lake and surrounding area.

"The Agency's network runs on multiple frequencies simultaneously, which makes it near impossible to crack," I pushed. "But not for you. And it has a flaw. To maintain their lies, they don't just transmit. They have to receive."

He dropped his gaze, a wry grin twisting the corner of his mouth. "Fine." As I watched, he initiated the decoder, ran multi-hertz broadcasts, and initiated a software I hadn't seen before. Within minutes, we were logged into The Agency's system.

Raven stepped forward. "My god."

Hundreds of thousands of lines of data, each linking to an individual, scrolled up the screen. After moving Brocco out of the way, I searched for Talia, for Mina, for any information on either of them. But I couldn't find a thing.

Trying to avoid my growing despair, I called Brocco over. "Here, I have a picture of Talia. Load it in every system you can hook into." I forwarded him the digital picture using an anonymous email I'd set up a month ago. I sent him Mina's picture as well.

Together, he and I searched the massive, underground storage farms The Agency saved of people's links for any image since the day Talia was shot, my fingertips becoming numb from pounding on the touchscreen's keyboard.

We got a number of hits on Mina, though most were from her recent broadcast. When we screened those out of our search, the number of hits dropped to one: of her boarding a plane in San Francisco over a month ago, accompanied by a man and woman I didn't recognize. We took screenshots of the couple and processed them, but other than a partial hit at a gas station outside of Dallas a week later, we couldn't find them.

Nothing came up for Talia. Not one goddamn thing.

"How can there be nothing?" I asked in frustration. "Kieran and his team saw Mina and Talia at Free Isle—and must've seen them when they transported them to wherever they took them. If nothing else, Mina should have images. She never would've left Talia's side."

"They don't save Agents' memories," Brocco said.

"Why the hell not?"

Monroe spoke up. "The Agency wouldn't keep proof of their crimes."

My hopes were dwindling. "What about Mina?"

"Maybe her memories are locked," Brocco said.

I almost lashed out at him, then considered. She could've seen things The Agency wouldn't want recorded. That would make her exempt from their archives—which meant unless she looked at Talia in real time, my daughter wouldn't appear in our search.

I had to come up with something else. "Can you trace calls?" I asked Brocco.

He could, so we traced Mina's calls, Raven tense beside me, a mixture of anxiety and distrust and hurt. Yet nothing came up: not with the phone companies, not the third-party transmitters, nor the satellite relay companies.

"She either used a burner phone, or it was some sort of government phone with special software," Brocco said.

I turned on him. "How come you can't find her? You're the best at this shit. This is my daughter I'm looking for."

He held up his hands, his face thinner than before. "I tried. You can keep searching, though." He left through the double doors, his voice floating toward me as he started up the stairs. "Always told you kids would warp you."

CHAPTER TWENTY-SEVEN

I lay in one of the guest beds that evening, a thin sheet draping my body, exhausted—but couldn't sleep.

I'd used Brocco's equipment for hours last night, doing everything I could to find Talia. I'd focused on Texas, using Mina's cryptic clue, even searching for facilities with barbed wire. When I filtered "barbed wire" with "medical facility", I came up empty. If I removed "medical", the search engine listed over four hundred locations, which was nearly as bad as none at all. We couldn't research even a fraction of those hits before our teams attacked the nodes.

Adding a filter for farms with the medical search yielded nothing.

Raven and Valor helped by searching for Talia in various ways using Brocco's other equipment—searching patterns in medical communications, abnormal police reports, recorded emergencies—both keeping their thoughts to themselves. Monroe had left, I assumed to insure the house was secure, not even returning to eat the leftovers Brocco set out after sunset.

Monroe wasn't the only one to stay away. Brocco avoided us all evening.

He'd been furious with me years ago when I created the software linking the country's camera systems. I'd thought he was jealous, as communications was his field. Now I wasn't sure. The way he'd acted then, the way he acted today, wasn't jealousy.

Or pettiness. He seemed fearful.

If only I'd had that same fear. I never saw the risks my network posed, never ran a single negative scenario through my head, too seduced by the benefits and too trusting in the police to think anyone would warp what I'd created.

I had to get over myself and figure out how to find Talia. I worried she truly was dead. It would explain why we couldn't find her.

If she was dead, Mina had lied to me. And I'd lied to myself.

I wanted to call Anya to hear her voice, confide in her, but it would've risked exposing her to The Agency's surveillance.

I climbed out of bed and went to the window, which revealed a large deck that extended the length of the house, the lake visible past it in the faint moonlight.

I spotted Monroe making his way across the deck, stopping occasionally as he searched for threats. His shadow became more pronounced, which I realized was from an increase in ambient light. Someone was in the broadcast room beneath him, though they'd kept most of the lights off.

I left my room and returned to the basement.

Raven stood before a pair of monitors, the screens the only source of light. She looked small and alone, worry creasing her face, her hair pulled back in a haphazard ponytail.

My memory of when Talia had tried to entice her into playing a trivia game after Adem's death resurfaced. A week after the incident, I was working on a prototype of a lightweight bicycle when Raven arrived home from softball practice. Minutes after she disappeared inside, I heard yelling.

I followed the voices to Raven's room, where she accused Talia of "breaking" the robo-butler, pieces of the robot strewn across her hardwood floor. "You ruined him," Raven yelled, her hair slipping from her ponytail.

"I was looking for his voicebox. I wanted him to speak in funny accents. Then maybe you'd play with me again."

"He's not yours."

"At least he talks to me. Mom won't snap, Dad tinkers, and you avoid me."

"That doesn't give you the right to destroy my stuff."

"Blinky is mine, too!"

"The butler? He doesn't have a name—and giving him one doesn't make him yours."

I entered the room, told them how much they meant to me, and hugged them, but a rift had formed, one I couldn't fix.

Watching Raven now, I wondered how many of her memories haunted her as mine did me.

"Hey."

She lifted her head. "Hi."

"You should be sleeping."

She'd turned on Brocco's hidden equipment, initiated the decoder, and hooked back into The Agency's network. Data scrolled up the screen, bands of activity mocking me in my failures.

"It's disturbing," she said. "I could spy into these people's lives if I wanted."

"Is that why you're down here?"

"I can't believe not a single doctor or nurse or anyone has seen Talia."

"The Agency must be hiding her. A wounded girl in one of their facilities would prompt a lot of questions."

"How about if we tracked medical deliveries made in Texas? The Agency would need supplies to care for Talia: needles and IV bags and stuff. Maybe the data could lead us to her."

I started to search. I wasn't a great hacker, but I was able to access the logistics programs of the major delivery firms. Raven and I spent hours tracking delivery routes and trying to match them with medical purchases, focusing on specific purchase items—small-sized needles, kid-sized gowns, and type O-positive blood deliveries—but came up empty.

We were so engrossed we didn't hear Brocco come in, wearing a blue-and-purple striped silk robe over old-style pajamas and carrying a small bowl. "Thought you'd be down here. Raven, this is a pleasant surprise." He sat on a nearby counter. "Want to explain what you two are doing?"

Raven gave me a look of warning. "Not really," I said as I leaned back and stretched. Outside, the sky began to brighten.

"I can't help if you don't get me up to speed."

"You want to help now?"

"Since you don't take a hint, I figured the sooner I do, the sooner you leave."

Raven gave me another look, but I relented.

Brocco ate pistachios as I talked. When I finished, he set the bowl aside. "It wasn't fair to say kids 'warp' you. I know you want to make the world a better place—unlike Zion, who just bitched about crowds and population numbers. But Adem's death changed you, Dray. You became more stubborn. Less collaborative. Less you…though you became so high and mighty about saving everyone, it wasn't a completely bad thing."

"Is that supposed to be a compliment?" I asked as Raven stiffened beside me.

"Have you followed deliveries purchased directly by The Agency?"

Raven spoke up. "They're a division of the federal government, so any purchases would be lumped in with other agencies."

"Not necessarily. Here, step aside."

Over the course of the next hour, he worked his keyboard, finding The Agency's federal purchase codes, then searched for medical purchases. With his help, we discovered a number of purchases for children, even including dinosaur-themed band-aids, but every delivery went to regional warehouses. Though he tried, he couldn't find any online records that revealed when and where The Agency shipped supplies from Texas-area warehouses.

As hopelessness seeped in, he swiveled to a screen behind us and began to type. "Confession time. Seeing you made everything in your broadcast real. And you bring up some bad memories. That's for another time, though. I want to show you something. It's a program I created. Didn't think it would help with your girl, but it does. Shocked you didn't think of it, actually."

He brought up a program that showed an outline of the country, but instead of showing implant feed, it displayed larger dots with edges streaking outward, like tiny stars.

"I've never met an Agent, but I've seen them. They have multiple implants connected to different networks. My program combines that data to locate each recipient." He watched us for a reaction. "You're looking at the location of every Agent in the country."

Raven looked as stunned as I felt. This was invaluable information. None were close to our location, thank god, the closest being three in Kansas City. A large cluster was located in Denver, which didn't surprise me. There were more on the West Coast, a massive cluster around Washington D.C., and other Agents across the country.

"There are hundreds of them," Raven breathed.

I hadn't realized how many there were. We couldn't defeat them all.

Brocco clapped his hands together. "This is the first time in ages I out-programmed you. It feels good. Now you know the jealousy we felt."

I didn't feel anything other than despair—and a little confusion. "How can this help us with Talia?"

He typed a command into the console, and names appeared beside every tiny star. "You know which Agent shot her, right? They would know if she's still alive. You need to confront whoever that was."

CHAPTER TWENTY-EIGHT

Raven clenched her fists as if she was going to launch herself at Brocco. "You want us to confront *him*?"

Brocco appeared surprised by her reaction. "The Agent—I assume it's a he from your reaction—can tell you where Talia is."

As she trembled, Brocco looked at me—and the force of his words hit me. Facing the man responsible for Talia's death and for nearly killing me. I still felt his six-foot-plus frame pinning me down, his hands around my throat.

I forced the words out. "Kieran. That's his name."

Brocco typed on the old-style keyboard.

On the second monitor, one of the stars brightened, and Kieran's name appeared next to it. The view zoomed in: first on Texas, then on Dallas, Kieran's star in the center of the screen, the black-and-white map expanding to a house north of downtown. An address appeared, the information burning into my mind, along with the schematic of the large, story-and-a-half house.

"He's your best chance," Brocco said. "If your daughter is alive, he should know."

My mind spun with anguish, regret, and a doomed inevitability, only vaguely aware that dawn had broken. I looked at Raven. "We're running out of time."

"Dad."

I didn't say it—I'd given Brocco too much—but from her expression, she knew. Less than two and a half days until the node attack. Fifty-odd hours to find Kieran, make him talk, and get to Talia.

* * *

Valor and Monroe went full guard mode when they saw Raven and me, nearly attacking Brocco before I pulled them back. My announcement that we were leaving—and his promise to free Monroe's weapon—were the only things that placated them.

Brocco followed us out, though it seemed more to make sure we left than to see us off.

I didn't thank him for his help. Didn't have the energy.

As Valor drove us away, she and Monroe took the news about us going to Kieran better than Raven had, but not by much. "You want to go to an Agent's house? And confront him?" Valor asked. When I nodded, she didn't say a word, but I saw how hard she gripped the steering wheel.

"We can't," Raven spat. "I won't do it."

Good. I didn't want her near him. My need to stop her from continuing on this journey was magnified by the fear of him capturing her. "You should stay here. Brocco will protect you."

Valor slowed the car, though Raven told her to keep going before turning on me. "What about the war? Our friends?"

"Go meet up with them—or help those heading to Kansas City. There are two nodes there. I'm sure they'd welcome the help."

"You're not fighting Kieran alone. You nearly died the last time."

That wasn't her only fear. Kieran had violated her when we had tried to escape L.A., forcing an implant into her skull against her wishes.

I leaned toward Valor. "Look for a truck or car parked on one of these farms."

"To dump the SUV?" Monroe asked from beside her.

"No. I want you two to take Raven to Jex."

Raven grabbed my arm. "Are you really going to face Kieran just because of what Mina said? She chose a hologram over us. How can you believe *anything* she says?"

"I've wondered how Talia could possibly be alive. Then I remembered the nanobots that helped me when I was stabbed. Maybe somehow they helped her."

"Dad, they shot her in the chest. She..."

Raven didn't finish her thought. Didn't need to.

* * *

We continued to argue, or Raven did, arguments chased and tears shed. Each one cut me, for they cut her. Just the thought of the pain she carried, of what facing Kieran would do to her, nearly turned me away from my path.

I couldn't, though.

I should've known he was my journey. I'd hoped I was done with him.

I'd fooled myself.

Memories came quick: Kieran approaching me at City Park; confronting us when we tried to flee L.A. and my failed efforts to stop him from ramming an implant into the hole in Raven's temple; fighting him above the San Francisco skyline; finally defeating him and ripping out his primary implant. Yet I hadn't defeated him. If Mina was right, he'd won before he'd even entered the node.

Other memories came: Talia leading us through the alleys of Free Isle with a confidence that hinted at the woman she would've become. Another, years earlier, when I'd taken her and Raven to see a musical at the Walt Disney Concert Hall. I hadn't been sure if either would enjoy the show, and for much of it, Talia had typed at something using her datarings. When the show ended, she sent me what she'd worked on: she'd figured out the algorithms the architects had used to design the hall and told me which seats I should buy next time for optimal sound.

The memory that hurt the most was the light leaving her eyes. It cycled so many times in my mind, each version laced with a desperate hope that I might have been wrong and she actually survived, that I no longer knew if they were memories or fantasies.

What wasn't a fantasy was Kieran's howl when I'd taken

his implant. Horrified. Angry. Primal.

His vengeance would be out of control.

The only thing that had saved me was hiding from him.

* * *

We were tense when we reached I-70. Agency reconnaissance and inspection drones dotted the air, though as we drove under the interstate, we didn't seem to trigger any notice. Still, we remained on alert through the rest of the state.

Our trip through Oklahoma was uneventful, though longer than normal, as we avoided every major city and highway, nearly always staying under the speed limit. As we traveled, the land gradually surrendered wheat fields to hills, brush, farms, homes, and forests, anonymous lives being lived that I hoped our efforts would save.

We seemed to have the state highway, which had dropped to two lanes, to ourselves.

Mile marker 50 passed on my right. Almost to Texas.

"What're you doing?" Valor asked, breaking the silence.

Raven said, "Texting Jex."

Both Monroe and I leaned forward. "How?" I asked.

"We set up a private account. It's fine."

"Sever the connection," Monroe said.

She shot him a glare. "Nearly everyone is in position, though the teams in the Northeast are still traveling. There's just under forty hours left. Everyone's OK. Anya and Garly say 'Hi,' by the way."

He glared back until she removed her datarings, then raised his eyebrows. "Hey, let me see your hand."

She hesitated, then removed her glove and twisted in her seat so he could inspect it.

He held her modified hand gently. "They installed a nine-ringed magnetic pin, didn't they? That's a great weapon."

She carefully wiggled her finger-shaped plasma cores. "Seriously?"

"Did Garly show you how to fire it?"

"Yeah, by flexing my finger."

"The cores are designed to work in different ways. If you fire quickly, you can shoot up to three rounds per second. But if you hold in the trigger, when you release it, the cores will fire a larger blast."

Her face brightened for the first time in hours. Maybe days. She settled back in her seat; from the reflection in the side mirror, I could see her moving her metallic fingers.

Monroe settled back as well—then suddenly whipped around to look behind us. I looked as well, though the road was empty. Something must've triggered his sensors.

He glanced at me. "Grab your shields."

His face had turned granite; in that moment, I saw his Special Forces training.

I lunged over the back of the seat for Garly's duffel bag and hauled it back onto my lap, in my anxiety not bothering to turn back around to face forward. I unzipped it to find the chest plate on top, weapons underneath. Whatever Monroe had seen spooked me. I wanted to grab the chest plate, weapons, all of it, but pushed them aside and snatched one of the two hand shields. "Here," I barked, reaching behind me to hold out the shield to Raven. "Put it on."

She took it, and I removed the other hand shield.

As I buckled it on, a blur out the rear window caught my eye, the object slowing just enough for me to note a metallic body and legs before it leapt into the air, disappearing from view—

And slammed onto the roof of our SUV.

As Raven cried out and Valor swerved into the next lane, claws punctured the roof. Three sets, each set a cluster of four reinforced-metal claws, two angled toward the back and one above Monroe's head. A fourth set slammed into the roof above Valor's headrest and swiped across the width of the car in a shriek of metal. The next moment, the roof peeled back like the cover of a sardine can, wind rushing in—then tore away from the SUV and landed in the road, turning our vehicle into a quasi-convertible.

The severed piece of roof flipped back as it landed in the

roadway to reveal the thing that had attacked us: a weaponized robot. It was the size and shape of a Rottweiler, its jaws stronger, metallic teeth razor-sharp. I'd never seen a robot like this but had heard rumors.

Valor floored it, the dog dropping from view as we accelerated, but a strange-looking vehicle, sections carved out of the front half like massive launch tubes, appeared a dozen car lengths behind us. The vehicle had no roof or doors, just a windshield—with Britt behind the wheel. As I watched, a dog leapt from one of the tubes, ran so fast I could barely track it and leapt into our SUV.

Monroe pulled his gun and fired not at the mouth but a spot on its chest—

And the robot snatched the gun from his hand with its teeth.

As he reached for his other pistol, the robot sank its front claws into Monroe's chest, causing him to cry out, and leapt from the vehicle, taking him with it.

Though I still had the duffel bag in my lap, I lunged for Monroe, but it happened too fast to save him. The robot spun with him as it flew backward and landed in the roadway on top of him. From the impact and the way Monroe lay sprawled, I knew the robot had killed him.

I stared in shock as Valor struggled to get us away, the wind pouring in from the sheared roof shaking the SUV.

The road curved away, the trees crowding the side of the road blocking my view of Monroe—and Britt.

A blur warned me a fraction of a second before the first robot reappeared. It landed in the rear of the SUV, crushing the rear window in the process, then lunged at me, though Valor jerked the steering wheel, causing the robot to fall short, straddling the rear seat instead. Its front claws knocked the chest plate away and dug at the duffel bag laying across my body as it scrambled to attack me, claws gouging the machine gun pinned inside the bag—and its head jerked forward to bite my face.

I activated the hand shield, the edge of it deflecting the

robot's head at the last instant, lethal teeth flashing as the energy deflected its attack. The robot reared back and slammed its head into my shield. Biting at it.

Through the blurriness of the shield, I made out the robot's multi-wave-detection eyes, wide snout, and diamond-edged teeth. Past its neck, a metal plate curved over its chest, extra protection for something. The body of the robot was a compact mass of wiring, energy sources, and motors trying to kill me. Though the robot wasn't heavy, from my angle, with my feet under me and back pressed against Raven's seat, I didn't have the leverage to throw it off.

The weapon redoubled its efforts to chew its way through my shield.

The hand shield warmed as it vibrated against my hand. It hadn't been designed to fend off this kind of attack.

Movement caught my eye as Raven rose up in her seat, the other shield covering her right hand, and fired her pistol left-handed at the robot but missed.

I lifted my hand shield, pushing the shield and robot upwards so she could get a better shot. The next one caused sparks. I couldn't see what she hit from my angle, but the robot jerked back. My eyes flickered down at its body and spotted the edge of a bright yellow square partly hidden by the curved metal plate. Of course. The robot had been made too compact, designed for quick attacks, and the enclosed space of the SUV worked against it. The robot's CPU, its core brain, was in its chest. Protected.

The robot lunged forward, angling down to use my shield to block Raven's gun, still straddling the back seat.

As Valor yelled at Raven to take the wheel so she could fight, I grabbed the robot's shoulder, held it as I lifted the machine's body with my shield, then twisted and shoved the robot against the passenger door, pinning it against the door with the duffel bag between us. I reached in my pocket for my ion blade, extracted it—and pain shot across my left shoulder as the robot's right leg slipped under my shield and sliced me, claws scraping bone. Fighting the pain, I activated my ion blade and plunged the blade into its chest just under the metal plate.

Orange light flashed, then the robot stilled.

"Watch out," Valor shouted.

There was a thud, and the SUV tilted momentarily as the second robot dog landed in the SUV, its front paws on either side of the headrest where Monroe had sat minutes ago.

I was vulnerable, twisted on my side and entangled with the robot I'd disabled, its claws still embedded in my shoulder, my back to the second robot.

With a cry, Raven leapt from her seat, the wind shoving her hair forward and into her face as she threw herself at the robot. At virtually the same time, there was a crunch of metal, and the SUV shuttered as something slammed into the front passenger's door. A third robot. Bigger than the first two, so it was slower but just as lethal. Maybe more so. The bigger 'bot ran alongside our SUV and head-butted the door again, rocking our vehicle.

Valor was yelling, but I couldn't catch her words.

The second robot shoved Raven back. She fired twice, the shots ricocheting off the robot's body, one into the sheared edge of what was left of the car's roof, the other into the window beside me, and the robot used one of its paws to swipe the gun out of her hand, cutting her hand in the process. As she cried out, I lunged forward before the robot even reared back, yet I was almost too slow. I just caught the robot's snout with the edge of my shield before it reached Raven. My body twisted awkwardly as I strained to protect her, left shoulder throbbing.

She reacted as well, shoving forward with her shield, and together we thrust the motorized beast backward. I spotted its CPU, but my ion blade was underneath me, the blade slicing into the fake-leather seat.

"You got him?" I shouted. Behind us, Valor started shooting, probably at the robot running beside our vehicle.

Before Raven could reply, before I could pull back, the robot shifted nearly too fast to see and lunged at me. I somehow managed to block it again, the hard, curved edge of my shield catching in its mouth.

The robot began to chew at the shield. For a moment, the compressed-wave shield held. Then a spark emitted from the hand shield's glove, and a tiny piece of the shield disappeared.

The individual projectors had been designed to surge when their portion of the shield was attacked, but they couldn't maintain that level of energy, especially with the hundreds of pounds of pressure exerted by the attacking robot.

The mechanical dog-weapon dug in more, chewing at more of the shield to get to me.

There was a slam as the robot outside hit our car again.

Another spark came from my glove. Two more projectors went out.

I was pinned, ion blade out of reach, legs under me. The robot above me charged again, jaws moving rapidly.

Then Raven acted. Empty-handed, her shield seemingly forgotten, she leaned forward, grabbed the robot's head with her left hand, and shoved her right hand at it—which she'd clenched into a fist. She extended her robotic fingers—

And a burst of plasma burst from her hand, nearly blinding me.

Behind us, there was a loud crunch as the front passenger door was ripped away.

As I blinked to clear my vision, I made out the creature's head, which had melted from the heat and energy of the plasma charge. Raven had followed Monroe's instructions and unleashed a lethal blast.

Abandoning my blade, I grabbed her right wrist, pointed her fingers at the robot's CPU, and yelled, "Shoot."

She did, unleashing another blue-white bolt of plasma, and the robot collapsed on top of me, its circuits destroyed.

Valor yelled from the front seat—and the vehicle shifted as the third robot, larger and twice as thick as the other two, leapt into the front seat, rear claws scraping against the doorframe. It pivoted, climbed in farther, and reared up over me, front claws tearing at the back of the seat.

I was on my back, blade under me, weapons in the bag

beside me—but underneath the first robot. Useless.

Raven spun, rose up, her hair thrown back by the wind, and slammed her reactivated shield into the robot's head, her war cry lost in the noise.

I shoved the robot laying on me to the side, twisting in my seat and freeing myself to help Raven, when Valor suddenly shouted.

"Hold on."

She had been following a curve in the road but straightened before the road did and floored the engine. The next moment, we slammed into the railing of a bridge at an angle—

And launched into the air, the SUV's rear end rising as we began to flip and twist.

A river appeared beneath us as the world tilted. Raven flew out past my vision, Valor a fleeting shadow as well, both sailing toward the river. Though the vehicle's momentum tried to throw me as well, I was pinned in place.

The water came up fast as the SUV continued to rotate, my body finally coming free, the disabled robot and weapons bag jarred from the vehicle as I fell. I barely had time to shove my shield forward to cushion the impact before I plunged into the river.

I hit the river bottom hard, panic seizing me as the SUV landed almost at the same time beside me, its back bumper hitting the bottom—and the vehicle falling toward me. I flipped off my shield and shoved away, barely getting out from under the SUV before it settled in a swirl of cloudy water, wheels up, on the river floor.

Readouts appeared in my vision. My implant had reconnected with the network.

I yanked my cap back down over my implant, cutting the feed, then got my legs under me and swam to the surface, cresting after a couple of strokes. The river was eight or nine feet deep where I'd landed, though very wide.

I desperately scanned the area as I took in deep breaths. For the moment, it appeared I was the only one around. I feared for Raven, for Valor. Had to find them. The remaining robot was somewhere.

I needed my weapons.

Without waiting to discover where they'd landed or if they were injured, I dove under and swam to the wreckage, pushing through the green-tinted water.

When I reached the vehicle, I grabbed the edge of the rear passenger door's frame. I spotted my bag jutting out from under the crushed rear door, which remained attached to the vehicle, the window a web of glass. Relieved, I grabbed the bag's handle and pulled—but the bag wouldn't budge. Setting my feet against the muddy bottom, I strained to lift the SUV enough to get the bag. My sliced shoulder was bright with pain. But I couldn't free the bag.

Movement caught my eye, the remaining robot thrashing in the cloudy water toward me. It hadn't been designed for water, so it wasn't as fast as it was on land, but it was still damn fast.

The robot approached from downriver, having been thrown from the crash.

I rose to the surface for air, took a breath, and heard a cry. Valor stood in the river a dozen yards away, the water just to her waist. Past her, I spotted Raven. She stood near the shore, clutching one of our backpacks and grimacing in pain. Their eyes widened as the river between us churned from the robot's efforts to get to me.

The churning came closer. Twenty feet away.

I could try for shore, but my shoulder was injured, and my body felt beaten up from the crash. I had one chance. "Get out of the water," I shouted.

Without waiting for a response, I dove under and swam to the weapons bag, grabbed the zipper, and opened it. Before I could reach into the bag, the air clouded around me, warning me just in time. I spun as the robot rushed at me, mouth open and claws slashing, and activated my shield again, which made the water thrash and vibrate from the waves it emitted. The robot backed off for a second, and the force from the waves pushed me back against the side of the downed SUV, but before I could adjust to the propulsion, the robot attacked. Claws and metal teeth flashed through the water as it dug at my shield, which was weakening. I couldn't get away, though. When I tried, the robot shifted, keeping me pinned against the vehicle.

The bag lay just out of reach.

Even if the robot didn't break through my shield—though as I watched, chunks broke off—it would drown me. And I couldn't stop it.

Desperate, I brought my legs up under the robot's body and shoved it off me, the water working in my favor, then lunged for the bag. I reached it, but before I could shove my hand inside, the robot was on me again, hind leg claws sliding into my thigh. I caught the robot's teeth and front claws with my shield, struggling to keep it at bay as I slipped my free hand inside the bag.

Above me, the water started to clear as my shield weakened. A third of it was gone.

My lungs began to burn.

I felt around inside my bag. Felt the 3D printer. Binoculars. Barrel of the grenade launcher, which was pinned by the SUV.

The shield failed to block one of the robot's front clawed paws. It swiped at me and sliced at my left arm, the water slowing its attack just enough that the cuts weren't deep.

I struggled not to breathe.

My free hand closed on the bolt-emitter. Hoped it would work in the water—if not, I would die in this muddy river—and hoped Raven and Valor were safely away. As I pulled it out, my shield shorted out completely. The robot paused for the briefest moment, as if unsure what had happened, so I grabbed it by its thick throat with my gloved hand, shoved the emitter into its large chest with my other hand, and triggered the device, unleashing a blast designed to take out an Agent.

White energy filled my vision, bursting in every direction, fingers of electricity spreading out in the water, surging up over the surface, wrapping around the robot—and into my body. My muscles went rigid, my teeth aching as my jaw clenched, my back arching, the robot's metal throat burning my hand.

Then all went black.

CHAPTER TWENTY-NINE

I felt a blow, though it was muted, like I wasn't connected to my body.

The blow to my chest came again, harder this time. Other sensations came: wet clothes, lungs on fire, hard earth under me, searing cuts. The sound of crying.

The third blow made me flinch—and I suddenly curled to the side and expelled water that had been trapped in my lungs. Heaved in air. My body acting without my direction.

I forced my eyes open. Raven straddled me, tears streaming down, hands together in a fist. When she saw me, she separated her hands, then shoved me. "Damn you."

She got up and stumbled along the edge of the river toward a body lying farther away. Valor.

I lay mostly out of the water, though the river covered my legs.

I rolled onto my hands and knees, muscles flaring, and started to crawl toward Valor, but she was already coughing. "You two okay?" I croaked.

"'Okay'?" Raven cried, her voice raw. "I had to pull you out from under that damn robot, drag you to shore, and bring you back to life! How do you *think* I'm doing?"

"You pulled me out, too?" Valor asked.

Raven sat back and gave a brief nod, hands trembling. The glove that had masked her right hand was missing, her metallic fingers in stark contrast to her pale skin. "I saw what I thought was the bag Garly gave Dad, so I grabbed it, hoping to get a weapon, but it was empty. I ran back to the river, and that's when the water lit up." She shot me a look that was half accusation, half fear. "You did that, didn't you?" When I nodded, she reached out to Valor. "You were standing in the water."

"I don't remember a thing," Valor admitted.

"The blast shoved you back, and tiny lightning bolts crawled all over you. When they stopped, you collapsed into the water. I pulled you out. Then I dove in again." She looked at me and drew up her knees.

I glanced at the river and spotted small objects bobbing on its surface. Dead fish.

I could fill in the rest of her story. I crawled to her and, moving slowly in case she resisted, wrapped my arms around her. "You saved our lives."

She began to sob as her adrenaline drained away, and I held her.

After a few seconds, she forced herself to stop. "I saw Britt. She pulled up to the bridge right after the blast. I hid in the weeds, so I don't think she saw me, but she saw you starting to float down the river," she said to Valor. "Then she drove off, probably to grab us downriver somewhere."

We couldn't stay. Nor could we retrieve Monroe's body or stop to mourn him.

I stood, my body aching all over, and started to walk along the river's edge, pushing myself to move. I bled from four different cuts: shoulder, arm, thigh, and one I hadn't even been aware of on my hip.

"The dogs came from her, didn't they?" I heard Raven ask Valor.

"Guess so. Kieran has drones, so I guess her thing is killer dogs."

Grimacing, I waded into the river and dove under the murky water, my sliced muscles at partial strength. After a few strokes, I reached the SUV, where I'd almost died. The dog

I'd fried lay on its side, curled as if it had been a living thing. Grabbing the doorframe with one hand, I salvaged everything I could: the handcuffs Garly and I had made, the energy absorber, my repair pack, a flasher ball, and the bolt-emitter. The actual weapons, the grenade launcher and machine guns, were pinned under the SUV, as was the chest plate. And my ion blade was gone.

As I climbed out of the river, Raven and Valor joined me. "I think I'm hurt," Valor said, holding her abdomen, hatch-mark tattoos more prominent as her skin had paled. Patches of mud stuck to her wet clothes, and both she and Raven were peppered with cuts.

I transferred the items I'd salvaged to one of the backpacks Raven had found, then put an arm around Valor's waist.

On the road above us, a car approached the bridge. Lights flashing. Cops.

We hurried off, Raven leading the way, first through the thin marsh and then into the tall grass. The ground was firmer in the grass, but we still left tracks.

Within minutes of us leaving the river, two more police cars showed up. We kept low as we hurried, but drones would be launched, possibly ones with tracking capabilities, if the local enforcement had the budget for them.

We ducked into a small cluster of trees and looked back. As I scanned the growing crowd of cops by the river, Raven tapped my arm and gestured behind me. Up a nearby hill was a large barn structure, upgraded in the last twenty years or so.

Voices shifted from the river. By the change in tone, I suspected the police had found our tracks and started to follow them.

We hurried to the barn, keeping low, though my legs fought me and my arms were stiff. I didn't have time to dwell on the fact I'd nearly died. From the way Raven acted, I suspected she'd struggled to bring me back. Maybe almost gave up. My fingers and toes tingled, my lungs burned, and the muscles in my neck felt like they'd been replaced with iron rods.

By the time we reached the sprawling, multi-leveled barn structure, the three of us were sweating, Valor worst of all. We flinched at the smallest sound, fearful more robot dogs would attack. I tried the door, discovered it was unlocked, and we slipped inside. As I closed the door behind us, two policemen appeared at the bottom of the hill.

Shit.

The barn's interior was dark and still, the farmhands or machines or whatever ran this place seemingly done for the day. We moved deeper into the structure, moving cautiously through the darkness.

"Where to?" Raven asked.

Before I could answer, we heard the crunch of gravel as a car pulled up outside. A voice hailed the others. More police.

I remembered the cuts we'd suffered. Even if the authorities didn't have DNA scanners, they'd take samples of the blood we'd left and enter their findings into a centralized database. Among the three of us, we probably left a decent trail leading to the barn.

The Agency would swoop in like a swarm of hunter-drones.

Valor steered us down a different pathway—but when a thick channel of light suddenly burst across the path before us, we ducked behind a tractor.

As footsteps cautiously entered the building, we scanned the area for a way out.

The light from the doorway illuminated piping that ran along the walls, a well-worn workbench, hand tools, and a series of toolboxes marred with nicks and dents. Nothing that helped.

A new set of footsteps grew in volume as someone approached, then stopped in the doorway, blocking part of the light. "We found the car," a female voice said. From her tone, she had to be a cop, joining the ones I'd spotted. "The dive team is on their way."

Flashlights clicked on, multiple beams gliding over the farm equipment scattered about, up to the rafters overhead, and then down to the floor. Our flight through the grass and woods had cleared the water from our feet, so we hadn't left any tracks, though as we hid behind the equipment, water pooled under us from our wet clothes.

The three cops inside the building angled to their left and slipped out of sight.

From the change in the timbre of the voices inside the building, they must've entered the largest portion of the barn, which was three stories tall.

I cautiously led Raven and Valor to hide behind another machine, an older generation bailer.

With my eyes adjusted to the darkness, I spotted three AG-M1300 robots from the Gen Omega agriculture line. Man-shaped and bulky, each stood six feet tall, designed to handle nearly any chore with the right attachment: hay rolling, thrasher, etc. Each one could lift upwards of five hundred pounds; we had sheathed them in layers of metal graphite to protect them from farm accidents. They were the only agricultural products my old company sold but had been very popular. We'd never bothered with rolling stock, though we'd studied the possibility. I hadn't realized it at the time, but that research had been the source of the tech I'd used to create the hand shields with Garly.

The memory almost made me miss it: a tiny, flashing light located down a pitch-black passage I hadn't noticed.

I motioned to Raven, then hooked my arm around Valor and led them toward the flashing light, my backpack draped over my other shoulder. We moved quietly, though Valor had to stifle a moan as she walked, which made me worry about her.

We passed the ag robots and entered the narrow corridor, the cops' voices farther away. When we reached the light, it abruptly stopped blinking. I paused, confused, then noted a faint, thin vertical line to the right. A door.

The three of us approached it, though I hesitated. The cops were still in the barn, but they sounded as if they'd entered a different area. Had to risk it. I opened the door—and sunlight blinded us. We stumbled outside, and I quickly shut the door behind us. We stood on what appeared to be a rarely-used concrete pathway that led into thick woods. The fact it was concrete would conceal our footprints.

We hurried down the path, glancing to either side to make sure we weren't spotted—and checking the skies for drones—then plunged into the forest.

* * *

Three hours later, a gunshot stopped us.

We'd moved through the woods as fast as we could, pausing just long enough to patch each other up with the limited medical supplies we had, though Anya would've laughed at our efforts. If it hadn't been for the underbrush and our injuries, we would've run. I'd started to think we might be safe until we heard the gunshot.

We anxiously looked around. Valor swayed on her feet, clearly exhausted and in pain.

Another shot rang out.

We ducked and scanned the woods. The sound was thin. A .22 caliber, maybe. Agents used stronger weapons. Still, even if it wasn't an Agent, The Agency would find our trail. Agents, cops, robots, or drones could show up any second.

We didn't have any weapons other than Valor's and Raven's pistols, what I'd scavenged from the river, and Raven's plasma-loaded fingers, but the pistols didn't work. They might be salvageable, as they'd been dunked in fresh water, but until we cleaned them, they wouldn't fire. I didn't know if her fingers had any charge left, but when I tried to inspect them, she backed away. "I'll see who's shooting," she whispered.

We all moved cautiously through the trees. The gunshot sounds were sporadic, falling quiet and then popping in rapid succession.

A backyard appeared, carved out of the forest with a faded yellow ranch house on the far side, the sliding door to a walkout basement left open. Other homes were just visible in the distance past the house. We hadn't encountered a lone residence; we'd reached the edge of a development, what could be the edge of a town.

The barrel of a rifle rose in the air and fired.

The shooter was a pudgy boy standing in the middle of the yard. He hadn't reached puberty yet, though there was a hardened quality about him.

A drone fell to the ground.

Raven and I exchanged a glance. The kid had shot it. "I'll talk to him," she whispered.

"You can't let him see your face," I whispered back.

She took in the sunlit clearing, then started toward the left. It took me a moment to realize what she was doing. When I did, I nodded in admiration, though it was risky.

Beside me, Valor trained her useless pistol on the boy.

I set my feet, prepared to run into the clearing, though I didn't think I could run fast enough if things turned sour.

Raven stepped out of the woods.

The boy didn't notice her at first. He hadn't even bothered going after the drone he'd shot down. He continued to scan the skies instead, his gun raised.

She stepped over a downed drone, one of a half-dozen or so, and said, "Hi there."

The boy swung his rifle toward her—but squinted in the bright sunlight. She'd approached from the west so he wouldn't be able to see her face clearly.

She raised her empty hands. "What's your name?"

"What's yours?"

"Betta," she lied, using her best friend's name instead. "I went for a hike and got all turned around. I lost my friends, too. Dumb, huh? Then I heard you shooting, so I followed the sound."

He relaxed a little. "Highway's that way," he said, jerking his head to the side.

"Have you been shooting down drones?"

"They took away the next town."

Raven took a step closer, causing my anxiety to increase, though she stayed masked in the sunlight. "Who took away… what?"

"Dunno who. There were cars with flashing lights, but they

weren't no sheriffs. The town was small, but it was there. I used to see it when we'd go fishing. Dad said there was an accident, and we all have to stay away, but I snuck off the last time we went to the creek to see for myself. It's not there anymore. None of it."

Raven seemed to take this in. "So, you shoot down drones?"

"I don't want them taking my town, too."

She slid her backpack off her shoulder, reached inside, and removed a dark knit cap. "Would you mind putting this on for me?"

The two continued to talk, but I was distracted. Raven held Talia's old cap, the one she had patched up what felt like a lifetime ago. I carried the missing piece in my pocket like a talisman, but I hadn't realized she carried the rest of the cap with her.

Raven placed the cap on the boy's head and stepped to the side so he could see her. Once he saw her face, he couldn't stop staring.

Valor and I cautiously entered the back yard. When we did, Raven pretended we were the ones she had searched for.

A minute later, we followed the boy through the sliding door into his house. The finished basement was safe for the moment, the boy's implant blocked by Talia's cap.

"We can't stay," Valor said quietly.

"Who're you?" the boy asked.

She squatted down. "I'm Valor."

"Isn't that a slogan?"

"It's not my real name. I call myself that because I failed to be courageous when I was your age. It reminds me never to make that mistake again."

"Is that when you got your eyepatch?"

"It certainly was."

"Does your 'patch make you sad?"

"Not like it used to."

A car pulled up. "Dad's home," the kid said. He then

noticed Raven's metallic fingers and recoiled in confusion.

While Raven calmed the boy, explaining how her fingers worked, Valor and I hurried upstairs to the main floor, reaching the living room as the boy's father closed the front door. Valor leapt ahead of me, blocking me from view, and slapped a blocker over his implant before he could react. When she stepped back, I discovered he was almost my age, with the look of one who worked with his hands. I scanned the room's pale green walls and the pressboard entertainment center for pictures to determine if he was married or had other children, but it appeared it was just the two of them.

"Sorry for the treatment," I said, indicating the blocker. "If you understood, you'd thank us."

He suddenly rushed me. I held him at arm's length as Valor pulled her weapon, though he only fought harder. I realized he wasn't trying to attack me. I stepped aside, and he ran over to his son—who I hadn't heard come upstairs—and hugged him tight.

Raven, who'd come up as well, retreated to give them privacy. Valor did as well, following Raven into the kitchen.

I closed the living room blinds, careful to stay out of sight from the street.

When the man looked at me, I saw my familial fears reflected. "We won't harm either of you," I said. I explained about the implants and The Agency. They had a right to know.

"This related to Hodville disappearing? Cops said there was an accident, but I saw people with silver hair before it just disappeared."

Raven and Valor reappeared. "You have any weapons?" Raven asked him as Valor peered through the blinds.

"Other than Jacob's rifle, no," he said as he tried to watch the three of us at once. His son, on the other hand, seemed delighted to have company.

Raven set down her pack and dug through it. As she did, I spotted the edges of her curved blades, and my brow knotted. The thought that struck me was cruel, yet it was a solution. I calculated how to implement the idea.

"We need a vehicle," Valor announced. She motioned toward the father. "Yours looks in good shape."

I asked, "Interested in selling?"

He shook his head.

"Know anyone who is?"

* * *

An hour later, we were on the road.

Raven grumbled about the car's price—for eight thousand, we could've gotten one better—but we hadn't had time to haggle. I'd given Valor my account info, she'd transferred the cryptocurrency, then she picked us up in the fifteen-year-old Kia, but not before retrieving Talia's cap and the implant shield from the boy and his father.

I drove. While that carried risks, Valor was still hurting, and Raven's reluctance was growing.

Motioning to the car's GPS, I told Raven, "Look for a gun store."

"Too dangerous. Jex told me they have redundant surveillance, and each one has to provide a dedicated feed to The Agency."

Of course. It was another way to control the populace.

I considered for a moment. "I have another idea."

She found what I suggested, although it meant backtracking. I turned around and steered north, both Raven and Valor shifting in their seats as I did, their anxiety becoming evident.

We reached our destination without encountering any Agency forces—human or otherwise—though I felt we were pushing our luck.

I pulled into the lot beside a long, cinderblock building. There were two other vehicles, so I parked in the rear, and we waited. We didn't have the time to spare, but this was important.

At my insistence, Valor handed me her pistol. This had been my idea, after all.

Wishing Monroe was still with us, I headed toward the door, set along the side of the building near the front. A camera watched the entrance. Its lens faced away from me as I approached. While the camera was set high, the wire from it ran down the wall almost to eye level before disappearing into the cinderblock. I grabbed the wire and ripped it out of the camera, then continued forward.

Someone emerged from the building, and I slowed. The man, not much older than Raven, wasn't aware of my presence as he turned to lock the door for the night. I quickened my pace and reached him right before he stepped away. Pressed a pistol into his back. "Let's go inside."

"There's no money. OK, some in the register."

I stuck a shield onto his implant, which made him flinch. "Any cameras inside?"

"No." He stiffened, then slumped. "You destroyed the one out here, didn't you?"

I steered him into the building and flipped on the lights, which revealed a retail area with glass cases. A wall of windows past the cash register displayed the shooting area: a row of a dozen or more stalls inside a concrete room with torso-shaped targets lined up at the far end. The last station to the left was separate from the others, reinforced with concrete its entire length.

"We don't want money," I told the man.

His face grew mystified as Valor and Raven joined us. "Then what do you want?"

"You sell weapons."

"Just ammunition. We don't have a license to sell weapons."

Valor inspected one of the cases. "All I see are T-shirts."

"We also sell ear protectors and glasses." He shrugged fearfully.

Raven demanded ammunition for her Glock, and Valor ordered ammunition and a cleaning kit, but I was frustrated. We couldn't fight Kieran with two pistols and some gadgets. We'd be massacred.

Raven found a pair of shooting gloves. As she pulled them on to mask her fingers, I inspected the store more closely.

A television played in the corner, the sound muted. Across the bottom, the words "Mandatory curfew" flashed. The far side of the store contained a small office, but there weren't any weapons there, either. Not even a shotgun under the counter by the cash register.

Defeated, I swept the building one last time. That's when I spotted it: the reinforced stall contained a mini-plasma cannon, the technology's equivalent of a 50-caliber gun. The four-foot-long weapon was bolted into place. Patrons could pay to experience the thrill of firing something so powerful.

I entered the shooting area and approached the cannon. As the employee squawked a feeble protest, I worked the bolts, disengaged the weapon from its cradle, and lifted it free. I wondered how we would use the fifty-pound beast, then discovered the cylindrical weapon had a rod that could be extended to create a single-leg stand.

The cannon contained a nearly-full plasma cartridge. Though I wasn't familiar with this kind of weapon, the cartridge should contain more than enough plasma for our needs.

When I lugged it into the retail part of the store, Valor said, "Holy shit." Raven stared in wonder.

We returned to our sedan minutes later. I'd left cash; it hadn't been enough to cover what we took, but it would ease the sting. I felt bad about tying up the employee, but we couldn't risk him alerting the authorities before we got away.

After we stashed the cannon and ammunition in the trunk, Raven smiled. I had to admit my spirits improved as well.

That didn't last.

I had just turned back onto the state highway heading south when a hoverbike shot past overhead.

"Shit. They'll come back around," Raven said.

"Drive normal. Don't speed up," Valor said.

"I have this," I said, though my palms became sweaty as I gripped the steering wheel. The hoverbike turned in the air back toward us. If the Agent scanned our vehicle for implant signals, they'd come up empty. Might as well flash a sign telling them to stop us.

"Get off the highway," Raven said.

I took the first right and risked gunning it. Almost too fast. "We need to get off the road. Help me look for a place to hide."

"What's that?" Raven asked, pointing ahead.

It was an abandoned-looking road. I would've missed it, as it was partly overgrown.

I turned onto the road, which quickly degraded from dusty blacktop to gravel. Trees crowded in, though not as much as I would've liked. I kept an eye out for a place to stop, something with a deep groove in the earth. Had to be big enough. After two dozen yards, the ground dropped off sharply to a creek on our right. I wrenched the steering wheel and angled toward the drop, nearly driving over the edge.

"Dad," Raven cried.

I stopped at the last second, the front bumper sticking out over the edge, and turned off the car. "Quick, get out."

I led them to the front and took a few steps down the hillside. "Get under the car. The engine will mask our body heat. Hurry."

With my help, Raven shimmied under the car.

When I turned to Valor, she backed away. "You go. I have an idea."

The hoverbike's distinct sound grew. The Agent had tracked us.

I climbed under the vehicle next to Raven, although there wasn't as much room as I'd expected and brushed the side of my arm against the hot oil pan. With a hiss, I jerked my arm away and pulled myself the rest of the way under the car, pressing against Raven, who had curled herself into a ball. I swiveled and brought my legs up, my head nearly touching the front right wheel, my feet hooking onto the front left wheel to keep me in place, my ass sticking out a little.

The hoverbike grew louder, then paused above us.

Raven's face was close to mine; when the hoverbike stilled, her eyes widened. We were in no position to fight hidden under the damn car—and I was unarmed.

The hoverbike remained in its spot. Then I heard something else. We both did. A trickling of water.

Raven's expression went from scared to perplexed, then to amusement as the volume grew. Valor. She was peeing out in the open.

Giving the Agent a reason why she'd parked.

I was certain she'd exposed her fake implant as well—which should have codes that wouldn't trip any watch lists.

With a change in pitch and a burst of jet, the hoverbike flew off, and Raven began to laugh.

* * *

After extracting ourselves from under the car, we climbed onto the road where Valor waited, blushing hard.

"It's all I could think to do. Just…pretend this didn't happen."

"Oh, it happened," Raven said, smiling.

We got in the car, but instead of retracing our route, I continued along the now-dirt road, heading deeper into the forest.

"What are you doing?" Raven asked.

"Seeing if this goes anywhere," I said.

My curiosity brought us to a barbed wire-topped chain-link fence. *Keep Out. Quarantine,* the sign proclaimed. The dirt road continued past the fence, a small cluster of buildings just visible from where we stood.

I parked to the side, in a spot covered by trees.

We returned to the fence and followed it into the woods until we found a gap, the sections of the fence not perfectly aligned. With some effort, we slipped through.

As shadows stretched in the late afternoon light, we reached the structures we'd spotted from the road. They consisted of a gas station, a small grocery store, and an independent pharmacy, the names—Gas-N-Go, Holly's Grocery, Sixteenth Pharmacy—still visible. Yet the doors stood open, the shelves empty, the pumps dark.

We exchanged wary glances. This had to be the missing town.

I extracted my flasher ball but wished I'd grabbed the cannon; although I could carry it and fire it, the weapon wasn't designed for quick, close-quarters fighting if it came to that. Still, the idea tempted me. There was something unsettling about this place.

We walked down the street between the store and pharmacy. A small manufacturing building followed on one side, a two-bay mechanic's shop on the other, three vehicles parked out front covered in grime and rust. Homes appeared after that, narrow two-story buildings with a few wide ranches. If there had been people about, it would've looked like any other town. Some had modern conveniences such as AI-monitored home security systems and M-band satellite dishes.

Yet the only sound came from the rustle of leaves as they skated down the street, the noise like one of those scary movies Raven used to watch.

I tried the door of the corner home, one that didn't appear to have a security system. To my surprise, the door was unlocked. Raising my flasher, I stepped inside, ignoring Raven as she quietly insisted that she go first.

Tensed for an attack, I found a dust-covered couch and cheap furniture—a side table, lamp, vid-screen stand without a screen—occupying the front rooms. In the kitchen, I found cans in the cupboard and rotten food in the refrigerator, the smell almost enough to knock me out. Upstairs, I found what could've been spots of blood, although the stains were too old to be sure. Threadbare clothes clung to their hangers in the two closets. A pair of boy's Keds sneakers poked out from under one of the beds, curled in age.

The women had followed me inside, although I was the only one to go upstairs. I rejoined them and led them outside, where I described what I'd found.

"What happened here?" Valor asked, gripping her gun.

"Everyone was run out. Or attacked," Raven said.

"But why? If it was because of some sort of outbreak, it would've made national news."

I glanced at Raven. "Face the other way and expose your implant."

Her expression revealed she'd already guessed what she would discover.

She did as I asked, yet even though she'd suspected, she inhaled sharply. "I don't see a town anymore. My lenses make this look like an extremely thick forest, with huge boulders where some of the buildings are." She replaced her implant shield and looked at us. "That boy was right. They hid it all."

* * *

It took some convincing before they agreed to stay the night. "Agents will be able to see this place, but local police might not. And normal people definitely won't," I said. "It's the safest place right now."

"So, we can get a good night's rest before we confront Kieran," Raven said, anger flashing. "Because a little extra sleep will make all the difference."

Valor said, "He has a point. We try to drive tonight, we'll stick out."

I returned to our car to retrieve our meager possessions while they squabbled.

Nearly getting caught, finding the strange town, and now facing what we were going to do tomorrow heightened our emotions. We couldn't delay, either, as our friends would take down The Agency's network in a day and a half—which meant we had to confront Kieran, make him tell us where Talia is, then get to her before the nodes exploded.

At the car, I opened the front pocket of Raven's pack and found the burner phone she'd hidden, the one she'd used to reach out to Jex. While I didn't like using her phone behind her back, she'd brought it without my knowledge, so I considered us even.

I turned on the phone and dialed the number Garly had given me weeks earlier, one that he claimed was untraceable, though he never showed me how he did it.

"Hello?" Garly said uncertainly. Of course. He wouldn't have recognized the number.

"It's me."

"The only and greatest! How is your journey?"

"Difficult. We lost the soldier." I didn't want to trip any spiders by saying Monroe's name.

"Oh no! He was a walking weapon—and a good cat." He paused. "You're exposed. I'll send reinforcements."

"It's okay. We're still on the move." There wasn't time to shuffle plans to get additional help. "Is the doc there?"

"I'll get her. And hey, I'm on it. I got you."

I almost said his name but caught myself and just said, "Hello?" a couple of times, not sure what he was planning.

After a few seconds, Anya came on. "*Hi.*"

Her voice felt like a balm. "How are you?"

"I'd be better if you were here. Your plan is almost ready. Everyone is excited."

I wouldn't have missed that for the world, or left her, if not for Talia. "What about you?"

She sighed. "I'm worried you're on such a dangerous mission—and you're depending on what your wife claimed. Be careful. And come back to me."

Her words echoed as I walked back to the town, the land darkening with the sunset.

I wished we'd stayed on the phone longer. Wished we were together. Then I chided myself. I'd taken enough risks because of what I wished.

I returned to the house we'd selected with our meager supplies, all except the cannon, which I left in the trunk.

Raven and Valor waited on the front step, Valor clutching her middle. They were no longer squabbling, though I felt some animosity. I led them inside. "You need to lie down," I told Valor.

"Not yet. Have to do this for Monroe. And Senn." She extracted two candles from her pack, both burned down to nubs, along with a tiny bouquet of dried flowers that had been pressed between two sheets of plexiglass, and a large coin with the symbols of a half-dozen religions etched into its face.

"I'd thought my uncle was a preacher when I was little," she said as she laid out her objects on the kitchen table. "When I learned he wasn't, I felt lied to. But I've since realized a piece of paper doesn't make someone closer or farther from their god. Actions do." She lit the candles and arranged them to either side of the flowers. "It's not much, but it's my process."

Raven asked, "Where are the flowers from?"

"That's a long story for a brighter time." Valor straightened as best she could, an arm pressed against her stomach.

"Lie down," I told her, but she shushed me. Instead, she bowed her head, as did Raven.

I found myself hesitating, not because I didn't want to mourn Monroe or Senn, but because of the anger I felt at their deaths, and fear that if I started to mourn for them, I would fall down the chasm of heartache I had been on the verge of falling into for weeks.

Yet they deserved to be recognized. And I needed to let myself feel at least a little of the sorrow I carried, lest I become so hardened I lose myself.

I bowed my head before Valor's makeshift shrine.

When she determined we'd grieved enough, she blew out the candles and let me steer her to the couch. After she settled on the cushions, I made her show me her abdomen. It was bruised, the deepest shade following the curve where the SUV's steering wheel had been. "Is it getting better? Or worse?"

"Better."

I raised my eyebrows.

She snorted. "Seriously, Dr. Dray. I'll be fine." The fact she simply rolled over and went to sleep, however, told me her pain was worse than she'd admitted.

I took a breath to steady myself, then approached Raven. "Do you have the curved blades Garly gave you?" I asked, though I knew the answer.

She rifled through her pack and extracted them. "I've had them for weeks," she said with a hint of a smile.

"They might've gotten wet in the river. Let me check them."

With the blades in hand, I disappeared into the kitchen. The rest of the day's light was fading, which cast the room into darkness. A flick of the light switch confirmed there was no power, so I closed the window shades and withdrew a small work light from the repair kit. By its fluorescent glow, I disassembled each blade to make sure water hadn't gotten inside. There was just one section that appeared damaged. Over the course of a half-hour, I carefully repaired the damage, then reassembled it. The other blade was in perfect condition.

I hadn't known whether Raven would watch me work. The fact she didn't told me we weren't okay. I took advantage of her absence and extracted a small remote receiver from my repair kit, which had been a leftover part from a plasma launcher. Working quickly, I attached the receiver to the trigger mechanism, careful not to sever the wiring apparatus. It only took a few minutes; when I activated the remote, instead of the electricity from the trigger activating the plasma-coil mechanism, it would redirect the electricity to the metal handle. The charge would be enough to knock her out.

My actions would scar her, but at least she would be safe.

When we reached Kieran's, I would zap her and lock her in the trunk. Valor and the cannon would be enough to help me defeat him, especially if he was still weakened.

Finished with my addition, I triggered both devices. The glowing blades lit up the room, attracting Raven's attention, their brightness almost too intense to look at. Satisfied, I turned them off and handed them to her as she entered the kitchen. "Good to go."

She took them into the next room. I heard blinds being drawn, then the searing hiss of the blades igniting. The light from the blades moved and shifted as Raven spun and twirled, either repeating choreographed fighting moves or pretending to spar, I didn't know which.

My need to parent and guide her remained as strong

as ever, though it was no longer welcomed. She acted as if she wanted to be my equal. I hoped she would grow into a better person than me. I believed she would, assuming she survived all of this.

I felt disgusted with myself for pursuing such a horrible plan.

As she continued to work the blades, I retrieved the devices I'd salvaged from the river and began to repair them. By the time I finished, the cuffs worked again, the absorber checked out, the flasher ball was fine, and the bolt-emitter was in good shape, from what I could tell. Since I couldn't charge the emitter in this dead town, I fashioned a crude USB-6 adapter to plug into our car's electrical system.

My hand shield was another story. While it had worked in battle, the battery had drained, and I didn't possess the materials I needed to replace the portions that had shorted out. I activated the shield—but just over a third formed, and the modified glove shook, the device unstable.

At least the hand shield I gave Raven still worked. It had escaped undamaged.

Not that she would have a chance to use it.

Pushing the thought aside, I cleaned and lubricated her and Valor's pistols, using the kit Valor obtained at the shooting range and admiring the etchings she'd done as I cleaned hers.

After I finished and stored the devices in my pack, I stood and stretched my back. Raven had stopped her movements, the blades extinguished. I stepped outside, figuring she might want some space. When she emerged from the house a minute later, I realized I was wrong.

In the starlight, I could tell she'd worked herself up, maybe from playing with the blades. Or because of where we were heading.

"Why do we have to face *him*?" she asked. "There has to be another way to find Talia."

"If we're going to get her out of wherever she's being held, our only chance is to do it during the node attack."

"You're assuming he'll tell us anything."

"I'll make him." When she didn't look convinced, I avoided her gaze. "I thought about killing him the night I defeated him. I almost did. But it would've been wrong—even though it meant I might have to fight him again someday."

She wavered, then took a few steps, gripping the unlit blades in her fists. "You can take him, right?"

"Garly and I developed weapons for the fight." I would've felt better if I still had the augmented sleeves, I didn't add.

"Don't even think of trying to ditch us. I took the car keys while you were working. You need us to have a chance."

"Do you really think you can fight him?" I asked, my voice more hostile than I'd planned.

"Britt didn't attack me like he did."

"You're too close to this—"

"How can I *not* be? We're going to fight the bastard who violated me, warped Mina, and probably killed my sister."

She's Mom, not Mina, I didn't say.

Emotions I'd suppressed rose up. Looking back later, I realized I began to speak to her not as a father to a daughter but as one wounded person to another. "I will redeem myself with Talia, even if she's really dead."

"By sacrificing yourself? Because that's what you seem to be doing."

"Please, go to Jex. Help him take down the nodes." My throat tightened. "I have to do this. The guilt is crushing me."

"*Your* guilt? I started all of this. If it wasn't for me, Talia would be alive."

"I didn't stay on Free Isle to save her."

"This isn't some sick contest. One guilt can't wipe out the other."

"I know that."

"Mina turned on us, and I froze twice now, and I've probably hurt Jex by not letting him come with us." Raven walked back to the steps that led up to the back door and sat on them. Even in the faint light, her misery was evident. "I've been torn between going after Talia—hoping so much that she's really, actually alive—and being a part of something bigger."

"You can still be a part of something bigger. The war won't end after they take down the nodes."

"I'm not sure I can face Mina. Not after what she did."

"She loves you. She just lost her way."

"Is that what this is about? To reconcile with her?"

I shook my head. "It has nothing to do with her. I left Talia behind. I… I didn't do anything to try to save her," I said, the admission wrenched from the deepest part of me.

She stood and clenched her fists. "I know. I'll never forgive you for that." Her face twisted in anguish. "Or myself."

Chapter Thirty

The mood in the car was strained the next morning as I drove us away from the deserted town, unresolved issues and corrosive accusations occupying the air we breathed. Valor was angry we didn't tell her what had transpired while she slept, though she could feel its aftermath. Her abdomen bothered her less, so she replaced her grimaces with glares. As for me, I hadn't recovered from Raven's hostility. I had never forgiven myself for my kids' deaths, and her anger and self-loathing were similar to what I directed at myself. I worried how much her emotions would scar her.

Until last night, I hadn't realized how much she'd blamed herself for everything that had happened. It explained her cockiness and need to rush into danger. She was trying to make up for her failures.

And maybe more.

A couple of days after she and Talia had fought over the robo-butler those many years ago, Raven asked me to help make one for her sister. She wanted it to be smaller, with ports Talia could access to change the robot's operating system. I brought parts home from the office, and we constructed the robot over the course of a week. The final version was cruder than Raven's and looked more like a robot armadillo than a butler, but she thought Talia would love it. She scooped up the gift and went to find her—but quickly returned, the gift still in her arms. "She's gone."

Talia's backpack and some clothes were missing, along with her school tablet and a box of her favorite snacks.

I broke multiple speed limits as I drove us through the neighborhood, searching for her. Raven suggested areas to look, then thought to pull up my Uber account. Talia had booked a ride using my card. Within minutes, I contacted the driver and met him ten miles from our house.

When I pulled up behind his vehicle, Raven told me to stay in the car and hurried to Talia, who looked ready to bolt, backpack slung over her shoulder. I could just make out their conversation as she apologized for their earlier fight.

After they made up, Talia said, "Scurry away with me. Mom and Pops need to cry together without us around."

"I made you your own butler. You'll be able to change his voice to whatever you want, and he lights up."

"You don't want me to play with yours?" I could hear her pain.

"Yours is better. That's what I want to do for you, little stinker, make things better. I'll always be there for you."

"Schmaltzy," Talia said, though she smiled.

The two hugged. When they pulled back, Raven glanced at me, as if making sure I'd stayed in the car. "We can't run away. Mom and Dad need us. But we need to watch out for each other. It'll be our secret."

"Like still fight at times but not for reals?" When Raven nodded, Talia said, "I'm so in."

I pretended I hadn't heard them when they climbed into our car, but even if I hadn't, I would've noticed the change in their relationship. They still bickered after that, but they became closer than most siblings I knew.

"Cole posted an update last night," Valor said, referring to an anonymous message board they'd set up weeks ago. "The attack happens tomorrow at 1:30. Thirty-one and a half hours."

I squinted as the morning sunlight pierced our windshield. "Good. If Talia is alive, we'll need the distraction to have a chance."

I knew I wasn't being friendly but couldn't stop myself. I was too conflicted and angry and nearly overwhelmed by the thought of facing Kieran.

Still not trusting the interstate, I took the state highway south. I drove past endless farms, a return of the wheat fields like we'd passed up north.

"At least we'll be free when the nodes fall," Valor said, more to herself. "The thought of Agents watching me from everyone's eyes freaks me out."

From the back seat, Raven asked, "What did you do before all this?"

"Created marketing ads for a fin-tech company. At night I made mixed-media art pieces, mostly sculptures. Did a small art show once, but the critics were vicious."

"I'm sorry."

Valor shrugged. "I've done pretty well for a girl from South Carolina. Spent time in the National Guard, won two local bodybuilding competitions. Should have my head examined for taking on this life."

"Dad's company could arrange that. I remember them sticking wires to my head when I was little." Raven's tone was accusatory.

"We created a miniature scanner," I told Valor. "An entire line of medical devices, actually. We didn't have a contract with Washington, so we had to create products that worked independently of everyone's neural nets. We sold off most of our creations, though we still provide robotics that gives mobility to the disabled."

"No one cares," Raven said.

Valor threw her a weird look, then me. When neither of us responded, she told me, "There was also a note from Nataly. Said there are some 'strange things' online related to you. She thinks they were supposed to be negative propaganda, but they were replaced by random content: missing kids' posters, armored car ads, stuff like that."

"Maybe some of the hackers survived Kieran's attack," I

said. That sounded like their handiwork.

We dropped into silence again. Or rather, Valor did. Raven and I weren't speaking to each other.

We passed a sign that we'd reached Texas.

The prospect of facing Kieran grew more real. We were three hours from his place. Maybe less.

A massive combine trudged across the field to our right, sunlight glinting off its unmanned cab, an equally large harvester trailing it.

I slowed, then pulled over.

"What are you doing?" Valor asked.

The combine drew me, though it took a moment to realize why.

I was losing Raven, our issues and her self-anger eroding our bonds, and my betrayal would exacerbate it. I'd thought my actions would protect my girls, not drive one to rebel against the federal government and the other to seemingly die in a firefight. Even so, I had to protect Raven.

She was all I had.

As for Talia, I didn't know what to believe.

I pulled my damaged hand shield from my pack. I'd lost my ion blade in the river, so I reached into the back seat and snatched one of her curved blades from her pack—noticing a couple of electronic devices hidden underneath.

"Dray?" Valor asked as I got out.

"Stay here." I quickly scanned the farms to either side. As I'd suspected, all of the combines were in use, scattered among the various fields. I'd have to do this the hard way.

Using both hands to protect my face, I plunged into the field and ran a zigzag pattern across the field, down and through the narrow rows, the wheat wiping at me as I ran. I started to feel disoriented, as the wheat stalks stood higher than me, augmented strains that generated twice the yield of the natural plant, so I just pushed between them, moving perpendicular to the rows.

I heard the combine's mechanical thrashing up ahead, the sound augmented by the throaty growl of the engine, one of the last commercial diesel vehicles still being made. As I grew closer, the smell of cut wheat wafted over me, along with a hint of diesel smoke and grease, the air taking on a haze as tiny bits of chaff drifted to the ground.

The cacophony of sound grew sharply louder. I stopped, unsure where the combine was—when it suddenly cut across my path less than five feet in front of me, the roar tinged with the hum of a four-foot-wide, translucent orange disk that protruded from the front edge of the thresher. The next moment, the combine passed, leaving an open, cut field.

I stepped into the open space. The combine continued to cut a precise line down the field, followed closely by a computer-guided harvester that collected the shorn wheat. The vehicles weren't going fast, but I would have to run to catch up.

I broke into a sprint, angling for the rear of the combine.

The ground was rutted where the rows had been, which didn't help. I pushed harder and got in front of the harvester, aware that if I tripped and fell, the vehicle's warning system wouldn't be able to stop it in time. A few more seconds, my arms and legs churning, then I managed to grab the ladder that led to the combine's cab and climb on before I ran out of energy. Still, I hung on for a moment to catch my breath, letting the combine carry me down the field.

My goal was the end of the thresher. Unfortunately for me, this combine was one of the larger models, which meant the thresher attached to the front of the automated machine was nearly sixty feet wide.

I pulled myself the rest of the way up the ladder to the walkway that led around the cab, my wounded shoulder flaring again though not as badly as yesterday. I didn't want to stop the vehicle, as that might attract unwanted attention, so I stepped from the walkway onto the connector and then onto the loud thresher itself.

The green-painted thresher contained spinning, circular metal blades that sliced the wheat and propelled the pieces toward a collector attached to the rear of the thresher like a large dustpan, which funneled the wheat into the combine's main body. The thresher portion, while sixty feet long, was only about five feet wide—at least that was the width of the metal "roof" I stepped onto that covered the top of the spinning blades—and of that, only three feet of the roof was level. The final foot on either side curved downward, which meant I'd either fall off behind the thresher or fall forward—and down into the blades.

The roof was ridged but slippery.

Wheat slapped against the front edge of the thresher as the combine mowed down the field.

I made sure the hand shield was firmly on my left hand, and Raven's curved blade was in my right. I knew the shield would turn on instantaneously if I needed it, but the blade took a moment to ignite, so I went ahead and activated the blade. Then I turned to my right. The far end past the edge of the thresher was free of wheat, that part of the field already cut down, so it was the logical choice.

Both ends of the thresher were capped by projection shields—the orange disk I'd spotted when the thresher first passed me. The electronically-generated shield kept the wheat in adjoining rows from getting sucked into and jamming up the thresher; it was the technology Garly and I had used to create the hand shields. It was also the tech used in screen shields, which deflected plasma blasts. I wasn't certain which version came first, but it didn't matter. One of these would replace my damaged hand shield, as they emitted a strong enough shield to deflect anything plasma-based and, potentially, bullets, depending on the caliber.

I'd need one of the shields to battle Kieran. He was a highly-trained operative with enhanced strength and healing abilities. If I didn't get more protection, I would lose.

I started down the thresher's length, though I had to move cautiously. The machine hadn't been designed for anyone to walk on it. I lowered my center of gravity and took another step, then another, the wheat slapping at the edge inches from my left foot, the metal shaking underneath me.

I reached the halfway point. Fifteen feet to go.

My legs burning, I stepped forward, when the wheat suddenly stopped hitting the thresher. That was my only warning, for the next moment, the combine began to turn. We'd reached the end of the section that needed to be cut down, so the combine was changing direction to go down the next row, the thresher swinging wide.

The sudden movement threw me off my feet.

I landed on the roof, angling toward the left to compensate for being jerked back to my right as the combine swung—but I overcompensated. Instead of falling in the center of the roof, I fell to the left and started to slide toward the spinning blades.

I jabbed Raven's blade into the rooftop, metal screeching, then triggered my hand shield. Raven's blade arrested my fall—but the circular blades, free of wheat, spun in a blur of lethal metal, the edges coming at me as I slid. I thrust my hand shield toward the blades to stop my fall, my fist shaking, shoulder aching, and my shield held, the blades beating rapid-fire at the damaged projection.

With a grunt, I pulled myself back onto the center of the thresher's rooftop.

The combine continued to turn, heading for the next section of uncut wheat.

I realized when it started down the next row that the projection shield I'd targeted was about to be swallowed by the unharvested wheat, which would make my goal even harder. But there was no way I was turning around to head to the other end of the thresher.

I planted my feet under me and with the help of Raven's blade, launched myself forward. I slid the last few feet along the top of the thresher, my blade poised over the curved side to my right, ready to use it so I wouldn't slide off the back.

The new row was coming around as I reached the end. I had seconds.

The projection shield was sloped, the forward edge extending past the front corner of the thresher as a kind of glowing bumper. The back half jutted out, so the wheat in the adjoining row would be pushed backward. The actual projector was attached to a metal bar about two feet across, the bar bolted to the side of the thresher, wires running up the middle.

Gripping the rooftop as well as I could with my left hand, I swung the curved blade toward the bolts. In one swipe, the blade severed both bolts and the power to the glowing shield. The shield winked out, and the projector fell away, striking the ground and bouncing three feet due to the centrifugal force.

The edge of wheat came at me. Ten feet away. Five.

I shoved against the edge of the thresher, pushing my body forward—and off the roof.

I landed at the end of the wheat, the blades deafening as they sliced into the next row, the combine and harvester proceeding away from me.

With a groan, I picked myself up, acknowledging the new pains I'd given my body, and shuffled to the projector. It appeared undamaged. The combined device and bar were pretty heavy, although nothing I couldn't handle.

Standing on my toes, I searched for the car across the field of remaining wheat but couldn't see it. I couldn't see the road either from where I stood, though I could make out the top of a barn on the opposite side.

I jogged down one of the uncut rows until I reached what I estimated was my entry point, then dove into the unshorn wheat and shoved my way through row after row toward the highway.

When I emerged from the wheat field, I paused. Our car was thirty feet away—but a sheriff's car was parked behind it, lights flashing. Raven and Valor sat on the ground by the front of our vehicle, gazing up at a man clad in a gray shirt and black pants who had to be the sheriff.

Raven's eyes flickered toward me, her only acknowledgement of my return. Valor didn't change expression, although she could've watched me via her eyepatch.

I tried to be quiet as I approached, though I only made it partway before the sheriff turned, whipping out his pistol like some cowboy wannabe.

"No reason to shoot," I said, cursing that he'd looked at me. Had looked at Raven. The Agency would identify us from his feed. We had minutes, if that.

"What you got there?"

I glanced at the projector attached to the metal bar. "I picked it up from the field."

Raven lashed out and kicked the sheriff's leg. He stumbled, caught unaware, and I broke into a run as he regained his balance.

As he rounded on Raven, Valor jumped on the man, who was thin but managed to shove her back and bring around his gun. Raven joined the battle, grabbing the wrist that gripped his pistol and shoving it downward. Valor wrapped a hand around the barrel as I neared and ignited Raven's blade—and the sheriff gave up struggling. "What the hell's that?" he cried as he stared at the blade inches from his face.

I hid it behind my back, not wanting The Agency to know more than they already did. Raven turned him over, and Valor used the man's own cuffs to secure his wrists behind his back, then fished out an implant blocker and covered his 'net.

* * *

"We should kill him," Raven said after we'd calmed down from the fight.

"Why's everything so brown?" the man said, staring at the sky. His nametag identified him as Sheriff Hocks.

"You're seeing for the first time," I said as I frowned at Raven. I told him about the implants and how they were used to mask the smog-filled world we lived in. "The planet is running out of oil. What you're seeing are the burnt additives."

"We shouldn't hurt him," Valor said.

I stared at the man, who we'd propped against our front bumper. His weathered face, poor shaving job, and gray-and-black uniform made him appear harmless, though I knew better. I checked his gun. It was standard issue, not locked to any one shooter. Amazingly, I could use it.

I retrieved an extra clip from his car, then squatted before him. "I'll make you a deal. I'm taking your gun, but I'll give you the keys to your cuffs—and let you keep that blocker. Don't let anyone from the government discover you have it. They'll ask what happened here—they'll watch the feed through your eyes—but tell them you got knocked out, don't know what happened."

"Through my *what*?"

I quickly explained. "Be careful, Sheriff Hocks. I'm putting you in more danger than you realize."

* * *

"We should've killed him," Raven said as Valor drove us away. I was in the back again, the projector on the seat beside me.

"Then we're no better than they are," I said.

Raven stared at me, then looked away.

I didn't pretend my actions swayed how she felt. I also knew my decision to spare the sheriff was dangerous. I only hoped I hadn't made things worse.

As Valor picked up speed, I turned my attention to the projector. I had two hours before we reached Kieran's—and twenty-nine hours to find Talia.

CHAPTER THIRTY-ONE

An hour and forty-six minutes later, Valor drove us past Kieran's house. It was surreal and nauseating to think he went about his day, free and unaffected, while Raven and I and so many others suffered.

The modified story-and-a-half sported tall windows to the left of the front door and a lower, stone-covered façade to the right. It was much nicer than the house a government employee might afford. But he wasn't an ordinary employee.

The building stood on top of a small hill. Of course. He could keep an eye on anything that approached. There was grass, but not a single tree or structure on his lot that would obstruct his view. We'd be exposed when we made our attack. His driveway extended off of a back road that snaked between forests and manicured fields, no other homes or structures visible.

We could wait until nightfall, but that would limit the time we'd have left to get to Talia. Even if Mina had told the truth and they were in northern Texas, it could take too long to reach them. We had to be in position when our teams attacked the nodes.

Valor continued past the house, not stopping until she reached the next forest, which blocked his house from sight. She pulled off the road, taking a spot among the towering trees just big enough to fit our car. "Are you two nervous? Or is it just me?" she asked.

"Jex gave me something," Raven said. She reached into

the back seat, grabbed her pack, and pulled out the recycler I'd spotted earlier. "It intercepts whatever feeds are transmitting in a fifty-foot radius, copies the feed, then rebroadcasts it. We can use this to create a loop."

"One less headache," Valor said, although we wouldn't know what it captured, as it would record a thirty-second loop and then broadcast the clip at a stronger output level to drown out any other data. It could show Kieran reading a book, which would be ideal—or him staring at a house alarm we triggered.

I gritted my teeth as we got out of the car with our packs, went to the trunk, and popped the lid. I didn't like what I was about to do.

As Raven strapped on a protective vest, Valor stepped between us and secured the thresher's bar to my right forearm, both working quickly. Even though no one was visible, a car could pass by any second. "You see his house?" Valor whispered. "I bet there are sensors and tripwires. There's no way to sneak inside."

I thought Raven would respond, but she seemed distracted, her hands resting in her pack.

"We're going to have to do a frontal assault," I said. Jex's recycler would help, though so much depended on luck.

Valor attached the shield projector to my forearm with wire in four spots, strips of cloth underneath it so the wires wouldn't cut into my skin, the power pack taped to the bar. When she finished, she stepped back. "What's the plan—and how are we going to avoid him triggering an alarm? It's the middle of the day. I thought I saw movement inside. He's a big dude, right? Six foot or so?"

Raven glanced at me from the corner of her eye. Tense.

I slipped my left hand into my pocket and wrapped my fingers around the remote. The cannon rested in the trunk, but once we removed that, there would be plenty of room for her after I knocked her out.

She pulled both blades from her pack and gripped them in one hand. Faced me. "Yeah, Dad, what's the plan?"

I wanted to plead with her, explain the position I was in. I couldn't risk one daughter's life to search for the other. Raven needed to learn the truth as badly as I did, but I could tell her after. Maybe that would lessen the blow. I knew it wouldn't, though. She still carried the black-and-white worldview that youth possessed, that most were forced to modify by their own actions as they aged. This was the last time we'd be… whatever we were.

My thumb rested on the button.

She'd be safe out here—though as sunlight slipped from behind a cloud and illuminated her hair, my doubt revealed a horrible thought: if Valor and I failed, Raven would be vulnerable. She'd be knocked out, helpless.

Kieran would find her. Enslave her.

I'd hand her to him on a fucking platter.

I let go of the remote. I couldn't do that to her. Couldn't risk it. Better she at least fight for her fate, though the thought of her facing Kieran made my heart beat faster.

The knuckles of her hand whitened as she squeezed the handles. "You going to do it?"

I jerked my hand out of my pocket. "Do what?"

She held up one of the blades and tapped her metal index finger at a spot above the hilt. "You rigged this. I recognized the receiver. I've been waiting for you to knock me out."

"Wait, *what*?" Valor nearly shouted.

"I didn't. I'm not going to," I said, though even as I spoke the words, I knew they were meaningless. Her entire life, she'd been my shop helper. Of course she would've spotted the receiver.

Raven pulled the recycler from her pack and looked at Valor, her voice cold. "Grab the cannon."

Without waiting for either of us, she started toward Kieran's house.

Valor eyed me warily as I helped her with the cannon and shut the trunk's lid. We hurried after Raven, who reached the edge of his lawn. "Once inside, you go left," she told Valor. "I'll take right."

We'd both seen the house's schematics at Brocco's. Raven wanted me to go down the center.

Act as bait.

I wanted to talk to her as she quickly described her plan, make this right somehow, but she acted as if I meant nothing to her. We were divided before we'd even stepped into Kieran's house.

I didn't blame her. I'd left the rebels, endangered her and Valor, almost betrayed her, and now we planned to face off against the man who'd traumatized her.

We had no time to reconsider our options. Raven was already walking across Kieran's lawn toward the front door. I followed, Valor barely keeping up as she was weighed down by the plasma cannon. We came at the house from the stone-front side, avoiding the tall windows, though as we hurried, scanning the house for any sign of movement, I caught a glimpse of the side of the house, which had even more windows down its impressive length.

We reached the front door.

Raven pressed the recycler against the door and activated it. After it finished recording, she nodded, and I dropped to one knee, slid Jex's guiding rod into the lock, then eased in the tumbler rod. As he'd taught me, I felt for the tumblers—my adrenaline causing my hands to shake a little—and managed to disengage them.

With a soft click, the door unlocked.

I entered the house, pack slung over my left shoulder, the sheriff's pistol raised. Valor was a step behind, cannon over one shoulder and pistol in her free hand, with Raven bringing up the rear.

We stepped into a wood-lined, modern foyer. Directly ahead stood a hallway that ran through the center of the house. It was dark, with light visible at the far end. To the left of us, a doorway led toward a high-ceiling room illuminated by the tall windows. To the right was a narrow, formal living area, with suspended steps to one side that led up to what appeared to be an open, second-floor suite.

All was quiet.

Valor headed to the left, her pistol extended, the cannon leaning against her shoulder, and quietly disappeared.

Raven tilted her head at me, indicating the central hallway, then started to the right, moving as silently as Valor.

I went straight, the hallway decorated with various pictures I ignored. There was a bathroom partway down, followed by a small, office-type room with a built-in, L-shaped desktop containing a pair of clear monitors and pieces of neural nets, framed pictures covering the walls.

Continuing forward, I crossed the last dozen feet and entered a vast, open space that took up the entire rear of the house. The space contained a family room, sitting room, and a dining room which extended to the right and around the corner past where I stood. A long table with about twenty chairs was visible in the dining area, while the other two areas were more casual. Cream and white colored couches and armchairs prevailed, with reading nooks and even a wet bar, as if Kieran held frequent soirées. Everything was pristine.

Then I saw him.

He sat in a chair in the sitting room almost directly in front of me, near the tall, drapery-lined windows that stretched across the back of the house and along the side to the left toward what I suspected was the kitchen area. He looked healthy and dangerous. He didn't have the circular device around his head anymore; instead, a silver transmitter jutted out from the spot where his primary implant had been, as if it had been impossible to shove a regular neural net all the way back into his skull. Whatever it was, he wasn't as vulnerable as I'd hoped.

For an instant, he looked stunned to see me. Then his face tightened, and a wild look appeared in his eyes. A need to attack. To destroy.

I felt the same.

Kieran leapt from his chair—and I raced forward, only dimly aware I was shouting. I fired twice, hitting him in the arm and upper chest, but it didn't slow him. At the last second, I triggered the projector. The orange energy disk formed, the vibrating, humming shield coming close to my ear as I cocked my arm back and swung it forward. I slammed into him, using the shield as a battering ram, my adrenaline temporarily muting the toll on my body.

Kieran's momentum was nearly as great as mine, and for a split second, he hovered in the air, the shield and my body absorbing his blow—and then I shoved him to the ground.

My savage thrill didn't last, as he was on his feet almost immediately. He punched me in the chest, sending me backward with a burst of pain. If I hadn't been as thick as I was, the punch would've taken me down. I stayed on my feet and was starting for him again when Raven rushed him, firing her gun, her hand shield activated, the vibrating shield confusing him for a moment. She plowed into him and held him in place.

I quickly pulled off my pack and opened it. "Kieran," I shouted.

He swung his head to me, his expression one of growing anger. I held up the flasher ball and triggered it, the light not only blinding him but pixelating his lenses and shorting his infrareds, forcing his implanted system to run repair diagnostics.

Raven shoved him back as he covered his eyes too late.

The flasher expended. I dropped it and charged forward. Together, she and I pushed him backward, the shields buzzing where they touched, into the living room, Kieran off-balance from being blinded.

I heard a faint chime, grabbed Raven's shoulder, and we ducked.

Kieran straightened in confusion. Exposed.

From the kitchen area, Valor triggered the plasma cannon.

A cylinder of plasma blasted across the space and slammed into him, the thick, bluish-white bolt of energy throwing him backwards. His feet clipped the back of a nearby couch and flipped it over as he crashed into the wall between two of the windows, cracking both of them. Even though the plasma missed us, it passed close enough that I felt its sharp heat.

I straightened, not sure what kind of shape he would be in. A blow like that would've sent a normal person to the hospital if not the morgue. Yet Kieran rose from the carpet, woozy but livid, shirt charred and skin red, straining to see enough to locate the cannon.

Valor had already started the cycle again, which took a few seconds. There was another faint chime, we ducked aside, and she shot him again, the blast throwing him against the wall, shattering the nearby window. He collapsed as shards of glass fell around him.

I led Raven to the fallen Agent. He was on his back, dazed, covered in glass though he wasn't cut; he bled a little from where I'd shot him but not much. Damn enhancements. Though his shirt was shredded, his skin was no worse than a bad sunburn. That might be the extent of his injuries—which was why we had to hurry.

As he began to scoot backward to try to get away, Raven jammed her gun into her pants and pulled the specialized handcuffs from her pocket. I stepped forward, and he reached for me with his left hand, his eyesight starting to return. Raven slapped one of the cuffs around his wrist—but though he jerked back, he wouldn't be able to get the cuff off, not even with his strength.

We dropped to his side simultaneously and tried to get his other arm, which was under him. He twisted and fought to get away, so I activated my shield again. He punched at it with increasing strength and ferocity, recovering from the cannon blasts.

I drove him backwards as he fought to get up. He nearly threw me to the side, but I just managed to hang on. Beside me, Raven activated her hand shield, and together we pinned him in the corner of the family room near his quartz-lined fireplace. I managed to catch his uncuffed right hand in my larger shield, though it exposed my left side. Raven tried to get the cuff around his right wrist, but he jerked his arm back at the last second, using my shield to block her efforts. The three of us struggled, him to avoid being cuffed and us trying to capture his wrist. Once we cuffed both wrists, the two individual cuffs would draw together like magnets, though a multitude stronger. Once they came together, even he wouldn't be able to break free.

Though we couldn't get to his wrist, we pinned him into the corner; with his back against the wall, his feet stretched out, he couldn't gain any leverage to overpower us. Yet he continued to fight, thrashing about and shoving us backward.

Kieran suddenly arched his body, pushing us a step back, but instead of fighting, he used the space he'd created to maneuver his left hand toward the wall. He pulled back and punched the wall, breaking through the drywall. I didn't understand until he jerked his hand back out—with his fist holding the end of a wire. He'd torn it from the nearby electrical outlet, the plug half ripped out of its spot in the wall.

The wire was live.

Before I could react, Kieran jabbed the wire at my thresher-projector shield. A massive spark erupted—and my shield winked out, the commercial-grade, refractional projectors smoking from the damage.

He'd overwhelmed the electronics, shorting out my shield.

I was exposed.

Kieran raised his leg and kicked me, sending me flying. I flew over the overturned couch and landed beside a chair, pain flaring.

Raven scurried backward as Kieran rose, her focus laced with fear, her plan falling apart.

Valor triggered another cannon blast, but he'd expected it and ducked out of the way. The blast slammed into the wall behind him.

I climbed to my feet and charged, hitting him over and over. Raven attacked as well. She'd lost her gun but didn't pause. She turned off her shield to get at him, grunting as she attacked with quick, martial-arts-like attacks, and I felt Kieran weaken, though he punched her and threw me back. I landed on the ground, and the cannon erupted again.

I got to my feet and leapt at Kieran once more, only partly acknowledging that he was still up, still fighting. There was a trickle of blood on the side of his face, but I wasn't sure he felt it. He didn't seem to feel his injuries. I punched him as hard as I could instead, full in his chiseled face, though he countered with a blow to my stomach. As I straightened, he cocked his arm back to punch me; Raven activated her shield again and swung it forward two-handed, throwing the Agent toward the sitting area. He regained his footing, but a blast from Valor's cannon sent him flying into another section of wall, cracking it as well and buckling the floor nearby.

She lifted the cannon from her spot in the kitchen and brought it into the family room before planting the cannon's adjustable metal leg to keep it upright.

Kieran picked himself up. His skin was bright red with blisters appearing, and I could make out some bruises, but his anger burned brighter. "*Come on already.*"

Raven turned off her shield glove, extracted her curved blades, ignited them, and ran at Kieran. "For Talia!"

Whether it was Raven's war cry or her glowing, curved ion energy blades, Kieran froze as she approached. She sliced across his chest, which would've cut him open if he hadn't snapped out of it and jerked back at the last second. The blade still carved through his shirt and skin, and she continued after him, slicing his arm, then swinging at his face. He blocked her arm, then jumped back as she shoved the blade in her free hand at him. He hurried backward as she went after him.

I ran over, grabbed my pack, and upended it, my devices falling out. I went after the bolt-emitter, which I'd recharged on the ride here, snatching it as Raven cried out.

Kieran had jumped up and ripped down one of the curtain rods. He spun the rod to block her blow, the curved laser energy catching the curtains on fire. He ripped them away, seemingly unbothered by the flames, then blocked her next two blows and hit her in the side of the head with the rod. She stumbled back, then started forward again. I hurried over to join the fight, yelling Kieran's name. Neither he nor Raven responded, locked in a battle that sped up as smoke billowed into the air past them. His swings came fast, her counters almost as fast, his strength versus the lethal energy curving around her fists.

He blocked two of her attacks, shoving her arms upwards, then hit her shoulder. The blow spun her, so her back was to him; before she could react, he dropped the rod, grabbed her arms, left hand wrapped around hers, and drove the glowing blade in her hand into the quartz blocks that rose up the wall above his fireplace. The blade slid into the quartz—and Kieran twisted Raven's wrist, causing the blade emitter to shatter, the pieces falling to the fireplace below.

Raven jabbed backwards with her right arm, her elbow catching him in the face. As he stumbled back, she switched her remaining blade to her left hand and sliced at his right hand. He jerked back with a snarl, letting go, then scooped up his rod, ducking from under her next swing, and jumped back.

She activated her shield, came at him again and sliced at the rod with her remaining blade, shortening it, yet he bashed at her shield-covered arm, sapping her strength.

I could see the outcome and had to stop it.

With a slice, she shortened the rod more, an angled cut that turned the rod into a sharp-edge spear. As Kieran raised the rod, I leapt forward, not caring if Raven cut me, and plowed into Kieran.

The Agent threw me backwards, then grabbed Raven's right arm and spun her around, driving her blade-covered fist toward her body. She turned off the blade at the last second, then swung her free hand and slammed the edge of her shield into the side of his knee.

Kieran cried out as he buckled, then pivoted on his good leg and threw her.

She sailed through the air across nearly the entire length of the family room, before crashing to the quartz-littered floor.

Jumping to my feet, I pointed the bolt-emitter at Kieran

and triggered it.

Electricity reached out with disjointed, glowing arms and grabbed him. He shuddered, his back arching, and he dropped to his knees when the energy stopped.

I ran to him, raised my metal-bar-covered arm, the shield destroyed, but the bar was a solid weapon by itself, brought my arms back to magnify the blow I was going to deliver—

Kieran snatched a lamp that had been knocked off a side table and swung it, the thick base hitting me in the chin.

As I stumbled back, dazed, he stood and slammed a fist into my sternum.

I crashed into a credenza near the central hallway I'd used.

It felt like my ribcage had been broken. My skin was soaked with sweat and probably blood.

I heard the telltale chime—but so did Kieran. He pivoted almost too fast to see and threw the lamp at Valor, hitting her and causing her to fall back. As she did, the cannon fired, the glowing projectile punching through the ceiling and roof.

Kieran was bent over, but he was still standing, flames rising behind him. I couldn't let him win. Raven would suffer, would become his prisoner, if not worse. I thought I heard her moan where she lay, though I wasn't sure.

Grimacing, I stood. Raven and Valor were down.

I had one last chance: my pistol. I pulled it from behind my back, where I'd wedged it, and fired at him, just remembering at the last moment I couldn't risk killing him. I shot him in the shoulder instead, then the same thigh Raven had cut.

Kieran lurched at me, snatched the gun and threw it past the dining room table, which was about the only undamaged piece of furniture left, then grabbed me by the shoulders and lifted me off the ground, though his arms shook. "You can't defeat me."

I heard the faint chime.

He did, too, his face almost comical in his surprise.

The next moment, Valor fired the cannon. Both she and the weapon lay on the floor where they'd fallen, but she'd aimed it at Kieran. When she fired, the projectile shot out from the edge of the kitchen, across the carpet—leaving a charred streak in its wake—and slammed into his foot.

He cried out as he collapsed, taking me with him. I landed hard, though he looked worse off. The bones in his foot had been shattered; it looked as if it had been crushed, the skin blackened.

His gaze refocused on me, his body and his training able to take the pain. I scrambled back, needing to get to my feet, when I saw the absorber lying within reach. It was meant for machines, but I snatched it anyway, thumbed the safety, and as he grabbed me, I jammed the absorber against the side of his head and triggered it.

Kieran shuddered, his breath coming in short gasps, then I felt it too. A dissipation of thought. Of motor skills. He no longer gripped my shirt but didn't let go. His muscles needed direction to do that, direction given by electrical signals. Thoughts, movement, all electrical, the machine drawing from both of us, his hand connecting his body to mine. I couldn't let go if I wanted. My body didn't respond; it grew heavy, detached.

A shadow appeared above us. Raven. She cocked back, the broken rod held like a baseball bat, and swung at Kieran's skull.

CHAPTER THIRTY-TWO

I shook my head again to try to clear it of the absorber's lingering effects. As I did, I caught sight of Raven. She stood a dozen feet away, hunched over with her arms crossed, an empty fire extinguisher she'd used to put out the fire laying on the burnt carpet behind her. Her remaining blade, the one I'd boobytrapped, lay at her feet. Distrusted.

She straightened as I forced myself to my feet.

I faced her, but Valor spoke before I could. "Need some help."

She'd dragged a heavy dining room chair over and had somehow gotten Kieran's body onto it—but he started to slide off, still knocked out, when she tried to tie him in place.

I hobbled to her, my body stiff and disjointed, and grabbed Kieran's shoulders, pushing him back into the chair so hard I nearly tipped him over.

Valor snaked the rope around his waist and under his arms. I glanced back at Raven. She'd stayed in place, posture rigid, her expression void of the love and trust that I'd always seen from her.

Valor maneuvered me as she worked, and I ended up behind Kieran, his body between Raven and me. Valor finished looping the rope around his torso for a fourth time, then started looping the rope under the seat and around his waist.

I lifted my gaze to Raven. "You okay?"

"Nothing's broken, body-wise."

Her tone. Cold and dismissive.

Kieran's body shifted.

I jerked on his collar, which caused him to shift the other way.

"Could use better help," Valor muttered.

She pushed me to the side and stayed low, as if not wanting to get between Raven and me, to bind Kieran's arms together behind his back, running the rope all the way to his shoulders.

Raven's expression was guarded, but I could see her turmoil. She'd always had me and Jex by her side. But he wasn't here, and I'd destroyed her faith.

The combined rooms were a wreck. Occasional bits of ceiling where Valor had blasted a hole sprinkled down, air blew in from the hole and the shattered windows, and most of the furniture appeared broken. At least the fire was out.

As Valor tied Kieran's legs together, running the nylon rope around the legs of the chair, I worked on the cuffs to get them operational, then secured his wrists in place. Even with his strength, he wouldn't be able to break free.

When Valor stood, I gauged her health. She seemed mostly unhurt. Raven, on the other hand, had a limp. She and I had both suffered some cuts, and my muscles ached, especially my back and chest.

We didn't have time to rest or absorb what we'd accomplished. We had a monster to wake. His leg continued to bleed where Raven had cut him, and his foot was a crumpled mess, but his other injuries already seemed to have healed.

I looked at her. "We need to cover his implants."

She'd been staring at him, but her gaze swiveled to me. I caught the moment when realization dawned on her. "No."

"I hate it, too."

She removed Talia's cap from her pack and angrily shoved it at me.

With my lip curled in disgust, I forced the cap over Kieran's head. After I'd covered his entire head, the cloth stretched tight,

I tried to wake him. When he didn't immediately respond, I punched the wound in his thigh.

He jerked awake, his confusion quickly fleeting. He scanned us and the room, getting his bearings, then tested the rope and cuffs.

I leaned forward. "You're going to tell us where Talia is."

His eyes flickered with sadness and what seemed like remorse at the mention of her name. The next moment, he struggled harder to break free. It wasn't until Valor sat on him that he stopped.

I faced him. "Is she alive?"

His eyes registered that he was trapped, yet he seemed to war with himself.

My hands began to tremble. "Is she?"

"I need to atone for my actions," he said. "But don't ask me about her."

"Why the hell not?" Raven asked.

His eyes swiveled to me, then back to her. "You don't know what you're doing."

"Don't bother signaling for help," Raven told him. "We've blocked your implant. You'll answer our questions."

"You think I haven't been cut off before? I was cut off after your father's stunt. I have better technology now. I'll crush you."

I couldn't tell what he'd been implanted with. I needed to remove it, study it, neither of which I had time for. "What you did was horrific."

"I was carrying out my mission."

"Your 'mission' was shooting a twelve-year-old girl?"

"I didn't shoot her. I tried to save her. I had my team rush her to our medics to get her heart going. They had to hook her to some machine, but she lived. She's alive," Kieran said, visibly struggling to push the words out as if he'd held them in too long. He dropped his feverish gaze. "I couldn't bear it. I took every punishment The Agency gave because of what they did to her."

I dared looking at Raven and Valor. They looked as stunned as I felt.

The thought of Talia actually alive, which I'd hoped for so long, felt unreal. "Why didn't you say anything at the L.A. node?" I demanded.

"I thought I would defeat you—and I did until the last second. It doesn't matter. You abandoned her."

The pain and shame in his eyes triggered a rising panic. "What aren't you telling me? What did they do to her?"

Valor climbed off of him. "Dray, he's trained in psychological warfare. Don't buy any of it."

But Raven stepped forward. She must've seen his emotions as I had. "Where is she? You have to tell us. You're responsible for all of it."

He sneered. "Neither of you were any better. You failed to protect her, then you left her. I saved her. Me and Zion."

It took a second for the name to register. "Zion? My old partner?"

"He's won the war. It doesn't matter that you know. You can't change it. You can't help her." Kieran's tone was forlorn. "It's too late. She's a part of the system now."

"What does that mean?" Raven demanded.

"She's not your sister anymore." He looked up at me, anguish and sorrow and penance blazing forth. "She's not your daughter. Zion made sure of that. He's behind this. He's the head of The Agency."

CHAPTER THIRTY-THREE

The last year of undergrad, I came home to a trashed apartment.

Sharing an apartment with Zion had been fine at first; between my coursework and football practice, I was rarely home, and he spent most nights at the lab.

I'd caught glimpses of his temper before, but not to the degree I experienced that night. When I came home, he'd smashed our plates and glasses, destroyed our vid screen, overturned our cheap bookcase, and was in the process of destroying the flimsy table and chairs we'd bought at a second-hand store, one of the last remaining pieces of furniture. He didn't say a word.

I grabbed him to stop him.

For a second, I thought he was going to fight me. Instead, he said, "I'll pay for it."

It took a few days to coax him into telling me what had happened. I'd known a physics professor had been involved in a gruesome accident. What I hadn't known was that after she fell into a coma, Zion suggested installing a bionic interface into her brain. This was before implants became a way of life. Bionics were Zion's field of study, and he was very convincing. He'd gotten the professor's husband, children, and the school board to agree—but her surgeon refused. Nothing Zion said changed her mind.

Because of her refusal, he'd decimated our apartment. Then he filed bogus malpractice claims that nearly ruined her, he admitted months later, drunk on Patrón Platinum.

A week later, I moved out of our place and in with Mina. I told Zion it was because she and I were in love, which we were, but I didn't want her around him.

I should've warned Nikolai, Tevin, and Brocco about his temper when their talks of forming a company grew serious. But I never conceived it would end up like this, my former friend running an organization bent on destroying us—and holding my daughter hostage.

Beside me, Raven wailed with grief, a cry that shredded my heart. "How could you?" she yelled at Kieran. She punched him. "Where is she? *Where*?"

Kieran looked at her, then me, sorrow shading his gaze.

"Answer her question," I said, my voice thick.

His face hardened. "If I destroy you two, I won't feel so terrible about what was done to her." He tried his restraints again. From where I stood, I saw his fingers straining to reach the nylon rope.

"Tell me," Raven said, cocking her fist back.

"You're too late."

A rage that I'd carried since Free Isle flared inside of me. He'd caused Talia to get shot, caused the pain Raven and I had suffered. He wouldn't tell us anything—which meant he didn't serve a purpose anymore.

Before Raven could swing, I snatched the gun from her belt and aimed it at his head.

"Do it," he said. "I'll haunt you like she's haunted me."

If I killed him, I wouldn't be any better than him. I'd told Raven that.

If I pulled the trigger now, I would harm her more, maybe irreparably, and still wouldn't have Talia back. But I wanted vengeance.

My finger began to squeeze.

Valor stepped in front of my gun. "You jury and executioner now? This how your version of America goes?"

"You don't understand."

"You don't think I've felt the horror of seeing someone you love die at their hands? We aren't this."

Kieran's voice floated up from behind her. "He can't be reasoned with."

Valor turned to him. "Where's the girl?"

"Not talking."

She leaned down, grabbed his damaged foot, and twisted. He screamed and passed out.

She dropped the foot. "Shit. Too much."

Raven glared at him—then me. Without a word, she stumbled off.

"Should I wake him?" Valor asked, unsure.

I stared at Kieran. While a part of me had enjoyed his cry of pain, he wouldn't tell us what we needed to know, though I wasn't sure why. I would've assumed it was out of a sense of duty, but with the way he'd just acted, it seemed to be a sort of self-flagellation.

Not that it made anything better. And it didn't ease my rage. Or loss.

"We can't stay," Valor said.

I checked the time. Twenty-six hours and eight minutes until the attack. I set a countdown using my implant, the numbers visible in the bottom of my vision. "Keep an eye on him."

Though I felt I'd let Raven down, I didn't search for her. I needed to find the information Kieran refused to reveal. Yet I was reeling. The way he'd talked, I feared Zion planned to turn Talia into an Agent. She was smart and perceptive, but she was still a little girl, malleable enough to be warped into believing Zion. He was an old family friend. She didn't have any reason not to trust him.

I remembered his obsessive need. Cunning and ruthless, he didn't care about ethics or morals when it came to his work. To him, the end justified his actions, which included pushing people to his will. His only weakness was his inability to reason with someone—and he was immune to it as well.

Worst of all, he'd have access to our old company's

technology, which meant anything I'd created could be used against us.

Zion would've used many of my designs to manipulate and coerce others. He craved power, and The Agency would've been the ultimate source. He hadn't created The Agency, but someone had appointed him to head the organization. That's when The Agency had really taken off. The augmented Agents should have clued me in. He had never been satisfied with the human body's limitations.

His superior—probably the President—wouldn't have known the threat Zion posed until it was too late. Unless, of course, the President wanted Zion to take over, so the President could remain in the Oval Office permanently.

Zion wouldn't have targeted Talia, but when she was brought in, he must have seen an opportunity—and with her hacking abilities, she had the potential of becoming an exceptional Agent. Just like she would've been exceptional at anything she'd pursued.

I searched the combined rooms, picking my way through the destruction. Underneath one of the couches was the holopad Kieran had been watching when we came in. A video was paused. When I hit play, Britt appeared. "Dray Quintero is to blame. He's a traitor—" I stopped the feed, which was a taped national news segment. I needed answers, not propaganda.

I went to the office I'd passed earlier. The pictures on the wall were a mystery to me: beachfronts and dilapidated buildings, gravel paths and long, nondescript structures. One framed picture was of a group of six male soldiers, young, caught mid-laugh, a cliff visible behind them. I realized Kieran was one of them. His hair was normal then, a sandy-blonde color. Another frame held a map of Houston, which Kieran had marred with black marks, what I realized were the sites of the 2032 terrorist bombings. Other framed pictures showed the devastated sites, gaping holes and crumbled buildings deformed into monuments of suffering and fear.

There was also a diploma of some kind, an official-looking

government certificate.

I searched through the few papers left on the desk. The bottom sheet was an official document. Kieran had been demoted to Field SubCommander. Almost two months ago, right after I'd neutered him.

The other papers discussed various domestic terrorist groups. As I skimmed the documents, I spotted my name three times.

This was getting me nowhere. I had to find Talia. I had a flash of her with silver hair. She'd have to be brainwashed before they'd let her join. Maybe that was why Mina was so scared, because Talia was being warped into something that wasn't our daughter.

I collapsed in the chair, the counter running in the corner of my vision. Talia could be anywhere. Brocco had been wrong. Kieran wouldn't tell me anything. He and I were enemies.

And Talia would be, too.

I struggled to focus as my fears assaulted me. Zion and his people would need time to warp her, to first heal her and then operate on her. Then she'd be lost to me forever, as Kieran appeared lost from his past.

I snapped my head up, then stood. Searched the frames again.

The diploma.

* * *

Raven had righted one of the cushioned chairs and sat in it, holding a Smith & Wesson 9 mm. She wore a thin woman's glove on her right hand, having replaced the one she'd previously damaged.

I took a deep breath. "I think I found Talia."

Valor grabbed my arm. "Where?"

"Zion was always wary of me. Maybe it was my size as a running back or the way I distilled his ideas."

"So?" Raven interrupted impatiently.

"Where would you hide something if you knew the person you feared would come after it? In the most secure location possible. Besides, if I'm right, she'd be there to become groomed as an Agent." I jabbed a thumb at Kieran. "After soldiers fail Special Forces' training, they're given a chance to join The Agency. Many take it, but the process is brutal, not only due to the training, body modifications, and brainwashing but because of the multiple implants The Agency installs."

"That's where Talia is?" Valor asked.

"There's a plaque in Kieran's office, a certificate for completing advanced training at the Acceleration and Transformation Facility. It has to be where Zion creates his Agents—which means it'll be heavily guarded."

"We need more weapons," Valor said.

Raven held up the 9 mm. "There are some upstairs."

She led me to Kieran's second-floor bedroom, which had a low king-sized bed and modern, horizontally-paneled walls. Two pictures occupied the nightstand: one of Britt, the other of a high school. On the far side of the bed, a section of the wall stood open. Inside, Glocks, Smith & Wesson 9 mms, an LR-500, a Remington R4A, two Colt CM901s, and others hung on hooks, while drawers underneath held ammunition. And four percussion grenades. He'd created a mini arsenal for himself.

I snatched the Remington, a Glock, then paused. Checked the triggers.

"We can't use these," I told Raven, returning to the living room. "They're keyed to him. They won't fire for us. We can take ammunition for our guns, and the grenades will work, but that's it."

Raven put the 9 mm aside with a sigh and motioned to Kieran. "What do we do with him?"

I couldn't kill him. Should, but couldn't.

Valor spoke up. "I have an idea."

* * *

Having summoned our car into his garage, Raven opened the trunk as Valor and I carried Kieran through the garage, struggling with his weight. He wasn't just muscular, he felt denser than a normal person. When we reached our car, we dropped him into the trunk—causing a muffled cry, as we'd taped his mouth after untying him from the chair, though we'd tied his arms and legs back together—and I tugged Talia's cap tighter over his head.

Maybe it was fitting after all that he wore it.

Raven programmed the car, and we sent it on its way. As it disappeared, Valor asked, "Where are you sending him?"

"The Petrified Forest. By the time he reaches it, the nodes will be destroyed."

"I'll send people to retrieve him. We'll make him stand trial."

Or maybe drop him in a deep well, I didn't say. I tossed her the keys to Kieran's Cadillac Sparna sedan. "Let's go."

Chapter Thirty-Four

We paused just long enough to switch vehicles, trading Kieran's sedan for a beat-up, extended-cab pickup truck we found parked on the outskirts of a large construction project. I'd wanted to leave a note, but the keys on the Cadillac's front seat hopefully made our intentions clear.

It was a tiny bright spot in what we were about to do.

I had too much time to think as Valor drove. Too much time to imagine the horror my child must've endured, surrounded by enemies who would've twisted her fears and love against her, made her doubt me and Raven. They would've used Mina to sell the message that I was an uncaring father.

I felt responsible, not only for Talia's suffering but for the oppressive, monitored world we lived in. I needed to make sure my daughters didn't suffer any more than they already had.

The click of metal drew my attention back. Raven. Loading bullets into an extra clip she'd taken.

Her fingers seemed shaky, but her face was wrathful. Almost unrecognizable.

One damaged daughter at a time—assuming we rescued Talia.

We passed lush, green land. Large swaths of Texas had been transformed, the overflowing waters of the Gulf desalinized and piped north to turn the area into new farms. Texas was now one of the largest producers of crops in the country. We'd traveled over two hundred miles west of the Dallas/Fort Worth area; farms claimed the land around us as we approached our destination, some family-owned, others massive.

A semblance of normalcy, its inhabitants unaware of the silver-haired demons in their midst.

Valor took a series of side roads before pulling over beside a field of nearly-grown hay. "We should approach on foot."

The journey from Kieran's had taken long enough that the sun set as we neared this place, and other than a quick glance from up the road, I'd kept us away. There was so little traffic that any vehicle would attract attention, and I hadn't wanted to tip our hand. We'd slept four miles away, parked in a dark corner of a fast-food parking lot, though I didn't get much rest.

Today would change everything.

When I got out of our truck, I spotted an old barn to the north with a harvester parked beside it. To the south were more fields, cotton maturing and winter wheat sprouting. Trees stood farther back behind us, a thicket surrounding a shed and an area electrical grid. The land rose past that, but all I could see were other farms.

Raven and Valor pulled their pistols and led me along the edge of the field heading east, staying low so the hay would mask our approach. When we reached the end of the field, we surveyed our target.

Two sets of chain-link fence, constructed one inside of the other, stretched away to either side of a guarded entrance before turning east and continuing into the distance as far as I could see, the fencing topped with barbed wire. I suspected it was electrified.

The setting fit Mina's description. It had to be the Facility.

Inside the enclosed property sat a whitewashed structure that looked old, probably built in the 80s or 90s. One story in height, it contained a reinforced-double-door entrance, a couple of narrow windows to either side and a handful of bushes along the front between the building and a row of parking spaces. The Facility had no signage of any sort or indication of its purpose, just a warning that trespassing was forbidden.

"I don't see any DNA scanners or feed disrupters," Raven said quietly.

"A bunch of cameras, though," Valor said.

"And an old alarm system," I said. There were four megaphone-shaped alarms visible from where we hid.

Then I saw why the Facility contained so many alarms.

A cluster of eight people rounded the corner, jogging, all clad in light-gray outfits. And they all had silver hair.

Agents.

Raven, Valor, and I exchanged a look. We'd taken down Kieran, but that had just been one. Not eight.

"Why do I have the feeling there are more inside?" Valor asked.

I'd feared Talia wouldn't be here. Now I feared she was.

"Only a few have all-silver hair," Raven said. "Others have a mix."

"A process," Valor said. "To turn into The Agency's lapdogs."

"There could be dozens inside."

I shared their feeling. Our weapons—two pistols, a cannon, four grenades, and some gadgets—seemed woefully inadequate.

If I had more of my devices, I'd detonate disrupters to scramble their feeds, sow confusion, light up the place with plasma cannons and an entire army of rebels. But we didn't have any of that. Not even an EMP would help. Manufacturers shielded virtually every product nowadays, ever since an EMP nearly destroyed Silicon Valley in 2036. Even if we did have an EMP, a blast would hurt us as well as the Silvers.

I recalled when Talia started fourth grade. Already the smartest kid among her peers, she'd been placed in an advanced class. But on the second day, I'd been summoned to her school. I found myself in the principal's office, Talia bobbing in annoyance beside me.

"Your daughter argued with the teacher," the principal announced.

"She was pandering to me," Talia said.

"Do you know what that word means?" the man asked.

Talia looked up at me with her big brown eyes. "My god, it's an epidemic."

I'd laughed so hard I clutched my belly. When the principal calmed me down, huffed up in his tweed jacket and dated haircut, I gave him some advice. "If you ever think Talia won't understand something, you're wrong. She's the smartest person on this campus. Maybe the entire state."

Talia eventually became the teacher's favorite student. She always did.

I flicked my gaze at the counter running at the bottom of my vision. *One hour, fifty-seven minutes left.*

* * *

We retreated to the truck.

I started to climb into the back of the cab, but the barn, which stood two hundred feet from the Facility's entrance on the opposite side of the road, drew my gaze.

At my urging, Valor took us there. She didn't fight me, though her actions were those of someone overwhelmed. I could relate but couldn't let it stop me.

She drove onto the farm's property like we owned the place, drumming the wheel anxiously. The truck we'd stolen fit into the surroundings, but still, with being this close to The Agency's Facility, we were taking a big risk.

As I'd hoped, there weren't any cameras pointed our way, as they would've taken in the Facility as well. Zion wouldn't let anyone record what he was doing.

The sliding door was unlocked. I led the way inside the barn.

The building had modern upgrades: insulation, electricity, and computer systems that monitored the fields, weather, and soil moisture levels. The main portion of the barn held a tractor, a loader, various attachments, and hand-guided farming equipment.

Raven shot me a questioning look. I wasn't sure why I'd

brought us here either.

Tackle and grooming supplies were stacked to one side, near a row of stalls that contained horses.

I passed the animals—and discovered why I had been drawn to the barn. Four charcoal-gray Gen Omega robots stood along the back, their honey-colored eyes dark.

The man-shaped robots, the same model we'd encountered after the robot-dog attack, each sported the articulated "hands" they needed to roll and move round bales of hay. Other attachments hung on shelves behind them.

They not only handled a number of jobs but also sported a "defend" program. Amarjit and I had thought it would protect an owner from a bucking farm animal or possibly a robber, but it had an aggressive mode as well, features I hadn't thought would ever be used.

As Valor guarded the door, I booted up the four robots. They were perhaps a dozen years old, not even a third of a way through their designed lifespan. Since my implant was covered, I opened the nearest one's chest plate and logged in manually. The four were linked, so within seconds, I pulled up the shared program that controlled them.

I wasn't sure how they'd help, though as I ran through possible scenarios, an idea struck me. I removed my wire interface from my pack, slipped the curved end under my cap and hooked the wire to the lead 'bot. Pulling up my credentials, I synched with them and issued a series of commands.

Checked the time. *One hour, twenty-three minutes.*

The 'bots were just one piece, though, and not the most important. I recalled the time Nikolai had interfered with my commands when I'd tried to light the fusion reactor—and the weakness Agents seemed to have.

I searched for Raven and found her standing in the corner, talking quietly. Horrified, I hurried to her. "What the hell are you doing?"

She said, "You too," then hung up. "I doubt we'll survive this, so I called Jex. I wanted to hear his voice."

"You might've just tipped our enemies to where we are. Goddammit, Raven, you have to think."

She crossed her arms, her tone sharp. "He's fine, by the way. They all are." She glanced at Valor, who joined us. "Everyone's ready to strike."

Valor scowled at us. "You two need to work out your shit. I don't wanna die because you are too stubborn to talk to each other."

Raven walked away. I felt I should go after her, but lately, that hadn't been my strong suit. And we didn't have time.

I approached the large tractor instead. It had a detachable screen, which the owner could use to maneuver the machine remotely. Using a crowbar, I cracked open the cradle it normally rested on and located the receiver chip. It was small, only an inch long, and was actually a backup, a second receiver to extend the tractor's range. Recalling what I remembered of the old security systems I'd learned about back in college, I connected the handheld display to my implant and wrote an override program, then made sure the handheld was still synchronized to the receiver chip.

"Can I help?" Valor asked.

"Look for something small but sharp that would be able to pierce rubber."

"Like a nail?"

I nodded. "When you do, solder it to this chip. Also, find adhesive or something to keep the board in place."

As she got to work, I went to the tractor's engine compartment, unlatched the cover to the energy packets, and pulled out a plasma-energy battery. We'd stopped using plasma batteries in our products because of their volatility, but the tractor's manufacturer hadn't. I pulled out a second battery, then a third. As I did, I found Raven beside me. Without a word, she took it and placed it next to the others as if she knew my plan. I handed her the fourth as well, then went to retrieve more wires.

I should've asked how Jex and Anya were. I cared about them. Yet I felt I'd lost my right to ask—and was worried my efforts wouldn't be enough. The plan forming in my head was layered with guesses and wishful thinking.

I should've taken Raven away from all of this. After my broadcast, I should've taken her out of the damn country. Actually, I should've taken Kieran's job offer. It would've protected my girls, the rest of the world be damned.

I shouldn't lie to myself. His offer would've protected *me,* my girls be damned.

Raven didn't say anything as she helped, working as efficiently as if I'd told her exactly what I had in mind, echoing memories of when she'd helped me on projects as a little girl. Jex was right. We were too similar.

Yet, she was her own woman. Tough, frustrating, with so much life to live.

I spoke softly as I focused on the batteries. "Whether Talia is there or not, this is where I'm supposed to be: confronting the man behind it all. You need to stay behind."

She didn't jerk away. Didn't explode. Instead, she said, "This will work. It has to. If not, then what happened to her, to Trevor, to you and Mom, was all for nothing."

I considered arguing with her. Then I looked at the batteries, which would make powerful bombs. I'd use them to bargain for Raven's and Talia's lives if I had to—and take the entire place down. The realization was calming in an odd way.

"Will you be able to shoot Agents if it comes to that? Shoot to kill?" I asked.

She removed the protective absorber from the last battery. "They're keeping Talia like some sort of trophy. If anyone gets in my way, even if they're unarmed, they've earned their fate."

CHAPTER THIRTY-FIVE

The process, including programing the loader, took longer than I'd wanted. Thirty-nine minutes, nineteen seconds, until the attack on the nodes.

We finished loading the pickup truck with rakes, hoes, and a canvas bag we'd found that might've served to carry hand-held farm equipment in the past but now contained our weapons. I'd also fashioned a four-foot metal rod and covered one end with rubber.

After I settled the bag carefully in the back, making sure the tarp concealed the three robots hidden underneath and put the rod in the bed of the truck, I held out my hand for the keys, which made Valor frown. "What, I don't look the farmer type?"

She didn't, as the clothes we found didn't mask her eyepatch or crazy hair—Raven and I at least wore flannel shirts we'd found that smelled of hay and looked authentic—but that wasn't the point. "Only Raven and I are going."

"I told you my stomach doesn't hurt anymore."

"It's not that."

"What is it, some family bullshit? You need me." Her eye widened. "This is a suicide mission. That's why you didn't want Jex going."

I removed the bracelet linked to Raven's tracker and gave it to her. "Whatever happens, Raven will need your help getting out of here. You can gauge her movements, anticipate when they're coming out."

"How are you gonna make her leave that place without you?"

I shook my head. I didn't know. "Find a car and park behind the complex. I'll have Raven take Talia out the back."

"You save them. You're their father. Better yet, don't go in there."

"I have to do this." And so did Raven, I accepted.

Valor scanned my face, the camera behind her eyepatch making faint sounds. "Where the hell am I supposed to get a damn car?"

"There's a farmhouse up the road. Use the last robot as a protector. I've already coded it, so just motion to it. It'll do the rest. And leave the barn door open."

She glanced over her shoulder toward the farmhouse. "Your plan sucks ass."

"Don't wait too long for us, and don't park where Agents could see you. If we don't come out within fifteen minutes of the nodes blowing, leave. Get back to the others."

"I'll come in after you."

"No. Others need to know about this place. Once the nodes are destroyed, this will become one of The Agency's strongholds. We can't let them regroup and fight back. Besides, if you don't leave, no one will ever know what happened." I leaned close. "Think about what that will do to Jex. To Anya."

I realized she could be recording this. I hoped not. I needed her to do as I asked.

Worry twisted her face. "I hate you for this."

I rested a hand on her shoulder. "You've been a great bodyguard and a good friend."

She hugged me, then shoved me back. "You die in there, I'll never forgive you."

Raven came over and hugged her. As they whispered to each other, I climbed into the cab of the truck; after a few moments, Raven did the same. "Get the car as quickly as you can," I told Valor as I settled behind the wheel. "Don't let anyone see you."

"If I tell you how I got my eyepatch, will you let me come with you?"

I smiled sadly. "I'm not done guessing."

She grabbed the door before I could close it, her emotions lining her face, and handed me her Glock. "You get your girl and get out of there. *Both* of you. I'll be waiting. We'll come back later and blow the whole damn place up."

"Deal."

It gave her some hope, at least.

* * *

My heart thudded in my chest as I pulled up beside the gatehouse that guarded the Facility.

"Help you?" the guard asked. He had brown hair, not silver. Looked like a local. A bored one. He didn't know a revolutionary war had started.

As soon as the guy looked at me, I risked being identified by The Agency's software. The sunglasses I wore did little to hide my appearance, so I kept a hand to my lower face, resting an elbow on the open truck window. "We're the new landscapin' crew," I drawled.

"I didn't get no call you were comin'."

I shifted to raise the ID I'd fashioned while Raven began to lift the metal rod she'd hidden under the dashboard when four Agents, all fully silver-haired, jogged toward us, following the fence line.

My heart pounded as Raven hid the rod.

I forced the words out, keeping up the façade with the guard. "No one's called? Could come back later, but it'll be a week or two."

He grumbled as he lowered his head and started typing with his datarings.

The Agents jogged past us.

The air was warm and thick. We were exposed. Other cameras watched us. Raven kept her head down. Landscapers normally didn't look like attractive young women. I had to be quick. Those Agents could turn back, decide something wasn't right.

"Ya ain't in the system. Gotta go through proper channels," the guard said.

The Agents were heading toward the far side of the building, but they still had twenty yards to go. "Check again. I don't want your boss gettin' all riled up."

The guard sighed and dropped his head again.

Raven flashed me a look. I knew I was laying it on thick. I resisted the urge to shrug.

Of all the people to do this with, it scared the shit out of me that she was the one, yet I appreciated she was with me.

The Agents disappeared from view, so I turned back to the guard. "Here, let me give you my ID." I held out the blank card I'd fashioned, careful to keep it close to my wrist so he wouldn't notice the wires coming out of my long-sleeve shirt.

Exasperated, the guard reached for the card, his fingers clamped onto the metal end—and his body went rigid as a flash surge of electricity coursed through him.

Raven swiftly handed me the metal rod, keeping it as much out of view as possible.

Taking the end closest to her, I raised the rod and jabbed his chest, hitting him with the rubber-covered end. As I'd planned, the blow pulled his hand away from the card, severing the connection as he fell back, the jolt enough to knock him out. He dropped into his chair—but his head flopped backward. Shit.

I pulled the rod back into the cab of our truck, turned it around with her help, grabbed the rubber-covered end, and shoved the rod back out the window, this time aiming for the gate. I made contact with the arm's hinge, then touched the card to the metal. The electricity switched the magnetic polarity that kept the arm in place, and the gate rose.

I pulled the rod back, gunned the truck, and we made it inside before the arm dropped back down.

"What do we do about the guard?" Raven whispered.

"Nothing. Act natural." I'd kept the rod as low as possible. It might've been enough to avoid detection—I didn't hear any alarms—but it wouldn't last.

I quickly drove to the front of the building, angled our truck, and backed into a parking space.

Thirty-three minutes, fifty-one seconds.

We got out, both of us acting awkwardly as we tried to hide our faces and seem like legitimate landscapers. Neither of us were the gardening type.

I handed her a rake, which she held like a weapon, and grabbed the canvas bag.

We couldn't barge our way in. The double doors were reinforced steel, with an old-style sensor pad as its only access, the pad similar to the one I'd hacked back in Los Angeles. I wouldn't be able to do that this time, not with one of the cameras focused solely on the door. I led Raven along the building's front instead, risking a glance up to trace the cables that ran under the eaves. I kept a hand to my face to avoid giving the cameras a good look at me.

The cables had been painted white to blend with the building. I'd spotted them from the street, but now that we were only feet away, I could follow them easily—but when I glanced at them a second time, my breath caught. The cables that ran between the cameras and the alarm system went into metal piping that had been nailed to the building's façade. I wouldn't be able to penetrate that. With a growing despair, I traced the pipes as they met and plunged downward, the vertical pipe slightly larger than the ones near the eaves. The vertical pipe extended all of the way down—

Then ended six inches above the ground.

The cables curved out of the pipe, briefly exposed, before disappearing into the building's brick exterior.

We had a chance.

Except for the walkway that led to the double doors, small bushes lined the entire front of the building, acting as a buffer between the building and front sidewalk.

I set the bag down on the mulch that covered the landscaped area, unzipped it just enough to reach inside, and pulled out a hand rake. I then approached the building, as did Raven. I pretended to rake away some of the dead grass, keeping my head down, and glanced at the exposed portion of cable. It was only a foot or so away. I scooted around the small bush, scraped away more dead grass with one hand, and slipped my other hand into my pocket. Being careful to seem normal, I pulled out the receiver chip, the nail Valor had found digging into my skin. I started to back up as if I'd cleared the brush, then angled forward again, brought down my hand-rake—and with my other hand, slid the nail into the rubber, pushing it in until it encountered metal.

In the silent air, a phone began to ring inside the gatehouse.

Raven glanced at the gatehouse, then back at me, her eyes wide. Someone had noticed the guard.

Abandoning the hand-rake, I returned to the canvas bag, opened it wider, and looked inside.

The handheld display flashed a message. "Connection Made. Execute step 1?"

I pressed the "OK" button on the screen and heard a soft click.

Raven flinched. She'd heard it as well. She continued to rake, though her acting didn't improve.

The handheld flashed a new message. "Execute step 2?"

I heard voices from Agents jogging around the perimeter, but they weren't visible. Not yet. Maybe they weren't jogging. Maybe they were coming to investigate the guard—and us.

I stood, reached down for the bag, hit the second "OK" button displayed, then took the bag's handles and straightened.

When I stood, Raven went to the pickup truck and lowered the gate.

The Agents' voices changed. My software began to fluctuate the fence's electrical levels. It would distract them—for a few seconds, at least.

Raven pulled off the tarp to reveal the AG-M1300 robots, the middle one holding the plasma cannon between its legs. As soon as she removed the tarp, the robot on the end sat up, scooted out of the truck, then turned and picked up the cannon, prompting the other two robots to climb out as well. As they got to their feet, I headed to the front doors, which my program had unlocked, opened one of the doors, and stepped inside. Raven followed, carrying her rake with her to avoid delay. The three robots entered the building after her, and the door closed behind us, relocking.

My senses were on high alert. We didn't know what we'd find: receptionist, guards, more barriers, or something else.

I removed my sunglasses, tensed for an attack. Slate-colored hallways stretched to the left and right of us, as well as directly ahead. The hallways to either side ran along the front of the building, with what appeared to be empty offices stemming from both branches, while directly ahead, the wide, hospital-like hallway—recessed fluorescents overhead, plastic dark-gray railings lining both sides of the hallway, shiny seamless flooring—plunged through the center of the building for over one hundred feet.

With a wave to the three robots, I led them and Raven down the central corridor, past the first room, before stopping at the second. A glance inside showed it was occupied by a manager-type person focused on a screen, so we hurried to the third. It was empty, so we ducked inside, the robots' movements quiet but audible.

Raven shut the door behind them as I set down the canvas bag and opened it.

The display blinked again. "Execute step 3?"

I pressed "OK" and placed the handheld by the door as a series of commands scrolled across its screen. Raven set aside her rake and discarded the checkered shirt she'd worn, revealing her dark shirt underneath. I discarded my flannel shirt as well, as our charade was over.

The one I'd programmed as the lead robot lifted the plasma cannon, easily handling its weight.

"How long until it arrives?" Raven whispered.

"Thirty seconds," I guessed.

"Dad," she whispered, holding out her hand.

Her smile, which I'd always known would be trouble, had been missing for some time. In its place was the look of an adult. Hardened, scarred, single-minded in focus. I was proud of her, though I'd wished it had been under different circumstances. A different life.

I handed her a grenade, then nodded at her blade emitter. "Will you be able to fight them up close?"

She hesitated, then gave it to me. I slipped it into a side pocket on my pants, then removed my pack, which had the rest of our supplies.

Suddenly, we heard crashes, shouts—and a thunderous boom. Alarms followed, ringing throughout the complex. "Attack, attack," a synthetic voice announced. "Front entrance. All personnel respond."

I grabbed the handheld and pulled up its live feed, having hooked into the Facility's central computer system. The loader had driven out of the barn which was up the road, crashed through the front gate, and hit the building halfway between the front doors and the side, though per my instructions, not hard enough to break through the wall.

Shouts filled the hallways as the Facility's inhabitants responded to the alarm. Through the noise, I caught doors opening in different parts of the building as Agents and others dashed outside, doors swinging shut behind them.

On the live feed, Agents appeared, aiming pistols at the loader's cabin.

I looked at Raven. "Once we start, we don't stop. You can't hesitate for one second."

"I know."

More nervous than I'd ever been in my life, I closed the live feed and pulled up the program I'd written for our assault. A new prompt appeared: "Execute steps 4 and 5?"

I recalled Brocco's attack when we had broken into his house. I hoped he'd given us the key.

I clicked "OK".

Throughout the complex, every exterior door bolted into

place. Then a 120-decibel, screeching sound erupted from the exterior speakers. Even from our spot inside the building, we winced from the sound; outside, the Agents would be debilitated, possibly deafened by the assault, their multiple implants making them especially vulnerable to the piercing vibrations.

I didn't like harming others, but they drew first blood when they'd invaded Lafontaine's headquarters. And they had my daughter.

Twenty-five minutes, three seconds.

CHAPTER THIRTY-SIX

My senses so heightened I felt my shirt scraping my skin, I entered the hallway. The shrieking from the outside speakers was nearly deafening in the hallway, which was empty other than an occasional bench, not even a security camera that I could see. Joining me, Raven activated her one hand shield. I activated the other, which I wore as Kieran had fried my thresher shield, the energy spitting and wavering as it emanated from the damaged device.

I gestured to the robots to take up positions around us in the hallway, the leader and one other before us, the third behind. "Defend," I said. They leaned forward as their bodies widened, exterior metal skin unfolding as their arms thickened, ready to protect us, and the leader activated the cannon. I'd confirmed its parameters. Target adults only.

I motioned them to proceed, and they began to lead us down the hallway. Though it was still empty, my trick wouldn't work for long—and there was no guarantee everyone had rushed outside.

Each interior door contained a narrow window, which enabled me to glance into the rooms we passed. Offices occupied this area, along with a conference room and break room. No computers, though, other than the clear monitors that occupied most desks.

We continued silently until we reached the end of the

hallway, which intersected a passageway running perpendicular.

Raven leaned close. "Which way?"

Doors lined the intersecting passageway in both directions, with exits to the outside at both ends. Amidst the artificial screeching, I could hear pounding. Agents were trying to force their way inside, though so far, the exit doors held.

I motioned to the left, where another hallway branched off that led deeper into the complex.

When we reached the new hallway, we found it capped by a pair of thick fire doors propped open. I adhered one of the tractor-battery bombs I'd made to the top of the opening, the bomb linked up to one of the programmable motherboards I'd had in my repair kit.

What I hadn't told Raven, but Valor had figured out, was that a single bomb would obliterate this building. By my estimate, the four combined bombs would destroy everything in a quarter-mile radius.

We continued deeper into the Facility, the new corridor sporting hallways that branched off to either side up ahead.

The robots spread out as we walked to cover more space.

A man about my height suddenly emerged from one of the rooms. We all froze for a second, surprised to see each other. He wasn't a full Agent; he only had three implants I could see, and his hair was only partly silver. He stood closer to us than any of the robots, having stepped inside their circle of protection; they swiveled back, but he was twice as close as they were.

I brought up my Glock, as did Raven—but he rushed me before we could shoot.

I barely had time to react; the robot behind me hurried forward but was too far away. As the Agent-trainee lunged at me, I stepped aside at the last moment and swung my hand shield, catching him in the head. He crashed against the side of the hallway, then fell to the ground. Before he could get up, the robot smacked him with the back of its metal fist, and he collapsed.

The door the trainee had emerged from opened to a hand-to-hand combat room, one of what I realized were many in the facility. Posters lined the walls:

THE AGENCY IS PATRIOTISM.

THE MORE YOU SACRIFICE, THE HIGHER YOU ASCEND.

WE ARE GREATER THAN FAMILY.

If Zion had warped Talia with this brainwashing bullshit, I would tear him apart.

Gripping my weapon tighter, I led my group forward.

A shadow passed the window of another door we passed. Raven turned—and gasped. Three Agents were inside. Before we could react, the nearest one jerked the handle to open the door. To attack.

But the door stopped after two inches. Then slammed shut.

The Agent tried again but couldn't open it.

I wasn't sure what was going on, but we couldn't let them get out. I pulled the bolt-emitter from my pack, and when a second Agent grabbed the door handle as well, I touched the emitter to the handle on our side.

Electricity coursed through their bodies until I turned off my device. When I did, the two collapsed, and the third Agent backed away.

The sound outside dropped in volume, then dropped further.

"They're ripping down the speakers," Raven said.

She was right. The Agents outside had somehow overcome the acoustical onslaught.

We turned the corner—and gunfire erupted ahead. Two silver-haired Agents stood farther down. We ducked from the assault, but before we could dive back around the corner, one of the robots dove between us and the Agents, bullets pinging as they struck it instead of us. The next moment, the lead robot fired the plasma cannon, taking out one of the Agents. The other disappeared around the corner.

Raven tossed her grenade. It detonated as it reached the junction where the Agent had disappeared, and the man cried out.

We hurried to him.

He laid curled in a ball a half-dozen yards from our hallway, having been thrown by the explosion; past him, doors led to an indoor swimming pool and what looked like an obstacle course of some kind.

Others would've heard the explosion. I took Raven's shoulder. "We need to move." The sirens had mostly stopped. With their combined strength, the Agents we'd trapped could force their way back inside.

We hurried down another hallway, the robots rushing to catch up, passing posters that grew more warped, proclaiming The Agency was worthy of any sacrifice, that it came above all else, that procreating together served The Agency.

Footsteps warned us, though we almost didn't stop in time.

Four Agents, two women and two men of varying levels of transformation, emerged from a hallway behind us, armed with machine guns. We turned and opened fire, the robot carrying the cannon now behind us, unable to fire for risk of hitting us.

Raven pulled me toward a nearby door and fired two more shots, then ducked behind me to switch clips. I fired at our attackers, hitting one of the men and forcing the others back. The nearest robot positioned itself between us and our attackers, while the robot without the cannon ran at our attackers, drawing fire. Raven shoved me into the room—a weight room with mats, equipment, and a hyperbaric oxygen tank—and fired twice more at the Agents before ducking inside.

Horrific sounds filled the hallway, screams and the shriek of metal, sparks and gunshots.

In seconds, the sounds stopped. Silence settled.

Raven let me out of the room. The Agents lay on the ground, along with the robot that had attacked them. Somehow, the Agents had managed to nearly rip apart the robot with their bare hands. But the robot had taken them out as well, its remaining arm still wrapped around one of the men's throats, the others bent in unnatural ways.

I pulled Raven away from the scene—and felt a flare of pain as a bullet gouged my shoulder, luckily missing bone. Two more Agents, coming from the other direction. I shot at the one who'd grazed me, then with a boom, the lead robot fired at the two Agents, the plasma cannon taking them both out.

More Agents were coming. We could hear them.

Twenty-one minutes, forty-one seconds.

I led our small group deeper into the complex, taking a side hallway, following one around a curve and then taking another, smaller corridor.

We passed a surgical recovery room that had a large observation window.

Bandages covered the heads of men and women who had recently been operated on, two of them twitching, others fighting their restraints. All Agents in the making. Two nurses, who kept glancing toward the ceiling as if the battle noises came from above, administered to the eight bandaged bodies.

I slowed just enough to attach another bomb, this time to a pipe that ran across the hallway's ceiling the next door down.

Footsteps grew from those hunting us.

Moving quickly, we passed a series of windowed rooms. The first contained a surgical robot surrounded by medical-grade canisters that held silver fibers, adherents, cutting tools, and adjustable cranial immobilizers. The next contained a large apparatus with needles jutting from a thick, white arm, a xenobiological machine that I suspected was part of the Agents' genetic modification process. Other rooms held machines used for synthetic-biology modifications: engineered musculature, reinforced tendons, carbon-fiber bone wrapping, and other procedures I couldn't identify. The genetic modifications would result in some instances of mutation—which meant there were probably a few deformed bodies buried somewhere on the property. I'm sure Zion deemed it a small price to pay for the creation of human killing machines.

More Agents appeared, two behind us and three ahead. Blood had seeped from their ears and dried on their jaws, staining their shirts. They appeared almost inhuman, they were so enraged.

We fired at them, one robot in front of us and the other protecting our back, the cannon triggering again, the force of the weapon jerking the lead robot as the plasma charge barreled through the three front Agents like a bowling ball knocking down pins. "Cover my back," I yelled, then stepped out from behind the lead robot. Raven stepped out with me and turned to face the two behind us, both of us using our shields to deflect gunshots.

The cannon had taken out two of the Agents ahead of us, but the third got back up. I fired twice, hitting him, though he fought back, gunshots hitting my shield, which flickered as it weakened.

One of the Agents Raven fought went down, but the other remained standing.

I squeezed my fist as if that would strengthen my shield and charged the last Agent before me, though the lead robot was faster. It charged forward as well, switching the cannon to one arm and grabbing the Agent with the other, then pivoting and throwing him at Raven's remaining Agent. The two silver-haired men crashed into each other and went down. When they did, Raven and I dashed around the corner, the robots following, ran down the next hallway—then passed a corridor with more than a dozen Agents.

We continued past the corridor, but I stopped, as did Raven and the robots. I then hurried back to the corner and tossed a grenade, my second-to-last one. We took off again as shouts rose from the corridor with the grenade.

The detonation cut them off.

It wasn't strong enough to wipe them out. The blast might have hurt two of them. If that.

We took the next corner. This hallway was clear—for the moment—so we ran faster.

A set of fire doors stood open ahead. I slowed.

"What's wrong?" Raven said, both of us out of breath.

I glanced at my shield. It continued to spark and falter.

Hers flickered as well, though not as badly. I led her and the two robots past the doors. "More Agents will come."

"Are we going to be able to get out of here? After we find her," she added with a bit of uncertainty.

I checked the time. Eighteen minutes, four seconds. "We have one shot."

As I reached for the double doors, bloodied Agents appeared in the hallway.

I slammed the doors behind us—bullets striking the metal as I closed them—and motioned to the hands-free robot. It moved into position, hunkered down, placed a hand against each door, and locked its joints.

"Come on," I told Raven.

I started down the hallway, Raven glancing at me doubtfully as she and the lead robot, our last one, followed. Behind us, gunfire erupted, bullets pelting the door. As we neared the end of the hallway, there were a series of booms behind us. The Agents crashed into the door repeatedly, trying to break through. The robot held, though it started to twist. It hadn't been designed for this kind of assault. I wasn't sure how long it would hold off the Agents coming for us.

I placed my last bomb against a structural support beam and continued forward.

The hallway terminated in a wide foyer that contained three doors, one directly ahead. From the steel reinforcement of the door in front of us and the foyer-like design of the hallway, I suspected we'd reached our destination.

As I started forward, the door opened, and an Agent emerged. Huge shoulders. Thick neck. Silver, close-cropped hair.

It was Thys Gunnar, the muscular, ruthless Agent who had killed Senn.

* * *

Raven stepped back. So did I.

Gunnar smiled.

He shut the door behind him, though not all the way.

I wondered if Talia was on the other side. I'd only caught

a glimpse of lights in the room, what could have been a readout of some kind, possibly medical.

He started toward us, hands clenching into fists.

I heard a soft chime beside me, and the lead robot fired the plasma cannon.

The blast nailed Gunnar in the chest.

He flew backward, the blast lifting him a few inches off the ground, and slammed into the wall next to the door.

As the blow wore off, he held onto his chest but stayed on his feet. Glared at us.

"Shit," Raven whispered.

She and I started forward in unison, shields held before us. He wasn't armed, as far as I could tell, but he didn't need to be. He *was* a weapon.

He ran at us.

We opened fire, the bullets seeming to pierce his skin but having no other effect. He slowed to a jog, throwing a hand to his face as we fired, but he still continued forward. My gun suddenly clicked, out of bullets.

I didn't have time to switch clips.

I dropped my gun—and pulled out Valor's, my flickering shield before me. As I prepared to fire, Gunnar tackled us, a massive hand nearly breaking my arm as he pinned it across my body. Fighting to break free, my shield nearly in my face, I fired twice into his stomach. The shots seemed to zap some of his strength, and Raven fired into his side, her shield pushing him away from her.

The timing should be right. "Up," I shouted.

We both shoved him upwards, exposing him to the cannon.

But it didn't fire.

I craned my neck to look behind me. The lead robot had the cannon aimed but was peering down at it.

I realized it was out of juice. It had been cycling slower and must've run out.

Above us, Gunnar yelled and shoved our shields aside,

then grabbed Raven and threw her. She smacked into a wall, and he rose up, picking me up as he stood. He was going to kill me. I fired at his chest, the bullets hurting but not stopping him, then bent back and swung my shield at him, the jagged edge catching the side of his face.

He dropped me as he stumbled back, then spat blood-tinged phlegm onto the floor—and leapt at me so quickly I couldn't react in time. He grabbed me in iron hands. I fired again as he swung me around, adding to the bloody spots that peppered his body, and he threw me at the wall. I crashed into it near where Raven had landed, but my pack, which somehow stayed on, gouged into my shoulder. My pack!

I slid it off my shoulder as Raven raised her gun and fired at Gunnar again. Before I could reach inside, Gunnar dropped to a knee, grabbed and lifted both of us, then threw us back to the ground. As he rose up, both hands curled into fists—

And the robot slammed into him.

It had abandoned the cannon and launched itself at the Agent, driving him back.

Gunnar reached for the robot as it clung to him, trying to get it off him. As he grappled with the robot, I snatched my pack.

Raven struggled to pick herself up, bruised and battered.

As I frantically rummaged through my pack, Gunnar pinned the robot under him and slammed his fist into it repeatedly, denting, then crushing its chest, and then its head. The robot was unable to fight back, its blows ineffective.

My fingers grabbed the absorber, the bomb detonator, flasher ball—then the bolt-emitter.

I pulled out the emitter and aimed it at Gunnar.

He looked up at the last moment, and as I triggered the device, he jerked backwards, raising one of the robot's arms—and the bolt struck the arm. The Agent twitched from the energy, but he was feeling only a partial effect; the majority of the electricity raced from the arm down into the earth, away from him.

As soon as the blast ended, Gunnar came for me. Hoping to surprise him, I dropped the backpack, then grabbed the curved blade-emitter from my side pocket, activated it, and sliced at him, catching him across the jaw and cheek. He reared back, a seared mark across his face. I lunged forward to finish him—and he seized me.

Before I could react, he spun me around to face Raven, who'd aimed her Glock at him, about to fire. She let go of the trigger, not wanting to risk shooting me. Gunnar grabbed my blade and threw it at her, causing her to flinch backwards.

He then slammed me to the ground and wrapped his thick hands around my neck.

He started to squeeze.

I struggled to get away but couldn't. Couldn't breathe.

The glowing, curved line of the blade-emitter erupted and Raven, struggling by being so close to Gunnar, sliced his arm with a yell, tears streaming.

His grip on me relaxed as he bellowed, letting go as he swung around at her, still straddling me, and swatted her, sending her back.

I heard a soft chime. The cannon! It wasn't empty after all. It had one shot left.

I clasped my hands into a fist and drove it upwards into Gunnar's jaw. He didn't see the blow coming and fell back from the impact, rolling off me. I heaved my body toward the cannon where the robot had dropped it. I felt dizzy; I was coated in sweat and sheathed in pain, but I pushed myself forward.

Gunnar started after me, but he slipped in the oil that leaked from the destroyed robot, giving me the chance I needed. I swiped the cannon and brought it around as I sat up. I needed to stand, to brace myself, but I didn't have time. I brought the end around, jabbed the back end against my stomach, aimed at the Agent scrambling toward me—

And fired.

My stomach flared from the impact as the cannon jolted backwards.

Through the pain, I saw the blast slam into him, throwing him back. From the way his body had been angled, he hadn't had a chance to defend himself. Instead, he absorbed the full force of the blow. His body flew backwards, nearly a dozen feet.

He landed face-down. And didn't move.

With a groan, I pushed the cannon off of me, managed to get my feet under me, and stood. Gripping my stomach, I picked my way among the robot parts and spilled oil and blood to Raven, who sat up, wide eyes locked on Gunnar as if expecting him to rise up at any second.

"You survive?" she asked, voice shaky.

"Barely."

I turned off my shield and helped her to her feet. She'd turned hers off as well.

After grabbing my pack and the blade, I turned to the door, which was still cracked open. Checked the time. Nine minutes, eighteen seconds, until the nodes fell.

The door to the right revealed a short hallway that led outside, sunlight visible through the far door's window.

"You should go," I told Raven. "Meet up with Valor—"

"Dad."

"I'll be fine here."

"You want to make things right with me? Let me finish this."

I understood her need—which was why I gave in.

I slung my pack over my shoulder, and we walked to the reinforced door, my stomach twinging in pain with each step. I didn't know what I'd find. My hopes and fears, worries and doubts, magnified as we approached. Talia. My lioness. I hoped we weren't too late.

I grasped the edge of the door, pulled it the rest of the way open, and together we stepped into a large command room.

There were enough control panels, command modules, datatanks, and substations to run the entire country from this room. While the rest of the Facility had been older, with decades-old furnishings, this room contained the latest technology, with cables, fiber optics, and waterlines tracing the walls behind the panels and modules before disappearing into various holes punched into the walls. Free-standing structures that looked like command towers stood in random spots about the room, each displaying various holograms and data. Two other doors led from the room, with the one to the rear the type seen in hospitals with large square windows occupying the top half of the door.

The impression of the room hit me in a flash, but my focus was pulled to someone kneeling in the center of the room, the only person there. Waiting for us. Mina.

Her skin was paler, hair stringy. She'd aged this last month or so, though her eyes lit with hope when she saw me.

Then she shifted her gaze—and paled further when she saw Raven.

"Oh no," Mina breathed. "No, no, no."

CHAPTER THIRTY-SEVEN

Mina wore maroon clothes that reminded me of a prison outfit, long-armed and utilitarian, her shoes gray canvas, nothing like she'd normally wear. Her expression, a mixture of fear, grief and anxiety, was also foreign on her. The weeks since I'd seen her hadn't been kind.

Raven and I approached.

"You weren't supposed to come," Mina told her.

"You act like you had a plan," Raven said. "Did you?"

"Yes—"

"Did you tell anyone what the hell it was?"

"I couldn't. Your father—"

Someone entered the room behind us. "I had a plan, and it went impeccably."

I knew that voice.

Zion, my former partner. Former friend. He had aged well, though he was vain enough he'd probably had plastic surgery. He was nearly my height but thinner, tanned, brown-eyed, hair swept back, just a touch of grey at the temples as if for accent. The bastard probably had it done on purpose.

The side door opened, and Britt entered along with two other Agents, none of whom looked injured.

Eight minutes, eleven seconds.

I slipped my pack from my shoulders, removed the bomb detonator, and flipped the switch to arm the bombs. "Don't move, or I'll blow this place."

"With your family in it?" Britt asked.

"What do we have to lose?" Raven asked as if she knew my plan. As if the bombs were a bluff.

Zion glanced off, reading from his lenses. "We've disarmed one of your bombs near the entrance. How many others did you hide?"

Before I could reply, Britt lunged forward, punched me and ripped the detonator from my hand.

Desperate and terrified—of what they would do to me, of what they'd do to Raven—I raised my gun to shoot the Agent, but she hit me in my bruised stomach and wrenched the Glock from my hand.

She smiled at Zion, who narrowed his eyes. "Forget something?"

She stopped smiling, dropped to her knees near Mina, placed both the detonator and gun on the floor before her, and bent her head.

Mina fearfully scooted away from her.

"Good to see you again," Zion told me, as if we'd randomly run into each other at some symposium.

"Nothing good about it."

"If you'd accepted my invitation to join us, it might've been different." He swiveled toward Raven. "I tried to capture you, complete the pair and all, but you managed to get away. I would've been impressed if it wasn't so aggravating."

Raven raised her gun to shoot him—but one of Britt's fellow Agents fired a concentrated-energy dart, hitting Raven in the shoulder. She froze, every muscle locked. The other Agent pointed a gun at me. I prepared to activate my shield. If I timed it right and deflected the bullet to strike Zion, we might have a chance.

The door opened again, and Kieran entered the room with three more Agents.

My resolve faltered.

I wondered if we'd really knocked him out and sent him

off in the trunk of a car. He had a limp where Raven and Valor had both struck him, and his foot was in a cast, so it hadn't been a dream.

Beside me, the Agent disarmed Raven, removed the dart so she could move again, forced her to her knees, then trained his gun on me until I joined her.

I mentally ran through the rest of my weapons. We each had our shields, though they were spotty. I had the absorber and a flasher ball in my pack. Against seven Agents.

I'd planned to take them out, to destroy all of this. Now, I was a prisoner.

As was Raven.

Kieran nodded at me—whether out of respect, mockery, or as some sort of formality, I couldn't tell—then frowned when he saw Britt on her knees. "What's this?" he asked Zion with a flicker of anger.

"She sent the hounds after them. I wanted them alive, but she tried to kill them. She'll be punished."

I would've enjoyed the annoyance in Zion's voice under different circumstances. Instead, I glared at Kieran. "You warned Zion we were coming."

"There was no need," said my former partner. "Kieran and I manipulated you to come here. I feared you would figure out the truth, but he was right. In fact, this was all his idea. Destroying your rebellion was mine, though."

"Figure what out?" I asked, my voice tight as Raven flinched beside me.

"I could've just called you, told you to come here, but I needed time to put everything in place. Besides, this way was better, getting your hopes up, using Mina to lure you in, letting you think you had a chance."

His tone changed. "Though you beat Kieran. He was supposed to crush you, validate his return, but you humiliated him." He turned to Kieran. "For your efforts, I'll reinstate you, though your next performance review won't be complimentary. Welcome back to the team."

I caught something on Kieran's face, a subtle shift Zion didn't seem to catch. Remorse, conflict, and something else, his eyes flickering to Britt. I could see his love for her.

"We have new hardware for you," Zion told him. "It'll be another surgery, but you'll take it, won't you? I'd planned to promote you as well, but your failure has delayed that."

Kieran's eyes flickered to Britt again.

"That's all this was?" Raven asked Kieran. "Luring us here to get your fucking job back?"

Zion said, "There's a lot more. You don't realize you've already lost."

I checked the time, just a quick shift of focus. Four minutes, five seconds. I needed to stall. "No, you have."

His cheeks flushed with an old rage. "Arrogant and oblivious as always. I was fine with you staying at Gen Omega after I left, enriching me and the other shareholders with your breakthroughs—yes, I kept my shares. Then you started to rebel. I'd hoped you would stop, especially after Talia was shot, but you didn't. Then you did your damn broadcast. Always were a hassle."

"Where is Talia?"

"You really want the truth?" he asked, angling his head, his rich suit out of place in this setting. "Spare yourself."

"Where is she?" I asked as Mina dropped her head.

When he didn't respond, Raven asked, "What did you fear Dad would figure out?"

He smiled at me. "We've cracked the last defense you have. We can see what you see—and now we can read your minds."

He held up a small object, what I realized was an unfired burrower. "I designed it myself. They travel through the bloodstream to the cerebrum, lodge there, and send probes to different areas of the brain to map you. With the data collected from those we've injected, we deciphered the wiring in the human brain. Reason, suspicion, and deceit reside in the same areas of every person's mind, and I've deduced how to read them. As an additional achievement, I've figured out how to get this information using everyone's implants. The next time we update the neural net software, we'll know who is considering rebelling against us. We'll eliminate them before they even pick up a gun—or broadcast a ridiculous call to fight," he said with a flash of annoyance. "We used Talia to refine the process. She's a remarkable girl, more complicated than most. When we finally cracked her, we used her to calibrate the process, and the others we studied fell into place. Now we can read everyone's thoughts."

"You're a monster," Mina said, trembling. I'd never seen her so livid—or horrified. Her hand signal, the one during her broadcast when she'd announced Talia was still alive. It had been legitimate.

"You know machines are superior to humans," he told me. "Now I can control humans. Including you."

I said, "You won't be able to read everyone. There are too many variations, too many variables."

"All my software has to do is figure out how to read the slight differences in someone's wiring to interpret the imagery and triggers a person has—which takes less time than you'd think. With the predictive algorithms of the past thirty years, this was the inevitable conclusion."

As I reeled, Raven lifted her chin. "People will fight even harder. They'll figure out what you're doing."

"I'm *protecting* everyone. This way, we won't have rebellion or chaos or anarchy. We'll all be safer."

If he was telling the truth, he and his successors would be able to control the country, even the world, for generations.

Maybe forever.

The rebels were our only chance. I checked the countdown. *Two minutes, ten seconds.* We needed to keep stalling—and be ready. I glanced at Raven. She was tense, visibly worried but focused. I was terrified she was here.

"We'll detain would-be traitors before they can agitate others," Zion said. "It's an ideal solution. Besides, we have too many people for this planet, which I've been saying for years. I'm trying to fix that."

Mina spoke up. "People are good. You don't like them because every single one of them is better than you."

He glanced at her in surprise. "I've let your daughter live."

"What you've done isn't living."

The reinforced door opened wider, and an Agent trainee entered. "We've found all the bombs."

Zion frowned at me. "Another failure." He considered. "Though we haven't been without failures of our own, as you disabled the scanner my Agent injected you with. We'll inject you with another—which you won't be able to disable—and measure you as we torture you. We'll add the results to our database. You were an extreme example, so your data will further strengthen our algorithms. Think of it as a last way to help society."

I wanted to rip him, his disciples, and this place apart piece by piece. I kept my mouth shut, though. Let him talk like he always did. Thirty-one seconds. Thirty.

He leaned closer. "Before I kill you, I want to figure out how someone who was just a glorified assistant became such a pain in the *ass* when he should've stayed in his place."

Kieran seemed to suppress a smile, though he looked angry. He'd positioned himself just behind Britt, his leg lightly touching her side. The other Agents were stoic, silver hair unmoving.

Twenty seconds. Nineteen.

"Time for the show, don't you think?" Zion asked.

Surprised, I jerked my gaze to him. He smiled. "Haven't you been listening? We know everything, Dray."

With a flicker of his hand, three Agents approached nearby control panels and keyed in commands.

Ten seconds. Nine.

The control screens went blank, then showed feeds from various cameras. From the angle of sunlight and the scenes themselves, I could tell they came from different parts of the country: Florida, Vermont or upper New York, and what I recognized as Seattle. Armed men and women in black appeared on screen and began to fire at guards standing before unmarked doorways. Images switched: a woman planting bombs beside luminous datatanks; gunfire causing bystanders to run as more figures in black raced toward a government building; figures running through a doorway underneath stone-carved archways.

I felt my stomach drop. Beside me, Raven let out a shuddering breath.

"I must say, your people coordinated this well," Zion commented. Oh god. He wasn't concerned at all.

Explosions blotted out one feed, then another. A third switched to a view from a skyscraper, which showed four explosions erupt under the streets of Manhattan, which caused people to run in fear. Another feed switched to a news anchor. With a nod from Zion, the Agent played the sound.

"...initial reports are that these attacks are happening across the country," the anchor said, her voice heavy with shock. "We don't know why or how many casualties there are, but officials are reporting that these acts of terror are the result of domestic terrorists led by Dray Quintero, a man whose delusion warped scores of his fellow citizens to turn on their country."

Zion approached me. "Every bit of chaos, every injury, every death, will be blamed on you. There will be a lot of death today."

Fury and horror gripped me. He'd twisted the great things we'd tried to do, the sacrifices we'd made for the country, and the risks we'd taken to help others.

He leaned down. "You're going to be a reminder that if we don't stay united as a country, we could lose everything. See for yourself." He removed my cap, exposing my implant.

It was the first time it had been uncovered since the river, though it didn't matter now. I was caught.

As my implant connected to the network, I realized I would go down in history as a traitor and mass murderer.

Zion removed Raven's implant shield, then stepped back and faced her. "What did I fear Dray would figure out? That we'd realized the nodes were vulnerable, so we eliminated our reliance on them."

Images began to play on my lenses, to either side of my main vision, more devastation Zion wanted me to see: people running in fear, smoke and destruction, structures falling. On the console displays, doors swung closed seemingly on their own, rebels still inside, followed by explosions larger than the previous ones. On my lenses, which also displayed readouts as my implants continued its normal startup sequence, someone stared wide-eyed at a large, black structure sitting underneath a control screen, five times the size of the bombs being used. There was a timer: 0:03. 0:02. 0:01.

A flash, then all went black.

A new scene displayed, and I spotted Anya. Raven stiffened beside me as Jex appeared as well. There was confusion; he had a hand to his ear, and Anya and those with them started running for a bright doorway.

Another explosion followed, and Raven cried out.

I tried telling myself they'd made it, that they could've escaped the blast, but other feeds filled with explosions and smoke and terror flickered across my lenses.

Overwhelmed by the nightmarish visions and the utter collapse of everything around me, I closed my eyes—though I couldn't avoid the scenes that played, a half-dozen images to either side of my central vision—and dropped my head in defeat. Anya. Jex. Probably Garly and Cole and the rest of our friends. Our adopted family. Gone.

I'd never felt so gutted in my life.

We'd failed. I'd failed. Failed them all.

No one would know the truth of the implants, of the government's actions. They'd never be free again.

CHAPTER THIRTY-EIGHT

As I knelt in the command room, my eyes closed, I spotted a flicker in the darkness between the images of death and destruction.

The flicker turned into my neural net loading my normal feed layout as it connected to the public news sites I followed.

It seemed a sick irony, the technology I'd tried to destroy coming back online to reconnect me to a world too dangerous to live in. News summaries began to scroll across the bottom of my screen, along with various headlines, all of which contained my name.

Beside me, Raven groaned. She must've seen them, too.

Among the reports and readouts, which seemed almost foreign to me now, I spotted something strange. A program or communication of some kind. I didn't remember if I'd left a program running the last time I'd covered my implant, but I didn't think so.

"Don't you see?" Zion asked. "This is for the greater good."

The interface connected, and a familiar layout formed on my lenses. My brain took a second to recognize it—and realize the ramifications.

Garly.

His reinforcements.

My mouth nearly dropped open as I realized he'd sent the swarmbots to help me.

Mina suddenly spoke up. "The 'greater good'? Killing

people you're supposed to protect?"

"Now you ask?" Zion asked. "You've spent so much time hovering over Talia, I didn't think you cared. Congress approached me because of our dwindling oil reserves, seeking not only a way to hide their actions but to find a solution. A grand one."

Mina still knew me well enough to read my body language—and was distracting Zion. As she baited him, I used my gaze to focus on the commands I wanted, since I didn't have my datarings. I pulled up the map icon, which displayed a radar-like schematic. It took me a moment to figure out, but I realized the swarmbots were traveling in a long-range helicopter; they hadn't known my location until just now when Zion uncovered my implant. As I watched, the bots launched out of the helicopter in…a rocket ship? No. They *were* the ship. They used a jet similar to the one they'd used when they formed as a hoverbike.

Garly must've deduced we were somewhere in Texas and had sent them to find us.

"Our leaders have jeopardized humanity's future with their decisions. How do you think people would react if that became public?" Zion asked as more explosions and screams issued from the console's speakers. "They would tear our government apart. This was the only way."

"They're still going to revolt, as soon as they discover the truth," Raven said. "You stole control of this country."

"I kept the *might* of this country. If everyone knew, they'd thank me."

"Why don't you tell them?" Mina asked. "See how they react."

I returned to the main menu and searched the commands, frustrated at how slow the process was without my datarings. I found their program to attack, then pulled up their parameters. The bots' commands were limited, but I found one: SUBDUED. Those identified as subdued were selected not to be attacked.

I hoped it would be enough.

Zion said, "We're fighting for the future. You must agree

there are too many people. I'll save us—and make sure the United States remains united."

I glanced at the map showing the bots' location relative to me. They'd reach the Facility in twenty seconds. I opened my eyes and risked a glance around, then closed them again. Found the list of commands and told the collective to breach the building.

Their forward radar revealed the entrance doors were open, having been ripped out by the Agents.

Raven said, "With what you're doing, there is no future."

"The America you're thinking of doesn't exist anymore," Zion shot back. "Our founding fathers wanted to create a government that was fair, and it was to a degree, but our citizens aren't the persecuted, kicked-out people who were around when the Constitution was written. They're now the giants of the planet, and unless you attack them directly, they'll accept the system that's made them great.

"But they're lazy. They want the easy solution, the magic pill that erases a lifetime of bad choices. That's what PIVOT was. America was failing, and the implants made us the best again. *I'm* the one who made us the best. Remember that."

A prompt flashed onto my lenses. *Proceed through building to target before disengaging engine?* A square formed underneath to execute the command.

Zion suddenly grabbed my chin and lifted my face. My eyes flew open.

"You're quiet," he said. "Why?"

This close to him, what he'd done, the lives he'd taken, I felt enraged and disgusted. I tried to pull from his grasp, but he held tight. Demanding I answer.

I hadn't wanted to reveal my hand, but the swarmbots were getting close—so I dropped my gaze and focused on the box.

ACCEPT flashed in acknowledgement.

Zion's face hardened. "He's communicating with someone. *Kieran*."

Kieran and his team started toward me—but paused

as a sound rose from within the building, one that, from their expressions, they couldn't identify. But I could.

I took advantage of their confusion by leaping to my feet, grabbing Zion's lapel, and punching him in the face as hard as I could.

Beside me, Raven leapt for her pistol, which still lay in front of Britt. One of the younger Agents jumped forward to stop her—but Raven triggered a blast of plasma from her fingers greater than I'd seen. She must've been building it up for some time; the force of the blast blew him backwards and made the other Agents recoil.

Readouts flashed on my lenses. *Inside structure. Find owner.*

Raven activated her shield as two of the Agents shot at her, deflecting the bullets, then snatched her Glock and fired back. Outside of the room, the sound grew to the deafening roar of a jet engine—then stopped.

A weird scurrying rose instead, getting louder.

I spun, grabbed Raven and Mina, and pulled them behind one of the four-foot tower structures.

The next moment, the scurrying grew to a thunderous clattering as swarmbots poured into the command room. Tens of thousands of small robots, four or five times the number I'd ridden on, flooded into the room. They swarmed over the closest Agent, then the next, then over Zion, who screamed, all three thrashing about.

Two of the other Agents leapt forward and tried to uncover my former friend, swatting at the robots, but the bots scurried up their arms and started to cover them as well.

Bots scurried over to me carrying my pistol. I didn't know how they'd gotten it, but I took it, pointed to my bag, then stood. I fired at an uncovered Agent, turned when I spotted Britt still kneeling on the floor, watching expressionlessly as Zion flailed, aimed at her—and Kieran stepped between us, blocking Britt's body with his own. He grimaced, raised a gun of his own—

And a shield appeared before me. Raven.

Shit, my shield. I activated mine as well. "Save your

mother," I told Raven.

Kieran hesitated, either looking for a shot or figuring out his next attack, I didn't know, when he jerked his head down.

Swarmbots started up his legs, swirling upwards.

He started to fight them, stomping on as many as he could.

"Hey Kieran," Raven said. When he looked at her, she fired a bolt of plasma from her finger. He jerked back to avoid the blast, but his prodigious reflexes weren't fast enough; the plasma sheared off a line of silver hair as he flew back. He fell to the floor, and more bots swarmed.

Britt leapt to his aid, though there were more bots than she could swat away.

More Agents rushed in, the lead one pointing a plasma rifle at me. I swung my shield up, the Agent fired, and the plasma slammed into my shield, fragmenting into small, jagged rays that pierced the panels to either side behind me, shorting out controls. Eyes dazzled by the flash of light, I aimed at the Agent and shot him, though more were coming. Yet so were more swarmbots. Some had been crushed, but half of the room was thickly covered in the chittering, swarming robots.

My shield sputtered. It was barely functional anymore. Another hit would wipe it out completely, and possibly me as well.

Four more Agents rushed in, two from the rear, hospital-like door. I was exposed, the nearest tower the one Raven had hurried to.

Out of instinct, I threw up my arms—and the swarm rolled across the room in a wave that crashed into the new arrivals. The Agents disappeared in the surge; when the bots pulled back, swarming back across the room, the arrivals collapsed to the ground.

Zion and the first two Agents who'd been covered were on the floor, still fighting the 'bots that sliced them with their hooked claws, though one of the Agents stopped moving. As I watched, Zion managed to swipe away a handful of 'bots, enough to free his mouth, his face marred by a half-dozen cuts. He pulled a radio from his pocket and yelled into it. "Send reinforcements! *Now.*"

We couldn't stay. Agents were crushing more and more swarmbots under their feet; there were thousands, but the Agents were tireless. Britt's arms were blurs as she swatted at the ones going after Kieran and somehow knocked them away faster than they could cover him.

I hurried to Raven and Mina, who'd heard Zion's order. They both stood, and the three of us ran from the room via the rear door, Raven using her shield to make sure no one shot us on our way out.

We stepped out of the chaos of the command room into a hospital-like area with white, railing-lined hallways running in different directions, similar to the front part of the building except brighter. Colder. As we slowed, I glimpsed patient beds in various rooms.

I turned to Mina. "You know where to go?"

She nodded, her eyes downcast.

Raven handed me her shield. "Keep it," I said, though she refused. I put on the hand shield, activated it, and led the way as Mina directed me. I thought to bring the swarmbots but wanted them to keep attacking the Agents. They'd hurt the silver-haired bastards, even killed at least a couple, but more reinforcements would arrive. We had a minute, if that.

The hallway was clear, our hurried footsteps the only sound—that and the noise from the control room: the news reports and cries, gunshots and chittering.

"You need to do what's right for our daughter," Mina told me as she led us.

I frowned, not understanding, but we didn't have time. "We have someone outside. Valor. Once we grab Talia, we'll head out the back and get both of you away from here."

"No. You'll see," as she continued down the antiseptic hallway.

I caught flashes of bodies lying in beds, multiple wires and feeds and instruments just visible.

She stopped before a door. "It's this one."

The door was like the others, a curtain drawn across its window, yet it felt different. Only a very faint light came from inside—and the area gave off a kind of sadness.

I turned off my shield.

The three of us paused. None of us were ready to enter. I wasn't sure I was.

Raven opened the door and entered the room. I followed, Mina right behind.

The room seemed like any other. Instead of three beds, though, there was one to the left, the right side of the room occupied by a scattering of equipment. To my surprise, much of the equipment was non-medical: next-gen holograph interfaces, satellite rapid uplinks, multi-phase communicators—the type used on ocean expeditions of all things—and devices I didn't recognize.

A curtain masked the lone bed in the room, but I could tell a child rested there. Small. So small.

I approached the bed, hesitated, then pulled aside the curtain and saw the face of my little girl. Talia.

There seemed to be a lump of some kind attached to her chest, though it was hard to tell from how she lay. She rested on her left side, facing toward me, knees drawn up.

Scared to believe it, I looked at her face again. It really was her—and she was looking at me, her eyes wide and wet.

Behind me, Raven sobbed.

I fell to my knees before the bed. I felt like a piece of myself had returned.

One of Talia's hands slid out from the sheet and reached for me. I took it gently. "Hi, my lioness."

"Hi Daddy," she said, barely above a whisper.

"I'm sorry I left you. I'll never leave you again, not for the rest of your life."

Mina grabbed my shoulder. "Dray, you can't promise that. You have to end—" She choked up, unable to complete her sentence.

Shouts rose, and the sounds of weapons being loaded drifted toward us.

"Dad," Raven shouted.

Talia's expression was one I hadn't seen before, her eyes conveying something I couldn't read, and she squeezed my hand twice, though I barely felt it, her strength a fraction of what I remembered.

I tore my gaze away and looked over my shoulder. Raven stood by the door, peering through the curtain. By her feet, a handful of swarmbots slipped under the door into the room. Not enough to do anything.

"Dray. Save her, please," Mina cried. She looked beside herself, eyes darting to Talia.

Amidst the growing uproar, I heard Talia whisper, "Gotta motor."

I turned to her. "You're right. Time to go." I stood, then leaned forward and carefully slipped one hand under her legs, the other under her neck. I'd carry her out.

My brain registered the wires as the nagging I'd felt grew to a level I couldn't ignore. She hadn't sat up. Had barely moved. The wires. I encountered them when I slipped my hand past her neck. Something was wrong.

I pulled my hands out from underneath her, then leaned over her and moved aside a towel I hadn't noticed before as she protested weakly. Gleaming cords, three of them, disappeared into the base of her skull, while a fourth wire slipped under her toward the device on her chest, the cords connected to various machines, readouts reflecting various levels, many of the numbers meaningless, though the heartrates, the graphs, told me enough.

They had her hooked in.

It's why she hadn't sat up.

The machines kept her alive—but at the mercy of The Agency. And maybe more, their purpose a mystery.

There wasn't any hope of getting her away.

I looked at Mina and saw the truth in her eyes. "She's a prisoner," she said, her voice tortured. "Because of me. Because I betrayed our family."

I turned back to Talia. Her cheeks were slightly hollow but not overly so. Her skin looked healthy. Yet it was artificial, propped up by The Agency's care. I reached out with shaky fingers as my mind reeled from the nightmare they'd put her through. I stroked her hair, my fingertips grazing the cords. This wasn't life. It was enslavement.

"It's why I pleaded with you. I've been trying to tell you. Zion made me reach out, I knew he wanted you to come here, but I wanted it too—not so you'd become his prisoner but to help me."

"I thought you were his good little soldier," Raven spat.

"He's tortured Talia, barely kept her alive. He doesn't care about her or anyone but himself. Dray, you need to free her from this. Unplug her. I can't do it." Mina's voice cracked.

Numb with shock and grief, I leaned over and kissed Talia's forehead. "I dreamed of you."

With an effort greater than any I'd done before, I straightened, my legs shaking, and reached for the wires—

But Zion spoke first. "She's been helpful. The key, in fact."

He stood inside the doorway, suit torn, left arm hanging askew, but alive. Had broken free of the swarmbots, which meant they'd been destroyed—at least enough of them for him to get away.

The fury I'd felt toward him before was nothing like what I felt now. "You did this to my *daughter*."

"She was nearly dead when she arrived here. I just utilized the condition you left her in."

Now I understood his earlier claim. He had trolled Talia's mind, violating her, studying her, using her intelligence and ingenuity to test their systems until they could fine-tune their vile brain map.

I reached him in three quick steps and pinned him against the wall. I wanted to crush him. This close, I could see the sweat on his skin and the pain he tried to mask.

Hands grabbed me and threw me back. Kieran. Blood

coated his forehead. Three Agents filled the doorway behind him, also beat up. Kieran didn't look triumphant. Or angry. He looked shaken and troubled, his gaze flickering toward Talia.

I glanced at her. From the brief change in her expression, I could tell she understood Zion's words—and what they'd done to her. My heart broke. Then I remembered the bodies in the other beds I'd seen. More victims Zion had used.

"Don't bother fighting," he told us as more Agents entered the room and fanned out. "You think you hobbled us by blowing the nodes, but you didn't. Your broadcast in Los Angeles revealed our vulnerability. So, I built a second network, which has been in place for a few weeks, broadcast via a web of communication drones."

The final piece locked into place: the twin feed I'd discovered at The Agency's office. It was the new web, the one Zion created. It was a doubling of information because it *was* a double. A twin.

I recalled the solar-powered drones I'd seen in Kansas. They had to be his.

"We no longer need the nodes," Kieran said, his voice flat.

Zion nodded. "Even if some of the new drones become disabled, there's enough redundancy to ensure continued, consistent, unavoidable coverage. In fact, we would've decommissioned the nodes but wanted to draw in your rebels. As for you, Dray," he went on, clearly savoring this, "you'll be blamed for the worst domestic attack in the history of this country."

With a twirl of his dataringed fingers, he sent a new set of images to my lenses: news reports and vids and snapshots until the slaughter he'd orchestrated filled my vision: places exploding, police gunning down rebels I knew, panels like the ones that had fallen at HQ raining down as if attempting to capture those responsible, though I knew better. Jex suddenly appeared in one of the feeds—but my relief was wrenched away as someone shot him from behind, and he collapsed.

"No," Raven cried.

I launched myself at Zion, wanting to make him feel the pain he'd caused Jex. Before I could reach him, Kieran's Agents blocked me and shoved me back.

"We'll be able to locate any rebels who survive. With their clans destroyed, they'll have to expose their implants to rejoin society—and then we'll read their traitorous thoughts." He wiped away the images, restoring my vision. "To think I was jealous of you all those years. You're nothing but a glorified technician."

I had my vision back, but I didn't have a plan. I was too stunned, too overwhelmed. Raven was crying as Britt—who I hadn't seen come in—held her from going to Talia, the Agent not looking to Zion but to Kieran for guidance. He had an arm on Mina, though she didn't move, her face gaunt.

In that moment, I realized. My need to protect my family had blinded me. Had doomed our rebellion. Zion and Kieran had manipulated me, driven by Zion's jealousy and Kieran's desire to get back in his good graces. And I'd let them.

One of the swarmbots limped toward me, two of its appendages damaged, a last tiny warrior.

Kieran gave a resigned sigh and started toward me. I knew what came next. I thought briefly of Valor parked somewhere behind the complex, waiting for us.

I returned to Talia, wrecked over her being half-alive.

I knew I should end her suffering. I reached out for the cords. One tug was all it would take. I suspected the wire connected to the lump on Talia's chest was critical, even in this darkest moment the engineer inside me calculating how to solve the problem. End her life.

But I couldn't.

As if she'd read my mind, Talia looked up at me. "It's okay, Daddy," she whispered.

My lioness even now.

Kieran's fingers encircled my arms like steel clamps, and he turned me to face an Agent who aimed a burrower rifle. The man pulled the trigger, and the burrower pierced my stomach, which I didn't feel. As I looked down, the bulbous end pulled back, then injected Zion's mind-reading device into my body.

"Your rebellion is over, Dray," he announced. "You're part of the collective now. Welcome to the future."

To be concluded…

Acknowledgements

I completed the rough draft of *The Price of Rebellion* in February 2020, two months before the release of *The Price of Safety*, and one month before the world fell into a global pandemic.

Because of other demands, I shelved that first draft for most of 2020. While it was frustrating to have to pause my work, the time away gave a fresh perspective when I picked up the story again. I think the pandemic lent a darker edge to the tale. The middle section of a trilogy is normally darker, but even I was surprised by some of the twists that formed as Dray traveled down his difficult path.

You may be cursing me as a result of some of those twists, but stick with me. You'll be glad you did.

A number of wonderful, generous people helped me through the process of creating and editing *The Price of Rebellion*. I want to acknowledge their efforts, especially since I probably drove some of them nuts.

I want to thank my wife, Janelle, for her encouragement, unwavering support, and helpful comments. Thank you to Dad for your honest assessment of the rough draft. Because of you, the story is better. Thank you to my sister Lisa for your exceptional editing and insightful notes. Thank you to Debby, Jeremy, and the rest of my family for putting up with my writing quirks. I love you all very much.

Thank you to my other Beta readers: Sarah Greenwell, Nancy Broudo, Dorothy Mason, Judy Sachs, and Chris Eames. I particularly want to thank my writing brother Robert Kerbeck for your constant support, keen insight, and fantastic notes.

To Dorothy Mason for the incredible cover. You are truly gifted.

To Betsy Mitchell for your keen editing. To Karen Fuller and everyone at World Castle Publishing, thank you for your support.

Lastly, I thank you, dear Reader, for continuing with me on Dray's journey. I truly hope you enjoyed *The Price of Rebellion*. The concluding novel is on its way. I'd tell you more, but I'd hate to ruin the surprise.

Michael C. Bland

Michael is a founding member and the secretary of BookPod, an invitation-only online group of professional writers. He pens the monthly BookPod newsletter, where he celebrates the success of their members, which include award-winning writers, filmmakers, journalists, and bestselling authors.

One of Michael's short stories, "Elizabeth," won Honorable Mention in Writer's Digest 2015 Popular Fiction Awards contest. Three of the short stories he edited have been nominated for the Pushcart Prize. Another story he edited was adapted into an award-winning film.

He also had three superhero-themed poems published on *The Daily Palette.*

Michael currently lives in Florida with his wife Janelle and their dogs Nobu and Pico.

His novel, The Price of Rebellion, is the second installment in The Price Of trilogy.